FINDING
Us

DEBRA PRESLEY

Dear
Shannon,

Keep Rockin'

Debra
Presley

Debra Presley

Finding Us

A Nucci Securities Novel

© Copyright 2015 by Debra Presley

Cover Design by: Cover Me, Darling

Edited by: Scriptease Editing

Contributing Editor: Andi Marquette

Formatting: Brenda Wright – Formatting Done Wright

Published by: Debra Presley

table of
contents

Contact Debra Presley:
http://authordebrapresley.com

http://facebook.com/authordebrapresley

http://facebook.com/thebookenthsuast

Disclaimer:

This book is not suitable for young readers. There is strong

language, adult situations and some violence.

Dedicated to:

Genna, Vincent and Vanessa. Always follow your dreams.

Debra Presley

chapter
one

The house lights went on, and Abby Murphy took in the full stadium. They were cheering for her to give them one more song. Some held signs that read "I love you, Abby!" Others tried to hold on to the memories of the night by taking pictures and recording the show with their phones.

She'd spent the last two hours entertaining her fans with an elaborate show that included dancers, pyrotechnics, jugglers, acrobats, and circus animals. She wasn't a fan of all the glitz and glamour, but she wasn't the ringmaster of this show.

As much as she disliked the politics of her career, she hated disappointing her fans even more. "You want more?" She smiled and waved, and the audience roared. The noise gave her goose bumps up and down her arms. She signaled to the drummer, and he pounded out the intro to her next single "Beg Me." It seemed appropriate since the audience was doing exactly that. Her dancers jumped out from the openings in the stage floor. They flanked Abby, and she gave her fans a performance they'd never forget. Sweat dripped from her face and poured down her body as she sang her last few notes. Finally, fireworks exploded around her.

The show was over.

"Thank you, Vegas!" she shouted. "I love you. Good night."

They cheered, and with one last wave, Abby moved downstage. She stopped by her guitarist, Sean Haken, and gave him a quick kiss and then ran behind the curtain to her security detail. They whisked her off to her dressing room.

Once there, Abby sighed. The room was packed with staff, media, and random groupies, all vying for her attention. She hated this part of the night, and the high she got from the stage was lost as soon as she glanced around the room. The only thing she wanted after hours under the spotlights was a private area where she could recover. Looked like that wasn't going to happen. Again.

Her request for quiet never seemed to register with her mother, Vivien. All Abby needed was four walls, a door, and maybe a humidifier to keep her vocal folds healthy. But, no. Her mother insisted on a "pop star life," so Abby was met at every venue with a private, over-the-top suite filled with unnecessary things and unnecessary people.

This one had lavender walls and soft lighting to help "set the mood." The floors were cappuccino-colored hardwood, and an area rug that matched the walls was placed in the center of the room. A deep-purple sofa with accent pillows took up most of the space, and two cream-colored chairs with brown piping were on either side. A square, glass coffee table held freshly cut roses in various shades of pink. A humidifier was placed discreetly behind the furniture because Abby's mother thought such things were ugly and didn't match the décor. No matter that it was the only necessary thing in the room for Abby.

Her mother also insisted that lavender-scented candles in various sizes be lit at least one hour prior to their arrival, and a high-speed wireless Internet connection had to be available in the room. They were all things Abby didn't care about, but she'd stopped trying to change her mother's mind. Some days, though, it all made her want to run away.

Abby scanned the room and found her assistant Sophie Corradetti. Once she made it to Sophie, she'd be in the clear from all the people and noise.

"You killed it tonight." Sophie gave her a quick hug and handed her a bottle of water.

"Thanks, where's my mom?" Abby asked as she took a quick sip. Vivien Murphy was not only Abby's mother but also her manager.

"Your mother bailed as usual." Sophie gave Abby's arm a light squeeze to take a bit of the sting out of the statement.

"Thank God. I needed a reprieve." That was Abby's standard response. Logically, she should stop expecting anything different, but part of her was still a little girl seeking her mother's approval. She took another sip of water and saw Sophie's expression change.

"Don't get too excited. We might've dodged one annoyance, but there's another one waiting for you. Stephanie's heading our way. Don't worry; I'll save you." She patted Abby on the back.

"Ugh, what does that lady want from me? She's always in my fuckin' business." She groaned, knowing there's no way she could get out of talking to her.

"Well, she is a gossip columnist. It's kinda her job to be nosy." Sophie laughed.

"Not funny. You were my favorite assistant five minutes ago. Now you're just mean." She stuck her tongue out at Sophie.

"What if I promise to rescue your ass in about five minutes?" She poked Abby in the arm.

"I'd say you'll quickly become the best assistant in the world again."

"Here she comes," Sophie warned.

"Don't go far."

"I'll be over here, keeping close watch. Five minutes, and you'll be able to get some quiet."

"Yeah, right."

"Abby, sweetie! Wonderful show tonight." Stephanie placed her hands on Abby's arms and gave her an air kiss on either side of her face.

"Stephanie, lovely to see you," Abby greeted her.

"You and Sean looked cozy up on stage. Things going well?" She asked, obviously fishing for something.

"Yes, perfect. Sean's amazing. I'm very lucky to have him." Her prepared answer rolled off her tongue. If the world only knew how it really was between them.

"Oh, that's so good to hear." Stephanie's smile was cold and calculating, and it morphed into a wicked smirk in a matter of seconds. "Rumor is he was seen in a *very* compromising position with both a redhead and a blonde…not at the same time, of course." Stephanie paused, and Abby knew she was waiting for her to take the bait. "I'm glad to know the rumors are wrong."

Abby knew exactly who the redhead was, and she knew they were just friends. Kelly West had introduced Abby to Sean. She was a New York socialite who was famous for partying. She loved seeing her name in the spotlight, but no matter how much she flirted, there was no way she was having an affair with Sean. Kelly wouldn't betray her that way, and even Sean wouldn't stoop *that* low.

On the other hand, she had no idea about the blonde but couldn't be bothered to react. There was always some rumor about Sean with another woman. She'd accepted long ago that some of them were probably real, whether she wanted them to be or not. This was simply another blonde, and while it added to Abby's growing suspicion and discontent, it certainly wasn't a rumor worth a response. She wouldn't add her broken-hearted rage to Stephanie's tabloid fodder.

"Well, you can't believe everything you hear, can you?" Abby scratched her arm and hoped Sophie caught her signal. She was done talking to Stephanie.

"I suppose." Stephanie gave Abby a "yeah right" look.

"Excuse me, ladies," Sophie interrupted. "Abby, you need to get ready for your meet and greet. Stephanie, if you'd like to do a formal interview with Abby, give me a call and I'll set it up."

"Sorry, Stephanie, gotta go meet my fans." Abby gave Stephanie a quick hug and air kiss before Sophie ushered her away.

"Thank God that's over." Abby sighed. "She's relentless about Sean."

"I'm sorry." Sophie squeezed her arm and guided her through the mass of people, deftly avoiding anyone who might have wanted Abby's attention. She loved Sophie for that.

"By the way, you look *hot*, girl," Abby said, returning their conversation to a safe-for-public topic. Since Sophie *always* looked hot, it was an easy segue. She scanned Sophie's outfit to confirm it was true yet again. She wore a black shift dress with a thick white band down the middle and a square-cut neckline. To set it off, she'd selected a pair of black, sparkly four-inch platform shoes and pulled her reddish-brown hair into a bun. She was totally rocking the hot-for-teacher look. "That's the other reason I hired you. Your fashionista sensibilities."

"Learned it from you. Now come on. The inner sanctum awaits."

Abby followed her into the private part of the dressing area and sank onto a sofa. She closed her eyes, savoring the quiet.

Always efficient, Sophie retrieved her binder from the coffee table and took the seat opposite.

"Okay, tonight we have a meet and greet. It starts in about an hour and a half. We also promised you'd stick around to sign autographs and take pictures. I have an outfit set aside, and Amy and John stayed behind to help you get ready. Oh, and Ms. Sohm called."

"She did?" Abby smiled without intending to do so. Ms. Sohm was her former teacher and de facto parental figure.

She'd traveled with Abby for years and taught her everything her mother neglected. Abby loved her to bits. "Remind me to call her tomorrow."

"You got it."

Abby stood. She wanted to talk to Sean before she had to get ready for the rest of the night. She worked her way around the room, smiled, and greeted people as appropriate. Finally, she found Sean tucked in a corner, pressed up against a scantily dressed blonde with her tits hanging halfway out. *Not again.* The blonde giggled inanely at whatever Sean said as he ran his fingers up and down her arm.

Abby stared; she was shocked that he'd be so blatant. Stephanie was here, for Christ's sake. The woman lived to gossip about their love life. When she recovered enough to move, she ignored everyone else in the room and made her way toward them. She approached the pair from behind so Sean couldn't see her.

"Am I interrupting anything here?" she asked.

Sean moved away from the blonde. "Baby, I was talking to…"

"Brandi," the blonde snapped.

"Yeah, Brandi." He ran his hand through his hair. "She was telling me about a club we should check out."

"Oh, really?" Did he know Abby at all? She was all for a night out once in awhile, but with all that was required of her, she didn't do it often. Especially not after a show. "Too bad we don't have time. Can I talk with you for a moment, baby?" She tried to keep her tone even, doing her best to not attract any more attention from the small group of onlookers that had inched closer. She wrapped her arm around his waist and guided him to her private dressing area.

She double-checked to make sure the room was empty before saying, "What the fuck was that? I can't leave you alone for more than five minutes without you trying to get into some random skank's pants? Really?" She kept her voice low.

"I was being nice. She came up to me and wanted to talk. What was I supposed to do? Be rude?" He ran his finger across Abby's collarbone and looked into her eyes.

She always had a hard time resisting his touch, because no matter what else, Sean was *great* with his hands. She ran her fingers through his shoulder-length, brown hair and enjoyed the way the unruly curls caught against her fingertips enough to ignore the sweat left over from being on stage.

"Mmm. There, we're cool, right?"

"Fuck you, Sean. I've reached my limit with you. I'm sick of being made to look like a fool."

Sean stared at her. "I really am sorry."

Abby searched his face. He looked sincere, but she had no way of actually knowing. There was a time, in the beginning of their relationship, when she would've believed his apology, but he'd burned her too many times. When they first got together, they really were in love and not just faking it for appearances. When Kelly introduced them, they hit it off immediately. Sean was everything she thought she wanted in a man—attentive, loving, and he listened to her. They talked a lot. He was charming and persuasive. He even managed to change her mom's mind a couple of times. In Abby's experience, that was something that never happened.

Now, though, his suave ways had begun to wear old, and the truth never matched up with his version of events. Lately, she was starting to think the Sean she fell in love with was never real in the first place. And everything she believed back then was a lie just like everything he said to her now. The worst part by far was, along with the loss of trust for him, she also lost trust in herself. She didn't know if she'd ever be able to trust blindly again like she had with him.

When he claimed the blonde was a friend and all she wanted was to tell him about a club, she knew it was bullshit, but what did that knowledge get her? She knew he was lying, and he knew she knew he was lying. Everything else was just the costumes they wore in public. She could push the issue and start an argument, but with so many people within earshot, it wasn't worth it. Nothing would change anyway.

"Fine," she said, annoyed with life right now. "I have to get ready."

He shifted out of her way, but grabbed her hand before she could pass. "Where are you going?"

"I have an event that my mother set up."

"You can't get out of it?"

Abby rubbed her temple and sighed, letting go of some of her anger. "I wish I could." It wasn't the complete truth since she liked her fans more than her boyfriend at the moment, but she said it as a gesture of forgiveness. She was stuck with Sean, so she might as well make it as pleasant as possible.

"Um, sorry to break things up here, but you have to change now if you want to get back at a decent time." Sophie smiled, apologetic, and Abby wondered how much she'd heard.

"I'll wait up. Want me to have a bath ready for you?" Sean asked.

"That sounds nice." Abby gave him a small smile.

"How long are you gonna be?"

"A couple of hours, I guess." She looked over at Sophie.

"I have you scheduled for two hours, but the sooner we leave, the sooner you can get back to your room."

Abby smiled. "All right. See you later." She headed for the bathroom.

* * *

Abby sagged against the elevator wall, completely exhausted from her long day. All she wanted now was the hot bath Sean had promised, followed by blissful sleep. Sophie, along with her personal security detail, Danny Nucci and Ron Miller, stepped into the elevator with her.

"That wasn't as bad as it could've been," Sophie said.

"Danny was lucky enough to get cornered by that woman." Ron chuckled and pressed the buttons for their floors. "Left me to hold back all the squealing teenagers."

Abby fought the urge to roll her eyes. The woman was gross. She was dressed like a cheap whore. And, she was there with her daughter, not at some nightclub. She wouldn't leave Danny alone.

"You could've given me some help. She was disgusting." He shook his head exaggeratedly.

"She was quite fond of you." Abby laughed to mask her real feelings.

"Not one of you tried to intervene. I'm gonna need to shower for a week in order to get her perfume out of my nose. She reeked."

"Yeah, you do smell pretty," Abby goaded.

"I'll remember this. Just wait," Danny warned as the elevator door opened to Sophie's floor.

"Night." Sophie gave Abby a quick peck on the cheek before she stepped off the elevator.

"Night." Abby waited inside the elevator with Danny. He held the door open while Ron walked Sophie to her room.

"So, what are your plans for the rest of the night? A late night rendezvous with the smelly cougar?" Abby teased.

"Aren't you the funny one this evening. Well, baby doll, it's two-thirty in the morning, so I'm thinking sleep. Why? Did you have something in mind?"

She got lost for a minute in his deep-brown eyes that sparkled with mischief. She'd always thought he was hot, but she was caught off guard by the desire to touch his cheek, to smooth her fingertips over his dimples. This visceral reaction to Danny kept happening more and more frequently, no matter how much she tried to suppress it.

"Um, you still with me, Abby?"

She blinked, and her cheeks flushed with heat. "Oh, you want me to answer you?" she laughed to cover up her embarrassment. She didn't want him to realize she'd been daydreaming about how rough his five o' clock shadow would feel against the flat of her tongue. "I told you how I feel about your stupid nicknames." She tried to sound pissed, but didn't pull it off.

Ron laughed as he entered the elevator and pressed the button for their floor. Danny glared at him for a moment then started laughing with him.

Abby changed the subject. Much safer that way. "What time are we heading out in the morning?"

"Oh-nine-hundred hours," Danny replied.

"Okay, Drill Sergeant, I'll be ready." The elevator dinged, and the doors opened to the semi-private floor which held the suite she shared with Sean, along with another across the hall where Danny and Ron stayed.

"Well, Military Man, it's been a pleasure. I'm gonna go pass the hell out. Have a good night. See ya, Ron." She waved over her shoulder as she slid her keycard through the electronic lock. When the reader beeped and the green light came on, she gave the men one last smile before entering her suite.

She closed the door and removed the nude color platform pumps from her aching feet. Clearly, her shoes were made for showing, not walking. She made her way into the large sunken living room; the muted neon glow from the Vegas strip was the only light in the room.

"Sean?" Abby called on her way to the bedroom. She dropped her shoes next to the dresser.

Sean wasn't there, even though he'd said he would be. Abby blew out a puff of air, annoyed with herself for believing him, *yet again*. She wasn't lying when she said she'd reached her limit, but that didn't matter when he knew that it wasn't up to her anyway. Her mother would never let her leave him. She had plans, and it didn't matter what Abby wanted. Abby turned the light on then dug into her bag for her phone. It wasn't there. "Fuck," she muttered. She picked up the hotel phone and dialed Sean's number. It went to voicemail. She hung up. There was no point in leaving a message.

She dialed back to the operator and asked to be connected to Sophie's room.

"Hey, sorry to bother you, but do you have my phone?"

"No, I don't think so, but let me look. Hold on."

Abby chewed her lip, thinking about Sean. Where the hell was he? Worse, who was he with? A hard knot formed in her stomach as she thought about what he might be doing.

"Hey," Sophie said. "I don't have it."

"I must've left it in my dressing room." Typical, considering the way her luck had been tonight. "Sean's not here. You know what that means." She sighed. "I'm gonna go find my phone."

"Why do you even bother with him anymore? We've hashed this out before."

"It's late. Can we talk about this later? He's not here and right now I can't even think about what that means, but I know I need my phone." She was sick of it all.

"You shouldn't go alone."

"It'll take twenty minutes. Quick and easy." Thankfully the arena was connected to the hotel.

"Okay, but ask one of the boys to go."

"They've had a long night. I don't want to bother them. I won't be long, and besides, you'll know where I am. When I find my phone, I'll call you."

"Abby! Tell them. I get that you're upset, because Sean's disappeared…again but don't do something stupid."

"Fine. Will you come with?"

"I'll meet you at the elevator."

"Perfect. Thanks." Abby slipped on a pair of flats and unhooked the panic button from her purse and attached it to her bracelet. Danny insisted that she wear the damn thing. She insisted that it looked good as a charm she could wear hanging from wrist or attached to her purse. After all, security was important, but appearances could make or break her career. She didn't want it to look like she had a tracking device on her.

Abby double-checked that her keycard was in her pocket before she let her door close behind her, then she jabbed the call button for the elevator. She was about to knock on the door to Danny and Ron's suite, but a ding sounded behind her and announced the arrival of the elevator. "Damn." She decided to call the guys when she got her phone and hurried into the elevator before the doors could slide shut without her.

chapter
two

The girls quickly walked through the casino toward the arena doors, barely dodging a group of fans wearing concert T-shirts. This was why she shouldn't go anywhere without security.

"Look, it says the arena is this way." Abby dragged Sophie by the hand and hurried in that direction.

"Why aren't we going toward the manager's office?"

"Because we're closer to the arena than the office." Abby had no idea where the manager's office was but she needed to get into her dressing room, not somebody else's office.

"How do you know this?"

Abby saw a large group of people heading their way, and she panicked. She needed to get out of the lobby before someone spotted her. "I don't know."

They reached the end of the hall, and Abby searched around for some sort of clue as to which way to go. "Did we miss a sign or something?"

"The entrance is this way." Sophie pointed to the sign that hung high on the wall in front of them. Abby would've noticed it if she'd been walking like a normal person rather than with her gaze fixed on the floor.

"Good. The last thing we need is a mob of people following us." Abby wished she'd worn a hat or maybe sunglasses. There were too many people milling around for her to go unnoticed much longer.

"I told you this wasn't a good idea." Sophie picked up the pace.

"Just keep moving." *Shit, shit, shit.* Why were so many people still up? Didn't anyone sleep? It was nearly morning. Apparently Las Vegas was the "city that never sleeps," not New York. Why hadn't she called hotel management and asked them to look? *Because heartache apparently makes you stupid.* Sean's absence was eating at Abby.

"Come on, right over here." Sophie pulled on the arena door. "Locked. Great." She sighed.

"Of course it's locked. I just figured there'd be somebody here to let us in." Abby walked farther down the hallway to stay out of sight.

Sophie looked at her incredulously. "Why would someone be standing around with a set of keys? God, Abby you're so frustrating some days."

"Whatever."

"Don't 'whatever' me. If you'd given me a minute to find a few numbers, you'd already have your phone, and we wouldn't be on the verge of an ambush."

"Look, I'm sorry. Okay? I've got a lot on my mind."

"No, you have one person on your mind. When are you

going to throw that asshole to the curb? Enough's enough already."

"It's not as simple as that and you know it." It wasn't like Sophie was telling her something she didn't already know, but it was hard for her to verbally acknowledge even that much. She hated feeling like she wasn't in control and alluding to the fact made her even more uncomfortable.

"Let's go to the reception area and ask for the manager," Sophie suggested.

"You go. I'll stay here and wait." Abby pulled on the door Sophie had just checked to see if she would have better luck. She didn't.

"No. I'm not leaving you here alone. Come on," Sophie said.

"We've managed to get this far without anyone spotting me. How lucky do you think we're gonna get? I'll stay here. You go," Abby insisted, and as if to prove her point, a group of fans gathered near a cardboard cutout of her and took pictures with it.

She turned back to Sophie and realized she had her cell phone to her ear. "What are you doing?"

"Calling Danny."

She looked over at the crowd. "Shit, fine." She didn't want to admit it, but things were quickly spiraling out of control. All it would take is for one person to recognize her and they'd be overrun in seconds. Calling Danny was the right thing to do even if she'd have to apologize for being selfish and short-sighted. Saying sorry was better than being trampled on.

Sophie walked away as she placed the call. Probably because she didn't want Abby to hear her tell Danny what an ass she'd been, thinking they could run down to her dressing room, pick up her phone, and then run back upstairs as if she were a normal person. Normal simply wasn't an option for her. She'd been in the spotlight for so long, she didn't remember how it felt to run an errand by herself.

Abby tried to stay out of sight while they waited for Danny, but the group of people around her cardboard counterpart seemed to grow. *Who knew something so silly would be such a hot tourist attraction?* She looked around for an escape route. When she found nothing, her breathing picked up and her hands grew clammy. She was minutes away from having a panic attack.

There was nowhere else for them to go. After a few minutes, a set of doors opened, and a worker rolled a large garbage cart out of the arena.

Abby and Sophie looked at each other and then sprinted toward the open door. The arena was empty except for a few maintenance workers, and they didn't seem to notice Abby and Sophie. The stage was already broken down and on its way to the next location.

"We should wait until Danny gets here." Sophie stood mostly outside the door.

"No, I want to check the backstage doors."

"Don't you dare go off on your own," Sophie scolded. She actually sounded more motherly than Vivien ever had. The tone was foreign to Abby, and she wasn't sure if she liked it or not.

"I'm going to see if I can get someone to open a door for us; that's all." Abby traveled down the long aisle despite Sophie's protests. It was surreal to be on this side of the stage. She absolutely loved performing—in fact, it was the only time she truly enjoyed her career. But she couldn't remember the last time she'd been part of the audience. And lately, the shows felt more like work than something she was passionate about. Her life had been managed by her mother for so many years, Abby had a hard time finding herself in her work.

How long could she really keep allowing this to happen? Abby wasn't a teenager who needed to be supervised. She was a grown woman with her own ideas on how her life and career should go. But she was stuck. She simply didn't know how to make her way from beneath her mother's grasp.

She approached the door and heard muted sounds of music playing. It sounded like her band was still partying. Well at least she knew where to find Sean. Instead of making her feel better, now she was worried about who he was with instead of where he was. Over the past few months, he'd become very brazen with his infidelities.

Abby wanted to find the source of the music. Her patience was done. She walked back up the aisle to the first worker she found.

"Excuse me."

"Can I help… The maintenance man couldn't hide his surprise when he realized who she was. He smiled and said, "Ms. Murphy, how can I help you?"

"I left my phone in my dressing room. Could you

unlock one of the doors so I can get it, please?"

"Sure, but would you like me to look for you?"

"No. I'm good. I don't know exactly where I left it, so I'm going to do a quick search. My assistant is waiting for my security team to meet us. I'll only be a minute." She started through the door.

"Ms. Murphy?"

Abby stopped. "Yes?"

"Um, well, my kid...she's a big fan and it'd make me Father of the Year if I came home with an autograph. Would you mind?"

"No, no not at all." Abby always did her best to stop for fan requests. She didn't want to be mobbed, but one-on-one like this, she always found time no matter what else was happening. She smiled at the man as though she wasn't suffocating under the weight of her own life.

As if he'd known they would meet tonight, the man pulled a pen and notepad from his shirt pocket and offered it to Abby.

"Her name?"

"Oh, um, Tonya."

"How old is she?"

"Fifteen."

Abby wrote a short, personal message on the pad and handed it back to the man.

"Do you have a phone on you? Abby asked.

"Yes."

"Great." She waited while he fished it out of his back pocket. "Let's take a selfie," she suggested.

"Oh, I don't know… I always cut people's heads off."

"No problem. May I?" She reached for his phone.

"Of course."

"Smile." Abby snapped the picture. "Now, tell Tonya to tag me if she posts that on social media. Okay?"

"Absolutely."

"Perfect."

"Thank you so much."

"Of course. It was nice meeting you."

Abby rushed down the hall toward the music. Her band really lived the rock star life. They loved to party, and normally she didn't care. As long as they were fully functioning by the time the stage lights came up, she was okay with it. But tonight, it got under her skin. They stuck together and protected Sean when he cheated on her and knowing that made her sensitive to other things, like the partying that she otherwise didn't care about. They had a brotherhood, and she was on the outside.

She was about to barge into the room but thought better of it. First, she'd get her phone so that she could call Sophie and let her know where she was. She was probably already having mini-heart attacks, because Abby took off when she said she wouldn't. Oh well, another apology to add to her list.

She arrived at her dressing room. The gold star bearing her name hung on the wall canted to one side as if someone had bumped into it. She crossed her fingers and tried the doorknob. It was unlocked. Finally, one thing went in her favor. She didn't linger in the common area, but crossed immediately to the private section where she'd changed earlier. Her phone had to be there. It was the only place that made sense.

She stopped, puzzled, hand hovering over the doorknob. There was somebody inside. She listened for a few more seconds, and it dawned on her; she knew exactly what those sounds were. She slammed the handle down and shoved the door open.

The room was dark, but Abby could still faintly see— and hear—two people on the couch. There was no mistaking what they were doing. She blindly searched for the light switch on the wall, her gaze fastened to the scene in front of her. Abby *knew* it was Sean. She tried to mentally prepare herself for what was happening and what she'd see after she flipped the switch, but nothing she did stopped the torrent of emotions rushing through her.

She'd never caught Sean in the act before, but the signs had been there for a long time. Lipstick on his clothes, smells of foreign perfume, and of course, his many disappearing acts. But strangely, all those signs were easy to ignore. She was a master of dismissing a mountain of evidence as unimportant coincidence. But this was too much and confirmed what she'd believed for a long time. He was only with her to further his career. She knew it. He knew it. Still, this kind of blatant disrespect was a slap in the face.

Up until now, she was able to hedge, to tell herself that, even though he wasn't in love with her, he was still an okay guy, they looked great together which was good for her career, and he was really good in bed. She didn't expect happily ever after, but...hell, she didn't know what she'd actually expected. She was sure, however, that as soon as she turned on the light, her ability to pretend would be stripped from her.

She debated simply walking away, but her pride wouldn't let her. It was time to face reality. She braced herself and then flipped the switch. It confirmed her fears. "What the fuck?"

"Fuck!" Sean pushed himself off the blonde woman he was with. It was the blonde he'd been chatting up earlier that night. Abby didn't remember her name, but she remembered the vapid look on her face and the way her tits spilled out of her top. Only now there was nothing for them to spill out of. She was naked to her waist, with her skirt hiked up around her hips. Sean stumbled, trying to pull up his pants.

The woman stared at Abby, wide eyed. Abby had no time for her.

"Get out." Abby was close to violence, and part of her hoped the blonde would stay long enough for Abby to get a fistful of her hair. "Now."

The bleached blonde grabbed her clothes and shoes and hurried out of the room, tripping as she tried to dress and run at the same time. She left the door open behind her.

"You'd better fucking run, bitch," Abby yelled, then she turned to glare at Sean. "You have some fucking nerve."

"Abby, baby, I'm sorry. She followed me back, and I had a couple of drinks. It was stupid, I know. Please, *please*, baby, I'm sorry." He took a couple of steps toward her.

"Don't. Don't you fucking come near me. Get out. We're done."

"Baby, you can't do this," he begged, reaching for her. "You don't mean it. You know I love you. I made a mistake. Let's talk about this. You're tired." He tried to hold her, but she pulled away.

"You love me? That's fucking rich. I saw exactly how much you love me just now. Get out."

"Come on, baby. Let's have a drink and talk."

"I think you've had more than enough to drink."

"Be reasonable. Think about it. What are you going to do? Break up with me? You know your mom won't be cool with that. You don't have a say in our relationship anymore than I do. So, calm down and let's go upstairs." He smirked, and in that moment, she hated him more than she'd thought possible. And the worst part? He was right. She'd let her mom box her into this corner.

"No," she said softly. She was done. Done with pretending. Done with the lies. Done with the phony displays of affection. Just done. She had to take a stand at some point. Her mother might have control of her career, but no way was Abby letting her dictate her love life.

Not anymore.

"No, what?" he asked.

"No, we're not going upstairs together. We're done.

Get out! What don't you understand?" She turned her back on him, needing to get out of the room. It smelled of sex and betrayal. She was able to make it out of the private dressing area before Sean lunged and grabbed her arm. He'd stopped long enough to fasten his pants.

"Abby—"

"Let go." She tried to break his hold on her, but he tightened his grip. She pressed the round circle on her panic button and prayed it did what it was supposed to do. This was the first time she'd used it, and it was because her boyfriend had apparently lost his mind.

"Calm down," he pleaded. He sounded desperate. Good.

Abby's ring tone echoed off the walls in the next room. Her phone was in the bathroom. She'd forgotten the phone was the reason she was here in the first place. "Get. Off. Me." Again, she tried to pull free but couldn't. Her heartbeat picked up, and in that moment, Abby was genuinely frightened. She'd never seen this side of Sean, but the look on his face was sickeningly familiar, except she associated it with her father not her boyfriend. She'd seen it many times during her childhood when her parents argued. Her dad knew how to make things ugly, and she didn't blame her mom for throwing him out. He was a mean son of a bitch who drank too much and took his anger out on whoever was closest.

One of her first memories was of her mother bleeding on the kitchen floor, and her father yelling about his food being cold. Only once did he go after Abby. After that, her mother kicked him out.

Leaving her father was the only motherly act she remembered Vivien committing. At the time, Abby had felt hopeful, as if her mom might love her after all. It didn't take long to realize she was simply protecting an investment, not a child she loved.

She never thought she'd ever be in a position like this. Sean cheated, but he had never been violent before. Abby made herself a promise a long time ago that she'd never let a man lay a hand on her, and God forbid it did happen, she wouldn't stay with him. No way.

"We are going to sit down and talk." He sounded incredibly sober, his voice clear, concise, and no longer heavy with alcohol. "You're not going anywhere."

Her phone stopped ringing.

"That's probably Ron or Danny, so why don't you let go of me?"

"Fuck them," he said in a quiet, controlled voice.

"They're gonna look for me."

Her phone started to ring again, and Abby tried one more time to wiggle out of his grasp.

"Not going to happen."

He squeezed harder, and the look in his eyes made Abby realize she didn't really know Sean or what he was capable of doing. The Sean she knew was the one who would jam for hours; he joked around and flirted with everyone. This wasn't that Sean. With all their problems, he never lost his temper. He'd dismiss her and ignore her, sure. But never this.

From the hallway, a loud bang sounded. *Oh, thank*

God. She heard Danny calling her name. Sean gripped her arm even tighter and started pulling her deeper into the room. He applied more pressure to his hold. Her arm burned, and her fingers tingled from the lack of blood flow. Nothing she did made a difference, and she felt helpless and out of control. Without warning, the tears she'd been holding back began to fall.

"Fuck you." She used her free hand to push against Sean's chest. She wanted away from him. Now. "Danny!"

The main door to her suite opened with such force that it bounced off the wall and almost slammed back into Danny. He blocked it with his forearm, without slowing his charge toward Sean. Ron, Sophie, and hotel security were right behind him.

"Sean. Off. Now." Danny's tone was cold and hard.

Sean released Abby's arm, and Danny motioned for her to move behind him. She sagged against the wall and gulped for air. Her heart was beating so hard that she thought she might pass out. Danny grabbed Sean by his shirt.

"I'm sure she told you to get off her. I think you should've listened," Danny said, the timbre in his voice wasn't something Abby was used to hearing, but she wasn't scared. He was protecting her, and she knew she was safe with him.

"Fuck you," Sean over-emphasized both words.

Danny pushed Sean against the wall with so much power Abby felt it shake.

"Fuck me? You're a piece of shit. I should beat the fuck out of you for touching her."

Sean pushed away from the wall and glared at him. The two stood nearly eye-to-eye. "I'd like to see you try, pretty boy," Sean taunted. "Why don't you get your own piece of ass and leave my bitch alone."

Danny threw Sean onto the floor and punched him so hard his head thumped against the hardwood.

Ron grabbed Danny's fist mid-punch. "D! Stop it. That's enough, man." Sean lay on the floor, dazed, with blood dripping from his nose.

"Not. Worth. It. Come on." Ron kept his eyes on Danny, and after several long seconds, Danny got to his feet while Ron continued to act as a shield between him and Sean.

"Get up, asshole." Ron motioned at Sean.

Sean struggled to his feet and started toward Abby. Ron blocked his path. "The exit is that way." He waited until Sean walked to the door. Ron followed, ensuring he didn't go near Sophie. She stood quietly in the corner, looking as shocked as Abby felt.

"This isn't over, Abby! You can't avoid me," Sean yelled.

"Yeah, yeah. Keep walking asshole." Ron followed him until the hotel security took over and led him out of the room.

"There's no hiding from me. I'll fucking find you. You're mine, Abby!" Sean's threats rang loud in Abby's head. She exhaled hard, releasing all the tension that held her upright, as she slipped down the wall to the floor. With a sob, she lowered her head to her knees, wrapped her arms around her legs, and continued to cry. It'd been a long, crazy night.

"Nucci, hotel management wants to know how to proceed. They want to call it in." Ron's words brought Abby back to the here and now. *Police? No way.*

"No! They can't do that. My mother will go insane. Just let him go, please," she begged.

"Abby…" Danny started.

"Please. If he gets arrested, everything will get worse. She'll make my life hell." She looked between Danny and Ron. No one really knew how bad her mother could get. They didn't understand.

"Abby." Danny placed a hand on her shoulder, and she flinched. She didn't want to be touched right now. Danny retracted his hand.

"It's okay. We'll deal with this in-house," he conceded.

She exhaled. "Thank you."

"Let me help you up."

She stared at him. Sean was still out there, and she didn't want to see him. Not now and not ever again. How could she ever be alone with him again?

"Abby." He sat down next to her but didn't try to touch her again. Instead, he simply assured her that Sean had left. "I won't let him near you. Don't worry."

She looked back at him, bone tired and too scared to move.

"He's gone. Did he hurt you?" Something in his

inflection made her feel as if he would hunt Sean down if she asked it of him.

"I'm fine. I…" She started crying again, and Danny moved closer. This time she let him.

"What happened?" he asked, his eyes filled with warmth and concern.

She searched for something to say but came up blank. She took a deep breath and stuttered as she exhaled.

"Why don't you come sit inside?" Danny gestured toward the room where she'd found Sean. The thought of returning there made her shudder.

"No. I don't want to stay here."

"Okay, then let's get you back to our floor."

"I can't stay there, either. He has a key."

"Don't worry about him. I promise he won't get anywhere near you. You can stay in our suite." He stood and offered her his hand.

She took it, grateful for the warmth and strength in his touch, and she let him help her to her feet. She inspected her arm where Sean had grabbed her; it was red, and she could clearly see the impression of his hand on her arm. Bruises were beginning to form.

"Let me see." Danny examined it. Abby saw the muscles in his jaw clench. "I need to get you back upstairs," he mumbled to himself.

"Sophie?"

"I'm right here."

"I'm sorry." Tears slid down her face.

"Shh, I'm happy you're okay." Sophie wiped the tears from Abby's face. "I'm going to talk to the hotel manager and smooth things over."

"But…"

"I won't be long, and I'll ask hotel security to escort me upstairs. Go with Danny and get some rest."

"Come on," he said and led her out of the dressing room. "Ron, will you take care of Abby's room, please?"

"Will do."

Abby relaxed a little, glad that she didn't have to go back to her room alone. Danny was here to protect her and *finally* she was done with Sean. She didn't let herself think about what her mother would say or what this meant for the rest of the tour. All she wanted was to go to sleep. Danny and Abby walked back to the elevator in silence. She leaned into him, and he pulled her closer. She turned into him, hiding her dazed smile of pride.

Clearly, she was in shock. And scared as hell, but she finally did it. She stood up for herself. There was nothing anyone could say to her that would make her take Sean back. When the elevator doors opened, Danny stepped out, but Abby hesitated. Her fleeting moment of elation was gone when faced with walking onto their floor.

"He's not here, Abby." Danny motioned with his head toward the open door. She trusted him completely but was still frightened. Danny opened the door to his suite and guided Abby to the sofa and encouraged her to sit. "I'll get you some water."

Danny's suite mirrored Abby's. There was a large sunken living room with a brown U-shaped sectional, a set of glass-and-metal end tables on both sides, and a matching coffee table in the center of the room. A large flat screen television hung on the wall opposite the window that looked out onto the Vegas strip. Photographs from local artists hung from the beige walls. In the far left corner was a full bar with a mini-fridge.

"Abby, please talk. You're worrying me. What happened?" He handed her the water, and she took a long drink.

"I walked in on Sean fucking some groupie." She took another sip of water and then placed it back on the table. After a moment, she stood and silently walked over to the balcony then opened the door. Danny watched but gave her the moment she needed.

"I never thought we were a forever thing, so I don't know why I'm shocked." She looked out at the Vegas Strip, staring mindlessly at the lights and thinking about how she'd let herself be controlled for so long. How could she have misjudged Sean so badly? "Guess I was wrong, huh?" She looked over at Danny. "Anyway, I told him we're over and to get out, but he wouldn't. He tried to sweet talk me, and I wouldn't listen. Then he basically said that I wouldn't break up with him, and when I didn't back down, he grabbed me." She looked down at her arm; the angry red indents had faded to a mottled purple, and she could feel the bruise throb in time with her heartbeat.

"Fuck, let me call for some ice."

Debra Presley

"Don't bother. It's so late I don't think I'll be awake long enough for someone to show before I pass out for the night."

"At least let me get you something cool to put on it." Danny went to the mini-fridge. She returned to the sofa and collapsed onto it again. She kicked off her sandals, curled her legs onto the sofa, and made herself comfortable. "Here." Danny returned with a can of soda and a towel. He wrapped the soda in the towel and handed it to her.

"Thanks," Abby mumbled back as she held the cold drink to her bruise.

The main door opened, and she looked up to see Ron walking in.

"Update," Danny said simply.

"I sent the dirtbag packing, and his shit is being removed from your room, Abby." He closed the door behind him. Abby relaxed into the corner of the sofa.

"Thanks, man." Danny gave him a nod of approval.

"Sure. We shouldn't have any more issues from him tonight," Ron assured.

"Thank you." Abby managed to give Ron a small smile of appreciation.

"No problem. Your stuff was sort of everywhere, so I didn't touch it."

"I can pack later." Abby said.

"Well, I'm going to sleep." Ron waved goodnight.

"Night. Thanks again, Ron," Danny said.

42

"Go to bed," Abby said once Ron had left. "If you don't mind, I'll sleep right here." She placed the can of soda and towel on the coffee table. "I'll need a blanket. Do you think there's one in a closet?" She moved the small throw pillow from behind her back to the arm of the couch.

"Not happening. I'll stay out here."

"I can't kick you out of your room. I'll be fine on the couch."

"Get up. Let's go." Danny motioned with his head for her to follow him.

"But—"

"I can handle the sofa for a few hours. Follow me." Danny guided her toward his bedroom. Once inside, he opened his suitcase. "Here, take this." He threw her a T-shirt. She looked at it for a moment and then at Danny.

"You sure? I know this isn't how you wanted to spend your night."

"Go to bed, Abby." Without further discussion, he left her alone in his room.

* * *

"No!" Abby woke with a start, turned the side table light on, and looked around the room. She was alone, and even though the room looked familiar, none of her things were in it. Instantly, images of Sean flooded her memory, and she felt trapped. The room felt too big, and the bed too cold.

She sat up and tried to slow her heartbeat, but she kept replaying the last few hours over and over in her mind. She couldn't make it stop. Abby closed her eyes and took a few deep breaths, willing her emotions to settle. She did this for several minutes, but it didn't help. Going back to sleep didn't seem likely, so she got up. She pulled the blanket off the bed and wrapped it tightly around herself before she entered the living room.

Danny slept soundly on the couch. She quietly walked to the bar and grabbed a small bottle of vodka. She downed half in one swig. She leaned against the bar and took a moment to think about what happened. No matter how hard she tried, she couldn't quite wrap her head around it. She picked at the label on the bottle and thought about how she'd always loved Las Vegas. It always felt so grand, full of life and excitement as if anything could happen here. Tonight, all she felt was the emotional coldness of the city. The butterflies she always got when she visited were silent for the first time. In their place she felt fear and loss.

She downed the rest of the vodka, placed the bottle in the trash, and then padded over to where Danny slept on the sofa. He looked pretty comfortable despite the fact that Abby had stolen his bed. She felt bad, but with his military background, he'd probably slept in places that were much worse. He looked peaceful, too. Abby had a hard time believing he was thirty.

Abby sat on an overstuffed chair and watched him sleep. His breathing was deep and even. Her gaze roamed over his face, his rugged, hard looks were relaxed and soft in sleep. A blanket rested half-on, half-off Danny, exposing his toned upper body. Danny had just the right amount of hair on his chest and deliciously sculpted abs. A fluttering as if she were stepping on stage for the first time started in Abby's stomach, but she quickly dismissed it. Danny was her bodyguard and an overall good guy. She didn't want to ruin the friendship they'd established over the last year. Not to mention, they had another four months on this tour, and it would be difficult enough to replace Sean, even with the two-week break coming up. She didn't need any more complications, no matter how sexy Danny looked while he was sleeping.

Reluctantly, she started back to the bedroom, but didn't get far before she changed her mind. She turned around and went back to the chair. Facing that big, cold bed alone with only her thoughts wasn't something she wanted to do right now. Instead she curled up on the chair with her gaze focused on Danny. The thought of him protecting her was the last thing she pictured as she drifted off to sleep.

chapter three

The sun rose, and the rays seeped through the windows of the hotel suite. The brightness woke Danny before his alarm. He grabbed his phone to check the time a moment before his alarm starting blaring.

"Fuck." He pressed snooze and stretched lazily. From the corner of his eye, he saw someone in the chair across from him. His body and mind were in action, assessing the threat, before he realized that is was Abby. At some point while he'd slept, she'd moved from the bedroom to the chair. She was wrapped in the blanket from his bed, snoring lightly. Her head was tilted to the side, resting on a small accent pillow, and her feet hung over the edge. She looked utterly adorable, and Danny hesitated to wake her. After last night, she needed the rest, and he had work to do before they were scheduled to be on the bus. He'd let her sleep a while longer.

He decided to deal with Vivien first and dialed her number as he walked into the bedroom.

"Mr. Nucci," she answered. He wanted to roll his eyes every time she called him "Mr. Nucci." Everyone in Abby's entourage was informal except her. Danny tried to avoid dealing with Vivien. She and Abby had a complicated relationship that he tried to stay out of. It wasn't his business, and as long as it didn't affect Abby's safety, he didn't need to weigh in. Abby had hinted at a troubled home life when she was younger, but she'd never really shared that part of her life with him.

"Vivien, I'm not sure if you're aware of what happened last night, but—"

"I'm well aware of my daughter's impulsiveness."

Danny held his tongue. Vivien hated to hear about problems. She just wanted them to go away.

"I think we need to discuss this situation."

"What's there to discuss? Abigail knows what's expected of her."

"That's between you and Abby. I'm here to keep her safe, and last night she was assaulted. That warrants a conversation."

"I don't agree, but if you insist, we can meet for a few minutes this morning. I'll have my assistant call you with a time." She hung up the phone before Danny could say anything else.

He stared at Abby sleeping in the other room. If he wanted to prep her for their meeting, he needed to wake her now. Danny returned to the living room.

"Abby," he whispered and sat next to her on the ottoman. He shook her gently. Nothing. She didn't even stir. He watched her sleep for a moment then leaned over to gently push her champagne-colored hair away from her face. He took in her fair complexion sprinkled lightly with freckles and then abruptly stood. He needed to stop before his thoughts got the better of him. The last thing he needed was for Abby to see how much she affected him.

He worked hard at keeping things professional because he knew all too well what happened when he cared too much for someone. Since Vanessa, Danny hadn't allowed himself to get close to any woman, and he still wasn't ready to take that step. Shit, last night he nearly lost it when he saw Sean with Abby. It brought up too many memories that hit too close to home. He failed when it came to Vanessa; he wasn't going to let anything cloud his judgment this time.

He watched Abby resting soundly, but he couldn't stop thinking of his fiancé. He blamed himself for her death. And at the time, it nearly destroyed him.

Their tour of duty in Iraq had been tense, and his mind was on other things. He missed the signs that something was wrong, and after she died, nothing anyone said could convince him that he wasn't responsible. Not only were they engaged, but she was also a fellow soldier who he'd worked with since boot camp. They'd served side-by-side, both sergeants in the Psychological Operations unit, commonly known as Psy-Ops.

"Abby." He said her name louder but didn't touch her this time. Abby said something in her sleep, but he had no idea what. Danny chuckled because, really, she was just too adorable.

"Come on sleepyhead; you have to wake up," he coaxed.

"Go away." She gathered the blanket closer to her body.

"I can't. It's time to get up. Let's go." He pulled at the

blanket and saw that she was only wearing the T-shirt he gave her last night. He stared. Her legs were smooth and sexy, and there was a hint of her purple lace panties peeking out. Danny threw the blanket over Abby and stood quickly. He worked for Abby. He didn't need images of her half naked in his brain.

He walked behind the chair. Distance was a must right now. His phone alarm sang "Reveille" and instead of shutting it off, he increased the volume and placed it by Abby's ear.

She jumped, causing the ottoman to shift forward. Danny laughed at her expression but stopped when she lost her balance and fell to the floor. Like a scene from a sitcom, she landed on her ass, with her legs up in the air. Abby quickly covered herself with the blanket.

"Are you okay?" he asked.

"Screw you, Nucci." She looked up at him with narrowed eyes. "Now help me up, asshole."

Danny helped her stand, mindful of her bruised arm. The blanket fell to the floor, leaving Abby in his old New York Yankees T-shirt. Even though he knew what to expect this time, the sight was too much to ignore. He tried to avert his eyes but failed.

Abby laughed and walked slowly into the bedroom, shaking her sexy ass. "I'm gonna grab a quick shower. Can you get my suitcase or do you have another one of these I could wear?" Abby flipped up the end of Danny's shirt, giving Danny an eye full.

"I'll get your clothes." Danny sighed and looked up at the ceiling. He was clearly off his game.

"Thanks." Abby winked and laughed even louder. She closed the door and left him standing in the living room with his mouth hanging open. *Holy shit.* His mind raced with all the things he wanted to do to her, and he was thankful for the reprieve. He grabbed the keycard to Abby's room and left to go get her things.

* * *

Danny, Abby, and Sophie rode the elevator to the lobby in silence. He could tell Abby was nervous about the meeting with Vivien and the attorney for Murphy Entertainment, the company that managed her career. She hadn't stopped fiddling with her hair since they left his room.

"You'll be fine. Stop doing that. It makes you look like you did something wrong." Sophie broke the silence. "Which you didn't," she quickly added.

"She's right. Take a deep breath. I'll be right by your side," Danny assured.

Abby didn't say anything but offered a small smile.

"All right, I'm going to make sure the bus is ready so that when you're done we can get the hell out of here." Sophie gave Abby a quick hug and left to do her job.

Danny held the conference room door open for Abby then followed closely behind and pulled her chair out at the table. He sat next to her as a show of support. He hated that she had to meet with Vivien, but also knew it had to happen. Sean was Vivien's personal pet and getting her to see their side of things would be a difficult task.

"Abigail." Vivien joined them at the table, opposite Abby. Abby glared at her mother. Everyone knew she hated being called Abigail.

"Mother," she replied.

"I hear there was a tiff last night between you and Sean." Vivien looked bored and disinterested.

"It was more than a tiff," Abby said. "Sean attacked me after I broke up with him. I'd like him removed from the tour."

Danny impulsively took her hand and squeezed it under the table. He wanted her to know he was here for her. They'd spent the last half hour prepping for this meeting. He knew Vivien intimidated Abby.

"Attacked? I think you're overreacting, Abigail. You look fine to me." She turned to the attorney. "I don't see anything here that warrants releasing Sean from his contract."

"Excuse me?" Danny said. There was no way he was letting that asshole get away with what he'd done.

Vivien stopped and looked at him. "Do you have something to add, Mr. Nucci?" She narrowed her blue eyes at him, and for a moment, Danny couldn't deny the resemblance between Vivien and Abby.

"I think you need to get all the facts before you dismiss what happened. Abby needs to explain the entire incident." He hated the way Vivien steamrolled Abby when they disagreed.

"All right, Abigail, please continue."

Abby stared at her, hard.

Danny gave her another squeeze, silently encouraging her. *Don't let her walk all over you.*

"I walked in on Sean with one of his groupies."

Danny could see Vivien had already made up her mind. There was nothing Abby could say to make her change it.

"When I told him that our relationship was over, he threatened me and then grabbed me." Abby's shoulders relaxed as soon as she finished. He knew how hard that was for her.

"That's all?" Vivien and Abby stared at each other, and it seemed to Danny that they were having some silent exchange that he didn't quite know the meaning of. "He has an iron-clad contract, and I'm not going to pay a team of lawyers to fight him in court because your feelings are hurt."

"What?" Danny and Abby asked in unison.

"Not to mention, the press would have a field day with this," she continued, ignoring them.

"Abby, I understand your concern, and I sympathize, but Vivien's right. He really could fight us on this. It's your word against his," the lawyer explained.

"Danny, Ron, and Sophie were there. They're my witnesses. How can you say it's his word against mine?"

"Were they with you the entire time?"

"No," Abby admitted.

"And why was that? Why do I pay for private security

if you are roaming around by yourself? Why weren't you with her, Mr. Nucci?" Vivien tucked her platinum-blonde hair behind her ear. Danny stared at her; she didn't have a wrinkle on her face, and her nose was perfectly straight. She obviously had some work done, but he could still make out some features that were similar to Abby's. They both had an oval-shaped face, full lips, and eyes that spoke volumes with just one look.

"I didn't tell him I was leaving. Sophie and I ran down to look for my phone. When things got out of hand, Sophie phoned him. I even used the panic button when Sean grabbed me," Abby said.

"Without a witness, it's your word against his," the lawyer explained.

"He grabbed me so hard he left fingerprints on my arm." She lifted her sleeve and showed them her bruises. Vivien winced; it was slight, but Danny caught it. "A lawsuit and negative press isn't as bad as letting him stay."

"I agree with Abby," Danny wanted to appeal to Vivien. Abby's marks had spurred some emotion in her, and it was the first sign she might bend. "He not only threatened and assaulted Abby, but he also threatened and attacked me. I don't think it's wise to keep him on this tour. I'm no lawyer, but you have plenty of evidence to show that he's a threat. He's unpredictable, and I wouldn't put it past him to try something again."

"Well, isn't that what you're here for? Aren't you security? Isn't this your forté?" Any spark of hope Danny had was gone after that comment.

He kept his expression neutral. He didn't want her to see how frustrated he was. "Yes. And I'm giving you my professional opinion that he's not stable and shouldn't be allowed to continue to work on this tour."

"If we let him go, the entire tour would be bombarded with even more press at every stop. It'd be a Goddamn circus." Vivien pushed back her chair, stood, and straightened her bright-blue pencil skirt. "I'm sorry, Abigail, but it doesn't make any sense to let him go now. The tour is winding down. We'll let him finish out his contract, and we won't renew for the next one. That's the best I can do."

Danny snorted at the absurdity of this meeting. No one gave a rat's ass about Abby's safety or the fact that she was hurting. He looked over at Abby. She was picking the bottom of her shirt. Another nervous habit. He tapped her on the forearm. She looked up, and he motioned with his head that she should continue.

Abby looked over at Vivien. "I don't feel comfortable with Sean. I don't want him on this tour, and I am *not* going to pretend we're a couple. You're going to have to figure out how to make that happen."

"You'll do as you're told." Vivien stood there, her arms crossed defiantly.

"Last I checked," Abby stood, her palms flat against the table as she faced down Vivien, "it's *my* name on top of the marquee, and I'm the one people pay to see. I don't want to be anywhere near him. That includes on stage, on the tour bus, and at the hotel. Hell, the entire goddamned hemisphere. I don't give a shit how you do it. Get it done." She smacked the table, and the sound echoed through the room.

Danny kept his expression neutral, but his heart flushed with pride.

"Abigail. It doesn't work like that. So what if Sean hurt your feelings? Men do that. Sean is good looking and charming. He's also feeling neglected, and that's on you. A man like that will find entertainment elsewhere if you don't give him a reason to keep coming back to you. I'm not going to fire him because you didn't learn from my mistakes. If you need to go through this on your own to understand it, fine. But you don't get to stomp your feet and expect me to put this entire business in jeopardy simply because it will make you feel better. Suck it up, Abigail. It's what we women have been doing throughout eternity. That's not going to change just because your name is on a marquee."

What the hell was she going on about? Danny glanced at Abby, then back at Vivien. This was no longer about Sean.

"Learn this now. Men don't know how to be faithful. They aren't wired that way. You have so many advantages I didn't have when I was your age. You have talent and money. That'll keep Sean in line and coming back to you, and trust me when I say you'll want his attention on others. It's safer that way."

This was getting strange. Vivien had some twisted thoughts on relationships and was filling Abby with her poison. Danny stood. He wanted to get Abby out of this room before Vivien said anything worse.

"Come on." Danny touched Abby's elbow gently and continued in a low voice, "Let's go."

"We're not done here," Vivien snapped.

Danny put his hand on Abby's shoulder in support, and he stayed standing.

"If I've taught you anything Abigail, it's to not be a naïve little girl. There is no prince charming. No happily ever after. So his eye wanders. Who cares?" Vivien placed her hands on the conference table and leaned toward her daughter. "Get over yourself. This is the music business. Expecting fidelity is absurd. Let him beg another day or two before you take him back. Make him sweat. It'll teach him a lesson."

"But…" Abby tried to argue.

"He stays." Vivien's voice was firm.

The color drained from Abby's face, and Danny reacted instantly.

"Time to go." He turned to their attorney, hoping he'd see reason. "Figure out how to keep him away from Abby, or I will. Understood?" He hooked one arm around Abby's waist and pulled her from the room; she stood frozen in what he could only assume was shock. Her mother had lost it. Telling her that it was okay for Sean to cheat on her and that she should just forgive him for what he'd done. Danny barely managed to keep from slamming the door as he fought his own outrage.

"Let go," Abby said loud enough that she drew the attention of the people passing by.

"Not until we're somewhere safe," he said quietly in her ear. He wrapped his other arm around her.

"My mother just said that I had to stay with that asshole. Tell me where it could possibly be safe."

"Let's just get somewhere not so public, and we'll debrief."

"Down here," Sophie called from the end of the hallway.

"Perfect timing," Danny noted as he swiftly guided Abby toward Sophie.

"The bus is all packed. I need to get my bag," Sophie explained.

"Will this even get us to our floor?" Danny asked as the elevator doors opened and they hopped on.

"Not yours, but it goes to mine." Sophie pressed the floor button for her room. "Hopefully, we can get to my room from this end of the hotel. If not, we're gonna have to go back to the main floor." She leaned against the wall.

Abby stayed silent beside Danny, and that concerned him.

"This way," Sophie said when the doors opened. "I think if we go down here and make a left, we should be able to access my room. This all looks familiar. Yes, here's the ice machine. It's up ahead." She swiped her keycard through the electronic lock.

"Here we go." She held open the door for the pair. He guided Abby toward the bed and waited for her to sit.

"I'll get her something to drink," Sophie said.

"You're okay. Shh," Danny assured her.

"Here you go." Sophie handed Danny a plastic cup full of water.

"Thanks." He took the cup and placed it on the side table.

"Abby, look at me." Danny sat down next to her on the bed. He needed to get a read on her. She was too quiet and disconnected.

She looked up at him.

"I need you to talk to me."

"What do you want me to say?"

"Anything."

"Why? Nothing's changed."

"I didn't quite understand all she was referring to," he admitted.

"I can't talk about him right now."

That didn't help, but he wasn't going to push her.

"I have to get out of here," she whispered. He could hear the desperation in her voice.

"Yes, I know. But you can't leave like this. Here, take a drink." He offered her the water, and she downed the entire cup in one long drink.

"Good?" She handed him the cup back.

"Much better." He smiled, trying to reassure her. She still seemed out of it, but she needed to get it together, so they could make it to the bus.

Danny rose from the bed and waited for Abby. "You can do this, right? We'll get out of here and away from all the assholes. After that, you can kick the shit out of me if you want."

He saw the smile Abby tried to hide.

"Take these." Sophie handed Abby a pair of dark sunglasses.

"Oh, thanks."

"Ready?"

She nodded, and they left the room.

"I'm going to see if I can find some good coffee. Do you want anything before we load up?" Sophie asked as they entered the elevator.

"Maybe a soy mocha latte."

"With a shot of tequila?" Sophie joked.

"Ha!"

"Okay. Large?"

Abby nodded.

"Do you want anything?" Sophie asked Danny.

"I'm good," he said. "Thanks."

The doors opened to the elevator, and they all exited.

"Okay, I'll meet you on the bus." Sophie veered left toward the shops, and Danny held Abby against him as they made their way out of the hotel. The bus was parked in the side lot, and Danny was sure there would be a small group of fans waiting. There always was.

"Chin up," he said to her.

Ron met them halfway down the hall and took a

position on Abby's right. "There're about fifteen people waiting for you."

"They'll have to be disappointed. She needs to get on the bus," Danny said.

"No." Abby looked up at him. "I can't do that. Help me get through it quickly."

"I would really feel better if you'd bypass the crowd."

"I know, give me five minutes. Time me if you want, but I can't ignore them."

"Five minutes. That's it." Against his better judgment, Danny agreed.

"Thank you." Abby tightened her grip around him and then let go.

He stayed close as she walked through the exit door and over to her fans. She posed for pictures and signed autographs. "Hi, everybody," she said, and Danny relaxed a little because she sounded more like herself.

"Thanks for waiting. I love getting the chance to say hi." She smiled for a picture and signed a T-shirt for someone else.

"Abby! Abby!" an enthusiastic fan called. The girl had to be about fifteen and was jumping up and down. Abby smiled and walked over to her.

"Hi. What's your name?"

"Tonya."

"Tonya? Does your dad work for this hotel?"

"Yes!" She bounced with girlie excitement.

"Did he show you our picture?"

"I posted it on Facebook."

"Awesome. Would you like me to sign that?" Tonya was clutching a magazine.

"Oh, my God. Absolutely!"

Abby took the magazine, signed it quickly, and handed it back. It was last month's *Rolling Stone* featuring her and Sean on the cover.

"How about we take a picture of us together?"

"That'd be *so* cool." The girl smiled.

"Do you have a phone or camera?" Abby asked.

"Oh yes." She pulled out her phone from her side pocket and handed it to Abby.

"Say cheese." Abby clicked the picture and handed the phone back to the girl. "Now make sure you tag me when you post that one, okay?"

"Of course. Is Sean here?" Tonya asked, holding out the magazine. "I would love for him to sign this, too." Her voice raised about two octaves.

"I'm not sure," Abby said.

Danny stepped in. "He's working on some new material with the guys. He'll join Abby on the bus later." He tucked his hand gently under Abby's elbow and said, "Abby, I'm sorry, we have to get going."

"Okay, thanks. It was so nice to see you all." She

smiled and waved one last time. Danny turned his body to shield her from the growing crowd and guided her toward the bus. He didn't relax until she was safely onboard with the door closed behind them. The only thing left to do now was deal with the aftermath of this morning's meeting.

chapter
four

Abby climbed onto the tour bus and was greeted by the welcoming smile of her driver, Anthony. He'd been with Abby for five years, and she wouldn't let anyone else behind the wheel.

"Morning, Abby. Ready to roll?"

"Absolutely. How are you today?" She gave him a brief smile.

"Good. Excited to get to California."

"A few more shows, and you get to spend some time with the family." Abby patted him on the back and walked into the small living area. The smell of leather and stale air hit her nose.

She loved touring because she got to perform, but she hated this bus. Except her bedroom; she loved that. Her mother had designed the bus to fit her style, but Abby had fought hard to decorate her bedroom to her liking. The living room sat right behind the driver's seat and had two cream-colored leather couches that sat opposite each other and were encased in shiny, dark-brown lacquer. It reminded her of a doctor's office. Everything was stale and cold. And, as if one sterile, rolling doctor's office wasn't enough, her mother had a second one made for herself. She was not the sort to share her space, not even with her daughter.

She kept walking until she reached the small kitchen table. She sat down and waited for Sophie, Danny, and Ron.

"Here you go." Sophie's voice startled her, and Abby jumped. She set the latte on the table and leaned against the counter opposite Abby.

"You're a lifesaver." Abby took a sip and closed her eyes, enjoying the rich chocolate flavor.

"Oh and before I forget…" Sophie dug through her bag, and Abby took another sip of her coffee. "Here ya go." She handed Abby her phone.

"Thanks." She studied the phone, thinking about all the trouble it had caused.

"Ladies, ready for a road trip?" Ron clapped and rubbed his hands together, giving them a mischievous grin.

Danny's large frame caught her gaze as he stopped to chat with the driver before the bus pulled away.

"You're way too excited about endless hours on a bus." She shook her head then got up and went to the back of the bus. She passed the bathroom and bunk area until she arrived at the door to her private bedroom. It was the only area on the bus that felt like hers. She sat down on her full-sized bed, positioned in the middle of the space. A pretty red and cream-colored comforter with scattered throw pillows made it feel like home. She plugged her phone into a floor outlet.

Abby relaxed back against the cushioned headboard and tried to figure out how she felt about everything that had happened. She closed her eyes and took a couple of deep breaths. When she opened them, Danny was standing at the door with her coffee. She startled.

"Sorry," he said.

"You scared me." She placed her hand on her heart.

"I didn't mean to. You opened your eyes when I was about to knock," he explained. "Anyway, you left your coffee on the table. Did you still want it?"

"Oh, yes. I forgot all about it. Thank you." She grabbed the coffee, and he remained in the doorway.

"You don't have to stand over there. Here." Abby moved the pillows to the side and shifted over. "Come sit." She patted the bed and smiled at him.

"Thanks. Feeling any better?" He settled next to her.

"Not really. It's been a horrible twelve hours. I can't even begin to wrap my mind around it all." She took another sip of latte.

"I don't know what to tell ya about what your mother said back there." He lightly patted Abby's leg. "But I do know you don't have to worry about Sean ever touching you again. I promise you that."

"I think that's the one thing I'm not worried about. If he's dumb enough to come close to me again, then he deserves whatever he gets. What my mother said, that was all about my father." She shook her head but didn't elaborate.

"I'm sorry. Still, these are her hang-ups, not yours. Don't let her project them onto you." He looked into Abby's eyes. "I'll protect you from both of them."

"As sweet as that is, you can't. Not from her, anyway." Abby rested against the headboard. She needed time to absorb all that happened. Eventually, the lack of sleep and stress of the day caught up with her.

* * *

Abby woke, startled by the loud noise coming from her nightstand. She recognized the ringtone. Sean. She reached for the phone and pressed the ignore button and placed it back on the table. Abby sat up in her bed and looked around the room. *What time is it?* She glanced at her TV satellite box and checked the time. One o'clock in the afternoon. She stretched and cracked her neck, doing her best to work the kinks out. Her phone rang again. Should she talk to him? If she didn't, he'd call her incessantly. Maybe she should give the phone to Danny, but she didn't want him to have to deal with this, either.

She disconnected the charger. "What?" She answered, trying to sound angry, even though she was mostly scared.

"Abby, baby. I'm so sorry. Please, forgive me. I miss you, baby." Sean rushed his words out, and his voice cracked at the end.

"Go away, Sean. Lose my number," she said firmly before she disconnected the call.

Almost immediately her phone rang again. She hit the ignore button and then shut it off. Abby didn't have the strength to deal with any more of his shit right now. Throwing off the cover, she planted her feet on the dark, wood-laminate floor. Napping during the day wasn't something she was used to, and she had a bit of a headache because of it. Abby walked through the dimly lit hall that held four bunk beds, two on each side, and into the main area of the bus.

"Morning, sunshine," Danny greeted Abby with a smirk.

"Hey." Abby waved to everyone and sat down on the end of the sofa, pulled her legs up, and wrapped her arms around them. She leaned her head against the partition and stared at the TV hanging from the wall.

"Did she just let you get away with calling her sunshine?" Sophie asked Danny in a shocked voice. "You must be half asleep," she teased.

"I feel like a truck hit me. Where are we?" Abby yawned.

"Another couple of hours until we're in Reno," Sophie said as she looked out the window.

"Here." Danny handed Abby two Excedrin and a glass of water.

"Thanks." Abby smiled and took the pills.

"You passed out. We were talking one minute and the next you were snoring."

"I don't snore." She passed the glass of water back to Danny and folded her arms. She absolutely snored, and she knew it, but there was no way she'd ever admit it to him.

Danny laughed but stopped when Abby glared at him. She turned to Sophie. "Okay, distract me. Let's go over the schedule for the next few days. I'm thinking there's some rearranging that needs to be done, and it's good that the boys are here because they can add their two cents to the mix."

"Sure, let me pull it up." Sophie picked up her tablet. "Okay, come on over and let's check this out."

Abby scooted over and spent the next couple of hours reworking the schedule with Sophie and going over any logistical things with Danny. Before she knew it, they stopped in front of their hotel, and she was feeling a little better about surviving the rest of the tour with Sean still on it.

* * *

.

"We'll be next door if you need us," Danny said as he walked around Abby's hotel room. She watched him search the room.

"Okay, thanks. Um, what are you doing?"

"Making sure you're alone."

"Oh." She started to nibble at one of her fingernails then stopped. It was a habit her mother despised. "You don't think…"

"I'm not giving him the benefit of the doubt. I've seen too much in my career to take the chance now." He continued to search the room. "Okay, all clear."

"Thanks." Abby's shoulders sagged a bit. She hadn't even thought about Sean sneaking into her room.

"If you need anything, call. And remember if you feel

frightened use your panic button."

"Thanks, and I got it." She pointed to the keychain hanging from her purse. "I appreciate all this." She gestured around the room.

"It's my job," he said, and Abby's smile faded. She'd reminded herself about that several times recently, but it hit her harder when Danny pointed out that protecting her was his job.

"Oh. Of course. Well, I'll see you tomorrow." She followed him to the door, making sure to keep her distance. After all she was *just* a job. No need for him to get the wrong idea.

"Night, Abby." He turned and looked at her with a bright smile. That made her feel a little better after his brusque answer earlier.

"Yep. Night." She closed the door and leaned her head against it, trying to make sense of her feeling of disappointment. She thought back to last night and how safe and protected she felt with him. He had been so kind and gentle with her. It was as if he somehow understood what she felt, and he wanted to save her from the experience. Danny had never reacted so passionately, and it had Abby's emotions in a spin. But apparently she read him wrong.

The hotel phone startled her. "Who's calling me on this phone?" she muttered as she picked it up. "Hello?"

"Abby is your phone off?" asked Sophie, concerned.

"Oh, crap. Um, the battery went dead." She hoped her lie wasn't completely transparent.

"That's weird. I thought you charged it on the bus."

"Well, I don't know. But it's dead." She knew she sounded bitchy, and a knot formed in her stomach. She didn't want to explain why she needed to turn the phone off. "Why were you calling?"

"To remind you about the phone interview tomorrow morning."

"Right, I completely forgot." That was a bit of a stretch since she did interviews with local radio stations in every city the tour stopped in.

"Are you okay?" Abby heard the concern in her friend's voice.

"Yes, there's a lot going on, but I promise I'll be ready for the interview. So there's no need to camp out on my sofa."

Sophie laughed. "Am I that predictable?"

"Yes, but that's one of the many reasons why I love you," she said, trying to smooth things over.

"You know it, sista. Oh, not to sound like a total nag, but charge your phone."

"Yes, Mom." Abby laughed.

"Okay. Get some sleep. Good night."

"'Night." Abby hung up then took her cell phone out of her back pocket

As soon as she turned the phone on, it began to beep and sing back at her. She had twenty-seven voicemails and thirty-five text messages.

"What the fuck?" She knew most, if not all, were from Sean, and it scared her. She spent the next ten minutes staring at her phone, trying to decide if she should delete his messages.

Even though she knew it wasn't a wise decision, she eventually scrolled through the text messages and opened one at random. *Baby, pick up. I'm sorry.* Abby continued to scroll through, looking at the time stamps for each message. 9:45 a.m., 9:52 a.m., 10:17 a.m., 10:22 a.m. As the numbers on the time stamps grew higher, so did her anxiety level with each message she read. *I'm sorry.* Followed by, *Take me back.* Then, *I love you. Please baby answer your phone.*

Abby skipped down to more recent messages; they definitely had a different tone. He stopped apologizing and started threatening. Abby opened the last message. He'd sent it only five minutes ago, and the words on the screen made her body go cold.

You think you can ignore me? You think you hurt before? See what happens if you keep this shit up. You are Mine!!!

She dropped the phone on the bed. She didn't want it in her hands. She wrapped her arms around herself and rubbed them up and down, hoping the friction would ward off the chills. *What the fuck am I going to do? He's over the edge.*

Sean was not sane. She stood there trying to figure out how this all started. The only thing that made sense was that she finally told him she wouldn't take any more of his bullshit.

Maybe he snapped when she broke things off. Ending their relationship meant ending his time on the road and in the spotlight. He was talented, and at this point he really didn't need to be with her in order to get noticed. In fact, he hated being in her shadow. There were many times he was asked to step aside so a photographer could get a picture of Abby alone. During those times Sean stomped around like a child who didn't get picked first for the team.

Abby felt more alone than ever standing in her hotel room. Odd, since she spent more time in hotel rooms than she did in her own apartment. Sean's behavior had stalker written all over it, and it affected her in a way she'd never expected. Sure, she had some aggressive fans. Everybody in her business did. But they didn't make her feel unsafe. Sean, on the other hand, made her feel vulnerable, and she didn't like it at all. She paced as she tried to figure out what to do. There was no way to predict Sean's behavior, and that left her feeling unsettled.

She needed to tell Danny, but she couldn't knock on his door when she felt so scattered and lost. He'd think she'd gone mad right along with Sean. She went into the bathroom and washed her face. The cool water helped her to focus. She looked at herself in the mirror and took a deep, calming breath.

Finally, she was ready to deal with the crazy her life had become in the last twenty-four hours. Abby grabbed her phone and headed toward the door. She needed to get to Danny's room and let him know what Sean was doing. She knew he'd freak; she also knew she needed his help. All she had to do in the five steps between her door and his was figure out how to tell him in a non-hysterical way.

She had taken two steps out of her bedroom when her phone began to ring, and she knew exactly who it was. Abby stared at it, and in a spur-of-the-moment decision, she answered the call.

"What?" she growled.

"That's not a very nice way to say hello."

"Give it up, Sean. Stop fucking calling me. We. Are. Over."

"We are far from over, Abby."

"No, Sean. We're over. Forget my number before I take this to the police," Abby threatened. "I'm sure they'll agree that what you're doing totally falls under the 'crazy stalker' category."

"I'd think twice if I were you."

"Fuck you. I'm so over this. I don't care if the world knows just how fucked up my life is. It's way better than living a big fucking lie." Abby took the phone away from her ear and was about to press the "end call" button when she heard Sean.

"You'll want to know all about what your precious Danny is doing backstage."

"Go to hell." She clicked off the phone and had a strong urge to throw her phone across the room.

Her phone started to ring, "Ahhh!" She walked out into the living room. She needed to go talk to Danny, but first she needed to calm down. The way she felt at the moment, she wouldn't make much sense. She was fuming mad.

Abby plopped down onto the couch and looked at the ceiling. What an arrogant asshole! He thought he could harass her and get away with it. That she'd take him back because of it.

Her phone dinged, indicating she had a new email. She unlocked the screen and clicked her email app. It was from Sean.

The subject line read, *Look what your bodyguard's been up to.*

He'd gone too far now. Clearly, he wasn't going to leave her alone, and she was sick of it.

Abby started toward the door but realized she didn't have her keycard. She turned to get it, Sean's email taunting her the whole time. She should ignore it. She *wanted* to ignore it, but she couldn't. *Look what your bodyguard's been up to.* What was that supposed to mean? What did Danny have to do with any of this? Sean's parting words rang in her ears. What did he mean by she'd "want to know what Danny's been doing"? Probably just trying to get her riled up.

She found the card on the nightstand and reversed her steps. She stopped abruptly when she saw the little attachment paperclip next to Sean's name. *What was he sending?* Curiosity got the better of Abby, and she opened the email and scrolled down. She clicked the attachment and waited for the file to download. It took some time. What the hell did he send her? She was about to say to hell with it when a video began to play. The quality was really bad. Abby turned her phone so the video took up the entire screen. Who was that? Where were they? The faint sounds of her band played in the background. Was this at a concert? Abby tried to zoom in so she could make out who was in the video. She knew who it *looked* like, but she wasn't convinced. Danny wouldn't do that with a groupie while she was on stage. Would he?

She blindly walked back toward her bed and sank down on it. This just wasn't possible. The angle of the video prevented Abby from seeing his face, but it did look like him. She contorted her head, as if that would help her figure out what she was seeing. *Just turn around.* She needed to see if this guy on the video had a tattoo on his left arm like Danny.

A crowd cheered in the background. Well, this was definitely at a concert. After that realization, she quickly shut off the video and tossed the phone on the bed.

She curled herself into a ball and stared at nothing. She needed time to figure things out, but it was impossible to do with the video of Danny playing in her mind, battling for her attention against the memory of Sean with the groupie. Were all men assholes? Or was it just her special curse in life? The only thing she knew for sure in the moment was she didn't want Sean to release the video. Danny might not be the man she wanted him to be—the hero to Sean's villain—but that didn't mean he deserved to have his career destroyed by Sean's petty vengeance. There were so many things she needed to *really* think about—her mother, Sean, her career, and now Danny. But there was no way that was happening tonight. There was too much swirling noise in her head for any clarity to make its way to the surface.

Her phone buzzed. She ignored it. It buzzed again. And again. Finally, she slowly picked up her phone.

Sean.

That was no big surprise. She sat up in her bed before opening the text. *Did you enjoy the show?*

Bastard. She ignored the text, but another came through. He wasn't going to stop. She looked at the phone. *Have you decided to play nice?*

Should she answer him back? No, he didn't deserve an answer. The next text came in. *You'll end his career.*

She let those words bounce around in her head. It was like Sean could read her mind or knew exactly how to get Abby to bend to his ways.

She fell back onto the mattress and looked up at the ceiling. She didn't know what she was going to do. There was no way she could pretend to be with Sean, not after all that had happened.

He used to be so different. When Kelly introduced her to Sean, he was exciting and only had eyes for her. They hit it off right away. She loved to jam with him late into the night. He took her seriously as an artist and encouraged her to keep writing. No one ever took an interest in her in that way.

Prior to that, Vivien had kept her sheltered. She didn't have boyfriends as a teenager. She worked. While girls her age were going on first dates, or to prom and graduation, she was rehearsing, recording, and selling out arenas that held sixty thousand people.

All her firsts were with Sean. She loved him, and for a long time, they were happy and inseparable, but then her mother found out how talented he was and latched her claws into him. Before Abby knew it, he was touring with them.

He changed after that. It wasn't immediate, but Abby noticed the subtle differences. He'd hang out with the band more, and she'd dismiss it. He had to bond with them, right? He needed to get to know them. Then he'd stay behind when she had interviews planned, or he'd "catch up" with her later. Always freshly showered and in a new outfit. Seemed understandable after a show.

But then it became blatant. Hard to push aside things such as groupies hanging around him, smelling unfamiliar perfumes, or finding empty condom wrappers. She told her mother, but her pleas fell on deaf ears. After a while, Abby just grew to accept it as normal. There was nothing she could do about it, so she might as well find a way to adjust.

She groaned.

The constant loop of Danny and Sean raced through her mind, intermingled with her mother's words. None of this was going away on its own, and there wasn't a damn thing she could do about it right now.

Instead of dwelling, she decided to give herself a little help forgetting for the rest of the night.

She found six of those tiny bottles of vodka in the minibar. If that wasn't enough, she'd move on to the supply of tequila. She opened one and tossed it back in two gulps. The alcohol burned against the back of her throat, but it would also help her relax. After two more bottles, her brain settled into a nice gray fog where Sean and all the other bullshit couldn't penetrate. She turned on the TV and eventually drifted off to sleep with the QVC sales person chattering in the background.

She'd sort her crap out in the morning.

chapter five

Abby awoke the next day with a pounding headache that echoed the loud banging on her hotel door. *Crap.* She rolled over and felt the tiny bottles lumped beneath her. *Fucking hell.* She rolled back to her original position and slowly sat up. The knocking continued, and Abby was certain her head would pop clean off if the noise didn't stop soon.

"I'm coming," she yelled and regretted it immediately. What had been an excellent plan to help her forget had turned into a huge hangover and a bottle graveyard scattered across her bed. This was not her finest hour.

"Abby, I'm coming in," Danny said, and Abby could hear how annoyed he was all the way through the door.

"Shit." She ineffectively tried to gather the evidence of her bad judgment, but she couldn't get her hands and feet to coordinate with the rest of her body.

"I'm coming!" She yelled louder and immediately dropped the bottles she'd managed to collect onto the floor. She clutched the sides of her head, hoping the pressure would keep her skull together. She had to stop yelling like that. She finally made it to the door only to find a very pissed-off bodyguard on the other side.

"What the fuck?" He brushed past her into the room.

"Sorry. I was sleeping and I didn't hear you."

"Where is your phone? Sophie called you. I called you. She even called your room phone and no answer. You scared the fuck out of me. I was three seconds from kicking the door in."

Abby stared at him for a long moment. The dull rush of blood through her brain muted his words and made it hard for Abby to understand what he was saying. When his last comment registered, she felt confused more than anything. "Why didn't you use your keycard?"

"Goddamn it, Abby," Danny roared. She'd never seen him this upset. His hands and voice shook as he said, "I couldn't *think*. I didn't know where you were, if you were hurt, I just needed to get to you."

Danny wasn't speaking as a professional bodyguard, and Abby heard everything he said, including the emotion behind the words, with perfect clarity.

"I'm sorry. Really, I was sleeping. What time is it?" She followed him into her room. While he searched for intruders, she popped a breath mint in her mouth.

"It's ten o'clock, and you're due in rehearsals in two hours, but you missed a phone interview with some radio station. Sophie's doing damage control." Danny walked through the rooms, obviously still on high alert.

"Shit. I forgot." She trailed behind him and sat down on the sofa. Abby pushed her hands against her temples. All this movement, not to mention the noise, wasn't helping the

80

thumpity-thump drum line stomping through her head, and on top of that, she felt a bit dizzy.

"Well, she's trying to reschedule. Why didn't you answer your phone?"

At the mention of her phone, Abby's memories from last night rushed to the front of her muddled brain and she got pissed. Her conversation with Sean and the memory of watching Danny with some woman hit her with 3-D clarity and Dolby Digital Surround Sound. *How dare he question me?* She wanted to let him have it, but she had an enormous hangover and couldn't quite think properly. Her anger added to the fog rather than clearing it away. She was in no shape to confront him, especially since she wasn't even sure what she would be confronting him about. She might be pissed, but she still didn't want to rush ahead and make things worse than they already were.

Instead of arguing, she shrugged, and that movement made her head spin even more. She bent over and cradled her arms over her head, trying to get the spinning to subside.

"What's wrong?"

"I'm not feeling well. I think I'm getting sick," she raised her head.

"Sick?" He questioned, and his voice gave him away. Danny wasn't dumb.

"I decided to have my own pity party last night. I think I went overboard, and now I have the biggest hangover...ever."

"I doubt it's the biggest ever. Even though it wasn't the

smartest thing to do, I understand why you did. You had some heavy shit thrown at you."

"You got that right." She turned away. She found it difficult to look him in the eyes. "And now I'm nauseous and dizzy and so embarrassed. I need to call Sophie and apologize."

He sat next to her and rubbed his hand over her back. "You should rest. I'll tell Sophie you're not going to rehearsal." He didn't give her a chance to respond before he pulled out his phone and dialed.

"I'm with Abby," he said, then silence. Abby assumed Sophie was venting on the other end of the call. "She was sleeping."

Abby moaned. Her head and stomach were really causing her a lot of pain.

"She's sick. I don't think she's going to make it to rehearsal today." He covered for her.

"I agree. I'll get her back to bed. I'll keep you posted."

"Danny?" she whispered and slowly sat up.

"Perfect. Talk soon." He ended his call. "I'm right here."

"You don't need to cancel rehearsals. I'll be fine."

"Do you really want blaring music in your ears right now? Because if you do…"

"Point taken."

"Go back to sleep. You'll feel better with a few more hours sleep."

"Thanks. I feel kinda stupid now."

"We've all been there. Sometimes a night to escape is just what you need. I get that."

Abby stood so suddenly the movement amped up her dizziness, and she stumbled. Danny held her steady.

"I'll help you." He guided her to the bedroom with a firm hand on her elbow. "You good from here?"

"Yes. It's the getting up and the moving that makes things all jumbled in my brain."

Danny chuckled. "Rest."

"Will do."

He exited the room but left the door slightly ajar.

She felt so confused, only partially because of her pounding head. These past few days really fucked with her emotions. She didn't have much experience with men. Sean had been her only serious relationship, and she'd spent her childhood performing and her teenage years on a bus. Now, at twenty-three, her only boyfriend turned out to be a lying, cheating bastard who didn't hesitate to hurt her when his false promises of love stopped working. And, to top it off, her mother valued Sean as her new protégée more than she did Abby's safety. It seemed Vivien saw life in two columns, one with dollar signs, the other without. Everything else paled.

She wanted to think about what she was going to do, but before she could make a decision she slipped off to sleep. Danny's gentle nudges finally woke her up.

"What?" she said with a groan.

"It's time to get up."

"Already?"

"Yeah, if you don't get up now, you'll have to leave still smelling," he teased.

"I don't smell."

"You reek. For real."

"You're an ass." She tried to hide her smile.

"Just get up and get ready."

"Aye, aye Captain."

"Now, who's the ass?"

"I'm up. Shoo." She motioned with her hands for him to go.

Danny left, but Abby didn't head for the shower, instead she searched for her phone. There were a ton of missed calls and messages, but she ignored them and searched for the number of the one person who could help get her head straight.

"Ms. Sohm?"

"Abigail." Abby was filled with warmth at the sound of her voice. Ms. Sohm was the only person who could get away with calling Abby by her full name. When Ms. Sohm said Abigail, it was with love the way Abby always envisioned a mother using her baby girl's name. You could hear the warmth and sincerity in her tone.

"Sophie told me you called. Sorry I didn't call earlier. I had a late night…" She hesitated. If she wanted honest advice,

Ms. Sohm was the person to get it from. She was Abby's teacher from the time she was ten years old until she graduated high school, and their relationship was much more than student and teacher. Ms. Sohm was the mother she always wished she had.

"What's wrong? You don't sound right."

"Oh, Ms. Sohm, I've had a horrible couple of days." She hurried into the bathroom and closed the door.

"Tell me all about it."

Abby let it all out, explaining everything that happened over the last two days. Confessing it all was cathartic.

"Don't back down Abigail. You're an adult, and what you're asking for isn't unreasonable. Despite all you've seen, you've grown into a kind and loving person. You're someone I'm proud to know. Stand up for yourself."

"I'll try."

"As for your bodyguard, don't make any harsh decisions. He doesn't sound like the type of guy to do something like that. From what I've seen, and what you've told me, he seems quite fond of you. Regardless, he is a strict professional. I can't see him leaving during a performance for any reason. Find time to talk to him. Show him the video and trust your gut."

"Right," she took in a deep breath and battled with her emotions.

"Now, it's three hours earlier there, but I'm thinking you need to get moving."

"Yes. I'm back in New York soon. I'll come see you."

"I'll be waiting for you."

"Love you."

"Love you too, Abigail. See you soon."

"Yes, I'll call you in a day or two and tell you when I'm free."

"Perfect. Have a great show."

Abby hung up the phone, feeling relieved and focused. She turned on the shower and got ready to leave.

* * *

Danny, Ron, Sophie, and three other guards from the arena escorted Abby to her dressing room. The atmosphere felt completely different compared to her show in Vegas. Only essential personnel were allowed in her room. For the first time in quite awhile, she was relaxed sitting in her chair while her assistants took care of her hair and make-up.

Sophie was also a great distraction. She kept the pre-show routine as close to normal as she could, and as with every other night of the tour, when Sophie had Abby cornered in the make-up chair, she went over any news she should know about.

"Here's our updated schedule. After the show tonight, we move directly to the bus. We have two more shows, and then you fly to New York. I have you down for two commitments while you're there, and then you get the rest of the time to yourself."

"Great, thanks. Oh, I spoke with Ms. Sohm today. Please make sure I get to see her while we're on break." She gave her a small smile to show her appreciation.

"You remembered." Sophie teased.

"Shocking, I know."

"Ten minutes, Abby," a roadie yelled from outside the door.

"You okay?" Danny asked. He stood quietly beside her, keeping watch without imposing on her routine.

"I…" Abby studied Danny's face, it was on the tip of her tongue, but this wasn't something you dropped on someone and then left to do a show. They needed time when they could sit down and talk, one on one.

"What?" He scanned the room. "We'll be out in a minute," he told everyone, and they shuffled out, leaving her alone with Danny.

"Abby?" He waited for her to look at him. "Don't tell me what you think I want to hear. Are you okay?" he asked again.

"I'm all right. I wish I didn't have to spend the next two hours on stage with that asshole, but I'll survive. I'm just going to stay away from him. I'm a bit nervous about seeing him again."

"I'll be watching. I won't leave you for any reason. He starts shit or makes you uncomfortable, look at me. I'll take him down. I don't care who's around or what the consequences are. You know that, right?" He gave Abby a hug, and she leaned into his firm chest, but when the meaning behind his words registered with Abby, she freaked.

"You can't do that!"

"Yes. I can," Danny assured.

"No, he'll start trouble."

"Trouble? What do you mean?"

"He—"

A gentle knock at the door interrupted their conversation. "Guys? We have to go." Sophie's intrusion saved Abby from having to explain.

Abby left with her escort and headed for the stage. She did her best to get her mind ready for the show. Usually she got some butterflies, but tonight she had the added stress of worrying about what Sean would do. She inserted her earplugs in and was met with the sounds of her band and the intro to her opening song. She took a deep breath and was about to step on stage to find her marker when someone grabbed her hand.

She turned, and Danny was right there.

He removed one of her earplugs, "Nothing will happen to you. He isn't dumb enough to start anything in front of all these people. Enjoy yourself like you always do, and after the show, we're off to the next stop." Danny's words took those last few butterflies away. Abby smiled, placed the plug back in her ear, and ran onto the stage.

* * *

"I love you! Good night!" Abby yelled and air-kissed the crowd before running off the stage and bypassing Sean completely. Ron was waiting for her with several other bodyguards. Danny wasn't anywhere to be seen.

"Where's Danny?" Abby asked as she was rushed through the crowd.

"He had to deal with something." Ron guided Abby toward her dressing room.

"Anything wrong?" Danny always escorted Abby to her dressing room after a show. The fact that he wasn't there made her uneasy. Something was up, and she didn't like not knowing what was going on.

"No, nothing's wrong. Stop worrying."

She looked over at him and saw his wandering eyes scoping out a pack of groupies.

"Ugh, gross, Ron." Abby gave him her best disgusted face.

"Just looking. Nothing wrong with that." He winked. "I'll wait out here for you." He opened the dressing room door. The room was completely empty and for a moment she simply stood and enjoyed the quiet. She continued on into her dressing suite but stopped when she remembered she needed to talk to her tour manager.

"Hey Ron…" she opened the door, and he was nowhere to be found. "What the fuck?"

"Abby!"

She turned at the sound of her name. Stephanie was standing behind her, smiling like a sticky sweet predator.

"Just the person I wanted to see. I'd love to get a comment from you on the story I'm running tomorrow."

Shit. Where the hell was Danny and Ron? She scanned the area but didn't see either of them.

"Of course. Why don't you come inside?" Abby stepped aside, and let Stephanie through the door.

"This won't take more than a minute of your time."

"I always have time for you." She smiled, but really she wanted to roll her eyes.

"I got a *very* interesting email this morning, and I had to take the first flight to Reno. Let me just pull it up for you."

Abby waited while Stephanie fiddled with her phone. *What was going on tonight?* No Danny, now Ron was gone and Sophie wasn't around either.

"Here we go." Stephanie's voice jolted Abby out of her thoughts.

Abby turned her attention to the phone that was shoved in her face. It took a moment to realize what she was seeing. It was Sean. Sean and her mother.

"Feel free to scroll through them all."

Abby was stunned. This couldn't be. Her mother? No way. With shaky fingers, she swiped the phone and looked at the next picture. Her heart broke. These photos were not like the out of focus video Sean sent her. These were clear. Sean couldn't talk his way out of this. She was sure he'd try, but there was nothing he could say to convince her that it wasn't him. And her mother. She was used to Sean being a lying, cheating bastard, but her mother? She was a lot of things, but this was in another league.

Her mother's total disregard for Abby was the worst kind of betrayal. She felt a great loss, and it surprised her. She thought she'd stopped expecting anything from her mom a long time ago. They weren't close, and their relationship was strained, but nothing had prepared her for this. How could Abby ever forgive her? Nothing she could say would explain this away and make it okay.

"It seems Sean has a preference for the Murphy women." Stephanie's words registered in a distant part of Abby's mind, but she had no idea what she was actually saying.

The photos overwhelmed her. They had to be fake. But she knew they weren't. Suddenly, she felt sick. She took in an audible breath.

"Where did you get these?" Abby was short of breath, and her hands were clammy. She'd never hyperventilated before, but she imagined it felt a lot like this. If she didn't get herself under control, she was definitely going to faint.

"A reporter never reveals her source. These will be on the front page of every paper tomorrow morning. I assume you didn't know this was going on?"

"Get out," she whispered.

"What dear? Speak up, I want to make sure I get your quote correct."

"Get out! Now!" She threw the phone on the ground and smashed it with the heel of her shoe and didn't stop until little battered bits of electronic parts covered the floor.

"Abby?" Sophie's voice came from behind her, but she couldn't turn, she couldn't do anything. She was in a state of shock. Her mother and Sean? No, no, no. It couldn't be.

"You need to leave."

"Who's going to replace my phone?"

"Fuck you. Who gives a shit about your phone?"

Sophie continued to argue with Stephanie. Abby heard them exchange of words, but she couldn't concentrate on it. Their voices sounded as if they were in a tunnel. Nothing seemed real anymore. She felt like an observer in her own body, as though her body was there, but her consciousness was floating somewhere far away.

"Abby? Abby!"

"Sophie?"

"Just breathe for me okay? You scared the shit out of me."

Abby listened to her friend, and as she settled her breathing, she realized they were no longer standing by the door to her dressing room. Instead, she was sitting on the couch in the back dressing area. "How'd we get here?"

"Don't worry about that. Just keep breathing. I'm going to get you water. Don't move and just listen to my voice, okay?"

"Okay."

"Do you remember what happened?"

"Um, I opened the door to ask Ron something, and he wasn't there, but Stephanie was. She wanted me to comment on an email she got. And it was…it had…" She started hyperventilating again.

"Shh, here." She handed her a bottled water.

"Where are the boys?" Sophie asked.

"The hell if I know. Ron said Danny had to deal with something but didn't elaborate."

Even though Ron said everything was okay, she knew Danny's absence was significant. And she needed to clear the stream of heartbreaking scenarios running through her mind. After the video Sean sent her last night, she wasn't able to rule anything out. He could be hooking up with a girl or bleeding out in a stairwell. One scenario made her irrationally angry, and the other filled her with deep, gut-level fear that blossomed and grew with each passing moment. Neither possibility was even remotely helpful.

"Then he disappeared. Something is up, but right now I don't care about any of that. Sophie, my mother and my boyfriend." Tears stung her eyes. She didn't want to cry, but shit…her mother. Abby thought her mother had far too much control over her career and her life, but she never thought she'd do anything this hurtful. This cut. Deep.

Sophie wrapped her arms around Abby. "Just breathe, girl." Abby held her tight and tried to follow her instructions. How much more could she take? She was getting hit with one horrible thing after another.

"I don't know how much more I can handle."

"I know."

"This shit is going to be everywhere."

"I'll do damage control. I'll put on my fightin' clothes," she winked. "I know how to throw a few blows too. But first let's get you out of this get-up and on the bus. Then we can figure out what's going on with the guys and how to handle this other mess, okay?" Sophie gave her a reassuring smile.

"Fine," Abby wiped the tears away and got up.

They spent the next half hour getting Abby out of her sweaty outfit and ready for the long trip to San Francisco. When Abby was dressed in a pair of charcoal grey leggings, a white tank, and a loose fitting scoop neck tawny color sweater, Abby followed Sophie out of her dressing room. Danny stood next to Ron, waiting for her. Relief flooded through her, and she had to physically stop herself from giving him a hug, followed by a slap for making her worry.

"Where were you?"

"What's wrong?"

"Where were you?" she repeated.

He bent down and said quietly, "We'll talk on the bus."

"No. I asked you a question."

"Abby, I'll explain everything on the bus, please. This isn't the right time or place to talk."

"Okay," she said, but his tone didn't make her feel any better.

They walked through the doors to the parking lot, and were met with a larger-than-normal group of fans waiting to get a glimpse of Abby.

"What the fuck?" Danny said. Usually, she was greeted by a small group of fans who won a pass to see her before she boarded the bus. Tonight, though, Danny had canceled all passes, and this area was supposed be clear of fans and press.

"I thought you said we were all clear?" Danny addressed Ron and quickly closed the door.

"Fuck. I…I did, man. The arena security said it was all clear." Ron stumbled over his explanation.

"Obviously not." Danny's words were cold, and he gave Ron a death glare. There was definitely some tension there.

"We should bypass the crowd," Danny said as he took her hand and started to walk the other way.

"No way." Abby stopped and twisted out of his hold. She returned to the door. After the night she had, she needed to do something that brought her joy. "I'll do a quick hello and sign a few autographs. There are guards out there, too. It's not just you two. It'll be fine."

"Absolutely not." He gave her one of his stern glares. "This isn't a controlled situation. I cancelled all after-show passes. The fact that they are even here means someone set this up. I can't evaluate the risk because I don't know anything about this."

Abby understood his concern, she really did. But she also understood that fans like these, the people who stood in the rain to catch a glimpse of her, were the basis of her career. Without them, she would fade into pop star history. "I'm sorry, but it's a chance I have to take. One quick pass of the line."

"This isn't safe." Danny's firm, professional façade crumbled slightly, and the look of desperate anguish surprised Abby. She may be just a job to Nucci Securities, but there was no denying the emotion Danny showed her in that moment. She had no idea what it meant.

"The bus isn't far. I can't ignore all those people. You'll be with me the whole time. It'll be fine."

"Fine." He turned and gave Ron a look. Abby knew they'd have words later.

"Thank you." She placed her hand in Danny's and waited for him to guide her out. She greeted the crowd, signed a few autographs, and smiled for a bunch of pictures. Abby was posing for a picture with a fan when the crowd surged forward and the barricades fell. She tried to retreat, but stumbled and was quickly overwhelmed by the press of unfamiliar bodies. Within seconds, she lost sight of Danny. She was pushed and pulled toward the middle of the crowd, and panic swelled in her chest.

"Abby!" Danny's loud voice rang over the excited crowd.

"Danny!" She yelled back, but she was pulled deeper into the crowd. It felt as if she were in a mosh pit. She continued to search the crowd for Danny and yelled in vain. There was no sight of him or Ron.

She felt a strong tug on her arm and turned around expecting to see Danny pulling her to safety. She was wrong. Standing in front of her was a very pissed off ex-boyfriend.

"Sean." Abby gasped.

"Told you your pretty boy and his crew couldn't stop me." He pulled her around the bus and out of sight from the crowd. Abby screamed, but no one heard her through the chaos around them.

"All I had to do was send your devoted bodyguards a little free pussy, and my plan fell in place." His laugh sent shivers down Abby's spine. "This all could've been avoided if you would've just talked to me."

"I told you I have nothing to say to you."

"You don't have to say anything. Just listen. I get I've made a mistake, but we're off the road soon, and we can get things back to the way they used to be."

"What way is that Sean? Is that where I pretend you aren't sticking your dick in every groupie? Or is it where I say it's okay for you to abuse me and pretend life is just peachy? Or wait, I know, it's where I pretend I didn't just see pictures of you and my mother fucking on some couch? Is that what you were referring to?"

Sean stood there, speechless. While he was distracted, she started running. Unfortunately, she didn't get far.

"Where do you think you're going? We're not finished." He yanked her back against the bus. "Abby you don't understand. She took advantage of me. She said if I didn't do what she wanted, she'd make my solo deal go away. What was I suppose to do?"

"I don't know, maybe say no. Maybe tell me. There were a million different things you could've done." She paused, remembering the photos. "Although from what Stephanie showed me, it didn't look like you were being forced to do anything."

"Son of a bitch. That Stephanie is a nosy cunt, isn't she? She's had a hard-on for me since I rejected her. Don't get me wrong, she's hot. But I'm not about to touch that."

"Bastard."

"You need to remember your place. I didn't put up with you and your mother to get nothing in return."

The longer she listened, the more Sean scared her. She reached for her panic button. It worked last time Sean had her cornered.

"Not this time." Sean caught her hand and ripped it from her wrist. Then, threw it across the parking lot.

It flew through the air and hit a large boulder She prayed the contact with the rock set it off.

"So I've been nothing but a means to an end." Abby said, almost to herself. She struggled to keep her voice even. Damn him if he thought he could see her cry again after yesterday.

He inched closer and caressed Abby's cheek with his hand and a cold shiver ran down her spine. "Honey, what else would you be? Once I sign my deal, you can go on your way. For now, you play the loving girlfriend while we're out in public."

Abby shook her head in disgust. "It doesn't matter. Stephanie said those photos go live tomorrow morning. No one's going to believe we're still together after that."

"I'll handle her."

"Your plan's fucked. Your name and your face will be plastered over every social media outlet. Soon everyone will know the real you."

"Shut up!" Sean grabbed her injured arm and did a combination squeeze-twist that hurt so much more than the last time he'd injured her. Abby screamed, but he clamped his hand over her mouth.

"Nothing's changed. Play your part." He backed away from her, and when she was no longer able to see him, she ran to the safety of the bus. She banged on the driver's side window, startling poor Anthony. He opened his small side window.

"Abby, thank God. Stay close and don't move," he instructed.

She nodded, then crouched behind the front tire. It was a crazy-mob scene on the other side of the bus and she was in no hurry to move from this spot. *What the fuck happened?*

She spent several long minutes alone, waiting for Anthony to make his way to her.

"Abby!" Danny shook her out of her trance.

"Danny!" She wrapped her arms around him.

"Listen to me." He pulled her out of his arms. "We need to get out of here, but there's no way to get you on that bus without being spotted. Sophie's inside, and Ron will meet us on the other side of the building. You and I are going to take a short ride in the storage compartment."

"You're joking, right?" She looked between the two,

convinced they'd lost their minds.

"We have no time to argue. In you go." Danny pushed a few suitcases to the side, helped Abby in, and then climbed in beside her. Anthony closed the door, and a few minutes later they were moving.

"This is the craziest thing I've ever done," she said as she wrapped her arms around Danny.

"I've got you, don't worry." He pulled her closer.

She should have been freaking out. She deserved to freak out. But Danny was so close, his hard body flush against hers. She rested her head against his chest and listened to the pounding of his heart and inhaled his fresh clean scent.

The sound of the bus's horn startled her, and she burrowed closer. She wrapped her leg around his thigh, pushed her face tighter against him, and held on for dear life.

chapter six

The bus stopped a few minutes later and just in time, too. Abby was shaking, and Danny needed to get her out of there so he could assess if she was injured and find out what the hell happened.

"We'll be out in a minute," he whispered into her ear.

He was seriously pissed about this entire situation, but he didn't want Abby to worry about him. Right now, she was his main focus. Finally, the hatch door opened, and Abby buried her face into his neck.

"Shh, it's okay, it's Anthony."

He needed to help Abby out, but he was enjoying the heat of her body pressed up against his. Danny was willing to travel the rest of the tour in the storage compartment if it meant he'd have her wrapped around his body.

"You're good," Anthony called.

Danny removed himself from Abby's grip when he got the okay to exit.

"Come on." He took her hand and walked her around to the main doors of the bus. "In you go." He stated calmly, as if it were a typical day and they hadn't been ambushed by a few hundred fans. His goal was to keep her from becoming more upset than she already was. Clearly, she was rattled and on the verge of crying. And he really didn't want to see that.

He followed her up the bus stairs. "Sit," he instructed and then took his place next to her on the sofa. It was the perfect spot because he could see the arena doors and watch for Ron. He needed to have a conversation with him before letting him on the bus.

"Are you okay?" Sophie asked as she sat down on the opposite sofa.

Abby's body started to shake. A common reaction to the adrenaline rush she must have had after that crazy situation. She crossed her arms over her chest.

"Are you hurt?" He gave her a once over, relieved when he didn't see any blood or torn clothing.

Danny tucked Abby's hair behind her ear and placed his fingers under her chin. He tilted her head so she looked him in the eyes and he could check her out for any cuts or bruises. "You're okay. All you need to worry about is relaxing for the rest of the night."

She drew in a shuddered breath. It pained Danny to see her this way.

"What?"

"Sean," she whispered so low he thought he heard wrong.

He froze.

"Sean?"

She nodded.

"He was there?"

Abby nodded again.

"Tell me everything that happened."

"I…I was signing an autograph, and the next thing I know I was pushed back and you were pulling me toward the bus…and then everything went a little crazy."

"Okay, right. A group of guys pushed us apart, and I was arguing with them to move." He flexed his right hand. The situation had quickly escalated from verbal to physical.

"I didn't know it was possible to lose sight of you so quickly." She took a couple of steadying breaths. "I tried to get back to you, but I couldn't. Then I felt someone grab my arm, and I thought it was you. It wasn't."

Danny flexed his hands to help control his emotions. The last thing he wanted to do was to show Abby how angry he was. "Go on," he encouraged Abby to continue, surprised how calm he sounded.

"It was Sean. He dragged me behind the bus. I tried to get away but he…he's really strong. He said no one could protect me from him. And I need to learn my place." She paused and took in another breath.

She was clearly struggling, but she was also talking. He wasn't a therapist, but he'd sat through enough sessions after Vanessa was killed to know that talking was the first step to healing. Besides, he needed this information in order to do his job properly.

"Anything else?" he asked quietly. He wanted to

encourage her but not so much that she shut down completely.

"Sean said I'm ruining his career, and I had to remember my place and do as I'm told. He also said how easy it was to get me alone. That..." She stopped suddenly and stiffened.

"What else?" Danny kept his voice soft, so as not to upset her further.

"Where were you tonight?"

"I was in a meeting." A stupid, useless meeting, but Abby didn't need to know that. She had enough on her mind.

"Really? Why would you schedule a meeting during a show?" Her tone was different from what Danny had ever heard from her before.

"Since your mother called and demanded it. She wanted to discuss Sean. What does that have to do with anything?"

She didn't respond.

"Tell me what's going on."

"Sean told me it only took a little pussy to get my bodyguards distracted enough to get me where he wanted."

"What?" He stared at her. "Your mother wanted to discuss a tentative plan to remove Sean from the tour. Or at least that's what she said she wanted. But when I got there, she wouldn't talk about Sean at all. She said I need to do a better job." He kept his voice steady, even though he was thinking murderous thoughts. He wanted to smack the hell out of both Vivien and Sean. "That's when I left." He took Abby's hand in his. "I know she's your mom, but seriously, Abby.

104

She's not doing you any favors."

"So nothing happened between you and my mom?"

He stared at her. "Are you really asking me that?"

She refused to look at him.

"Abby," he said firmly. "Look at me." Her gaze immediately found his. "I'd never hurt you that way. Never. You're important to me."

He needed Abby to believe in him, but he didn't realize how much he'd revealed in his haste to comfort her until the words were already out. Hopefully, she was too distracted by everything else and didn't pick up on it. The last thing Abby needed was for him to add his weird, unsettling emotions to her list of concerns, especially when he had no idea what to do with them. Acting on them certainly wasn't an option.

"Okay," she whispered and nodded.

"Tell him," Sophie said. Danny was so focused on Abby, he'd forgotten Sophie was there.

"Tell me what?"

"Nothing." Abby shook her head.

"Abby." Danny looked back and forth between the pair. Something was definitely wrong.

"He needs to know. If you don't tell him, I will."

"I saw Stephanie tonight, and she had a pretty big story to surprise me with."

"When did you see Stephanie? And why did you see

her?"

"She was outside my dressing room."

"And where was Ron?"

"I…I don't know. He walked me to the room and closed the door behind me. Later, I opened the door to ask him a question, and he wasn't there. Stephanie was."

"He wasn't there?"

"No."

Danny held back his fury at his employee and continued to question Abby.

"What did she want?" he asked cautiously.

"She didn't really have anything to say; it's more like she wanted to crush my heart and the little trust I had left." She placed her head in her hands. Whatever this was, it was big. He could feel it.

"What does that mean?"

She turned away from him.

"Abby? You can tell me anything," he assured.

"Not this."

"I can't help you if you don't tell me."

"No one can help with this. How do you help someone whose world has been torn to bits? It's just not possible."

"Abby? If I can't help, then I can at least try to protect you from it."

"No one can protect me. Stephanie's gonna release

them. Once they're out there, there's nothing anyone can do.

"Once what is out there?" he tried again.

She didn't turn back toward him, but he heard her anyway when she told the wall, "My mother and Sean."

"Your mother and Sean? What does that mean?

"My mother *and* Sean. Together."

"Does that mean what I think it means?"

She nodded.

"Fuck." He ran his fingers through his hair. That woman was no mother. Who did that to her kid?

"Stephanie ambushed Abby. I heard her badgering her and came out to see what was going on." Sophie filled in some of the gaps.

Danny gave her a hard stare.

"I threw her ass out."

"I want Sean gone." Abby lifted her arm and winced.

"You're hurt," Danny said and a cold anger settled in his chest. Give him five minutes alone with Sean. That's all he would need.

"I'm fine," she assured him. He gently pushed up the sleeve of her shirt. The fresh fingermarks made him clench his teeth together so he wouldn't start swearing again. He released Abby's arm and looked out the bus windows as Ron exited through the side arena doors.

"Danny…" Abby started.

"Stay here. Can you get her some ice?" Danny ordered.

"Wait," Abby said urgently.

"Not for this." He turned and headed for the bus doors.

"Danny, it's not his fault." Abby reached toward him.

"Please, stay right here." He strode off the bus and headed directly across the parking lot to Ron.

"That was a fucking madhouse back there. Those people are fucking crazy," Ron said when Danny had nearly closed the distance between them.

"What happened? Where were you?" He kept his voice low and dangerous.

"Well…I…um," Ron started.

"I'm going to ask you one more time. Where were you?"

"I was outside Abby's room. What are you accusing me of?"

"You never left?"

"No."

"I know you left. So where were you?" Danny gave him his military stare, the kind that made people back off.

"I…" Ron stammered.

"What?"

Again, Ron had nothing to say.

"You know what? It doesn't even matter." Danny knew he sounded cold, but he was struggling to keep his true thoughts from coming out. He looked back at the bus and saw Abby looking at him. She looked so scared and frightened. It was a memory that hit too close to home for him. He thought of Vanessa, of her chestnut brown hair spilling over his shoulder as she collapsed on top of him with a satisfied groan, and of her infectious laugh that always sounded so carefree. Then his thoughts turned, and he remembered the harsh results of cover-ups and lies.

He couldn't have someone on his team that tried to cover up the truth. He knew the consequences. Danny needed to focus before he lost his temper with Ron. He needed to keep things professional.

"I'm sorry, man. I fucked up."

"Yeah. You did. I can't have people on my team that put their needs before their clients. You're fired. I'll have your final check for you at the next stop." He turned and headed back to the bus, expecting Ron to plead with him, but he didn't. For that he was relieved. At least Ron was man enough to acknowledge his mistake. Over his shoulder, he said, "I'll have another bus come pick you up."

"Danny? What happened?" Abby asked when he stepped back onto the bus. Sophie stood behind her, clearly worried.

"Ladies, I'm sorry to tell you that Ron will not be accompanying us on the rest of the tour. Sophie, could I please have the phone number of one of the other buses? Someone needs to pick him up. He's won't be riding with us."

Abby bit her lip.

"I can make the call for you," Sophie said, eyes wide.

"Thank you." He walked into the kitchen area and

placed his hands on the counter, willing himself to calm down.

"Sure," Sophie said, strain evident in her voice.

"Please, Danny. You're worrying me." Abby came closer to him and placed her hand on his back. Her touch felt good, but right now he was too pissed to acknowledge it.

Danny turned his head toward her. "I need a few minutes, okay? Don't worry. It's a guy thing." He offered a smile, trying to lighten the mood.

Abby nodded and left him alone.

* * *

A few minutes were more like an hour, and Danny was still pissed about everything that happened. Ron's failure as a security guard meant that Danny had a ton of administrative work to do. He called his New York office and left a message for his assistant to initiate all the necessary paperwork that came with terminating an employee.

Vivien added another layer to the mix of crazy these past few days. He couldn't fire her or Sean as if they were his employees, but *something* had to be done. He didn't even want to think about how bad things could've really gotten. What happened was bad enough.

On top of everything else, he'd been forced to acknowledge his feelings for Abby. He couldn't deny them with all the crap flying around. His need to protect her went well beyond professional obligation. And how stupid was it for a bodyguard to be attracted to the star he was guarding?

110

Bad idea. Now, instead of focusing on protecting her, he was overly emotional, and it made him irrational. Somehow, he needed to stay focused on getting them through this tour.

He joined Abby on the couch.

"Better?" she asked and placed her iPad on her lap.

"Yes. Sorry about that."

"What happened?"

"From what I can piece together, I think Sean and your mother set us up. Your mother called me to that meeting, and Ron then left his post, which left Sean time to do his thing. I'm not sure about Stephanie. She might have seen a rare opening to get you alone and took it. Or maybe she's involved. I'll put one of my men on it. Regardless, I'm pretty sure those guards outside were involved, too, but I don't have proof."

"Shit," she murmured.

"That's about right. I left Ron in charge when I met with your mother. I wish I'd known what she was doing, and I would have refused the meeting. Ron knew better than to leave you alone. That's a major failure in security. You don't leave the person you're guarding. Ever. I can't trust him, and that's why he's gone."

"Okay." She rubbed the edges of her iPad nervously.

"We should meet with your mother and your management team. If they don't do what I ask, we should go to the police. What happened today jeopardized your personal safety, and it's directly related to your mother and Sean. We need to start a paper trail. Sean's lost it, and I'm not playing by their rules anymore. You're my number one concern, and

I'm going to do whatever it takes to make sure he doesn't get near you again. Today was out of control, and I'm sorry. I underestimated him, and that won't happen again." This was personal, now. Sean had better watch his back.

"You have nothing to be sorry for. I don't blame you." She rubbed her hand up and down his back, a comforting gesture, but her touch had a totally different effect on him now. He couldn't afford those kinds of thoughts at the moment, so he shrugged away from her.

"Are you sure about the police? I mean we don't really have proof that he was behind this today. My mom's a bitch, but she doesn't want to hurt me. Well, not physically, I'm only her money; those pictures made that perfectly clear."

He focused on the issues at hand. "Absolutely. Sean is a loose cannon, and he needs to leave the tour. He's put you in danger personally and professionally."

"My head is spinning from all this. I don't know what to think or who to trust."

"Things have gotten out of control, but if we work together, we'll eventually reach a point where you feel safe again. Until then, though, you need to stay sharp. Don't let anyone intimidate you. Sean's not stable, and that means it will be hard to anticipate what he's up to. I know you're scared, but if he contacts you or threatens you, you gotta tell me. Not telling me something, however small, makes my job harder.

"I do have something else I'd like to talk to you about, but right now I'm just so confused with all that's happened. I need time to sort it out in my head." Abby looked bereft with her shoulders slumped and eyes downcast. She was sad and tired, and him pushing like this wasn't helping. He wanted to know what was on her mind, but he needed to let her rest. She was having a rough go of it and giving her time seemed like the decent thing to do, even if it drove him nuts.

"Okay, fair enough, but if what your holding back can cause you harm, I really hope you'd trust me enough to share."

"It's nothing like that. Right now, I just don't trust myself. Every time I think I've wrapped my head around things, something new pops up and makes me doubt myself." She rubbed her eyes and took a deep breath.

Hearing her say she didn't trust herself made Danny angry. How dare they do that to her?

He didn't like how they manipulated her as though it was okay to do. Her mother made excuses. Eventually, Abby needed to say enough is enough and put her foot down. He could see she wasn't in that place yet, but he hoped with some time she'd get there. Sophie was a good friend, and she'd listen and help Abby, but he wanted to be that person for her, too. Danny wanted Abby to trust him and feel as though she could come to him. They really did a number on her, and she needed to know she had people who were there for her.

"I care about you, okay? I don't want anything to happen."

Abby lifted her head, and she looked surprised by his words. If Danny was being honest with himself, he was shocked as well.

"You should rest." He went to stand, but Abby grabbed his shirt and he stopped.

"I'm sorry."

"Don't be sorry. Remember that the more you let them in your head, the more you give them control. How about you pick out one of your weird movies? You can watch it, and I can make fun of it? Sound good?"

"Sounds perfect. What are you in the mood for?" She laughed and walked to her room.

"You up for it, Sophie?" Danny hollered to Sophie, who was getting ready for bed.

"I don't know how you both have an ounce of energy left. I'm going to bed. Have fun bickering," Sophie said with a laugh.

"Your loss," he said and laughed, too. He followed Abby into her room, thinking this was a bad idea, but that didn't stop him. After all that happened tonight, he needed to be close to her.

chapter
seven

"We have to watch this one," Abby said.

"Which one?" he asked.

"*The Goonies*" she cheered and passed him the disk.

"The what?"

"*The Goonies*. You're joking, right? 'The truffle shuffle'?" She mimicked the dance. "Nothing?"

He shook his head.

"Come on?"

"Nope," Danny said and let the "p" pop at the end. He loved the sound of her laughter. And though he had seen the movie several times, he liked seeing Abby in a playful mood.

They watched the movie in her room because she had a fifty-inch television with surround sound, plus a bed that was a hell of a lot nicer than his bunk. Overall, it was a pretty comfortable way to watch a movie, especially with Abby next to him.

She didn't last thirty minutes before she fell asleep. Danny was comfortable lying on the bed with her nestled into his side, but he knew he couldn't stay. He slowly untangled himself, shut off the television, and quietly left the room.

Danny settled onto his bunk, but his brain couldn't rest. He needed to get to the bottom of what happened today, and the only way to do that was to talk to one of the masterminds behind tonight's events—Vivien.

He knew it was just after midnight, but he didn't care. He'd leave a voicemail letting her know they needed to talk. It wasn't as good as an actual conversation, but it was better than sitting in his bunk all night and stewing on everything that happened. Not once since he'd started this business had he run into such a fucked up situation. Abby's own mother was as much of a problem as Sean. Danny didn't want to wake Sophie, so he went into the kitchen and dialed Vivien.

"Do you know what time it is?" Vivien greeted Danny on the second ring. She surprised him by answering the call.

"Vivien?" He was a bit taken aback that she answered. "Are you able to talk now?"

"It's quite late."

"I understand, but I'd really like to discuss what happened tonight. Some changes need to be made."

"What's so important that it couldn't wait until morning?" she snapped.

"You're plan with Sean to scare Abby."

"My what? You've lost your mind. I have no idea what you're talking about."

"Really, Vivien, you can stop pretending."

"If Sean did anything to Abby, that has nothing to do

with me, and everything to do with you and your failure to do your job."

"That's my point. Your interference is making it impossible for me to do my job effectively."

Vivien sighed exaggeratedly. "Stop talking in circles and tell me what *issue* you have so I can get to bed."

His issue? It would take more than a few minutes on the phone to tell her all his *issues* with what an incompetent, uncaring mother she was. He paused a moment to collect himself. Allowing himself to get off point with this conversation might make him feel better momentarily, but it wouldn't in the long run.

When he was able to speak without yelling, he said, "My issue is that Sean told Abby that you helped him stage a mob outside the stage door. He used the distraction to kidnap Abby."

"What?" Vivien sounded truly panicked, and Danny realized what he'd implied.

"We have her, Vivien. She's safe now. Scared, but safe." It was odd, trying to comfort a woman who did nothing but hurt Abby and make his job harder.

"Then why would you say something like that? Are you really so incompetent that you would let a guitar player kidnap my daughter? Or are you just so stupid that you would lie about something so awful."

Danny considered his response carefully. He wasn't sure whether she was emotional about Abby or if she was simply baiting him into losing his temper. Ten years ago, he would have jumped all over it without considering the angles, but not now. He knew responding with anger wouldn't get him anywhere with Vivien. She enjoyed sparring too much. He needed to keep the focus on the main issue and not let her sidetrack him.

"I'm sorry I scared you just now. That wasn't my intention. I'm just trying to understand everything, and it's not easy. I know that you and Abby have...a complicated relationship. And it's none of my business. Until," he paused for effect, inhaling and exhaling fully before saying, "your...disagreements put Abby in danger. I don't understand what you have to gain from hurting Abby, but I know that it has to stop."

"You're out of line. I handle the talent. You protect it. If you can't handle that job—and from what I've seen recently, you can't—then you can leave. I'm sure I can find a more competent security company."

"You can *try* to fire me." And he'd love to see that. "But I won't leave Abby's safety in anyone's hands but my own. And I'm worried, Vivien. I'm worried about what would happen if the press found out that you protected the man who abused your daughter. Or if they found out that you knew about the abuse and allowed it to happen a second time. Or what if they found out that you were more worried about that man's career than you were about your own daughter's safety? How do you think that would go? Do you worry about that too?"

"Are you threatening me, Mr. Nucci? Do I need to remind you about the non-disclosure agreement that you signed? If you leak anything, I will *own* you. Nucci Securities will become Murphy Securities; do you understand me?"

Danny almost laughed out loud at the indignation in her voice, but caught himself just in time. "No, no threats. You don't need to worry about me. I'm just thinking about all the possibilities. That's what you pay me to do. The situation is volatile. Abby is scared. I can't promise that *she* won't go to the press."

"She'd never do that. Abby knows better. And if you encourage her, you'll only make matters worse. If you care about her as you say you do, you won't let that happen. You'd be better off focusing your worries there."

"Keeping Abby safe is the *only* thing I worry about. You hired me to protect Abby, and that's exactly what I'm doing. Even if it means protecting her from you." He'd remained as calm as he could for as long as he could. Tomorrow, he'd pay for being so abrupt, but tonight it felt good.

"And what do you propose would keep both Abby and I safe from vicious, unfounded rumors like that?"

"I think if you terminated Sean's contract before noon tomorrow, it would take the teeth out of any claim someone could make about you not caring about Abby's well-being." He tried to keep the smug satisfaction out of his voice, but he knew he failed. He couldn't help it. He'd actually backed Vivien into a corner and forced her to consider what he was saying.

"I'll give some serious consideration to your...suggestion."

"Thank you. That's all I can ask. Good night, Vivien."

Danny disconnected the call and returned to his bunk. He felt a tentative swell of pride bloom in his chest. His plan might actually work.

"What do you think she'll do?" Sophie's voice startled him.

"I don't know. But it won't matter at all if Stephanie releases those pictures." For Abby's sake, Danny hoped that Stephanie wouldn't release them, and that Vivien ended Sean's contract. That would be the simplest, easiest solution and would cause Abby the least harm. Regardless of how the next twenty-four hours played out, one thing was certain; Danny was ready to go to war if that's what it took to keep Abby safe.

* * *

By late morning, the bus pulled into San Francisco. Danny hadn't heard a word from Vivien, which could be good or bad. He never knew with her. He tried not to think about Vivien by focusing on Abby and making sure she was taken care of, especially after yesterday.

"Here's the plan," he said while standing in the door to Abby's room, the perfect spot to talk to both her and Sophie. They were both getting ready to leave the bus. "I have a buddy of mine meeting us at the hotel. He's going to help with security until we leave for New York. He should be waiting for us."

"Oh good. I was wondering what was going to happen

now that Ron's gone. What's his name?" Abby asked.

"Scott. I couldn't get anyone here fast enough from New York, so I called in a favor. All right, now the important stuff. Once we check in, can we find some food? I'm starving, and the schedule today is insane."

"This hotel is completely over the top. I've scanned their menu online, and we *have* to eat there. Trust me. I'm Italian. I know food," Sophie said from the bathroom. "I think we're a bit underdressed compared to you." She inspected Danny's crisp, black tailored suit.

"To hell with that. I'm hungry. You can drop me off at McDonald's," Danny teased. He glanced at Abby. She smiled but seemed distant. "What do you want to do?" he asked as he took her bag.

"Breakfast here is fine," she said in a small, tired voice, and Danny wanted to strangle Vivien for being such a horrible mother and allowing an abusive fuck like Sean to touch her daughter.

"Okay, food decided. Anthony said we'll be at the hotel in about ten minutes. I'm going to see if Scott is here." He left Abby alone, but he had bad feeling in his gut.

After they pulled into the hotel parking lot, he left the bus, greeted Scott, and quickly filled him in on the basics before checking back in with the girls.

"Ready?" he asked Abby.

"Yep." She stood in the kitchen, sunglasses in her hand.

He guided her up the stairs of the historic hotel and

through the black and gold revolving door. Sophie followed closely behind them.

Danny veered left when they entered, avoiding the large lobby of onlookers. He went straight to the concierge, sidestepping the line.

"Welcome to the Mark Hopkins, Ms. Murphy. We've been awaiting your arrival. I'm Jonathan," the gentleman greeted them.

"Good morning, Jonathan," Abby said. "I'm very excited to be staying here. I've heard nothing but good things." She greeted him with a bright smile. Danny stifled a laugh because he knew how Abby hated places that were filled with pretentious people. She was very much a down-to-earth kind of woman who would rather spend a night watching a Yankees game with good friends than hobnobbing with the rich and famous.

He scanned the large crowd, thankful he had Scott at his back. The crowd seemed to be growing, a common occurrence when people realized they were in the same room as Abby Murphy. He needed to find a permanent replacement for Ron, but Scott would definitely do until he had a minute to sort shit out. Luckily, there was a two-week break coming up, and he could go back to New York and handpick the perfect person.

"Your rooms are ready, Ms. Murphy. Here are your keycards, and your luggage will be brought up shortly."

"Thank you," Sophie said and grabbed the keycards.

Danny didn't wait for him to finish. Instead, he tucked Abby into his side and headed toward the elevators.

"You first," he directed Sophie to walk in front of him.

"This place is beautiful," Sophie said as she looked around.

"It's all right." Abby rolled her eyes and glanced Danny's way. They both knew how Sophie loved the extravagance of hotels like this one.

"Good morning, Ms. Murphy. The bellman greeted the group and ushered them in. They rode the elevator in silence.

The doors opened, and Scott walked out. He gave Danny the all clear, and Danny motioned for the ladies to follow. He heard Abby thank the bellman before she left the elevator.

"This way," Danny gently placed his hand on Abby's lower back and guided her down the hallway toward her suite.

"There are only three rooms on this floor," Sophie said as she handed him two of the keycards.

"Good. Makes it easier to keep an eye on things. Breakfast, half hour?"

"Perfect. I'm starved. Just knock on my door."

"Scott, check out Sophie's room please." Scott took the keycard from Sophie, and she followed him in. Danny moved down the hall with Abby close behind.

He opened the door to her room. "Stay right here," he ordered.

"Aye-aye Captain!" She smiled, and it gave him a little thrill. He couldn't stop himself from smiling back. It was automatic—when she smiled, he smiled.

"You think you're funny, eh?"

"As a matter of fact, I do." Her smile got bigger.

"Well, at least someone does. Hang on. I'm going to make sure the suite is clear."

"Yes sir." Abby saluted.

"You're too much." Danny entered the suite and swiftly checked the rooms then returned to the living room. "We're good," he announced.

"Well, that's a relief." She came in, and he followed her with his gaze as she traveled the short distance into the living room and sat on the sofa. That was his cue to encourage her to open up.

"I think—" they both began.

He motioned for her to start.

"I want him gone. I…"

"Talk to me." He said simply. The nagging feeling in his gut returned, and he finally understood it meant something was wrong with Abby. She wasn't herself, and he could see why, but he wanted to talk about it. Abby had admitted that she had something to share, he just hoped she was finally ready to talk. He sat down next to her on the couch.

"I don't want to be my mother. Staying with some man because she thinks she doesn't deserve better or because she's somehow dependent on him. I'm not her, and I don't want that to be my life, but she's forcing him on me, and it doesn't matter what I think or say. I can't go on like this anymore."

"I spoke with your mother last night after you fell

asleep." He figured there was no reason to sugarcoat it.

"What? Why?" She was clearly surprised, and he couldn't tell if it was good or bad.

"I couldn't sleep, and I needed to speak with her about what happened. I reminded her about what might happen if the press learned that she prioritized Sean's career over your safety."

Abby gasped. "You didn't?"

"The only thing I want is for you to be safe. Period. I'm willing to do whatever it takes. Whatever. It. Takes."

"I still can't believe you did that. She must have been so angry." Abby shook her head, a look of disbelief on her face. "I can't even imagine."

He picked up her hand and brought it to his chest and then he waited. Danny inched closer and looked into her beautiful blue eyes that held so much sadness and worries behind them. "Please Abby, let me keep you safe. I can't stand back and let this continue to happen. I'll do whatever you want, but you have to let me protect you."

She gripped his shirt in her hand and leaned over to lay her head on his shoulder. He knew she was struggling. He could feel it, but he wasn't going to back down. This was too important. *She* was too important. "He assaulted you, twice, and I'm no PR guy, but if that gossip lady really goes public with those pictures, the little privacy you have is going to disappear. Maybe talk to Sophie, but I'm thinking you'll want to be ahead of the story."

"I haven't spoken with my mom about them yet. I

don't even know if she knows they exist or that Stephanie has them. I'll talk to Sophie. I just need some time to think things over. I'm not mad you talked to her but please from now on discuss things like that with me."

"You got it. I'm sorry."

"Thank you." She sat up and dropped her hand. "What did my mom say?"

"She wasn't happy, that's for sure. She threatened and yelled."

"I bet."

"She did sort of fire me though, but I told her what I thought of that."

"You did not!" She laughed, and he was relieved that she wasn't screaming at him for stepping over the line.

"I sorta did." He grinned, feeling smug. "Now, breakfast?" He stood.

"What about Sean? He isn't going to go away quietly."

"I don't expect him to. He's stepped over too many lines, and your mother really has no choice, and she knows it."

"I know." She was quiet for a beat. "I'll have to replace him. Which won't be easy. He's actually a very good guitar player."

"Do you have anyone in mind?"

"Eric, one of the roadies, is my first choice. I heard him play during sound check once, and his riffs are a-maz-ing."

Danny shrugged. "I'm glad he's in house. That will make things easier. Now, can we go eat before Sophie knocks down your door, bitching that she's starving?" He motioned for her to follow him.

"Yes. I seem to have gotten my appetite back." Abby jumped up and gave Danny a hug.

He was taken aback for a moment, but soon closed his arms around Abby and held her tightly. He reveled in the feel and smell of her. He gave himself this moment but knew he couldn't take this further without crossing into some dangerous territory.

He still had occasional nightmares over the loss of Vanessa, and he couldn't risk getting involved with Abby. He didn't trust himself. If he ever let his feelings for someone he was supposed to keep safe overrule his better judgment again, and something bad happened because of that, he couldn't take it. He barely survived Vanessa, and it'd been nearly two years.

He needed to stay as detached as he could and keep sharp. If he didn't he knew he couldn't provide her with the protection she obviously needed, not only from Sean, but from her mother. Not to mention the general crazies out there.

"Don't think with your dick" was the advice he'd gotten from a C.O. he'd respected during his military service. He was dangerously close to doing just that. Before he ended the hug, he took one more breath so that he could commit her smell to memory. Getting this close to her again would be a mistake, and he hoped she couldn't tell how fast his heart was pounding.

"Let's go get Sophie," he said hastily and motioned for

Abby to walk ahead of him. He needed some physical space. The two paces she walked ahead of him wasn't much, but it would have to be enough. His self-control, and her safety depended upon it.

chapter eight

Abby waited right inside the door of her dressing room as Danny and Scott did a sweep of the area.

"You're a tiny bit paranoid, Nucci," she hollered as he checked the bathroom.

"I like to think I'm thorough." Danny finished with the bathroom, apparently satisfied that no crazy-stalker ex-boyfriend was hiding in the toilet. He smiled as he walked toward her.

"Thorough is good." She turned away, trying to hide the blush that stained her cheeks as she thought about the other things he might be thorough about.

"You shouldn't hide your face," he said as he passed her.

"What?" She wondered if she'd heard him right.

"It's all clear. You can get ready now."

Before she could press him about his earlier comment, her phone rang. She dug through her bag, and found her phone at the bottom of the mess that she liked to think of as an organized disaster.

Her stomach clenched. "Great. My mother."

She didn't really have the energy for this, but she was filled with an odd mix of curiosity and dread. Was she calling to say Sean was packing his suitcases? Did she know about the pictures or video? God, her life had turned into an episode of TMZ, and it wasn't nearly as amusing to live as it was to watch.

Danny smiled softly and nodded in a way that she'd come to recognize as his silent form of encouragement.

"Hello?"

"Abigail, you'll be pleased to know that Sean has been released from his contract. You can thank Mr. Nucci for that."

"It needed to happen." Abby moved to the back room.

"Well, it's done. Don't blame me for what happens next." Vivien's implied threat was impossible to miss. Her tone dripped with contempt and annoyance…and a strange tint of disappointment. Abby wasn't sure if she was disappointed about Sean leaving or with Abby pushing for it to happen.

"I'm sure it won't be as bad as when Stephanie releases the pictures of you and Sean fucking." Abby hadn't planned on confronting her mother over the phone, and the words probably surprised her as much as her mother. Vivien's attitude put Abby on the defensive, and so she blurted out things best said calmly and with tact. She'd wanted to be face to face with her so she could see her reaction. Was it regretful? Spiteful? Did she have any emotion at all? Or was she this stone faced person that Abby had come to expect? Too late for that now. What was done, was done.

Abby waited for her mother to deny it or say some snide comment, but beyond a small gasp, Vivien said nothing.

"What, you have nothing to say?" She raised her voice. Silence wasn't something she ever got from her mother.

Abby noticed a shadow at the door of the room. Danny was hovering just outside the threshold. He looked as if he was deciding whether to knock on the door and come inside. She could see he was worried and concerned. It would be so easy to wave him in and lean on him for support, but she wanted to take control of her life. That meant relying on herself to be strong, not everyone else.

"Abby, that was..." Vivien fumbled over her words. "He was—"

Abby cut her off, too impatient to wait for her mom to figure it out. "You know what? I don't want to know."

She ended the call and turned off her phone. Abby was done. There was nothing her mother could say that would make sleeping with Abby's boyfriend okay.

Abby sank onto the couch and took a moment to gather herself. She rested her head against the cushion and closed her eyes.

So much for her perfect life. She'd give up all the fame, money, and notoriety to have parents who loved her and didn't want anything from her except her love in return. Trying to maintain a shiny exterior when the rest of her life was crumbling in decay was exhausting.

She lifted her head when she heard a knock at the door. Danny stood there, and she felt bad for ignoring him before. He looked so worried for her. When was the last time that happened? No one ever worried about her? Or cared how she felt about things. She was the provider. The worker. The person that went out of her way to do for others.

"Can I come in?"

Her heart swelled with emotions. He was such a good guy, the kind she use to dream about. He was the type of guy she wished for when she was younger. The guy that put her before anyone else. The type of guy that cared for her and didn't want to hurt her. She could fall for him so easily—hard and fast. She wasn't sure she hadn't already. But her judgment was crap when it came to men. She'd trusted Sean once upon a time, too, but he'd turned out to be a controlling, manipulative, abusive asshole. Just like her father. She needed to be more cautious. To move slowly. Until she learned to trust herself a little more, it wasn't fair to get involved with anyone. Especially a guy like Danny.

"Sure."

"Do you want to talk about it?" He sat down next to her on the couch.

Did she want to talk about it? Not really, but she had to let him in on some of it. He needed to know. "Well, Sean's been let go. That's the good news."

Danny's shocked expression told her he was just as surprised as Abby had been. "That *is* good news. I really didn't know which way your mother was leaning. But if that's the good news that means there's bad news. Do you want to share it?" he asked, hesitantly.

"Well…" She sighed. Did she really want to share this with Danny? Or anyone for that matter? It was one thing for everyone to know about the photos, but it was another to say aloud that your mother really was as horrible as they all thought. She knew everyone thought Vivien was a bitch, but thankfully they were all too professional to ever say it outright. "I hadn't really planned on telling her about those pictures, but it just sort of came out. She was being all smug and condescending and I just couldn't stop myself. She didn't even try to deny it. I don't know why I thought she would. I guess I was just hoping that maybe…I know completely stupid and obviously they *are* real."

"I'm sorry."

"Don't be. At least I don't have to worry about Sean anymore. He's gone. That right there is a reason to celebrate. Thank you for that." She paused to find the right words. "I'm so grateful…I just…thank you." Abby was making a mess of this. Her voice defined her, shaped her life and her career, won her the adoration of millions, and now, when she needed it most, it failed her. How could she possibly explain how much she valued Danny? How much his care and kindness meant to her? She knew his feelings for her went beyond the normal client-bodyguard relationship, but he worked so hard to hide it. He didn't want her to know, and while she didn't like it, she had to respect it. In order to do that, she had to maintain at least a small amount of her personal dignity. Anything she might say to convey her gratitude would also reveal the depth of her feelings for him, something she wasn't willing to do when he clearly didn't want her to. Instead, he played this painful game of push-pull that drove her mad and made her feel vulnerable in a way that Sean or her mother never had. She just couldn't expose herself further. Not until Danny was ready. And if that never happened, so be it.

She stared into his brown eyes that sparkled back at

her with so many questions behind them. She loved his eyes. She could get lost in them. Abby inched closer to Danny, her gaze moving to his full lips. God, she desperately wanted to feel them brush against her own, to taste the sweetness of his kiss.

She'd tried to deny her attraction. How many times had Sean accused her of being hot for Danny? Too many to count, and now she was inches away from him, and all she could think was how much she really wanted to feel his lips, his tongue caressing hers. She couldn't tell him how she felt, but goddamn she wanted this. *Fuck it*, she thought as she leaned in even closer.

"Ab—" Danny started, but a knock at the door stopped him.

"Abby, you're needed on stage." Sophie stood in the open door, head down over her clipboard. She looked up, and her smile faded. She did a visible double take. "Umm…"

Danny shot to his feet, his movements too rushed to be graceful. He darted a glance at Abby then took a hasty step away from the couch, his complexion grew darker with every second. In any other circumstance, Abby would have found his blush adorable. Now, however, it was mostly horrifying.

"Oh, shit." Sophie stared at him then at Abby. "Um…it's time for your sound check," she managed.

Danny ran both hands through his hair. "I'll wait outside."

He left, and Sophie stared at Abby. "Is that a good idea for you and him?"

"Don't worry about it." Abby sighed. "Nothing happened." She stomped out of the dressing room, cursing Sophie's timing. Lately it seemed that all she did was make an ass of herself, and she was so fucking sick of it. To top it off, Danny ran from her like a fifteen-old-boy caught with his hand up his date's shirt. *Fuck my life.* The day had barely started, and she was already humiliated. And there was nothing she could do to change it.

* * *

Fuck!

Danny berated himself. Didn't he say earlier today that he needed to maintain his distance from Abby? And he'd done *such* a good job. But then she was *right* there, looking at him with those eyes, her face tilted toward him with her lips slightly parted. God, he wanted to kiss her. Everything inside him felt *perfect* as they moved close enough for him to feel her breath upon his lips. He would have kissed her. Completely.

What the fuck were you thinking, Nucci?

Now he needed to get through the rest of the day, which included standing in the wings and watching as she strutted her sexy little body across the stage for sixty-thousand people.

It took every ounce of strength he had to *not* let that kiss happen. Even then, it hadn't been enough. Thank God for Sophie and her bad timing. A few moments later, and she would have found them entangled with Abby beneath him as he fumbled to get the front of her pants open.

But now here he stood, watching Abby going over tonight's playlist with her band, and the only thing he could think was how her body told him everything he didn't want to know. She wanted him. It didn't escape Danny that during their almost-kiss her breath had skipped, then sped up as her body inched closer and closer to his. And her eyes—those damn fucking eyes—split their time between looking at him and looking at his lips. And he'd wanted to devour her. Just thinking about it, and he was hard again.

He knew what he should do. If any of his employees came to him and told him that they almost kissed the person they were hired to protect, he'd immediately reassign them. No question about it. Nobody could effectively do his job while constantly fighting the overwhelming need to possess his client, when all he wanted was to be so deep inside her that the world narrowed to the sharp, beautiful moment where only she exists. As he watched Abby, he could barely *think*, let alone function well enough to ensure her safety. So much for not thinking with his dick.

While he would immediately step in if an employee was in his situation, there was no way he could force himself to leave Abby. Knowing the right thing and doing it were two totally different fucking things. He was a hypocrite, and he didn't care. There was no way in hell he was going to let anyone else protect her. He would never step down. All he had to do was maintain his distance.

He needed boundaries. There was no way he could avoid her, so he had to figure out how to keep things professional. He found it hard to stand near her and not touch her. Guiding her through crowds would be hard enough. He always kept a hand on her, or an arm around her, in those situations. He simply didn't trust himself to be alone with her in private. Besides, he was her bodyguard, not her fucking counselor. If she was upset, he needed to take a step back and let Sophie handle it. He should have been doing that all along. But he hadn't, and he'd let himself get emotionally involved.

Next, he had to figure out a way to stop getting hard every time she smiled at him or laughed or walked or...

Fuck!

He needed to pull himself together. Fast.

* * *

"Good night San Francisco, I love you!" Abby yelled to the crowd, and they roared even louder. Danny waited in the wings of the stage to escort her directly to her dressing room and then straight to a waiting limo. The show's vibe was so much better without Sean. More relaxed and happy. Plus, Eric had indeed proved he was worthy of the chance, and if he did that well in the next show, she'd give him the gig on a permanent basis.

Abby ran off the stage and right to Danny.

"Hey you," he greeted. "Excellent show."

"Thanks. It felt good."

He ushered Abby straight to her dressing room where

she quickly showered and changed so that they could leave for the airport. There was no time to chat. Sophie had all her essential items out, and that made things run smoothly. Abby opened the door of her dressing room, completely dressed and ready to go, forty minutes later.

"Done?" Danny asked.

"Yes, I think that's a new record."

"I know it is," he teased, and Abby immediately felt like maybe things would be okay between them.

She smiled and tried to ignore the rush of butterflies fluttering in her belly. She averted her gaze. The last thing she wanted was for things to be weird, and she wasn't sure how he felt about the almost-kiss. Shit, she wasn't even sure how she felt, but she knew she didn't want their relationship to change because of one stupid, thoughtless slipup.

They walked in silence with Sophie behind them. The entire situation felt strange and awkward. Abby hadn't had a free moment to speak with Sophie, and she didn't really want to go there with her. She knew what Sophie would say, and it wasn't something Abby didn't already know. Hooking up with Danny would be disaster. He was her bodyguard. Hired to protect her. He wasn't here for anything more. She knew this, but that didn't mean there wasn't a pretty big part of her that was disappointed. She was in trouble. No matter how much she wanted him, it was the wrong time. And Danny wasn't the kind of guy to wait around.

"You rocked it up there." Someone shouted as they passed by a group of onlookers that had gotten their hands on some backstage passes.

Danny motioned for her to precede him. They walked in silence down the narrow hallway that led to the exit. The quiet between them brought a knot to her stomach. She desperately wanted to break the silence, but she couldn't think of anything to say. The buzz from the show was rapidly wearing off.

Danny and Scott moved her quickly down the hallway behind the stage, and three huge bodyguards that worked for the arena helped to protect Abby from the backstage onlookers. Before she knew it, she was in the backseat of the limo and speeding away from a crowd of fans that were running after them.

"How'd it feel up there tonight?" he asked as they settled into the ride.

A bit of the tension in her shoulders eased at the gentle concern in his voice.

"So much better than it has. Relaxed. I had a really good time."

"Good." He smiled at her then turned to look out the window.

There was definitely a strange sort of "thing" between them that made Abby wish she hadn't tried to kiss him. That easy-going, back-and-forth banter they always had was gone, and it felt as if they were two strangers sitting next to each other in a car.

Abby looked over at Sophie as she organized her binder. *Subtle*. There were only two options. One, she could address the huge fucking elephant in the car with them. Or two, she could ignore it. Abby thought it best to let it go. She leaned against the seat and closed her eyes. Maybe things would calm down in a few days.

* * *

The bus pulled onto the interstate. Next stop, Los Angeles. This would be the last gig on this leg of the tour. Abby planned to work for a portion of the two-week break in New York, but it would be nice to be in the same spot for longer than forty-eight hours. She had an apartment in the city and wouldn't have to be in a hotel or on the bus. That was enough to make her excited about the break.

"One more stop," Sophie said, clearly enthusiastic. They were finishing up a midnight snack in the bus's kitchen.

"Somebody's excited for some time off," Abby teased.

"I love you girl, but I need time in the same spot for more than a night or two. I can't wait to do nothing except shop."

"Should I call the ladies at the Jimmy Choo boutique on Fifth Avenue to give them a heads up?"

Sophie laughed and flipped her off.

"You flip off your employer?" She asked and put her hand over her mouth, feigning shock.

"Night ladies," Danny said, and Abby watched him walk toward the back of the bus.

"Off to bed already?" Sophie asked.

Abby narrowed her eyes. She had dodged Sophie's questions all night about what didn't happen in her dressing room.

"Yeah, I'm beat."

"You sure you don't want to join us? Abby doesn't bite. Usually." Sophie winked and started laughing.

"Knock it off," Abby said, injecting a clear warning into her voice. She glanced at Danny, but he was looking the other way.

"Night," Sophie said in a singsong voice. "Don't worry we'll talk low." Sophie winked at him.

"Actually, I'm going to bed, too." Abby got up, dumped what was left of her fruit in the trash, and put her bowl in the sink. There was no way she was going to talk about today with Sophie, especially not while Danny was within hearing range.

"What?" Sophie asked innocently.

"I'm exhausted. See you in the morning." Abby waved over her shoulder to both Sophie and Scott, who was watching TV. In a few days, this would all blow over, and Sophie would forget what she'd walked in on; she hoped.

As Abby approached her room, Danny was getting his bunk ready. Abby squeezed by Danny, like she did a hundred times before. "Excuse me," she said softly.

Danny straightened and stepped back to let her pass. At that exact moment, the bus hit a pothole, and she fell into him. They were jolted back against the other set of bunk beds behind them.

"Shit," Abby said, more shocked than anything else.

"I've got you." Danny pulled her against his chest. Abby circled one arm around his waist and held onto his arm with the other. She moved closer. He tightened his grip as the bus continued over a long, rough patch of road, and Abby secretly hoped it would stay that way for a while.

She let herself relax against him and surrendered to his voice, his smell, his touch. He surrounded her, and she didn't care that they were getting pushed around from the potholes. She was more focused on how good it felt to be in his arms, and that scared her. The last thing she needed was to fall for someone. She needed time to figure things out on her own. There was no question she liked him a bit too much, but that didn't mean she had to act on it. The timing was all off and as long as he was working for her, she couldn't let herself cross that line.

"You okay?" Danny asked.

"Yeah, thanks." She looked up at him and was again struck by his thoughtful eyes and sincere smile. He was so good. Goodhearted. Good-natured. And maybe she didn't know how to handle that. She liked him too much to screw up what they had now. But turning off her feelings was a lot harder than she'd thought it would be.

"You sure?"

"Fine, thanks," she whispered, nervously biting her lip as she untangled herself from him. "Night."

They both maintained their eye contact until she reached back and searched for the knob to her door. When her hand finally found it, she turned and walked inside her bedroom. Danny stared at her the entire time, and she met his gaze for one long final moment before closing the door.

chapter
nine

Abby woke, startled by her ringing phone and rolled over to grab it.

"Hello?" she answered, her voice still raspy with sleep. She was met with light breathing on the other end. She cleared her throat and tried again, "Hello?" Nothing. Whoever it was hung up.

She checked her call log but didn't know the number. After the incident with Sean and his crazy, she'd switched numbers and blocked him just to be safe. Still, this was too similar to the calls he made before he grabbed her last time. Or, it could be nothing. To be safe, she'd let Sophie know about it later just in case one of those services that sells celebrity phone numbers had figured out her number already. That was a pain in the ass, but a part of being in the public eye she supposed. And, if it happened again, she'd let Danny know, too, just in case. Abby powered down her phone. All she wanted was a little more sleep, and the phone already woke her up once.

Unfortunately, no matter how much she wanted it, sleep didn't want her. The conversation with her mother, her stupid almost-kiss with Danny, and Sean's escalating anger played through her brain on a repeating loop. The track grew

144

so loud she only had two options to deal with it. She could stay in bed and be pissed about being awake, or she could get up and do something productive. She threw her covers off and planted her feet on her plush throw rug that she loved so much. Slowly, she opened the door and snuck past the others who were still sleeping in their bunks.

"Morning," she greeted Anthony as he navigated the bus through a bit of traffic.

"Morning. You're up early."

Abby sat down across from him on the sofa.

"I didn't turn the ringer off on my phone. A wrong number woke me up a while ago." She tried her best to get comfortable on the leather sofa.

"If traffic stays light we'll be at the hotel in about three hours. I'm stopping for coffee soon. Would you like me to get you a cup?" That was the best question Abby ever heard. Coffee was a must and especially this morning. She had a headache, and her brain felt foggy.

"Yes, please. You're a lifesaver."

As promised, Anthony got off at the next exit and brought her a large coffee. She went back into her room and changed. It was probably better to greet the day in jeans and a T-shirt than her pajamas. She didn't have a show tonight, just some meetings today about her next album. After that, she was free to hang out by the pool and catch some sun for the rest of the day.

By the time she was finished dressing, Sophie was awake and sitting up front with Anthony. "Hey you," Abby said.

"You're up early," Sophie stated the obvious.

"Don't remind me." Abby turned to Anthony. "Thanks, you've saved everyone from a major bitch-a-thon."

"Yes, thank you," Sophie agreed, though she grinned at Abby.

Danny and Scott joined the group a while later, and they all spent the next couple hours chatting about nothing important. When Anthony gave them a twenty-minute ETA, Abby headed back to her room to grab her purse.

As they approached the hotel, they noticed several hundred people surrounding the entrance. "Well, this isn't good." Danny scowled.

"What the hell?" Abby stared at the mass of people and an unfamiliar sensation filled her chest. Before Sean, Abby's biggest concern about a large group of fans was whether her schedule would allow her to stay long enough to greet everyone, and if not, how many people would she disappoint? Now, instead of calculating the number of autographs and photos she'd have to pose for, fingers of ice-cold fear gripped her. Her brain went blank, then rapidly started cataloging all the possible escape routes. She looked at Danny. His brow was furrowed, and he pulled out his phone as he walked to the back of the bus. She felt slightly better knowing he was working to figure out what was happening.

"No one knows where you're staying besides us, plus your mother and her assistant. We keep your location a secret so this shit doesn't happen." Sophie sounded as pissed as Danny looked.

"Someone must have leaked our location. Maybe an employee at the hotel? My mom is pissed at me, but I don't think she would have done this." Even as she said it, Abby doubted the veracity of her words. Before this week, she'd thought she'd known the people in her life. Her mother was difficult, but she wasn't unrepentantly evil. Now, after she saw the photos of Vivien with Sean, and Vivien hadn't denied it, she had to ask herself what else Vivien might be hiding. The thought that she may have leaked the name of their hotel made Abby sick to her stomach.

"I'm going to circle the building until we can figure this out," Anthony said as he turned off his blinker and accelerated back up to the speed of traffic.

"You should see this." Sophie held up her phone for Abby to see.

"What?"

"Look." Sophie said.

Abby took the phone from Sophie's hand and saw several pictures of Stephanie plastered on the screen. She had been beaten to the point of being nearly unrecognizable from the deep purple bruises covering her face.

"Oh my God." Abby grabbed the wall for support before sitting on the edge of the couch.

Danny returned from the back of the bus, phone still to his ear. Abby couldn't focus on anything beyond the rush of blood through her head, so she didn't hear anything he said. She had an overwhelming urge to run but at the same time felt as if she was plastered to her seat. This could not be happening.

Finally, she heard Danny's voice but was still too shocked to speak.

"Abby?" Danny set his hand on her shoulder and squeezed gently.

She turned toward his voice.

"Just breathe. It says she's fine."

"You know he's responsible for that. Do you think my mother talked to him?"

"Right now, all I'm worried about is you. Breathe for me."

"Danny?" Scott interrupted the almost-intimate moment. "We're nearing the entrance again. What would you like Anthony to do?"

"Tell him to just keep driving. We won't be staying here. I'll have a new location for him soon."

"You got it." Scott inclined his head slightly. The security team spoke to each other with small gestures as much as with actual words.

"I need to make a few more calls." Danny gestured with his phone then left for the back again. He nodded at Scott on his way out.

She listened to their conversation and felt like an observer. Like this wasn't really happening to her but to someone else. Abby didn't particularly like Stephanie, but she never wanted to see her harmed. The details were sketchy, but Stephanie had been attacked last night, and the police were investigating. They didn't have a suspect, and Stephanie wasn't talking, a first for sure.

"Well, we all know the top two suspects. Please don't sugarcoat anything for me. I'm thinking the same thing you are. It was either Sean or my Mother. At this point, I wouldn't put it past either of them. That video would ruin them...and me." The realization made her sick to her stomach. There were actually three suspects. Sean, her mother, *and* Abby.

Abby stared out the window. Her mom said Abby was making the wrong decision. At the time, her tone felt ominous, and again Abby wondered if it was meant to be some sort of warning? The crowd in front of the hotel was the added bonus. The thought of them waiting for her made Abby feel claustrophobic.

"Okay." Danny's voice startled Abby. She was back to being a jumpy mess again. Thankfully, Danny didn't notice. He was in full take-charge-and-fix-this mode. "Change of plans. I've arranged a safe location for us in Venice Beach."

Danny's matter of fact tone made some of the fear Abby had subside. Danny slid into the spot that Sophie had vacated and explained what was about to happen.

"Scott and Sophie will stay behind." He turned his attention to Sophie. "I want you and Scott to check in at another hotel. Use your real name."

"Our real names? You're sure?"

"Absolutely. I want to make it appear as if we changed locations. If you register us with our real identities, you know it'll get leaked and distract everyone enough so that I can get Abby to the secure location."

"Consider it done," Sophie agreed.

"Good, because it's your job to find a hotel with available rooms. Once we get to Venice Beach I'm going to make a few more calls. It's too easy to jump to conclusions. Right now, we need to remain calm and let the authorities investigate. I'll reach out to the local police and report our experiences with Sean just in case there is a connection," Danny explained.

Abby nodded. This was all too much. She had begun to calm down, but with all these sudden changes and thoughts of Sean made her feel as if she needed to flee again.

"I trust you," she told Danny because she could see he was waiting for her to say something. "Whatever you feel is the right thing to do, I'll do it. How long until we can get off this bus?" She gripped the edge of the couch, afraid that if she wasn't holding onto something she'd run for the exit.

"We have a bit of a ride. Why don't you go lay down, and I'll knock on your door when it's time?" Danny patted her on the leg.

"Maybe later. Right now I want to know your plan. This is happening because of me…it's happening *to me*. I refuse to be the last one to know what's going on. I'm not fragile. I'm not going to break." And it was true; she wouldn't break. But that didn't mean she wasn't mentally freaking out. Still, this was her mess, and she needed to know what to expect.

"Okay. Let's go over everything," Danny said and turned so that he was facing everyone.

Abby settled back into the couch, ready to listen. What Danny said next would shape her life, and she didn't want to miss a word.

* * *

"Abby?"

She opened her eyes and searched for the voice that woke her. Danny was in the doorway. "We're here, but Connor is ten minutes out, so you have a few minutes to wake up before we have to go."

"Okay, thanks." She cleared her throat. Connor O'Brian, she learned on the drive here, was an Army buddy of Danny's and was helping them out today.

Danny left and she sat up in her bed, placing her head in her hands. She rubbed her temple, trying to ease the pounding bass drum keeping time in her head. She pushed the covers off and grabbed her phone from the nightstand.

She turned on the phone, and it beeped over and over indicating Abby had several messages.

"People need to leave me alone," she mumbled to herself and opened up her text messages. They were all from an unknown number. She opened the first message, unsure what to expect. Sometimes fans got her number, but text messages from unknown numbers were unusual.

We're not done.

Abby felt as if she'd been kicked in the chest. Logically, she knew all the air hadn't been sucked out of the room, but she still couldn't catch her breath. She opened the next message.

I'll be waiting for you.

"Fuck," she said softly. *Sean.* It didn't take a genius to realize he'd sent the messages. What she didn't understand was how he got her number? There were too many people to consider pointing a finger at one. Right now though, she needed to figure out what she was going to do? There was just so much going on. She needed to tell Danny, obviously, but was waiting for the right time. Except that never happened, and right now she'd settle for the *wrong* time as long as it was thirty consecutive, uninterrupted minutes. Clearly, Sean was capable of just about anything, and that frightened Abby more than anything. She had shared the same bed with him and didn't know the first thing about who he really was.

You are still mine.

She dropped the phone on the bed. He clearly wasn't going to go away quietly. After several minutes she picked up the phone and scanned her voicemail messages. Again from an unknown number. She was scared to listen to them.

As she was staring at the phone, wondering what to do, the phone rang and she jumped. Unknown. Should she let the voicemail pick it up or should she face her fear head on? Was she going to let Sean continue to harass and threaten her? No. If Abby ever wanted to be free of all this bullshit, she needed to stand up for herself and not depend on others to fight her battles.

The longer she rolled her options around in her head, the angrier Abby became. How dare Sean think he could harass her like this? He had *no right*. She deserved better. Fuck him. She pushed the button to connect the call.

"Hello?" She could feel the anger thrumming through her head, yet she sounded calm. Too calm. She wanted to reach through the phone and throttle Sean. She paced the short distance in front of her bed.

"So nice of you to finally answer. It's not very smart to ignore my calls. Haven't learned your lesson yet? I'm not going away, but *you* can make this all disappear. You know what you have to do."

She had learned her lesson. Sean would no longer instill fear in her. Abby needed to ask him a few questions, and she wasn't going to allow him to run her life through threats and intimidation.

"Did you attack Stephanie?" she demanded. She was done with his double talk and innuendos. It was all bullshit.

"I have no idea what you're talking about."

But Abby could hear the snicker in his voice. He knew *exactly* what she was talking about. She couldn't wait to tell Danny. He'd already communicated with the local police and could get this information to them as well. But of course Sean hadn't actually confessed. God, she hated this smug asshole.

How had she missed this part of him for the past two years?

"Fuck you Sean." She laced her voice with as much anger and venom as she could muster, doing her best to channel her mom's attitude of entitlement. Vivien made people cower with just a look, and Abby wanted that power over Sean right now. "Leave me alone. We're done. Nothing you can say or do will get you back on this tour."

Abby felt great. Superior, almost. *This* must be how her mom felt. No wonder Vivien always said what was on her mind without a care about the consequences. It. Was. Amazing.

"If that's how you want to play this. Don't say I didn't warn you." Sean ended the call.

She stared at her phone. The adrenaline high she felt a moment ago was fading fast. Shit. It probably wasn't a good idea to antagonize him that way, but she couldn't stop herself. She was so angry, and she needed to let it out. It felt empowering in the moment, but as the energy of the moment faded, so did her confidence. She was left with only the hard rock of fear in her gut. She shook her head. Sean wasn't stable. She should have let the voicemail pick up.

It was time to talk to Danny rather than waiting for the perfect moment that simply never came. He needed to know everything. She had to confess it all, the messages, the voicemails, the threats and about that video. Sean was gone. Fired. And that so-called video had not been released. Sean was obviously full of shit. She was done worrying if it was or wasn't Danny and trying to figure out how that made her feel. Sean had lost all sense of reason, and she couldn't take the chance that he would follow through on his threats. He was unstable enough for her to believe he was capable.

There was another knock at the door, and she looked up.

"It's time."

"I'm ready." She slipped on a pair of flip-flops and grabbed the few things she needed.

chapter
ten

A dark blue unmarked van was parked next to the tour bus with the back doors open.

"Hop in," Danny instructed. When she hesitated, he added, "We're getting you the hell out of here. Get in before someone sees you.

Abby looked at the surroundings. They were in the parking lot of an old, abandoned shopping complex. She didn't ask any more questions as she took Danny's hand and climbed into the van. She kept saying she trusted him, and this was exactly the situation for her to prove it. Danny followed and pulled the door shut behind them. The vehicle pulled away before either of them had a chance to sit down. The floor of the van was littered with fast food debris, and Abby kicked an empty soda can as she made her way to the seat. *Was this guy really going to get them to safety?*

"Now what?"

"Relax. We're getting the hell out of here." Danny smiled.

"Who's driving?"

"Connor." Danny motioned with his chin toward the

front of the van.

"Yo! Connor O'Brian, pleased to meetcha."

Abby stared at the man behind the booming voice who sat in the driver's seat. She couldn't get a good look at him because he was driving, but what she did see, she liked.

Connor worked per diem for Nucci Securities. During their time in the Army, they were both stationed in Iraq and were in the same platoon. They were brothers and trusted each other with their lives, and because Danny trusted him, that was good enough for Abby.

"This is Abby," Danny said. "Don't be a jerk to her or I'll kick your ass."

"Sure you will," Connor said with a laugh. "Hi there."

"Abby, meet Connor."

"Hi."

She watched Connor scan her from head to toe before he gave her a big smile. The van swerved.

"Whoa, eyes on the road asshole!" Danny commanded.

"Sorry." Connor laughed.

"Good to meet you too." She turned to Danny. "Is there a seatbelt in this thing?" she whispered.

"No."

"Great," she grumbled and held onto the bench seat while Connor continued to drive like a maniac.

"Does he always drive like this?" Abby asked through clenched teeth as she slid a bit along the seat on a turn.

"He's fine. Just showing off." Danny moved closer to Abby. "Take it easy, man. She's been through enough today."

Connor turned his head again, flashed a killer smile back at Abby and continued to drive. However, he did slow down a bit.

"How long 'til we're at his house?"

"We'll be there soon. His place is on the beach. Until then, just sit back. We're good." He placed his arm around her shoulder and pulled her closer to him.

"Well, at least I love the beach." She relaxed into his side and he laughed.

* * *

Connor pulled into a driveway, and Abby twisted in her seat to try to see where they were but the darkened out windows made it impossible to see any details.

"Home sweet home," Connor said and turned the van off. "I'll let you lovebirds out." He smirked.

"Fuck you, asshole," Danny said, then turned to Abby. "Sorry, He's a character. Don't take it personally." Danny removed his arm from around Abby's shoulder.

Connor opened the doors, and it took her a moment to adjust to the bright sun. Connor smiled easily, a charming, panty-melting smile that probably earned him more than his fair share of action. Were all Army men this hot?

Danny helped her out of the van, and she took in the

sea foam green house with white trim and large front porch. It had a beautifully manicured yard with a quaint stone path that led to the front door and also veered off toward the backyard.

Connor opened the door.

"Go on in," Connor said. "Make yourself at home."

She entered the house, and the inside surprised her with its light colored walls and modern furnishings. She didn't really have much of a chance to get a read on Connor, but she didn't picture him being a clean-lines and minimalist kind of guy. On the drive to Connor's house Abby had imaged Connor's house would mirror the inside of his van.

"Wow, this is beautiful."

"Not what you expected?" Danny asked behind her.

"No," she admitted.

"Well, I'm highly offended. What did you expect?" Connor asked with a gasp. He managed to sound both mocking and shocked.

She shrugged, opting for silence instead of embarrassing herself any further by admitting to them what she'd come up with in the twenty minute drive.

Connor moved past her toward what she figured was the kitchen. Connor was a couple of inches shorter than Danny. Both men were pretty muscular but Danny's biceps were bulkier and his muscles more defined. Plus he had a sexy tattoo on his left arm and shoulder that was made up of lines and symbols. Abby never had the nerve to ask, but it seemed meaningful. Still, she wouldn't complain about either of them.

"Make yourself at home. There's a pool in the yard, or

if you want, we can head to the beach. The bathroom is down the hall." He pointed. "I don't have much food in the house, but we can order something in."

She glanced outside at the pool, large and rectangular; it included a hot tub and small waterfall. And it invited her to come and relax.

"Thank you. I might take advantage of your backyard. It looks quite peaceful."

"Go on," Danny said, and he was so close that his breath tickled her hair and a shiver ran down her back. "Sophie canceled everything today," he continued. "So you're free to relax. No one knows where you are."

"It's been too long. Thanks." She opened the sliding glass door.

"Here, don't forget this." Connor handed her a beer.

She smiled at him, touched. Beer wasn't her drink of choice, but it was still sweet. She walked outside and noticed there was also an outside kitchen toward the back of the yard with a huge barbeque grill, refrigerator, and stocked bar. She'd check out the offerings later. Right now, she planned to indulge in this respite, no matter how brief, from all the crap that Sean and her mother had leveled at her. Sighing happily, she sank into a comfy longue chair and enjoyed the warm rays on her skin.

* * *

Abby spent the next few hours relaxing and chatting

with Connor and Danny. This was a rare treat for her, but considering the day she'd had, it was something she really needed. She even managed a short nap which helped to clear her mind. Abby knew it was time to talk to Danny about everything.

"Hey sleepyhead. Feel any better?" Danny greeted her when she turned toward him in her chair.

"Hey." She yawned and sat up. "I can't believe I fell asleep."

"You needed it. Are you hungry? We were just trying to decide what to order."

"Where's Sophie?

"Sophie and Scott will be here soon. Probably best to wait for them before we order."

"Before they get here, can we talk for a few...alone, please?"

"Yeah." Danny hesitated slightly before he agreed.

"Maybe inside? The sun's getting to me."

"Sure."

He got up, and Abby followed behind him, while Connor stayed in the yard. They walked straight into the living room and sat down on the couch.

"What's up?"

Abby didn't know how or where to start. She fiddled with her phone. None of this would be easy to say and she felt sick to her stomach. "Remember when I told you I had something I wanted to talk to you about?"

"I remember."

"I had to think on things." Her phone buzzed but she didn't even bother looking to see who it was. She was done with being terrified every time she heard her phone go off.

"Well, Sean, he... well... he sent me a video. Claimed it was you and threatened to release it if I didn't take him back." She glanced over to find Danny staring at her intensely. It made her nervous. "I don't think it was really you, but with everything that was going on...I didn't know what to think or who to believe. I mean, I didn't even believe in me." She tried hard to fight back the tears filling her eyes. "And he's been sending these awful text messages and calling..." Abby drew a deep breath and tried to collect her thoughts. "I don't know where he even got my new number, but he leaves these voicemails..."

"Wait. Back up a second. What video?" Danny's brow crinkled together, one more sign that Abby was right to doubt the authenticity of the video.

"I can show you." Abby fumbled with her phone for a moment, but was able to find the email. "Here." She handed the phone over and studied his face as he watched the video that had broken her heart.

"You thought this was me?" he asked.

Abby nodded but didn't make eye contact with him. She couldn't look at him. "I'm sorry," she said. In hindsight, she was ashamed she ever thought it was Danny in that video.

"Why didn't you tell me?" Danny's voice betrayed his emotions, and Abby knew she'd hurt him.

"I don't know."

"Come on, Abby. Of course you know." Danny tossed the phone on the coffee table in front of them.

"I didn't want you to get in trouble," she whispered as she wiped away her tears.

"In trouble? I don't understand."

"I'm sorry," Abby said again and sobbed into her hands.

Danny pulled her into his arms and held her. His strong embrace was comforting.

"It's going to be okay. Tell me everything," he ordered gently.

"I'm scared," she cried and buried her head into the crook of his neck.

"How long has he been doing this?"

"I don't know. A while," she mumbled against his shoulder. He smelled crisp and clean, with a slight hint of cologne.

Danny's hand gently rubbed up and down her back. His gentle touch felt so good, and she could feel her body calming down.

"Everything will be fine. Take a deep breath." His tone was soothing, but he pulled away before Abby was ready.

Abby felt the sudden loss of his arms. She knew he wanted to talk, but she wasn't sure what to say.

"He must've said something to you so you wouldn't

tell me. What was it?"

She rubbed her forehead. "I've been getting calls and texts from Sean since I caught him with that groupie. First it wasn't that bad, just begging me to take him back. I could ignore those. Then…" She hesitated. "Then he told me he had a video of you and some groupie and that he'd release it and your career would be ruined."

"What? Is that why you had Sophie change your number?"

"You knew?"

"Of course. Why wouldn't I? She had to tell me."

She didn't look at him. "You saw it, Danny. It looks enough like you to make people wonder. The video was shot during a performance. You can hear me singing in the background. Sean threatened to release it to the media if I didn't take him back or if I said anything to anybody about the texts and calls. I couldn't let that happen to you." Even if it had been him with the groupie, she couldn't bear for the world to see him like that.

Danny sighed. "I've never had a thing with a groupie. I wouldn't touch that. I don't know who's on that video, but it isn't me."

"He sent it to me."

"It isn't me." He stated firmly. The look in his eyes convinced her. "And besides, he's gone from the tour. Has this video appeared anywhere? Because I've not seen it, and I've not been contacted by anyone. No reporters. No cameras. Nothing."

"I know, but he's been texting and calling, and I didn't know what to do. He's crazy and violent and like I said, even if it wasn't you in the video, he could say it was and then you'd have to spend all your time fighting the allegation. You know how it works in celebrity-ville."

He paused, and at least he didn't seem disappointed anymore.

"That night in my dressing room," she said after a few moments. "Things escalated so quickly, and I didn't want you to get hurt because of me. Then when he left, I didn't want you to get in trouble or put your career in jeopardy. He kept telling me that you'd be ruined, and that's the last thing I want. I figured I'd change my number so he couldn't harass me anymore. End of problem."

"As much as I appreciate your concern for my safety and reputation, I'm more worried about yours. Changing your number won't stop him. Sure, it probably delayed him a bit, but trust me, it won't stop him. Guys like him always find a way to try to intimidate and frighten their targets."

Damn Sean. Why had she let him browbeat her into a corner where even common sense was suspect?

"I'm going to take care of this. You don't have to worry about anything. I've got it covered. Are we good?" he asked, searching her face with his gaze.

"You're not mad?"

He smiled. "No. I understand why you didn't tell me. Thanks for trying to protect me. But when it interferes with your own safety, it's always better to talk to me. I'm here to protect you. Not the other way around."

Abby nodded; Danny made it all sound so simple.

"Okay. Let's change your number again first thing tomorrow." He helped her to her feet and gave her a half-hug.

She relaxed into his side. She finally wouldn't have to worry about Sean. Danny was going to take care of it. "Okay," she said, not hiding the relief she felt.

chapter
eleven

"That was good," Abby said and threw out the plastic container her dinner came in. "But I can't wait until I can eat dairy. I miss cheese." She was counting down the hours until she could indulge in foods like pizza and cheese omelets.

"Why can't you have cheese?" Connor asked with an amused tone.

"Because it screws with my vocals. I have two weeks off to binge on cheese pizza and mocha lattes made with milk, and I can't wait."

"I guess I know where your first stop will be," Danny teased.

"Brooklyn," Abby and Sophie said in unison. Abby's favorite pizzeria was located in Brooklyn. Getting pizza and an ice at L&B Spumoni Gardens after spending the day on the rides at Nelly Bly was one of the few fun memories from her childhood. Sometimes her father took her in the morning, usually after one of her parents' epic fights. They were so loud. Her mom would yell, and her dad would yell louder. Then he'd stop yelling, and her mom would start crying and begging him to stop. Abby spent those nights curled up in the back of her closet, trying to block them out by quietly singing to herself. It never worked.

"How long until I have to get ready?" Abby asked Sophie.

"A little over an hour."

"Oh wow, would you all mind if—"

A knock at the door stopped Abby. "I have a visitor asking to see you Abby," Scott said.

Abby could hear her mother bitching in the background. Did she really want to deal with her? She was kinda nervous about it. Outside of Abby's angry outburst over the phone, she hadn't talked to her mom since Stephanie showed her those photos. Abby knew avoiding her mother wasn't the best option no matter how much she didn't want to deal with it. Now or ever.

"It's fine Scott. She's my mom."

Scott moved out of the way, and Vivien strolled through the door.

"Abigail."

"Mother." Abby waited. She wouldn't avoid her, but she wasn't going to initiate conversation either.

"I need to speak with you alone," Vivien announced to the room. Her voice just as arrogant as always. It almost surprised Abby. She had hoped she'd hear some kind of regret. She'd even take being uncomfortable as a sign of hope that her mother had a heart.

"I'm not sure now's the time to—" Abby began.

"Please…Abby, we really need to talk. Alone." Her

voice cracked, and something unfamiliar to Abby's ears broke through. Sorrow? Regret? She had no idea, but it was something.

Abby wanted to be heartless, to be cold. She wanted her mom to suffer just like Abby had when she first saw those pictures. But she just couldn't do it. Her mom looked so…pensive and contrite as if she might be genuinely upset. It was such a strange state for Vivien that Abby had no choice but to take pity on her. Besides, Ms. Sohm would be disappointed with anything less.

"Fine. Could you all give us a few minutes alone please?"

Danny and Sophie stared at her skeptically, but she wouldn't back down. She needed to talk to her mom as much as her mom needed to talk to her. She might as well get it over with now so it wasn't something hanging over her head while on break.

"We're good. I promise." She assured them.

"I'll go make sure the crew is on schedule," Sophie said and left.

"I'll be right outside." Danny hesitated but eventually he too left, and Connor followed behind him.

Abby waited until the door closed to face her mother. "What do you want?" Abby crossed her arm. She felt a battle brewing inside herself, and she tried to contain it. This conversation wasn't going to be easy. She doubted it would even be civil.

Her mother crossed the room and sat on the couch. "I'd

like to explain. Please, sit and listen."

"Why? What's the point?" She hated their sudden role reversal where her mom was being calm and rational and trying to talk things out, while Abby was being emotional and reactive. She was closed off to the possibility of compromise. She didn't want to listen. She just wanted her mom to admit she was an awful human being and then go.

"If you'd let me—"

"No. I don't want to hear it." Abby turned toward the door.

"Abigail. He knew." Vivien nearly shouted.

Abby stopped. *What did Sean know?* Vivien's statement was so vague, and with her it could mean almost anything. "Knew what?"

"About your father, about me, about our past."

"So?" Abby stared at her mother. "Who cares? He was an abusive drunk. No big story there. I could see the press spinning it for a while, but they'd move on. How does that justify you fucking my boyfriend?"

"Please Abigail, *please*…come sit. There's so much more."

Tears welled up in her mother's eyes. They even looked real. Abby was so conflicted. She didn't know what to do. She wanted to believe her mother had a real reason, but on the other hand, what could possibly make this okay?

"You have five minutes. No more."

"Please sit."

Abby joined her on the couch, but kept her distance.

"This isn't something I ever thought I'd tell you. Or even wanted to speak of again, but I've been left with no choice. We've never had a typical mother-daughter relationship, and I'm not trying for that now. I'm not stupid enough to think that this is going to change us in any way, but I'm *not* heartless." Vivien paused to wipe away a stray tear that fell down her cheek.

"Just say it. Whatever it is. Nothing could make this any worse."

"I suppose you're right." Vivien took a deep breath and squared her shoulders. Abby didn't like her change in demeanor. Whatever she was about to say was big, and suddenly Abby didn't want to know. Before she could get off the couch to leave, Vivien began, "The man you remember as your father wasn't. He…he was my…he let his friends…and others…for money…" Vivien nearly choked on the last few words. "I don't know which of them is your father."

Abby clutched the cushion beneath her. She needed something that made her feel grounded because right now nothing made sense. What did her mother just say? This had to be some sort of joke. Another cruel thing her mother was doing to her. Why? To punish her? Keep her in line? She didn't know the reason, but it didn't matter. This couldn't be true.

"Abigail? Abby, say something." Vivien's voice broke through the hazy fog Abby had fallen into.

"Wait. I don't understand… This can't… I'm not… You… You must be lying."

"God I wish I was. I never wanted you to know. Sean found out. I don't know how, but he did, and he threatened me with it. He was going to expose our secret."

"Our secret? This isn't our secret. This is yours."

"You're in shock. You aren't thinking clearly right now. This can't ever come out. This would ruin you. I did what I had to do to protect you. He wanted to take this to the press. They'd have a field day with this. Do you understand?" Vivien reached for Abby's hand, but Abby jumped up before she could make contact.

"Don't tell me how I feel and don't touch me. Ever. None of that has to do with me. How were you protecting *me*? How?" she shouted.

"Abigail, lower your voice," Vivien begged.

Abby turned when she heard the door open.

"Everything all right in here?" Danny asked.

Abby didn't know how to answer that. Physically she was all right, but mentally she was far from it. "We're fine. Thanks." She gave him a half-hearted smile.

"You're sure?"

"Yes, we just need another minute."

Danny hesitated a moment, then closed the door.

"Does he ever mind his own business?"

"I am his business. So what else, Mother? Is that it?"

"Abby...I was a very different person back then. My parents...were...not supportive. I had no money. No place to live. I did what I had to do to make it through."

Abby wiped away a few of her own tears. She swallowed down her emotions. "So what," her voice cracked. "I'm a product of some trick?"

"Yes. Probably." Vivien's voice hardened. Abby knew that tone. She wouldn't get any more out of her mother.

"And Sean found out and instead of telling him to go fuck himself, you decided to actually fuck him, right?

Vivien just stared at Abby.

"Right." Abby turned and headed for the door. "I have a show to prepare for. I really think you should leave."

"I'll see you in New York," Vivien said as she passed Abby.

"Don't count on it."

"Nothing's changed, Abigail. We still have an image to uphold and business to conduct. I expect respect," Vivien said and then opened the door. Nothing's changed? Wasn't that the biggest lie ever told? Everything had changed. Abby's entire world had shifted, but Vivien walked away smooth as ice once again.

"Are you okay?" Danny asked.

"No." She said simply and didn't elaborate. "I need to get to my vocal warm up session so I can get back here for hair and make-up."

"Sure."

Danny's face was drawn tight. He was worried, but she just didn't have it in her to share while her emotions were this raw. Hell, she wasn't sure she'd ever want to tell him what she'd just learned. Some things were better kept a secret. On this point, she agreed with her mother. Right now, she needed to get through this performance. After, she'd try to sort out her life. Lately it felt like every time she managed to claim a bit of independence, something would pop up and knock her back on her ass.

They walked silently down the hall with Connor and Scott trailing behind until they reached the room where her vocal coach Genna was waiting for her.

"We'll wait out here."

Abby just nodded before opening the door and stepping inside.

"You're late, lady." Genna teased.

"I know. I'm sorry."

Genna paused. "You all right?"

Apparently she must look the way she was feeling. "Just had a meeting with my mother. I'll live."

"Say no more, girl. Let's get you warmed up."

"Thanks."

Abby spent the next half hour getting her voice prepared for the show that night.

chapter twelve

After the show, Abby, Danny, Sophie, and Connor boarded the red-eye flight to New York. The concert went off without a hitch despite Sean's obsessive, stalker tactics and Abby's crazy emotions.

"I'm exhausted," Abby said as she settled into the oversized first class seat. She heard the sounds of Danny's low chuckle as he settled in the seat next to hers.

The flight attendant handed Abby a pillow and thick blanket. "Thank you." Abby yawned and smiled.

"Can I get either of you anything else?" the flight attendant asked, and Abby noticed that "Cindy"—as it said on her name tag—was smiling a little too sweetly at Danny, and she lingered too long in his personal space for Abby.

"No, thanks," Danny said. "We'll let you know if that changes."

Abby glared at her until she walked away. All she wanted was to sleep, but now she was annoyed with the flirty flight attendant and with herself for being jealous when she had no right.

Once they were up in the air, she settled down enough

to sleep.

"Here, recline back," Danny suggested. He reached over her to click the seat back, and she breathed in his clean, fresh scent. Even at one in the morning, he still smelled delicious to her. His closeness made her heartbeat quicken. She let her gaze linger on his jaw line and the scruffy five o'clock shadow. Even that made him look delicious.

"Thank you," she whispered.

"Get comfortable and try to sleep," he murmured in her ear.

She smiled and closed her eyes. Since she'd told him about Sean's messages, things seemed a little less tense between them, especially after the almost-kiss. She let herself think about what it would have felt like if they had actually gone through with it. Yummy, she was sure. And totally hot. She turned her thoughts to business matters because thinking about that when she was so close to Danny was not a good idea.

They were set to land at nine a.m., and she had the rest of the day to get over the jet lag. Abby was hoping to meet up with some friends because she needed a girls' night out desperately, especially since she was due in the studio the next day to lay down some vocals for her next album. The songs had already been picked, and the music was ready. All she needed to do was learn and record them. Very little participation was expected, which used to make her mad, but she had long ago resigned herself to staying quiet and toeing the line. There was no use in fighting her mother and the rest of her management team when it came to the recording process. At some point, maybe she would, but for now she had enough of a battle on her hands without taking on any more.

She loved creating music. Before the recent drama, she spent much of her downtime writing and composing new songs. Whenever she had a moment she'd sneak off to her beach house in New Jersey where she had converted her pool house into a state of the art recording studio. Magnolia Studios was Abby's baby. She longed for the day she'd be able to record and produce her own music from her little studio. For now, she had a small keyboard tucked away in her room on the bus. Someday, maybe she'd cut an album with her own songs and her own arrangements. Someday.

Her mind continued to race for the next few minutes but soon settled, and she fell asleep next to Danny.

Abby slept through the entire flight, which was a first for her. She woke up when she heard the flight attendant telling Danny they were getting ready to land.

"Morning." Danny's deep, gruff voice tickled Abby's ear.

"Morning," she said shyly. For some reason waking up snuggled against him on a plane made her bashful and maybe a little goofy.

"Did you sleep well?"

"Yes. Too well for being on a plane."

"I've been told that our luggage will be at the car so that we can hurry through the airport." Danny moved so he could stretch.

"Good." Abby set her chair upright and stretched as well. She wanted to hold his hand but caught herself. He was her friend. And security guard. There was no reason for her to hold his hand here.

The flight touched down smoothly, and they all exited the plane before heading straight for the waiting car. Danny and Connor escorted Abby through LaGuardia without an issue.

The group made it into Manhattan after hitting a bit of rush hour traffic. Abby had the day off, so she didn't really care how long it took to get to her apartment. She kept herself busy on her phone trying to make plans for the night. Sophie had spent her time yesterday alerting Abby's closest contacts that she had a new telephone number.

She dialed her friend Kelly to see what plans she had going on. She was always good for a fun time.

"Talk to me" Kelly answered on the second ring.

"Hey girl, watchadoin'?" Abby greeted her friend.

"Bitch! What the fuck, girl? I forgot you changed your number. Where are you now?"

"Just got into New York."

Abby heard Kelly mumbling to someone.

"Fucking awesome," Kelly continued. "I'm going to hit up Exit. It opened last week, and I keep hearing it's fantastic. Oh, and I heard that there's a bartender that's sex on a fucking stick. Finger-fuckin'-lickin'-good! Yeah, bitches! What's up?

"Sean and I broke up."

"Really?" Kelly sounded pretty shocked.

"What happened? You guys were so good together."

"He had a thing for groupies," Abby said. She wasn't about to get into everything over the phone.

"Shit, that sucks."

"It is what it is."

"You need to come out then, girl. I haven't seen you in for-fucking-ever. You need some fun and we need to catch up." Kelly had always been good for a night of fun and that was perfect for Abby since all she wanted to do was forget the last week.

"Text me the details, and I'll meet you there."

"Perfect. Okay, catch you later." Kelly disconnected before Abby could say goodbye.

She put her phone away and shook her head because Kelly lacked a filter. If a thought was in her head, she blurted it out. It didn't matter who was around. She didn't give a shit. She didn't have to; her dad was Billy West of West and Howard Modeling Agency, and he was notorious for his foul mouth and attitude. The apple didn't fall far from that tree. She did kind of admire her for that though and wished she could do the same around her mother.

"Who was that?" Danny asked.

"My friend Kelly. She's…" Abby trailed off. She couldn't think of a single word that accurately described everything Kelly was. "Unique," Abby finally said after considering various adjectives.

"You're going out tonight?"

"Yes, Dad." Abby batted her eyelashes at him.

"Cut the shit. I have my guys coming over later to install a new security system. That'll take most of the day, and we have a brief at my office. Tonight won't work."

"What?" Abby frowned over at Danny. "It's girls' night out."

"Guess again," he said, grinning at her.

She watched both Danny and Connor bust out laughing.

"What's so damn funny?" she asked defensively.

"You." He laughed. "You're being stalked by some crazy fucker, and you think it's a-okay to go traipsing around wherever without us. No. I'm sorry, but it's my job to ensure your safety, and I can't do that if you go out without me. And I can't go with you tonight."

"Please. It's a night out with my friend."

"You're right, she is funny when she gets all bossy on you," Danny said to Sophie, who was seated across from them in the limo.

"Right?" Sophie laughed.

Abby tried again. "All right, you can't go, but what about someone else? Nucci Securities isn't just you. I know you have a ton of guys working for you. Call someone in."

She waited as he considered her suggestion; she could imagine him trying to find an excuse to tell her no. But she knew she had him. He *wasn't* the only person.

"I'll see who's available," he said, begrudgingly.

"Yay, me!" She clapped her hands, bounced in her seat, and smiled at Danny.

"You're a nut," he commented as he picked up his phone.

"Whatever." She looked to Sophie. "Wanna come?"

"No, thank you. The last thing I want to do tonight is hang out in some crowded club. But have fun."

The limo dropped Sophie off at her building, and then the driver took the rest of them to Abby's building on the Upper East Side of Manhattan. Danny and Connor escorted Abby up to her apartment on the twenty-second floor.

"Stay with Connor while I check your apartment," Danny ordered. "You know the drill."

Abby shrugged and thought he was being a little paranoid but didn't comment. She lived in a secure building with a doorman. No one could get in without being on an approved list. "Is he always this paranoid?" Abby looked over at Connor as they stood in the hallway.

"It's his job. He's good at it."

Abby leaned against the hallway wall and waited. Connor stood opposite her.

"How long have you been out of the Army?" Abby asked simply to fill the silence. Connor still had a high-and-tight haircut where Danny's chestnut colored hair had grown out a bit. It was long enough to grab hold of. Heat crept up her neck from her inappropriate thought.

"About three years," Connor answered.

"That long?"

"You sound surprised."

"A little, I guess. You seem like you might still be in the military," Abby admitted.

"You can take the man out of the military, but you can't take the military out of the man," he said with a smile.

"All clear," Danny shouted from inside Abby's apartment.

"After you," Connor gestured.

She stepped into her apartment, and after being gone for nearly eight months, it seemed odd to be back. She walked through the long, narrow, cream-colored hallway that was laced in dark wood trim. Abby placed her purse on the slim mocha-brown table and continued into the living room where Danny was staring out the window at Central Park. She heard Connor behind her. He was hauling in their luggage.

"See? Perfectly safe. I don't need some new state-of-the-art alarm system that I'll set off by mistake every other day. The one I have is perfectly fine. Plus, I have a doorman. If someone isn't on my list, he won't get in."

"Doorman? You think that seventy-year-old doorman is going to keep you safe from Sean or any other nut that wants to get to you?" Danny gave her a look. "You're funny."

"Whatever." Abby waved off his comment and sat on the gray tufted sofa that faced the large gas fireplace. It struck her as amusing, that fireplace. She never used it but it gave the house a bit of character and added warmth. Her mother's house was like a museum where you viewed the things in them, but you never touched and you never felt comfortable or like you were in a home. Abby always knew when she was finally old enough to get her own place, she wanted to be able to sit back and relax, but more importantly, she wanted others to feel the same way.

With every property she bought, Abby made sure it fit her style. She didn't care about impressing any hoity-toity society folk. All she wanted was to feel like she was home. Her apartment was filled with warm colors and furniture you could put your feet up on and feel like you were welcomed and belonged.

Danny sat down next to Abby. "The boys will be here in about an hour." He leaned back on the couch and relaxed.

"I'm going to unpack. Don't mind me. Make yourselves comfortable," she said with a little snark as she rolled her large suitcase to her room. It would be nice not to live out of a suitcase for a couple of weeks.

* * *

Danny's employees, John and Aaron, arrived promptly to deal with the security system, and they worked through the afternoon and into the evening getting every room wired. Abby thought it was overkill, but whatever. Maybe she could program it to keep Vivien out, too, and that made her smile. She watched the men work. They looked like they should be on the football field instead of working in security. If they stood outside her apartment door for the next two weeks, no one would ever be able to get in.

When they were done, Danny called out for some food to be delivered.

Twenty-minutes later, Connor went down to the lobby to pick up the order. "Where're we eatin'?" Connor shouted as he walked back into the apartment.

"Kitchen's good," Abby called back.

She set out dishes, and thanks to her housekeeper, she had a kitchen full of groceries including beer and wine. Abby gave the boys a beer and poured herself a large glass of white wine.

"Here's your sweet and sour chicken," Connor said as he passed out the food.

"Thanks." Abby took it, and the smell made her stomach growl.

"What time did you want to leave?" Danny asked.

"I don't know. After I eat I'll hop in the shower and get ready." Abby said before she gulped down some wine. "I'll call Kelly when we're done eating and see what her plans are."

Abby continued to feast on some fantastic Chinese food while the boys planned and strategized. She let them do their thing. All she cared about was getting to have a little fun.

"That was some good dinner," Connor said as he leaned back on his chair.

"Yeah, I love this place. It's small, but it has the best food. I haven't had a bad experience, and they don't advertise that I eat there. So that makes them tops in my book." She swallowed the last of her wine. "I'm going to go get ready."

"Make sure you work your sexy ass tonight." Connor teased.

"You know I will," she said with a wink.

"Yeah baby, you gotta make my boys here earn their paycheck tonight." He laughed.

"Don't you worry. I'll make sure they earn every penny." She laughed.

"Cut your shit," Danny pointed at Connor.

Abby threw a cloth napkin at him, and their laughter followed her out of the room.

chapter
thirteen

Abby walked out of her bedroom ready for a night out with Kelly. They were going to meet up in the VIP area of Exit. Even though Abby would have two watchdogs at her back, she was still excited.

"I'm ready," Abby announced as she walked into the living room. The men were seated around the room, watching the television mounted above the fireplace.

They all turned at the sound of her voice and stared.

"What's wrong?" She hurried over to the floor to ceiling windows and checked out her reflection. Everything seemed to be in place.

She thought she looked good. She wore a pair of gold glittery boy shorts that were long enough to cover her ass and a bit of her upper thigh but not much more. She paired that with a nude-colored see-through blouse and matching bra. It was the beginning of June, but today it felt more like the middle of summer than late spring. She accessorized with a thick gold bangle bracelet, gold hoop earrings and a pair of four-inch nude colored platform shoes with a gold decorative chain on the back of each shoe. She loved these shoes because they made her legs look as though they went on forever.

"That's what you're wearing?" Danny asked, a strange expression on his face.

"Yeah, why?"

"Don't you think you're a tad underdressed?"

"Um, no. I wear outfits like this all the time." She walked past him and patted him on the shoulder. "Relax. It's a club. What do you want me to wear? A burka?" she sassed.

"I just think—never mind. Have fun."

"Oh, I will." She smiled.

"Hey, do you mind if I take a shower? I need to primp for my big night." Connor mocked fluffing his hair, and he batted his eyelashes.

The other guys laughed at him.

"Make yourself at home," Abby said. "The guest bath is on the other side of the kitchen." She pointed the way. "And you can use some of my make-up as long as you put it back where you found it."

John hooted at Connor. "Put on the bright lipstick."

Connor laughed, too. "Thanks, Abby. Have a good night." He grabbed his duffle bag from where it lay by the couch and walked down the hall.

"Ready, fellas?" Abby placed her phone in her clutch.

"Let's roll." John clapped his hands together.

"John, Aaron, remember what we discussed." Danny gave them a stern look.

"You don't have to worry, boss." Aaron gave him a

little salute.

Danny glanced back at Abby. "Did you program their numbers in your phone?"

"I sure did. See? I *can* be responsible."

"Thank you. Don't leave their sight, and if you and Kelly decide to go exploring or whatever womenfolk do on girls' night out, let them know so they can tail you at all times."

"Yes, sir," Abby mocked.

He sighed. "Look, I'm here to do a job. You can help me do it better. I sent one of my men to get the lay of the land there and he said that club was insane. It's packed every night, and the inside is dark. Lots of places for assholes to hide. So tonight's not the night to do anything stupid."

"Okay, fine. Yeesh, I feel like I'm a teenager again."

"It shows you he cares," John said. "Nucci's good at this. Let him help you. Especially since you have an asshole in your life."

She nodded, feeling a little bad that she was riding Danny's case. But it kind of stung the way he kept reminding her that she was just a job. She fought a frown.

"Stay safe," Danny said. "Use common sense."

"It'll be fine. Have fun at your stuffy, boring meeting. Who has a meeting at this time of night, anyway?"

"I do."

"Obviously. Okay, toodles." She waved and followed John and Aaron to the door.

* * *

She entered the elevator with the guys and caught their reflection in the mirror. It looked so odd not having Danny with her. She second-guessed her plans for the evening, and was about to turn around and go back inside when her phone chirped with a text message.

She fished her phone out of her clutch and took a deep breath before she checked to see who was texting her. As far as she knew, Sean didn't have this number but that's what she thought about the last one. Who knows how he got it? She wasn't about to let her guard down. Kelly's name flashed across her screen. Abby unlocked her phone.

Kelly—*Where are you?*

Abby—*On my way.*

Kelly—*Awesome! Did you escape the babysitters?*

Abby—*No.*

Kelly—*How fucking lame! Come on girl, this place is awesome. We can't have fun with babysitters!*

Abby—*I'm sure we can. I can't walk into a packed club in NYC alone. That's suicide.*

Kelly—*You'll be fine. I got ya back.*

Abby—*Yes, I feel 100% secure with you as my bodyguard. ;)*

Kelly—*Fuck, I still say ditch them.*

Abby—*I can't!*

Kelly—*Ugh!! FINE! Text me when you're here.*

They exited the elevator and proceeded to the waiting car.

"Ma'am," Vinny, her driver, greeted and held the door open for her.

"Vinny, I've told you a million times to call me Abby. You make me feel old when you call me ma'am."

He smiled politely as she got in the car, and he closed the door for her.

She texted Kelly. *On my way.*

Since Abby didn't know John and Aaron, she spent the car ride checking emails and answering a few text messages. Plus, she was still a little cranky about Danny.

Vinny stopped in front of the celebrity entrance of the club, one of the perks of being famous that Abby actually liked, especially since the front of the club was filled with so many people they spilled into the street. And at that moment, Abby was actually thankful for John and Aaron. There would be no way she'd survive inside if the outside looked this crazy. But she kind of hated it that Danny had been right.

The door of the car opened and Abby was whisked inside. She didn't even have time to wave to onlookers who were camped out behind the barrier waiting for any random celebrity to make an appearance.

Once inside, she stayed close to her guards. There was a short walk before they reached the VIP area. Luckily a few bouncers flanked them and made navigating through the crowd a bit easier. Before they reached the VIP area, Abby was able to get a quick glance at the club which had cages in the corners. There were nearly nude dancers displayed throughout the room, working the stages and putting on a show. The crowd surrounded them as they danced seductively to the music pounding through the speakers. There were also a handful of dancers on top of the bars. From what she could see, Exit had an anything goes policy once you made it past the bouncers at the entrance.

When they reached the VIP lounge, the bouncers left Abby with her crew, and they were able to freely roam the smaller, less crowded area. She loved how they set this section up as the two-story lounge. It was like a lounge within a club. No one in the main area could see what went on behind the closed door, so she could have the illusion of privacy. For Abby, even in a VIP section, she had to keep up appearances. Everyone was *always* watching her.

She slowly walked around looking for her friend. Kelly was a quirky dresser, so Abby wasn't worried about finding her. The crowd was smaller in here than in the main club, but the noise level seemed louder.

After making a pass around the first level with no luck, she climbed the stairs with the men following close behind her. About halfway up, she noticed a group of people standing off to the side and a petite blue haired chick was in the mix. Abby was almost certain that was Kelly.

She continued up the stairs through the small crowd. As she approached the group, Abby heard Kelly's unique laugh, which sounded like someone inhaled way too much helium. It brought back some fun memories of Abby, Sean,

191

and Kelly hanging out during breaks in between tours and recording sessions.

"Yo, bitch." Abby covered Kelly's eyes and yelled into her ear.

Kelly screamed with excitement. "Ho, what took you so long?" She pulled Abby into a tight hug and jumped up and down.

"It takes time to look this good," Abby yelled back, and they pulled away from each other.

"Don't I know it." They both eyed each other up and down, looking at each other's outfits.

"Whatcha drinking?" Kelly asked as she pulled Abby toward the bar.

"Sex against the wall," Abby shouted with a straight face to both Kelly and the waiting bartender.

"Make that two, sugar," Kelly chimed in while eye fucking the bartender. She only stopped when Abby snapped her fingers in front of her face, which made Kelly laugh.

"What?" Kelly looked at Abby innocently.

"You're drooling, girl," Abby teased as she continued to laugh.

"Sex on a fucking stick. I told you. My intel never fails." Kelly turned back to the bar.

"Can I get you anything else, ladies?" Mr. Sex On A Stick asked as he leaned on the bar and winked at them.

"Put these on my tab, sugar." Kelly winked back.

"Make sure to add a big fat tip for yourself," Abby shouted, straining to raise her voice over the raucous music.

"I could use a little help," Kelly said seductively as she leaned over the bar making her cleavage spill over and giving the bartender a show.

"Down girl," Abby hollered.

"Hey Mr. Hottie?" Kelly waved him back. Abby watched as she handed him her business card but turned her head when they started making out.

"Here." She handed Abby her drink. "Those two your babysitters?" She asked, glancing over Abby's shoulder.

"If they look like linebackers, yes." She sipped her drink.

"Not bad. Guess it could be worse. You could be stuck with a couple of big, hairy mouth-breathers."

"I'm sure there are plenty of nice guys with those issues," Abby said before she took another swig of her drink.

"Let's hit the floor," Kelly said.

Abby nodded, gulped down the last of her drink, and followed her toward the semi-full dance floor.

John and Aaron followed, but they also allowed her a bit of space, which she was thankful for. She wanted to dance and be silly tonight, and it helped if security stayed unobtrusive.

Abby and Kelly made their way to the dance floor. They danced and laughed, and it was just what Abby needed—a night where she didn't have to worry about threats and cell phones and mothers sleeping with boyfriends. Abby noticed Kelly was texting but before she could tell her that this was a phone-free night, she got distracted by a hot blond god who pulled Abby into his arms. He started to grind with her to the music. Abby waved off John and quickly got the man under control. As hot as he was, she didn't want to be groped by a total stranger on the dance floor.

When Abby turned, Kelly was still typing on her phone. "Who you texting?" she shouted into Kelly's ear. Kelly jumped and quickly tucked her phone back into her pocket.

"Fuck, you scared me," Kelly yelled back, clutching her hand to her chest.

"Sorry. So, who were you texting?" Abby asked again. "No work stuff. Tonight is all about fun." Abby threw her hands above her head and started giggling.

"No one you know. Making plans for later. Although, I might not need those plans," she stated, winking at Abby as she took hold of a passing man. There seemed to be a theme in this club. Every man Abby saw was more appealing than the last. She thought about Danny, imagining him in tight jeans and shirt, dancing close to her. The image was easily hotter than any of the men she'd seen so far tonight.

Still, it was nice to be noticed. Another guy brushed against her. She grabbed him by the shirt and pulled him closer. Between the wine earlier in the night and the drink she downed, she was feeling pretty bold. She danced, drank, and gossiped, and it felt great to be out. Danny was so wrong. This wasn't a bad idea. At all.

* * *

An hour had passed since Abby arrived at Exit, and she was feeling a bit off. She guessed it was the alcohol mixed with the dancing that was getting to her. She needed a time-out.

"I have to pee. Be right back," Abby shouted in Kelly's ear.

Kelly took Abby's hand. "I'll come with you. Give me a sec," she shouted over the music.

Abby nodded and waited while Kelly whispered something in her dance partner's ear, and then she and Kelly headed down the long hallway toward the bathroom, with the guys following. John cleared the hallway while Aaron checked the ladies room.

"Please," Kelly said as they waited. "Seriously? Pervs in the bathroom?"

"You'd be surprised," Abby said, suddenly feeling a little defensive about her detail.

"Whatever."

Abby started to retort but decided not to. She felt a little queasy, so she leaned against the wall and closed her eyes. Abby liked to have a drink or two and admittedly she had been using alcohol lately to help cope with the stress of Sean and her mother, but it never hit her this hard.

"All clear," Aaron said.

"Thanks, Sugar." Kelly brushed against him as she

walked into the bathroom.

Abby followed. She struggled in the stall but managed to do what she had to do then splashed cool water on her face. It didn't help make her feel any less strange. She gripped the sides of the sink to help keep her upright.

"Babe, can you get the boys? I really don't feel well. I think I drank too much. I gotta get out of here before I get sick and wind up on the next episode of TMZ." Abby splashed some more water on her face.

"You got it, girl. Don't move."

"Thanks."

She heard the bathroom door open, and she closed her eyes in hopes that the world would stop spinning.

A minute later, she heard the door again, and she slowly turned her head to explain to the guys what she was feeling, but they weren't there. Two women rushed in instead. *Fuck, where the hell are they?*

They were going on and on about a fight, and Abby was glad when they finally shut up because they were loud. Slowly, she moved toward the door but struggled to open it. She looked for John or Aaron, but neither was waiting for her. What the hell?

The hallway was empty but there appeared to be a brawl near the dance floor. That must've been what the ladies in the bathroom were going on and on about. She saw her bodyguards in the thick of it along with the club bouncers. She tried to walk toward them but after a few steps she stopped. Her head was too fucked up to even move. She leaned against the wall and closed her eyes. She searched for her phone in her clutch and when she found it she dialed Kelly's number. It rang and rang until her voicemail picked up.

"It's me," Abby said. "Where are you?" She hung up. Her eyes felt so heavy, and she wanted to sleep. She tried to call Danny, but before she could get the number to come up, she dropped her phone.

"Great," she mumbled.

Abby leaned against the wall and used it to guide her to the floor. She picked up her phone and after a couple of tries, she finally dialed Danny's number and waited for him to pick up.

Now she needed to get her ass back up. For a moment, she contemplated crawling to the guys, but she wasn't sure she'd even make that. She'd be lucky to get her ass off the floor at all.

"Oh, thank God," she said, relieved she'd made it to her feet. However, as soon as she had the words out of her mouth, she felt her body swaying forward. She was going down, and there was nothing she could do to stop it. She braced for the worst, but it never happened. Someone caught her. Abby was in the arms of a very solid being. She opened her eyes and found herself eye to eye with Sean. He pushed her up against the wall.

"Shit," she said.

"Abby?" Danny's voice came through her phone.

"Hel—" Abby attempted to yell.

Sean covered her mouth with his hand and took the

phone from her. He held her against the wall with his body.

"Mr. Nucci, so sad you're not here." Sean snarled before throwing the phone onto the floor.

Abby tried to push away, but her limbs felt as if they were filled with sand.

"Time for a little trip."

Abby hit his chest, her movements loose and out of control. And he was so strong, and she felt so weak. Her screams were muffled against his hand.

Someone see me. Someone help me.

Kelly. There she was. And she saw them.

Thank you. Relief flooded through Abby's system. Kelly would go get one of the boys.

But then Kelly smiled, waved, and turned her back on them.

Abby stared at her, confused.

Abby struggled to get free, but nothing she did helped. Her body and brain were no longer in sync.

"Now, let's go have fun," Sean whispered in her ear as he started pulling her down the hallway.

chapter fourteen

Oh God no! No, no, no, no, no.

What the fuck was happening? Sean was here. Kelly saw and didn't help.

She fought against him as he pulled her toward the emergency exit.

"I've missed you, baby." He trailed his fingers down her cheek.

Abby continued to struggle to get free.

"What was that, baby?" He taunted as Abby still tried to scream for help even though her cries were useless.

Sean kicked open the emergency exit, and the alarm blared. Before Abby could even register what was happening, he threw her over his shoulder and ran down the stairs. He jumped down the last few steps of each level. Her body was jostled and bounced off his shoulder and into the banister. The only good thing about this position was she was free to scream, and she did. As loud as she could and she didn't stop. Nobody came to help. Sean had her.

Cool air hit her face and she realized they were outside. What was happening? When did they leave the club?

The chill in the night air helped to clear her muddled brain. Still, all she could make out was a dimly lit alley.

"Fuck!" Sean kicked the brick wall. He paced back and forth with Abby still over his shoulder. She hadn't realized how strong he was.

"Where is it?"

He was on the phone, and Abby knew the voice on the other end of that line. She'd recognize it anywhere.

Kelly. But she couldn't tell what she was saying.

"Fuck."

She strained to hear Kelly's response, but she couldn't make out the words.

"You didn't think this was something I should know? Just get here."

He threw his phone and took Abby farther into the dark alley.

"Please, Sean, let me go," Abby said, fighting another wave of nausea. Maybe if she puked on him, she'd have a chance to get away.

"Shut up."

He roughly dropped her on the ground, and her head hit the brick wall.

"Uggh," she mumbled as pain shot through her skull. She tried to roll away from him.

"You couldn't play nice, could you? Had to run your mouth off to your boy toy." He kicked a stray bag of garbage, and Abby took her chance. She scrabbled to her feet, leaning on the wall for support, but she didn't get far. She lost her footing and tried to break her fall with her hands. It stung, adding to the pain in her head. She started to crawl. Anything to get away from here. Where were John and Aaron?

"Where do you think you're going?" Sean pulled her back to him and ripped her blouse. "I'm not done with you."

"Please, Sean," she managed. The words sounded thick and her head felt like it was stuffed with cotton. "We can work something out. Please don't do anything you'll regret."

"I don't regret anything except maybe believing your cunt of a mother when she told me that she could control you. I wish I had time to play with you." He shoved Abby's hair away from her face and pushed himself against her. She felt how excited this all made him, and a new kind of fear overtook her, coupled with revulsion.

Please, no. She was *not* going to be violated. No fucking way.

"No!" She pushed with all she had and kicked him squarely in the crotch. He doubled over.

Abby got up and ran. She was almost to the club door when she tripped over debris and fell. She gasped to catch her breath and struggled to her feet.

"Get back here," Sean called after her, rage in his voice.

Abby didn't look back, but she heard him running after her. She made it to the door, but there was no handle on the outside. She banged and banged but no one opened it. She tried to run again, but Sean quickly caught up with her and tackled her to the ground. She was trapped between him and the asphalt.

She struggled to break free, but he overpowered her. He took both of her hands in one of his and pinned them above her head.

"Please, Sean. Please don't do this."

"Shut up." He ripped the last of Abby's shirt before yanking down the right cup of her bra. He roughly squeezed her breast, and the pain and shock made her cry out. He took her nipple into his mouth.

"Stop!" She thrashed beneath him to no effect. "Sean, please, please stop. *Please.*"

"Now, now Abigail," he crooned and brought his lips to hers and brushed them lightly with his. "Let's play nice. You're not going anywhere," he whispered, causing a chill to creep down her back.

Sean released her hands and started to unbutton his jeans. *Oh, God. No. Please God, no.* She clawed, kicked, and fought wildly. She got another shot to his balls before he punched the right side of her face. The force of his blow caused her head to swing to the left and hit the pavement. A fiery burst of pain burst through her face, sharp and hard and overwhelming. It was like nothing she'd ever felt before. Her brain felt like it had shifted and everything was spinning.

"Please," she whimpered.

"Please what, Abigail?" Sean taunted. "Tell me, Abigail? What do you want?"

"Please," she implored, tears rolling down her face. "Don't hurt me. Let's talk. We can work things out. Let's go talk." She sobbed between her words.

"Oh, now you want to talk. I think the time for talking is over *Abigail*." He grabbed her by the hair and pulled her up. "I'm done talking. All *I've* done is talk to your voicemail. That's very rude." Sean's right hand curled around her neck, and his thumb pushed into her trachea. She gasped for breath and grabbed his wrist, doing her best to loosen his grip.

He pressed this thumb deeper into her skin. She clawed at his face, but her fingers couldn't find purchase.

She felt his hot breath on her neck when he whispered in her ear, "Talk, Abigail. I'm listening." He released his hold on her neck.

She sucked in a huge gasp of air and coughed, struggling to breathe.

"Please, Sean. I'm sorry, please," she croaked between gasping breaths. "You can come back. We can work things out. I promise." Anything to make him stop.

"Talking's done." He squeezed her throat again, harder this time, and pulled her up to him only to slam her back down to the ground.

Abby's head hit the blacktop, and her vision blurred. She was helpless, unable to fight as he pulled down her shorts. The last blow to her head completely undid her. Which was worse? Death or what he was about to do? *Please, God, somebody help me,* she begged silently.

A loud bang sounded, and she couldn't register what

was happening. Sean's weight lifted off her, but he grabbed her by her shoulders.

"Until next time." He pushed her back to the ground momentarily, and she heard his running footsteps. After that, everything stopped.

* * *

What the fuck just happened?

It took a moment for the situation to register in Danny's head before he was on the move.

"Round up," he ordered his crew.

"What's going on?" Connor asked as he jumped to his feet.

"That bastard has her."

"Fuck."

"All hands on deck," He told his men, and they moved into action.

He dialed John's number, then Aaron's, but neither picked up.

Fuck.

His heart was racing. Sean had her. Just like that bastard had Vanessa.

"I'm calling anyone in the area to get their ass over there," King announced. Mike King was one of Nucci Securities top guys.

Danny nodded.

He tried John and Aaron again, but still no answer. He wasn't about to wait around for them to return his call. Danny and his crew were on their way to Exit within ten minutes.

"Ricky is nearly there," King informed Danny. King navigated through the streets of Manhattan. Half the team was with them, and the other half in the car following behind.

Danny's phone rang. John. Danny took a breath as he answered the phone. He was overflowing with adrenaline and fear-fueled anger and yelling at his employees wouldn't help right now. He'd have plenty of time to kill people later. Still, he didn't bother with hello. "Sean took her," he said.

"Not sure—"

"No, Sean took her," he said, cutting him off. "He had her and called me. What happened? Why was she out of your sight?"

"Kelly had an issue and—"

"Is Kelly with you?"

There was silence on the other end of the line.

"I asked you a question."

"No. When the alarm sounded, we broke away and went to get Abby. When we returned, she was gone."

"Christ. Okay, we're ten minutes out. You need keep looking for Abby." He hung up, and his next call was to the management office of Exit.

"Club Exit. How may I direct your call?"

"Andrew Franco, please."

"Who's calling?"

"Danny Nucci, Nucci Securities. I spoke with your boss earlier today about my client. She was just kidnapped from your club. I think he'll want to take my call." *He'd better*, Danny thought grimly.

"Hold, please."

The manager picked up almost instantly. "Mr. Nucci, I've been notified of the situation, and we are working diligently to get it resolved. As I'm sure you know someone tripped the alarm on one of our doors. The crowd in the area thought there was a fire, so it was a bit hectic there for a while. Things are starting to look normal again. We are assessing things as we speak so—"

"Mr. Franco, my client was taken."

"Excuse me?"

"She called me in distress when someone took her."

"Uhhh…" the manager sounded at a loss for what to do.

"I'll be there shortly. I'm going to need your full cooperation on this."

"Of course."

"I have men there now."

"Yes, I've not had a chance to speak with them directly because I was dealing with patrons, but I'll find them now and get briefed on matters. Someone will meet you out front when you arrive."

"I'd appreciate that."

Danny hung up and didn't feel any better about the situation. Sean had Abby, and his men were clueless. This all seemed so surreal. Why didn't he listen to his instincts? He never should have let her go out tonight. He had been trying to convince himself that he wasn't emotionally invested in Abby. That he wasn't repeating his mistakes. He needed to push aside his personal feelings and guilt. Now wasn't the time to play the "what if" game. When Abby was in front of him and safe, he'd have plenty of time to beat himself up.

Danny's phone rang as the car pulled up to the club. Aaron, this time.

"Yeah," he answered.

"Where are you?" Aaron asked.

"Pulling up now. Got something?"

"Yeah. Abby."

Relief flooded every part of his body. "Where are you?"

"Back alley."

"On our way." He hung up. "They found her. Follow me."

chapter fifteen

"Where is she?" Danny demanded when he reached the scene.

Aaron met him at the alley's entrance. There was a commotion up ahead, lots of people milling around.

"She's just ahead. Banged up a bit, but it looks like she'll be okay."

Maybe physically. But what about mentally?

"What happened?"

"We escorted Abby and her friend to the ladies room, and while she was in there, this dick that had been dancing with her friend Kelly started getting rough with her. I went to defuse the situation. The guy attacked me, and shit got out of hand, and John had to assist. Then an emergency door alarm was tripped, and all hell broke loose. We searched the area and couldn't find her."

"Where's Kelly?"

"I don't know. She's in the wind."

"Find her."

Sirens sounded, and Danny figured emergency

personnel were on their way here. He turned and looked back at his team. "Secure the area and make sure the ambulance has clear access."

He followed Aaron. His heart was racing and nothing anyone could say would convince him she was okay until he saw for himself.

The men cleared a path, and there she was, lying on the ground with John next to her. From this distance he could see that her face was bloodied and swollen, but she was still breathing. She had a man's jacket draped over her body. He really didn't want to think about why. He clenched his fist and fought back his emotions. Abby didn't need to see any more anger tonight.

"Abby?"

John made room for Danny. "She wants to sleep, but I've been talking to her to keep her awake."

He nodded and kneeled next to Abby.

"Abby?"

"Danny?"

"Yeah, it's me." He smiled at her while he took in the injuries he could see. She had a nasty red mark on her face, her shirt was completely torn to shreds, and there were minor cuts and scrapes over her body. He'd feel better once a doctor checked her over. But there was no doctor in the world who would be able to fix Sean once Danny got to him.

"He found me," she said between sobs. "I don't know how and I tried—" she took a breath. "I tried to get away, but I couldn't."

"It's okay. He's gone, and I'm here. Stay still."

"I'm sorry," she said.

"For what?"

"I should've listened. I should've taken it more seriously."

"Hey, none of that. Let's get you fixed up first, okay? We'll talk later." He reached out to touch her hair but pulled his hand back. He didn't know the full extent of her injuries and didn't want to accidentally hurt her. And maybe the last thing she wanted after Sean was any man's hands on her.

Sirens blasted nearby then stopped.

"The ambulance is here, and we're gonna get you out of here."

"I want to go home," she said through her tears. "I don't want to go to the hospital. The press—"

"Don't worry about anything right now, okay?"

"The paramedics are here," Connor said.

Danny started to get up, but Abby grabbed his shirt.

"Don't go. *Please.*"

"It's okay. I'll be right here. They need to have a look at you."

"Danny—"

"Sir, can you step back, please?"

"Hold on," he said to the newcomer. "Abby, I'm not going anywhere. I need to let these guys do their job. I'll be right here," he assured her.

"Promise?"

"I promise."

"Okay." She let go of his shirt, and he got to his feet.

"I'm concerned that she's asking to go to sleep," he said to the paramedic. "Concussion at the very least."

"Let us have a look," the paramedic said.

He moved out of the way, and the paramedics went to work. While they did their thing, Danny rounded up his team, trying not worry about the extent of Abby's injuries.

"I'll be at the hospital with Abby. The police will probably say they have this shit under control, but I'm not waiting for them to gather the intelligence we already have on him. We hunt, and we find him." There was no room for compromise. He wasn't going to sit back and do nothing.

"On it," King said.

For Danny, tonight it wasn't just that Abby was attacked. They all were. There had been a security breach, and each man standing there needed to correct that.

"If you find him, bring him to me." He struggled to maintain his composure.

"That's a promise."

He glanced around, staring at the shadows accusingly, daring Sean to step out of them and face him man to man. "King and Aaron, hit the intel networks. I want security video pulled of the club and a three-block radius. Check in with NYPD for street views. John, get a team and run down this fucker's records. Check his phone, credit cards, bank accounts—anything and everything. I want to know when this asshole takes a dump and what toilet paper he uses. Connor, with me," Danny said as the rest of his team dispersed.

"Are you Danny Nucci?" A paramedic asked.

"Yeah."

"We're about to load Ms. Murphy into the ambulance. She's asking for you."

"What kind of injuries?" Danny asked.

"Probable concussion. Doesn't look like anything is broken. Bruises and scrapes."

Danny didn't ask any other questions. He wasn't sure he was ready to hear about the answer yet. He and Connor followed the man to the ambulance.

The paramedic gestured for Danny to take a seat in the back of the ambulance toward Abby's feet.

"Hey," Danny said as climbed in. "It's me."

Abby managed a smile.

"I'm right here, okay?"

She gave him a weak thumbs-up, and the paramedic shut the door as Danny settled himself onto the bench. He left plenty of room for the medic to tend directly to her. Connor got into the front seat with the driver.

"Moving," the driver announced, and Danny braced himself as the vehicle pulled out of the alley and started its lights and sirens. They swerved in and out of traffic, passing cars and trucks in his rush to get them to the nearest hospital. Within minutes, the back doors opened, and a medical team moved her quickly and efficiently into the building.

Danny and Connor follow closely behind her stretcher, but were stopped by a security guard.

"Gentlemen, only one of you can follow her back. The other will have to stay in the waiting room." He motioned to the double doors on the right.

"I'll wait outside. The guys should be here in a minute, and I'll give Sophie a call and let her know what's going on. Let me know if you need me back here." Connor patted Danny and left.

Danny headed to Abby's cubicle. There were several nurses working on her, hooking Abby up to machines and taking blood.

"The doctor will be right in," a nurse informed.

"I'm going to need to speak with whoever is in charge here."

"Let me find someone to help."

"I'd appreciate that."

Danny kept his eyes glued to Abby, who was laying on the gurney, motionless.

"Hello, I'm Nikki Moore. I'm the charge nurse. How can I help you?"

Danny looked her over. Youngish white chick, hipster glasses but she had an earnest expression. "I'm Danny Nucci, President of Nucci Securities and personal bodyguard to Abby Murphy. I'm sure there's going to be a mob of reporters and fans here as soon as word gets out. Also, for your security, she was attacked tonight. I'll have my team supply a photograph. We'll need to know what plan your security has in place. I'll also establish a schedule rotation to ensure she's protected at all times."

"Okay." The nurse tapped her pen against her clipboard.

"We need to register her under her alias, which may help to delay the media attention, but we shouldn't count on it. We're too exposed here. I'm going to need a private room for my client."

"I'll get her registered in the system. What name should I use?"

"Madeline Roberts," Danny answered.

A doctor entered the room.

"I'll get the paperwork started and inform the staff. I'll also have a private room set up for Ms. Murphy."

The nurse left, and Danny watched and listened to the doctor give his orders.

"Sir, I'm Doctor Phillips.

"Danny Nucci. I'm Ms. Murphy's bodyguard."

"I'll need you to step back and let us examine her please."

Danny looked down the gurney and noticed he was holding Abby's hand. He hadn't even realized he had picked up her hand. Fuck, he was really losing it, and that just wouldn't do. He needed to keep his shit together. Now wasn't the time to fall apart. Abby needed him. He released her hand

and walked to the corner of the cubicle and observed the hospital team do their job.

Her face was beginning to bruise, and he was sure she was going to be hurting soon, if she wasn't already. After several minutes, the doctor approached Danny.

"I want to send her for a CAT scan and a few other tests before I determine if I'll admit her."

"Is she okay?"

"We won't really know until the results of the CAT scan comes back, but right now she's stable."

Danny nodded. He knew the drill, but he still had to ask.

"Okay, let's get our patient up for the scan and please put a rush on her blood work," he told the nurse.

"Thank you, Doctor. I really appreciate that."

The nurse prepared Abby for the move.

"Danny," Abby mumbled.

He moved quickly to her bedside. He took her hand, and it felt small and vulnerable. His heart ached.

"Yeah? I'm right here."

"Don't leave me."

"I'm not going anywhere," he assured.

"Thank you." She let go of his hand so the nurse could continue, and he sent Connor a quick text to tell him he'd need him to help escort Abby for her tests. He wasn't about to chance Sean showing up and trying to finish what he started.

Within minutes they were all in the patient elevator on their way to the first of the several tests Abby would have to undergo.

* * *

"How long does it take for test results to come back?" Sophie demanded. "I'm going to find someone to tell me something."

Danny let her go. He knew there was no point trying to stop her. She was nervous and wanted answers. He was frustrated too, but Abby was sleeping soundly and her vitals looked good, so he wasn't as nervous as Sophie. He had bigger things to focus on.

Like the fact that Vivien had graced them all with her presence about an hour ago, and since then she hadn't stopped bitching. Concern for her daughter's well-being was quite low on the list.

"Have you seen the chaos that has ensued since I got here?" Vivien glared at him. "All because she needed to get her way."

Danny cracked the tension out of his neck and forced himself to ignore her. She was partially right, though. Since Vivien had made her overly dramatic entrance into the hospital, it had caused a huge spectacle and the place had been crawling with paparazzi and fans. NYPD had sent a few officers to help keep them from running around loose all over the hospital, which was helpful, but he was still tired and pissed and Vivien was the last person he wanted to deal with.

Thankfully, she shut up when Sophie came in with the doctor following her. Danny hid his smile. Leave it to Sophie to get a doctor to hurry his ass up.

"Okay, let's wake up our patient. I'm going to have to ask anyone that isn't family to leave, though."

Danny heard Vivien laughing, and he shot her a look.

"Sorry, Vivien," he said mildly. "The doctor is aware of the situation and has granted me a family pass."

"We'll be outside if you need us." Sophie said softly.

"I'll let you know ASAP," Danny said with an encouraging smile. He continued to ignore Vivien who muttered all the way to Abby's bedside.

"Ms. Murphy?" The doctor gently called.

Danny moved closer when he didn't see her move or react in any way.

The doctor pulled a small flashlight from his pocket and checked Abby's pupils. Danny took another step. In an instant, all the possible reasons for someone not waking up ran through Danny's head, and he clenched his teeth again.

Abby reacted. She turned away from the light and moaned.

"It seems our patient is being stubborn and doesn't want to wake up yet."

"Figures," muttered Vivien.

Danny glared at her and took another step closer to

Abby's bed. "Abby?" He leaned over the bed rail and moved her bangs from her face. "You need to wake up. Come on. Rise and shine."

She groaned, but after a few long seconds, her eyes fluttered opened.

"Hey, you," he said, his chest flooded with relief, and his muscles relaxed. "Thanks for joining us."

"Oh, you know me," she said. "I need to make an entrance." She tried to laugh but winced instead.

"Be careful," he warned.

"Ms. Murphy? I'm Doctor Phillips, and I have the results of some your tests. I'm still waiting on your blood work." He looked down at the chart then back at her. "Everything looks good. All your tests came back negative. No concussion, no internal bleeding, no broken bones." He cleared his throat. "No physical evidence of...ah...sexual trauma."

"Why would she need to be checked for that?"

The doctor looked at Vivien. "It was necessary under the circumstances."

He closed the file and looked at Abby. "You're very lucky. As a precaution, I'd like to keep you for twenty-four hours. Pending anything odd on your blood work, I think you can go home tomorrow."

"Well, then," Vivien announced. "Drama over. Be ready for the tour in two weeks. I'm going to see if I can salvage the rest of my vacation." Vivien grabbed her things and swept out of the room, leaving an awkward silence behind her.

How could you explain that to a stranger? Danny glanced at the doctor, who pursed his lips. Danny caught his eye in a shared moment of "what the fuck."

"Ms. Murphy do you remember what happened?" the doctor asked, breaking the tension.

"Um. I left my apartment with John and Aaron to meet Kelly at the club." The doctor looked to Danny to confirm and he nodded. "Kelly and I were having fun and dancing and then—then—I don't know. Everything is fuzzy."

"What's the next thing you remember?"

"Waking up a few minutes ago to Danny's voice."

"What about at the club? Do you remember anything from there?"

"No."

"Do you remember how you got here?"

They waited for Abby to answer. Danny could tell she was really trying to recall something.

"I can't remember. It's all sort of blank right now."

Danny took her hand. He waited for her to look at him. "From what John told me, and from what I know, Sean was at the club, and he was able to grab you."

"Sean was there?" She stared at him. "At the club?"

"Yes. There was a fight. Do you remember anything about that?"

"No. Was I in it?"

"No, not at all. It was a diversion, and it allowed Sean a window of opportunity to grab you without John or Aaron noticing until you were gone."

"I don't understand. How did he know I was there?" She gripped his hand.

Danny squeezed back, gently. "I don't know that yet, but I promise you I'm going to find out."

"Where is he?" There was fear in her voice.

"I don't know. The police and my men are looking for him."

"Ms. Murphy," the doctor cut in. "Is it correct to say you don't remember anything Mr. Nucci is telling you? None of this seems familiar to you?"

"No. But my head is pounding, so that could be why."

"What else are you feeling right now?"

"Just a bit dizzy."

"It could be lingering results of the trauma you suffered. The hit to your face would cause the headache and some dizziness. I'm a bit worried about the memory loss. Hopefully, that will fade. The brain sometimes protects us from traumatic memories. I'll be back with the results of your blood tests, and you'll let me know if you remember anything else. Sound good?"

"Yes, doctor. Thank you."

"Yes, thank you doctor for all your help."

"I'll ask the nurse to bring you something for your headache. Mr. Nucci, could I see you outside for a moment?"

Danny followed him into the hallway, anxiety in his gut.

"Since she can't remember what happened, I'd like to call someone in to do a more thorough examination and administer a rape kit."

Danny sucked his breath between his teeth. "You said you didn't find any evidence of that sort of trauma."

"Unfortunately, that doesn't mean a rape couldn't have occurred. Especially if any kind of drug was placed in her drink. I'm going to send someone to talk with her about it. It is, after all, a decision that she ultimately makes."

He nodded.

"I'll be in touch."

"Thank you."

Danny went back into Abby's room, and not long after, there was a knock on the door.

"Is it okay to come back in?" Sophie poked her head in.

"Sure." Abby smiled.

"How are you feeling?"

"Crappy. And I have a headache."

"Everything came back negative," Danny said. "He wants to keep her until tomorrow. Blood work is still pending, though." He didn't mention the rape kit.

"Negative is excellent news. Thank God." Sophie took Abby's hand. "What happened?"

"I don't know. I can't remember right now."

"Well, that's to be expected, I suppose, with the hit to your face."

The door opened slightly, and Connor peeked in. "Nurse," he announced. He opened the door wider so the nurse could enter.

"Hi, there," she said. "I'm just going to give you something for your pain. In a few minutes you should feel some relief. You really should try to rest some more, Ms. Murphy."

"Don't worry. I don't think my eyes are giving me a choice right now."

"Sleep. I'll be back to check on you in a little bit."

"Thank you."

"Well, I won't stay," Sophie said. "Listen to the nurse and sleep. I'll go do some damage control, and I'm thinking your two-week break will need to be a bit longer, so I have some rescheduling to do as well. I'll come back later. Love ya, girl and glad you're okay."

"Love you, too."

Sophie left, and it was Danny and Abby.

"Danny?"

"Sleep," he said sternly.

"I will." She paused. "You're staying, right?"

"I'm not moving. Don't worry about anything. Sleep. I've got you covered."

"Okay."

By the time Danny moved to the corner of the room to sit down, Abby was asleep.

chapter
sixteen

"I know what I'd like to do, but my mom is never going to allow it." Abby informed Danny and Sophie. It was the next day, and Abby was patiently waiting to be released from the hospital.

"I could make it work," Danny said. "I'd call in more men and cancel all backstage passes and events. No one would get to you, but I agree with you. I don't like the idea of being on the road, and Sean knowing your entire itinerary. It makes for a security nightmare."

"This is all too much for me to think about right now."

"So don't think about it. I've got it under control. I'll call your mom's assistant and tell her your canceling the tour, and by the time Vivien finds out, you'll be out of here, and I'll tell her how it will be. After how she acted yesterday, it'll be fun." Sophie winked.

Abby picked at a spot on her hospital gown.

There was a knock at the door, and the doctor walked in.

"Good morning Ms. Murphy. How are you feeling today?"

"Good morning Dr. Phillips. I still have a headache, and I'm sore, but other than that, I feel okay."

"I wanted to discuss your blood work with you before I release you."

"Okay." Abby didn't like his tone.

"Would you like everyone to stay?"

"Yes please."

"All right. You tested positive for gamma hydroxybutyrate acid or GHB. Better known as "the date rape" drug.

"What?" Abby, Danny, and Sophie said nearly in unison.

"That explains why you were nauseous, the headaches, and most importantly, your memory loss."

"But how? I don't understand."

"It's most commonly administered through liquids. The drug is odorless and colorless so it is very easy to hide in drinks."

"So someone drugged me?"

"It would appear so."

"Who would do that?" she asked but didn't really expect an answer.

"Will her memories return?" Sophie asked the doctor.

"It's hard to say. For some, they remember everything within a few days, and for others, maybe they remember certain parts. But there is a chance you won't remember anything."

"Great," Abby mumbled.

"I'm going to fill out the paperwork for your release. I'll prescribe something for your headaches. They should go away within another day or two. If they don't please let me know." The doctor handed Abby his business card.

"Thank you, Dr. Phillips, for everything."

"Don't hesitate to call if you have any questions. I'll fill out your release papers, and then you're free to go home." The doctor left the room.

"Drugged?"

"Who would drug you? And *how* did they drug you?" Sophie asked.

"I don't know. I wish I could remember. This is so frustrating."

"Don't force it. Stressing out about it surely won't help," Sophie tried to assure her, but Abby could see Sophie was just as freaked out as she was. Someone had drugged, her and she couldn't remember anything.

"I guess."

Danny hadn't said a word since the doctor left. She looked over to him, "Please say something. You're making me nervous."

"Sophie's right. You can't force yourself to remember. We'll go upstate, and you'll get some distance and hopefully that will help."

Something was off with him, but Abby wasn't going to

push it.

"Okay, I guess I'll get dressed."

"That's my cue. Connor should be at my cabin soon, and King is outside on guard. I'm going to make sure everyone is in place. I don't want that mob out there to get wind that we're leaving. Dress comfortable, we have a long drive."

Abby nodded, relieved. "Sounds good. I'm done with this place. I need quiet and calm right about now."

"I can guarantee you'll have that."

"Really?" Sophie asked, skeptical. "With Abby Murphy around? Is there ever anything calm?"

Danny snorted a laugh and left. Sophie looked back at Abby and studied her for so long that Abby squirmed.

"What?" Abby said after a few uncomfortable moments.

"I need the truth. How are you *really* doing?"

"I'm good." But she knew she wasn't going to convince her.

"Don't tell me what you think I want to know. I'm worried, and Danny's worried, and he doesn't know how to approach the subject."

"He's worried?" Maybe that's why he was so quiet?

"Of *course* he's worried. I've never seen him act so nervous."

"Nervous?"

"Yes. He's very good at hiding his emotions, but trust me, he was nervous when we went in that exam room." Abby had granted the hospital permission to run the rape kit, and Sophie had held Abby's hand through the experience. "I keep trying to tell you that he's crazy for you, but you won't listen to me."

Abby rubbed her forehead. "No, not true."

"Oh, my God. You're blind and possibly stupid if you can't see how he is with you. You've had other bodyguards, so you know how it goes. They escort you from point A to point B and then back again, but they don't hang out with you, get to know you and your friends, or stand up for you. And they definitely don't bring you up to their cabin in the mountains. Are you really this clueless?"

"Whatever."

Sophie threw her hands up in mock despair. "You're so frustrating. Don't believe me. Fine."

"Go away," Abby said, but she was teasing. She knew their relationship was different. They were definitely friends. But Danny had feelings for her? That thought put little heat waves into her chest.

"And then where would you be?"

"Okay, okay. You're right. I'd be lost without you. And maybe I'm not fine. Maybe I don't want to think about things right now. I want to get out of here and go somewhere that has nothing to do with anything that's happened."

"I know." You could hear the sympathy in Sophie's voice. "Let me help you get changed."

"Thanks." Abby was grateful for the help. She was bruised nearly everywhere and quite sore.

"Okay, I have to go. I'll get up there as soon as I can. I have a lot of shit to do. Call me if you need me or want to talk. Take this time to heal and relax. Don't worry about anything else." She bent down and gave Abby a quick kiss and left. Abby sat on the bed and thought about what Sophie said. She leaned back and closed her eyes. If only she wasn't such a wreck with all these issues. But if it were true, what could she do? She had too much to work through, and Sean was out there, somewhere. The thought chilled her. She turned on the TV to distract herself, but the little heat waves she'd experienced earlier had been replaced with unease.

* * *

"I'm good. I promise." Abby shooed Danny away. They were getting ready to leave the hospital, and she had changed out of her hospital gown and into something warm and comfortable.

"I want you to be careful," he said.

"I'm feeling much better. Dizziness is gone, and the headache is just a dull ache. I don't think I'll keel over. We're good." She patted his arm. He'd been kind of cute the past hour, like a mother hen or something. He seemed a bit nervous, which was so out of character for him. It made Abby think of what Sophie said earlier, but the last thing she needed right now was to complicate things between them. She needed to heal and get her life in order. Everything was coming at her from all angles. Her career, her love life, her mother, and adding Danny to the mix right now would not be smart. She needed him too much to add a bunch of crazy emotional stuff. Besides, what if Sophie had read the whole thing wrong? That would really be awful, to come on to him only to find out he didn't feel the same.

"Ready, Ms. Murphy?" the nursed asked.

"As I'll ever be."

"Let's get you in the wheel chair."

"Thank you." She situated herself in the chair, and the nurse wheeled her out onto the floor, and Danny along with four of his guards surrounded them. They traveled to the freight elevators and down to the basement without incident. Danny had explained the plan to her before, and it seemed things were going the way he wanted. There were four black Range Rovers waiting in the alley. She was thankful it was daytime because the idea of entering an alley made her anxious.

They arrived at the door that would take them outside.

"Thank you," Abby said to the nurse.

"Make sure you follow the doctor's instructions, and if the dizziness returns or the headaches start to get bad, please call us.

"Will do. Thanks again for everything."

"Anytime and thank you for the autograph. My daughter is going to flip."

Abby smiled. "Glad I could provide it."

Danny helped her out of the chair, and his hands were warm and strong around hers. She reveled in it for a moment before he let go.

"We're the second car."

She was a little stiff from not moving, but at least the dizziness was gone. And she knew her face was still a mess, but she had some pain meds to help with that. Too bad the meds couldn't help her with the other stuff.

Danny gestured at the vehicle. "Get in the back for now."

She stuck her tongue out at him.

"I think the drugs they gave you are making you loopy." He opened the Rover's door, giving her a stern glance, but she saw the smile on his mouth. She climbed into the backseat and settled herself before she put her seatbelt on.

"Probably."

"When we're out of the city, I'll stop and you can get up front," he said.

"Sounds like a plan." She smiled at him. Sophie's opinion about Danny's feelings had Abby a little nervous about going with him to his house. He got into the driver's seat and started the engine, and she stared out the window, trying not to think about what had happened.

Within a few minutes all four cars pulled out of the alley and went in different directions. Decoys. Like she was in a spy movie. He turned on some music, and Abby watched him drive for a while. She liked his hands, she decided, and she never really got a chance to look at them, but there they were on the steering wheel. Strong hands. But gentle. She moved her gaze to his jaw line and thought about kissing it. She jerked her attention out the window again, watching as the city and its traffic started to diminish.

"How're you doing?" Danny said.

"Okay."

"There's a rest stop ahead."

Almost every parking slot at the rest stop was occupied and groups of people milled around. Some were eating snacks while others congregated near the bathrooms and vending machines.

Abby decided not to get out of the car. She didn't have to go to the bathroom, so she climbed through the space between the two front seats and plopped down in the passenger seat.

Danny stared at her. "What are you doing?"

"It's crowded here. I'm saving us time."

"Are you trying to hurt yourself more?"

"What? It's not like I did it while you were driving. I thought about it, but I figured you wouldn't appreciate that, either." She gave him an innocent smile.

"Put your seat belt on, and I'll go."

"No problem." She saluted and clicked her seat belt in place.

"You think you're funny?"

She grinned. "I do."

He started the engine and backed out of the parking space. "I guess that's a good sign."

"And I'm thankful to be out of that hospital and away from my mother."

"Abby, with all due respect, she's a piece of work."

"She's something all right," she shot back, and the words were venom on her tongue.

"Don't stress over her, though. She has no idea where you are, and you can rest without her harping on you."

"I feel bad that I left Sophie to deal with her."

"If anybody can handle your mother, it's Sophie. Plus, it's part of her job description." He accelerated onto the interstate.

"I picked well. She likes a confrontation." Abby watched the asphalt out the front window; the lines on the road sort of meditative.

"Then don't worry about her. She'll call if she has to. Relax."

"Good idea." The painkiller she'd taken in the city made her eyelids feel like a hundred pounds each.

"Hit the button on the side for recline and make yourself comfortable."

Abby did that and within a few minutes she was out.

* * *

Danny lowered the radio to let her sleep. He cruised down the thruway, constantly checking to make sure they weren't being followed. Getting out of the city was easier than he thought. The media thought Abby was going to be in the hospital a few more days for monitoring, so that no doubt had helped with the escape. He liked thinking of it that way. An escape, like they were running away together.

He glanced over at her, glad she was sound asleep. The bruises on her face made a cold, hard anger sit in his gut like a rock. He'd find Sean. Sooner or later, he'd find him, and make sure he knew what it was like to be hunted. Abby made a little noise in her sleep, and Danny resisted an urge to brush a strand of hair out of her face. How he longed to gather her in his arms and feel her against him, feel her lips on his. He glared out the windshield.

Worst idea ever, especially after what had happened. They had a great rapport now, and he shouldn't screw that up. Whatever that one incident had been, he was pretty sure it was stress that drove her to almost kiss him. Though now, he wished she had so he could at least have that. He adjusted his position and stretched his back a little. *Thoughts like that will get you nowhere*, he scolded himself.

"Mmm. Where are we?" Abby yawned and looked out the window.

"Hello, sleepyhead. We're almost there."

"Really? I slept a long time."

"Good. You needed it." He took the Lake George Village exit and made a left onto route 9N.

He passed the tourist shops; they were preparing for

the summer season that started in a few weeks. When Lake George was busy, the local two-lane road was impossible to drive without constantly stopping because of the influx of traffic. Soon they were passing a huge statue of Uncle Sam, standing outside a theme park. He smiled, thinking about how his parents brought him and his sister here as kids.

"Earth to Danny. Hello? How do you know this place?" Abby sat up in her seat, and Danny glanced over at her as she stared out the window at the quaint shops.

"My family spent most summers here when I was growing up. We're going to a cabin I had built a few years ago. It overlooks the lake. I love coming up here."

"It's beautiful," she said.

"I have such good memories of this area that when I thought about buying a place I knew it had to be here. I searched for land and found the perfect spot. And that right there," Danny pointed to a small, almost shabby diner, "has the best breakfast you'll ever eat. That's all they serve. I think they close at one every day, then later in the afternoon, they open up the building next door and serve the best homemade ice cream way into the night. The chocolate is really good. We went there almost every morning for breakfast and begged our parents to take us back every night for ice cream."

"Did it work?"

He grinned. "A few times."

"Breakfast and dessert. That's ingenious. My two favorite meals."

"I'll make a note of that." Danny reached the stoplight

and turned right onto Lake Front Road and drove past the passenger tourist boats. He remembered going out with his family on the local steamboat, the Minne-ha-ha, for the July Fourth fireworks show on the lake, and how the bursts of color in the sky would reflect off the water. Maybe some time Abby could see that, too. They followed the winding lane up the mountain.

"How far up are we going?" Abby leaned forward to see out the front window.

"Another mile." He loved hearing some life in her voice. She sounded almost like herself again.

"Is that Lake George?" She pointed at the water below. The reflection of the setting sun made it appear nearly orange.

"Yep."

"God, it's beautiful."

"I know. That's part of why I love it so much." He turned left and traveled down Pond Road past two elegant homes before he made another left into his driveway. While moving up the long driveway, he pushed the garage door opener on his visor.

"This is yours?" Abby looked over at him.

"Yes. Surprised?"

"Maybe a little. I guess I didn't take you for the rustic log cabin, mountain man type."

"I don't think mountain men had two stories in their cabins."

"Or big stone pillars on their porches." She laughed.

"I'm a special kind of mountain man."

"Clearly. Oh, look at that. An outside staircase up to a wrap-around porch. It looks like something a Southern Belle would come down. In a big gown."

"I can arrange that for you," he said, and she laughed.

"Maybe later." She laughed along with him. "It's magnificent."

"I come up here when I need to get myself grounded." Danny pulled into the four-car garage and shut off the engine.

"I can see why." Their gazes locked, and Danny stared at her, fighting the urge to lean in and kiss her. "Let's go," he said instead.

Abby climbed out of the vehicle and stretched. Danny opened the back door to take the few bags they brought with them in the house. Abby looked around; Danny could already see a small difference. She looked relaxed, with a carefree smile on her face. He set the bags on the floor.

"Okay, want a tour?"

"Seriously? You're asking me that?"

He grinned. "This way, then, to the house."

Abby followed Danny through the door that connected the garage to the kitchen.

chapter
seventeen

"It smells awesome in here."

"Connor must have something in the oven. Let's hope it's something he brought in and that he didn't cook."

"I heard that," Connor yelled.

"Hi, Connor, where are you?" Abby yelled back.

"Hey, darlin'." He stood and emerged from behind the kitchen island, a hand towel over his shoulder.

"Tell me I don't speak the truth," Danny said.

"Pfft, whatever, dude." Connor flipped him the bird.

"Well, it smells yummy," Abby said. "Did you make it?"

"Hell, no. I can't cook."

Abby laughed.

"So it'll be totally edible," he added.

"Get back to work," Danny said, though he was smiling. Connor shrugged.

Danny looked at Abby. "Okay, let me show you around. We'll start with second floor. The bedrooms are up there, and we can drop everything off before I show you the main level and outside."

"Sounds good. Lead the way. I love how open the first floor is laid out," she said.

"You can see everything from the stairs."

"Thanks. I drove the architect crazy for a while, but the end result is what I had in my head."

"You have good taste."

"Why, thank you."

"Who knew?"

He huffed at her. "I assure you; I am a man of many talents."

"Yeah, yeah. Which room's mine?"

He guided her down the hallway to a room adjacent to his.

She made a little happy noise. "It's beautiful. And spacious. Exactly what I need."

"Glad you like it."

"I'm gonna take a quick shower and change."

"Hell, take a long shower. You're on R and R, girl." He set her bags down in her room.

"Well, all right."

"Come down when you're ready," Danny said. She nodded and shut the bedroom door. Danny sighed and went back downstairs.

* * *

"How's she really doing?" Connor asked when Danny walked in. He was sitting on a stool at the counter, a slice of pizza on a plate in front of him.

"Okay, maybe. I'm worried." Danny lingered by the oven, not sure he was hungry.

"Dude, she took a beating."

"It's not just the physical shit. They did a rape kit because she can't remember anything. She doesn't even know if Sean got that far. And if he did…" Danny shoved that thought out of his head. He couldn't even think it, let alone speak it out loud.

"Mmm." Connor nodded.

"And the biggest concern she's mentioned is how she's worried her mother will freak out because she's canceling the tour."

"Maybe it's okay she can't remember right now," Connor said, echoing Danny's thoughts. "But the rape kit is some heavy shit. She's going to need some time to process that. As for her mom, I'd flip too. Seriously, bro. Give her time. She's all fucked up, but she'll pull through. I think she'll surprise us all."

Danny nodded, hoping Connor was right. "It would help if we could find that fucker."

"Um, dude?"

"What?" Danny looked up from what he was doing.

"What's the latest on that?"

"We've got nothing. He's in the wind."

"Fuck."

"My contact at the precinct says they got jack shit, too."

Connor picked up the slice of pizza. "I'm thinking everyone's looking in the wrong spot."

"How so?"

"Well from what you've told me about Vivien and her relationship with Abby, she really doesn't have boundaries. You can't rule out that Vivien might be helping him. She's smart, so she has to know we'd be watching her."

"King says she's clean, but he's still following her." Danny confirmed.

"What about that alleged friend Abby met at the club?"

"Kelly." *Total skank.*

"Yeah. She was there. She has to know what happened, and even if she didn't, it's all over the fucking news that Abby was attacked. Has she even called to check on Abby?"

"Don't know, but I don't think so. I'm not a fan," Danny admitted.

"That's why I've got John looking into her," Connor told Danny.

This surprised Danny a bit, but it was a smart move.

"Good thinking."

"Kind of fucked up, how she went all radio silence after the attack." Connor took a pull from his Coke.

"I agree." Danny chewed on his lip, thinking. His money was on Kelly as responsible for some of this. He just wasn't sure quite how.

They both looked up when they heard Abby approaching.

* * *

Abby pressed end on the phone and wiped away the few tears clinging to her lashes. God, she was an emotional basket case lately, but it felt good to talk to Ms. Sohm. She always knew how to get Abby back on track and focused on the positive.

She smelled the food from the hallway, and her stomach growled, letting her know she needed to get to the kitchen before it protested louder.

"Hey," she said from the doorway. "You gotta love a hot shower. I feel so much better."

"Good," he said; his voice wobbled a bit. "Food's ready."

"Here take this." Abby handed Danny her phone. "I just talked Ms. Sohm."

"How was that conversation?"

Abby sighed. "She's worried and wants to come up here to check me out for herself, but I think I convinced her to stay home."

"Abby… I'm glad you called her, but are you sure you don't want her to visit? I could have someone drive her up."

Of course she wanted to see her, but she just couldn't; not like this and not when there was real danger surrounding her. She'd always been there for Abby. She had helped Abby deal with so much when she was growing up and trying to manage fame and being a kid. Whenever she needed a mother, she turned to Ms. Sohm. She provided comfort that Vivien never did.

But her life was a chaotic mess right now, and Sean made sure she was a liability to everyone around her. Abby loved her too much to put her in harm's way. There was no easy way to explain how she felt about it, and if she tried, she'd just end up crying all over again. Her emotions were just too raw.

"That's sweet, thank you, but I don't want her to see me like this." She gave Danny the simplest version of the truth and hoped he'd drop it from there.

"Oh Abby…" He reached for her hand but pulled back at the last second without touching her. He swallowed hard and glanced at Connor out of the corner of his eye. He gave her that look, the one that said he cared, that his feelings for her went well beyond their professional relationship. She loved when he looked at her like that. Part of her shifted in a small, indefinable way, and her heart yearned for him. That look said she belonged with him, and it was all she could do to hold herself still.

As much as she loved it, lived for that perfect, possessive, aching need so plainly written on his face, she also hated it. Because as soon as it appeared, it disappeared just as quickly. Instead of fire and passion, he stared at her with a carefully blank face, his professional façade taking over where his personal feelings used to be. And, inevitably, he would do or say something to remind Abby that he was just doing his job.

As predicted, by the time Danny spoke again, whatever internal battle he was having no longer showed on the surface. "If you're sure. Let me know if you change your mind."

"I will. But right now I just…I don't want to think or talk or do any of the other things that I'd have to do. That's why I'm giving you my phone. If Sophie needs me, she can reach me through you. I don't have the energy for anyone else right now."

"All right, let's eat."

* * *

Danny jerked awake, listening. Something wasn't right.

From across the hall, he heard Abby whimper and then, "No. Help!"

He jumped out of bed, ready to fuck somebody up. But Abby was alone and thrashing wildly in her sleep.

"What's going on?" Connor said from the doorway, and Danny caught the glint of a pistol in his hand.

"Nightmare. Go back to sleep."

"You sure?" Connor asked.

"Yeah."

"Okay." He withdrew, and Danny moved to Abby's bed.

"Hey," he said softly as he placed his hand gently on her shoulder. "Abby."

She snapped awake. "Danny?" she said breathlessly, blinking up at him.

"It's me. You were having a nightmare." He sat down on the bed next to her.

She covered her eyes; her breath was coming hard and fast as if she'd been running.

"On second thought, I'm going to do a quick sweep of the house," Connor announced from the doorway. He didn't wait for an answer.

Abby grabbed Danny's hand, and he gently caressed her arm with feather light strokes.

"What happened?" he asked.

She didn't respond.

"You shaved at least ten years off my life tonight, and Connor's ready to take down an army. Did you hear something?"

"No. A nightmare, I guess," Abby mumbled, and she repositioned herself so she could snuggle into Danny's lap, which felt really good but was a really bad idea. He wasn't very good at controlling how his body responded to Abby, and he had to restrain himself from wrapping her into a fierce embrace.

"Wanna talk about it?" he asked while his fingers started another slow path up and down her arm.

"I don't really remember anything."

A comfortable silence grew between them, and after a few moments, Abby's breath evened out. He glanced down and saw that she had fallen asleep.

He tried to untangle himself so he could go back to his room, but as soon as he moved, she tightened her hold.

"Abby?"

"Don't go."

"I can't stay in here."

"Why not?"

Because it would be a bad idea, me being this close to you. He didn't voice that thought. "Tell me what your dream was about," he said instead.

"It's fuzzy, but Sean was there and it freaked me out."

"He's not here. He can't hurt you here."

"Please, Danny. Stay."

He relented. "I'll be over on the chair."

"Why? It's a big bed."

There was no good reason for him to stay, but he was helpless to deny the raw fear in her voice. "Fine," he said, relenting.

Abby moved over and rolled the covers back for him. In the dim light, he could tell what she was wearing. Or rather, not wearing. She had on T-shirt and a pair of very skimpy night shorts. *This is such a bad idea*, he thought as he settled in beside Abby for the rest of the night. He lay awake for a long time, listening to her breathe, not daring to move too close. Finally, he managed to doze.

* * *

Danny blinked and was assaulted by the sun. He thought he closed the curtains before he went to bed. He turned away from the bright light and opened his eyes to take in his surroundings.

Shit.

He was tangled up in the blankets with Abby. He silently berated himself for staying in her room.

"Hey," she said in a sleepy voice that he found irresistibly sexy.

"Morning," he managed.

"Sorry I freaked out last night," Abby said.

"Don't worry about it. What was in the dream that upset you?"

"I wish I knew." Abby attempted to shrug.

"You don't remember anything?" Danny asked.

"No," she said too quickly.

"You were yelling. Scared the hell out of me and Connor."

"I'm sorry. I'm gonna get dressed." Abby pushed the covers back and nearly ran into the bathroom.

He sat up and a few seconds later heard the water from the sink. It was best to leave now before she came back out with nearly nothing on. His control was only so strong, and this was not the day to test it. Maybe later, she'd be willing to talk to him about the dream.

chapter eighteen

Danny hoped that a few days at the lake would help Abby, but he was beginning to think maybe that bringing her up here had been a bad idea. She wasn't working, so that left her with lots of time to think. Or rather, brood. Hopefully when Sophie got here, it would help pull Abby out of her mood.

He walked out onto his wraparound porch. He knew she'd be out here. It was her favorite place the last few days. She sat in an oversized wicker chair, sipping coffee and looking out at the lake. She'd done that a lot lately, too. And it worried him that she only seemed to sit and stare.

"I knew I'd find you here," Danny said as he sat down next to Abby and placed his coffee mug on the small table between the two chairs.

"It's so peaceful. I can sit here for hours and get lost in it all." Abby motioned to the vast scenery in front of her.

"I know. So how are you feeling?"

"I'm good. How can I not be when I'm looking at this?" She looked over at him and then back to the forest that had finally started to come alive with the change in the weather.

"You want to go exploring? Might do you some good to get out and about."

"I'm fine," she snapped.

He sighed. "But you really aren't, and I'm concerned. I don't want to push you, but I want you to know *if* you want to talk about it, I'll listen. I'm here for you."

"I'm fine," she repeated as she eased out of the wicker chair. "Really," she reassured him in an overly bright voice.

Danny watched her walk inside and wished he knew how to get her to let her guard down and confide in him.

* * *

Abby escaped through the porch doors and into the living room. She continued up the stairs to her room. Why did he have to push her? She wanted to forget the whole thing, but he wouldn't leave it alone.

She kept telling him she didn't remember, but she knew he didn't believe her. Danny was not someone she could lie to. What did he want her to say? They knew who attacked her. Admitting the rest wouldn't change anything. Besides, a lot of it was still fuzzy. She at least knew she hadn't been raped.

There was a knock on her door, and she turned.

"Can I come in?"

"It's your house." She immediately felt bad after saying it.

"Don't be like that. You can say no. I told you already to make yourself at home, and I meant it."

"All right then, no. I really want to be left alone right now." She stared at him.

He backed down. "Fine. I'll give you time. I'm sorry I pushed."

Abby waited until he closed the door before she curled up on the bed and cried.

* * *

Danny could hear Abby's faint sobs through the door. He wanted to comfort her, and he wanted to go hunt Sean down so he could beat the fuck out of him. It broke his heart to see her like this, but she clearly wasn't in a welcoming mood. He walked away from her door and back downstairs into the living room.

Connor would be here tonight with Sophie. Hopefully, she could break through and get Abby to open up. Regardless, he had work to do. He dialed his office.

"Good morning. Nucci Securities, how may I direct your call?" his receptionist answered.

"Hi, Paula. It's Danny. How are you?"

"Well, hi, there. What can I do for you?"

"Is King around?" Danny asked.

"Yes. Transferring you now."

"Thanks." Danny waited while Paula placed him on hold.

King clicked on the line.

"Hey, Nucci."

"What do you have for me?" Danny was eager to find out if there was anything new. Lack of information was the downside of being so far away.

"I'm sorry, man. He's a fucking ghost."

"Nothing? Still? How is that even possible? In this goddamn day and age, how is it possible to be nowhere?"

"I don't know. I mean we're so far in his shit that he can't do anything without us knowing. He has someone helping him, or he took the fuck off. We're watching his credit cards and debit card. He's hiding or operating on cash only because for the past five days not one damn thing has come up in his name. You know we're working 'round the clock shifts on this," King explained.

"Mother fucker." Danny raked his free hand through his hair. "Shit. We're gonna have to force him out."

"I'm hoping to avoid that." King didn't sound pleased with that option.

"If this shit keeps up, we have no choice." Danny wasn't thrilled with that idea, and he'd try everything before involving Abby.

"All right. I'll keep you posted. Let me know when or if you want to try something else."

"Yeah. Thanks." Danny hung up. The only thing that

would get Sean out of hiding was Abby. But there was no way she was prepared to act as bait. And how could he even ask her? She was clearly depressed, and he wasn't equipped to deal with it.

His phone beeped. He checked it and found a new web alert. He clicked the link. Christ, Vivien again. She was all over the damn media, trying to drum up sympathy for herself.

It made him want to puke. The press was camped out in front of Abby's apartment building, looking for any sign of her. No matter how many holes Sophie tried to plug, Vivien would make another one with more asinine statements, keeping the story alive. It was as if she was trying to force Abby's hand. Danny grimaced. Of course she was. That's how she operated. Good thing Abby had told Danny to put her phone in protective custody. She didn't know how much Vivien texted, called, and emailed. Danny didn't have Abby's password, but her notifications were turned on. Easy enough to see it on the front screen. Fortunately, nothing from any unknown numbers or emails.

He placed his phone down on the coffee table in the living room and turned on the television and searched for a game to watch. Connor and Sophie would be here later, and until then, he'd give Abby her space.

* * *

"No!" Abby woke with a start. Shit. She'd fallen asleep. She pushed herself into a sitting position and wiped her trembling hand across her forehead.

"Abby?" Connor called from outside her room. "You okay?" He opened her door slightly.

"I'm okay. What time is it?" She blinked the sleep from her eyes and noticed the sun had set.

"It's past eight." Connor opened the door some more.

"Shit. You can come in. How long have you been here?" Abby sat up.

Connor opened the door wide, "About an hour."

"Sophie's here?"

"Downstairs. You all right?" Connor sounded concerned.

"Yeah. I can't believe I fell asleep, or that I slept that long. I'll come down in a minute. I have to let my brain realize I'm awake," she joked.

"Okay. We saved you some take out."

"Thanks."

Connor left but didn't close the door.

Abby gave herself a pep talk as she tried to calm down. *Only a dream, Abby. Only a dream. Not real.*

Since her memories had come back, Abby hated sleeping. Every night she woke from a nightmare. She didn't like feeling so frightened by her own dreams that she had to lean on Danny to protect her. He did that enough already in her waking hours.

She padded to the bathroom to clean up before going downstairs. She splashed cool water on her face to help her wake up. Her head was killing her, and she was hungry, but she needed to look halfway decent so that she wouldn't face the Sophie inquisition. She headed downstairs for food.

"Hey, you're up." Danny greeted Abby with a warm smile.

"Hi," she croaked. "Great. I sound like I've smoked a pack of cigarettes." They were all sitting in the living room, watching a baseball game. Sophie looked pretty comfortable sitting next to Connor. His gaze was plastered to the television, but his body was angled toward her. Danny's gaze was on Abby.

"Hey, girl," Sophie said. "Eat. Get something to drink. You'll wake up and feel more like yourself."

"I can't believe I slept that long. I wasn't even tired. Or so I thought."

"Your body is still healing," Sophie said as if she was some kind of doctor.

"I guess." Abby went to the kitchen, and Sophie followed. "How was your trip?" Abby asked her.

"Interesting," Sophie said with a smile.

"Yeah, I can imagine being stuck in a car with Mr. Jokester. For nearly six hours."

"He's pretty funny. He's also really smart."

Something in her tone made Abby scrutinize her. "Oh, my, is someone crushing out on Connor O'Brian?" Abby said in a stage whisper.

Sophie blushed. "Whatever."

"Oh, my God. You *are* crushing."

"Shut up."

"You are totally in a crush. Oh, this is going to be fun." She searched for a plate and placed Lo Mein and boneless spareribs on it.

"No one's crushing on anyone so be quiet."

"Whatever." She placed the plate in the microwave for a minute.

"Don't. He's here to do a job."

"So, he could be here to do *you* too."

Sophie flushed again. "Clearly, all this free time has affected your brain, because you've lost your mind."

"Sophie and Connor sittin' in a tree…" she started.

The microwave beeped.

"Eat your dinner and keep your damn mouth shut. Geez."

Sophie went back into the living room, and Abby laughed and damn it if it didn't feel good. She poured herself a glass of wine, grabbed her plate, and joined everyone.

chapter
nineteen

Two really good days had passed since Sophie arrived. Sophie had brought Abby her keyboard, so she could play a little music, and the two spent time chatting and reconnecting as friends. It had been so long since Abby could relax and be herself, she'd forgotten how much fun it was to hang out with Sophie.

Connor had her in stitches from his Army stories and overall goofball antics. He even got Danny to loosen up a bit. But no matter how much they joked, there was always an undertone of seriousness. Danny was always watching, and though he pretended not to be concerned, Abby could tell he was. He never sat and relaxed.

"We ship out in ten," Connor called through the hall.

"I'm done," Sophie answered.

Abby was still fretting over her make-up. No matter what she did, she could still see the bruises, though faint, where Sean hit her.

"Hey sweets, you ready?" Sophie called.

"I'm not going." Abby threw her make-up brush across the bathroom.

"Huh? What's wrong?"

"What's wrong? I can't go out like this." She pointed to her face. "I can't seem to cover it, and the more I add, the worse it looks. I have like five pounds of foundation and powder caked on my face. I look ridiculous." She covered her face with her hands and began to silently cry.

"Hey, come on." Sophie took one of Abby's hands and guided her to the toilet. "Close the seat and sit down. Take a deep breath and let me see what I can do."

Abby followed her friend's instructions while wiping gingerly at her tears.

"You can't get so upset."

"Easy for you to say. You didn't cause all this shit."

"Oh my God, Abby, would you stop. You didn't cause this. Sean is crazy. He caused this, and so did your mother. They're both delusional and thought that you were their puppet to play with." She tilted Abby's head up. "I'll be honest, here. When you finally stood up and said no, you shocked the shit out of me. I could only imagine what they thought and when the issue was pressed you stuck to your decision." Sophie wiped away all the make-up from Abby's face. "Only someone not right in the head does something like this to someone. I repeat; this is not your fault. So you'd better stop thinking that now. Geez girl." She tilted Abby's head upward. "Keep your eyes closed."

Abby relaxed and let Sophie help.

"Have you been sitting here the past few days thinking that we all blame you for this?"

"Well…" Abby opened her eyes.

"I can tell you are. Ridiculous. No one blames you, so get it through your thick skull. I don't want to see you moping in the corner thinking we all hate you or blame you or whatever. Everyone in this house supports you and wants nothing but the best for you. And speaking of, you should take this time to figure out what that is. What do *you* want?"

"Hell if I know. This is the first time in a long time I'm not under the iron fist of the one and only Vivien Murphy."

"Now is your time to figure that out." She stopped messing with Abby's face. "Okay, go look."

Abby stood and walked to the sink. Sophie had done an amazing job. The bruises weren't completely covered, but you'd have to be pretty close to notice. She doubted Danny would let anyone get that close.

"You can hardly tell."

"I'm glad you're happy with it. Okay, let's get moving before the men start complaining."

Abby grabbed a tube of lipstick and followed Sophie out of the room.

* * *

"It's beautiful out here." Abby said as she admired the lush greenery and peaceful blue skies.

"I love this time of year because the tourists aren't flooding the water yet." Danny turned and smiled at Abby.

"Well, this view is amazing."

"Go relax. I'm going to ride us out a little further, and then we'll stop and break out a beer. Do you want me to bring you one?"

"No, I'm good. Thanks." Abby spent the next hour soaking in the sun and admiring the views from the top of Danny's two-story yacht. The first level had a small kitchenette and living space, while the second had a few spots where she could relax.

"You awake?" Sophie poked Abby in the arm.

"Yep."

"Feeling any better?"

"A bit. I've been thinking," Abby hesitated. The thoughts about her future were a little too new for her to be confident about sharing them. Sure, it was only Sophie, but Abby felt vulnerable nonetheless.

"About what?"

"Just…well…" Abby sat up and turned toward her. "I've been thinking about what my next step should be. I don't think I can go back to the city and act like my mother didn't stab me in the back or that she didn't try to keep someone on the tour that was violent toward me. She really took things to the extreme." Abby sighed. "We've never been close. You'd think that with the way my dad had treated us, she would've had some motherly instinct to protect me, but no. All I've ever been was her way out of our slummy neighborhood and into the limelight."

"Hey," Sophie said gently as if she was trying to

comfort her.

"It's okay. I'm over that. Trust me; he was no prize, so I'm not crying over it. But it sucks that I got fucked when it came to parents."

"You know I understand that."

Abby squeezed her arm in support. "I know, and I'm not trying to say I had it worse than you, but it's all getting to me. Too much to take at once, and I feel overwhelmed."

"What does your gut say to do about your mom?"

"To cut ties." Abby played with the end of her sweater.

"You don't say that like you mean it." Sophie wrinkled her nose.

"It isn't easy. We're tied financially. She has a contract, and she isn't going to let me go gracefully. She'll fight."

"Well, you have to decide what's more important. Your freedom. Or your money," Sophie said it as if it should be the easiest thing in the world for Abby.

"It's not that simple, but I get what you're saying."

"No one expects you to decide anything right now. That's one of the reasons you're up here."

"Oh, well, yeah," Abby said, sarcastic. "The other is because I have a violent asshole for an ex-boyfriend trying to find me and finish what he started." She got up and walked to the edge of the boat.

"Why don't you worry about the things that are in your control, instead of stressing over what isn't? You can't do anything about Sean so figure out what you want for yourself."

"I guess." But it wasn't that easy. Sean was out there somewhere, and it unnerved her.

"Let the guys worry about him. What I want to know is who the hell is helping him? You didn't drug yourself, and that wasn't some random act. It makes me worried that there is some mysterious someone out there screwing you over."

Abby turned, ready to tell Sophic what she remembered, but Connor called from the stairs, "Lunch is ready."

"Oh, good, I'm starved." Sophie got up from her chair. "Coming?" she asked Abby.

"Sure. I could eat." Abby put on a brave face and followed them to the first level of the boat.

* * *

"Enjoying yourself?" Danny asked.

He sat down next to her on the front deck. Abby had her feet up on the rail as the sun warmed her skin. "Yes. It's so relaxing. I can't remember the last time I felt this calm and stress free."

"Good." He smiled and stared out over the water. Abby recognized his recon look, and she tensed little.

"It really is beautiful out here," she said, trying to get back into her previous relaxed state.

262

"I couldn't agree more." He sounded a little distant, but he turned his gaze to her.

Abby chewed her lip for a few moments, uncomfortable under his scrutiny though she knew he was only concerned about her. "Um, can I tell you something?" She fumbled a bit with the question.

His shoulders relaxed a little. "You can tell me anything. You know that."

She took a deep breath and fiddled with her fingers in her lap. "I remember what happened that night." She watched Danny for a reaction. All she saw was attentive concern.

"Some things are still fuzzy…" she continued. "But I know I wasn't raped."

Danny exhaled softly, as if he'd been holding his breath.

"He tried but didn't get that far. I'm guessing your guys or somebody interrupted him."

"Do you remember anything else?" His voice was steady.

"I needed to use the bathroom and told Kelly I'd be back, but she came with me instead. It was in the bathroom that I really started to feel sick. I asked Kelly to go get the guys, and I waited, but no one came so I went to find them. When I left the bathroom, no one was there." She rubbed her head, thinking. "It gets a bit fuzzy there, but I vaguely remember falling against someone. When I looked up, it was Sean."

"Was he with anyone?" His voice remained steady.

"No. It was him, but..." she hesitated. "I tried to scream and get someone to notice us." Tears sprang to her eyes, and she turned away. "I tried. I really did," she whispered.

"I'm sure you did. You're okay now. Get it all out so that you can let it go."

She took a shaky breath. "Kelly spotted us, and she didn't help." She stared at her hands. "Why didn't she help? She smiled and let him take me. She saw the state I was in, and she did nothing." Abby wiped at the tears on her cheeks. "Sophie never liked her, and she warned me several times to cut ties with her, and I ignored her. And you..." she lifted her head so she could look at him. "You didn't want me to go that night, and I was too busy being immature to listen."

He was silent for a few moments. "You're absolutely sure you saw Kelly and she did nothing to help you?"

"Yeah. She even waved, I think."

Danny didn't respond, but the cold, hard expression on his face scared her a little.

"I'm sorry I didn't tell you sooner. I couldn't." She still couldn't promise that her memory wasn't off track. But it felt real. The choking fear from that moment rose like bile in her throat if she thought about it for very long.

He smiled at her, and the warmth in his eyes sank right into her heart. "It's okay," he said. "It was a lot to handle. Thank you for telling me. I'm so glad you did, because I had a feeling Kelly was involved somehow."

Abby wiped at her face again with her sleeve. "I can't

wrap my head around why she'd help him. I know they were friends, but I thought we were pretty close."

"Jealousy is an ugly monster," Danny said.

"Jealousy? Of what? Her father is Billy West of West and Howard Modeling Agency. They're the top firm worldwide. She has never had to work a day in her life to get what she has. As long as she keeps West and Howard in the press, her dad's happy."

Danny shrugged. "You might think you don't have anything for her to feel jealous about, but she might see it differently. You're very talented, and to most of the world, you have it all."

"But my mother—"

"I know your mother tries to control everything you do, but there aren't many that know that. Did you tell Kelly about your relationship with your mom?"

"No. I can't see why anyone would want all this crazy that is my life."

"They don't see anything other than the fame and the money," Danny explained.

She sank back in her chair. "I guess I know that. Doesn't make it any less frustrating. What am I going to do about Kelly?"

"Nothing. Connor and I talked about her already, and we've been watching her. I have an idea, but that's not for now. I want you to enjoy the day. Tomorrow we'll talk about what our next step will be."

"Okay." She picked at her nails. She'd wanted to tell

him, and she knew she couldn't hide anything from Danny. Somehow he always knew when she was keeping something. He also deserved to know, but that didn't mean she wanted to get into it all now.

"You still look like you have something on your mind. I'll listen if you want to talk."

"I've been thinking about my mother a lot lately, too, and how our relationship…I don't know."

She hesitated, and Danny waited. She loved that he could sense when she needed a moment. "I started out so young that I think I've come to accept how she is. There wasn't much I could do when I was a teen. She pushed and pushed. There was always an audition to go to or a person to meet. I never had a normal childhood. Once I got my break she became worse. She controlled everything I did, said, and wore. It was how it was, and I never questioned it."

"You said it yourself; you were young. No child would question a parent about those things. You were a kid, and it was her job to do right by you."

"Most teenagers rebel. I went with it. Now I'm nearly twenty-four, and I'm stuck with a mother that controls my every move, and I don't know how to fix it."

"You're not stuck. You're an adult, and if you don't like how things are being done, you can make a change."

"I wouldn't even know where to start."

"You know that's not a reason to not try. That's an excuse. Talk to Sophie about it. You know she's like super woman, and she'll help. Or if she can't, she'll know exactly who can."

"True, and we did talk a bit before. I'm at the point where I'd rather give it all up than have to live another day with my mom as my manager."

"I'm glad you started the conversation, but I think you really need to put your heads together and come up with a plan.

"Yeah, I guess."

"Promise me," Danny pushed.

Abby nodded, a solemn expression on her face. "I promise."

"Good. You don't have to do anything you don't want to do."

"I know. I mean it though I'd rather give it all up than spend the rest of my life unhappy. It's not worth it. Thanks for listening. It feels good to get this all off my chest."

"Anytime. Do you want anything out here? A beer? Soda?"

"No." She smiled at him, and he squeezed her shoulder. For the first time in a while, she felt a lightening between them, and maybe a little bit of a spark.

"Okay. You know where to find me." He stood, and she watched him from behind her sunglasses and appreciated how he moved. Maybe if there wasn't all this crazy in her life, there would be a chance—no. She wouldn't want the mess of her life to taint Danny's any more than it already had. But it did feel good to talk to him. She smiled and turned back to the view, feeling better than she had in a while.

chapter
twenty

"Hey, sunshine. We're going to be late," Danny said as he knocked on Abby's bedroom door. They had a dinner reservation at eight for one of his favorite local restaurants.

"Five more minutes," Abby called.

Danny heard her laughing with Sophie and having a good time. God only knew what women did when they were huddled together in a bathroom.

They were going to be late, but there was no way he was going to rush her when she sounded so happy. It had been so long since he heard her laugh freely. Since Abby opened up to him and confessed that she remembered everything that happened to her that night, she seemed lighter in some way. He knew he felt a huge sense of relief, so she must've felt similar. Since then Abby hasn't stopped talking to both him and Sophie. He leaned against the wall, thinking, then went back downstairs to the living room.

"Hey, are they almost ready?" Connor walked in from the garage.

"Who knows? I didn't get in the middle of what they got going on up there." He sat back on the couch and flipped through the channels on the TV.

"Yeah, Sophie might kick my ass…though that might be worth it." Connor laughed.

"Oh, so that's how it is between you two."

Connor smirked. "What? She's feisty. I like that."

"She'll eat you up then spit you out," Danny taunted.

"Like I said. I like that."

Danny laughed. "To each his own."

Connor watched the TV for a bit, then without turning to Danny, he said, "Are you going to talk to Abby about Kelly tonight?"

"That's the plan."

"It's the only thing to do," Connor sounded far too calm about a situation that was anything but.

"Doesn't mean I'm happy about it," Danny grumbled.

"It'll be fine. We can control things, and she'll never be touched."

"Really? The fucker has gotten to her twice." Danny worked hard to keep his voice level. The thought of putting Abby in a position of danger *on purpose* terrified him.

"If we all stick to the plan, he won't get through again."

"I'm still not thrilled." Danny clenched his teeth.

"Ultimately, it's your call, but you know the longer we wait for him to make his move, the worse it could get." Connor was being rational, logical, and Danny appreciated it. He needed that to offset his emotional overload.

Danny nodded, but he didn't like it.

"Okay, while you're down here messing with the TV, I'm thinking I need a good ol' fashion ass kicking. I'll go interrupt the secret rituals of the women."

"It's your funeral." Danny watched Connor fly up the stairs with a big smile on his face.

* * *

The trip to the restaurant, a local sports bar in the town, was only twenty minutes, and the group chatted about nothing special. Danny felt pretty comfortable here. He had owned his house in the area for years and knew most of the locals.

Danny parked a few blocks from the restaurant. This time of year, tourists took up most of the parking throughout Lake George. "We'll eat and then we can check out the sights," he said as they climbed out of the vehicle.

They walked in relative quiet. Danny and Connor flanked Abby and Sophie, keeping them close.

"Here we are." He pointed at the structure. Outside, several people were smoking and talking.

"Are you sure it's okay to go in there?" Abby asked, clearly worried.

He figured she'd panic a bit when she saw the crowd, so he had called ahead and spoken to the manager. "It'll be fine. I have it all covered. Come on." He took her hand and led her inside.

"Somebody might recognize me."

"It'll be fine. Keep your head down and come on." Danny gently pulled her toward the door while Sophie stood on her other side.

"Here." Sophie swiped Connor's baseball cap and handed it to Abby. "Keep your sunglasses on until we're settled."

Abby took the cap and pulled it low over her eyes and let Danny lead her to the door through the crowd.

"Welcome to Mystic Sports Bar and Grill," said the cheery hostess.

"Hi," Danny said. "I called ahead and spoke with your manager. He said he'd hold a table for us under the name Nucci."

Danny stood in front of Abby, helping hide her.

"Yes, here it is. Follow me."

Danny glanced back at Abby. She was fidgeting. He knew this had to be hard for her. They followed the hostess through the bar crowd and up a set of stairs. She walked them toward the outside deck. The room was separated from the main dining room yet Danny could still see everyone coming and going. Perfect.

"Here you go." The hostess motioned to the dining area. "Pick any table you'd like. We reserved the deck for you tonight."

"Thank you. Please send your manager my thanks as well." And Danny would be sure to include a lot more money for this opportunity. The manager lost a lot of business with these other tables not in use.

"Erin will be your waitress, and she'll be over in a few to take your drink orders." When they were all seated, she handed them menus. "The specials are listed on the first page. Enjoy your meal."

"This view is amazing." Sophie said with awe.

Danny turned his attention to where she was looking, and she was right; it was amazing. From the deck, you could see a panoramic view of Lake George. Tonight the lake looked nearly orange from the sun's rays reflecting off it.

"It is. It's one of the reasons I love this place so much." He opened the menu and glanced down at it.

"What's good here?" Abby asked.

"I haven't had anything bad yet."

"Hey y'all I'm Erin," said a perky young woman. Her dark hair was pulled back into a ponytail. "I'll be your waitress. Can I start you off with something to drink or an appetizer?"

The group placed their drink orders, and when Erin left, they all studied the menu.

"There are way too many choices. What do you recommend?" Abby asked after a few minutes.

Without looking up from the menu, Danny said, "The baby-back ribs are really good and so are burgers. But no matter what, you need to get the beer-battered fries. I think they're my favorite." Danny stopped and cleared his throat. Weird. This felt like a double date, and the realization made him both nervous and kind of excited as if he were in high school again. He glanced over at Abby, who was studying in the menu. She'd taken the ball cap off, and she looked pretty cute. Her forehead creased as she studied the restaurant's offerings. *All right, quit it*, he told himself. This is not a damn date. Head in the game.

"Mmm, I think I'll have the ribs and fries, then." Abby closed the menu and set it on the table in front of her.

"You won't be disappointed." He saw Erin approaching with a tray of beverages. "Do you guys know what you want?"

"Yep. I'm set." Sophie closed her menu as well.

"I'm good." Connor did the same.

"Here you go." Erin handed out everyone's drinks. "Do you need a few more minutes?"

"We're actually ready to order."

"Great, what would you like?"

They all ordered their meals, and Erin bounced away from the table back to the stairs.

"It's very nice here," Abby said. "Sorry I got a little freaky. Thanks for bringing us," she said to Danny and took a sip from her drink.

Danny picked up his glass. "It's good to get out, see what's going on." He relaxed a little, glad that she'd decided to brave the public. He glanced at Connor, who gave him a barely perceptible nod, recognition that he, too, was keeping an eye on things. Danny scanned the room again then settled into the banter and conversation, though he couldn't shake the feeling that this was some kind of strange double date. It felt good, but he knew having those thoughts would lead nowhere.

* * *

"Tonight was a lot of fun. Thanks for making it easy on me." Abby looked out at the darkened woods; she couldn't see much, but she didn't care. It was quiet and peaceful. She sat back in the Adirondack chair with a light blanket draped over her legs and sipped her tea.

"You're a lot stronger than you think." Danny sat beside her.

"Taking this time away from the spotlight has really helped me. I know what I want, and I'm not going to let fear stop me. I'm beyond worrying about everyone else. In a way, I'm almost grateful this happened because it made me open my eyes. Now that I'm seeing clearly, I know exactly who I can and can't trust."

"Good. Although I am not at all happy that you were attacked."

"That wasn't your fault," Abby said softly.

"Easy for you to say. I'm responsible in a lot of ways. Not for Sean being psychotic, but he was able to get too close too many times. That was my team that screwed up. And that reflects on me."

"How could they know? How could you know? I mean, I thought Kelly was my friend. I would've never guessed she'd do that to me."

"It's my job to know. I'm supposed to be able to predict things like that."

"You can't predict crazy."

He smiled, but it seemed forced. "I don't see it that way."

Abby shrugged and sipped her tea and enjoyed the sounds of the woods. "I mean…shit." She sat up in her chair.

"What?"

"Crap." How did she not make the connection sooner? She rubbed her temple with her fingers.

"Tell me."

"I'm so dumb. Stephanie."

"What about her?"

"During one of my many run-ins with her, she mentioned having a picture or something of Sean with a redhead in a compromising position. I wonder if that was Kelly? That chick changes hair color every other day. I'm so dumb."

"Your not dumb. First, you don't even know if that was her. Did Stephanie offer to show you those pictures?"

"No, but still. There was tons of evidence, and I knew he cheated. I just accepted it."

"You can't play the 'what if' game. It does no good now."

"I guess, but still I wish I had opened my eyes a lot sooner." Maybe if she had questioned things more, all this mess might have been avoided. And maybe, nothing would've changed because she always just did as she was told. Accepted everything even when she knew it wasn't best for her.

"We all have events in our lives we wish we could do over." Danny sighed, heavily. "Abby...I..."

"Spit it out already. I know you want to talk to me about something."

Danny chuckled, but didn't respond. "I guess you've been paying closer attention than I thought."

Abby laughed. "Thanks for the compliment, I guess. I've enjoyed this time to do some thinking, but I'm not totally in my own bubble." Nope, the other times she was swooning over someone that she couldn't have.

"I'll have to remember that."

"Yes. Do. Now talk." She tightened her grip on her mug. She liked the warmth against her palms.

"Well, it actually has to do with Kelly."

Abby frowned. "Okay."

"I'd like you to consider calling her."

"Why?" Abby turned toward him. He was sitting close enough that she could see him in the darkness. The thought of talking to Kelly, knowing she saw Abby that night and did nothing, sent a chill through her. No way.

"We need to put an end to this. If we don't, we're dancing to their tune. We can't sit around anymore and wait for Sean to show his face. Kelly drugged you. She must be helping him."

Abby forced herself to loosen her grip on her mug. She was afraid she'd break it out of anger.

"At the moment, she's our only direct connection to him. Calling her just makes sense."

"So what do I do?" She tried to sound brave, but really, was he nuts? Her direct connection to Sean was a reason *not* to call her, yet Danny was asking her to do the opposite. If her bodyguards didn't show when they did, that night would've ended in a totally different way. This might make sense to Danny, but to Abby it sounded as close to insane as it could get.

"You're not going to call to say 'what's up' or something like that. I want you to pretend you don't remember anything about her involvement."

"Then what? Ask her over for coffee?" She tried not to sound snappish, but she was pretty sure it didn't work.

"Not exactly, but close."

She took a deep breath. Danny wasn't crazy. He was highly trained. The least she could do was hear him out. "Okay, I'm listening."

"I want you to call her and mention that you're up here with me. Say that you've been spending time here healing, and that you want to come back to the city but can't until we find Sean."

"Wait a second." Abby stared hard at him, and she thought she saw him move back a little. "Seriously? You want me to tell her where I am?" That confirmed it. He was out of his fucking mind.

"Yes."

"Why?" And then it hit her. "Oh my God." If she did what Danny asked, then Sean would know exactly where she was. Danny *wanted* Sean to know. A wave of nausea rolled through her, and she choked down the urge to vomit. It would serve him right though. He deserved to be puked on for even suggesting something like this.

"Abby, hear me out—"

"You want Sean to know where I am." A chill raced up her spine. "You're setting a trap. And I'm the bait."

He cleared his throat, something he did when he was nervous. "When you put it like that—"

"There's no other way to put it, Danny." She gripped her mug tightly again. She stared across the lake and focused on her breathing. The calm darkness of the water transformed. Her feeling of safety, security fell away. All she could see was danger in the unknown. Every light that used to be someone enjoying the lake at night was suddenly a threat. Her perfect cocoon ruptured, and she was left exposed and vulnerable. Fuck him for taking that away from her. Fuck Sean for putting her in this position in the first place, and fuck Danny for making her feel safe only to tear it away from her with just a few words.

"Okay, listen, please. Yes. I want him to come up here so we can trap him. He's a ghost right now. And so is Kelly. No one can find him, so he's laying low and has at least one person helping him. We have men on your mother twenty-four seven so I doubt it's her. With what you've remembered and Kelly being MIA, it has to be her."

"So I tell Kelly where I am and then what? We wait?" Abby felt numb. She forced all her emotions, the churning unease, into a dark corner of her consciousness. She couldn't afford to let her fear rule her for one more day. She was tired of leaving her well-being up to so many other people, and it was time for her to reclaim some of the responsibility for her own life.

"Yes."

"What if he doesn't show?" But she knew that wasn't possible. From what she could remember of that night, Sean was a man possessed.

"He will."

She knew he was right. And somewhere deep inside, she actually wanted Sean to come for her. She thought about fear and anger and decided she'd let anger be her guide this time. She was fucking tired of running.

"Abby?" He said her name uncertainly. Maybe he thought she was a total head case. Or maybe he knew he was asking too much. His job was to protect her, not dangle her in front of her own personal psychopath ex-boyfriend.

Her thoughts were in overdrive. All the possible outcomes of doing this were running through her mind like scenes in a movie. So many things could go wrong, and she couldn't silence the twinge of doubt in her head. Could Danny really pull this off? Sean had been one step ahead of them this entire time. The only thing keeping her safe was that Sean had no idea where she was. Doing this could give them the upper hand. Did she really have faith in Danny? She wanted to. When he looked at her with that sincere, fierce promise of protection, she believed he could do anything. And if she said no, what then? Live in fear? Double and triple security? Live like a hermit because she was scared Sean might get close again? No. She was done with that, and she wanted her freedom and her life back. "All right."

"Look, it's the only…wait. All right?"

She laughed. There was absolutely nothing funny about this situation, but she'd surprised him, and it struck her funny. "Yeah. I'm tired of running."

"I…okay. Well. Um."

Did she just agree to do this?

"Okay." He cleared his throat again. "Nothing will happen to you. Connor and I have it all planned out."

"And of course you're going to tell me the whole thing, right?"

"Yes, but all you really have to do is make the call. The rest is on my team and me. You'll be here, and you'll be safe."

"Well, let's hope, anyway." She took another sip. She wanted to feel safe again.

"He won't get near you."

"He'll try," she said. "But I'm really tired of him. And I'm tired of my mother, and I'm really disgusted with Kelly."

Danny was silent for a long time, and Abby imagined the wheels turning in his head, trying to figure out where this new Abby came from. *I've always been here*, she thought. *I let shit get to me. I'm over it.*

"I'm sorry. I knew better than to let you go that night, but I didn't want to act like your keeper. After all, I'm your bodyguard."

Bodyguard. That stung. Again Danny reminded her about the boundaries of their relationship. "Let me know what you want me to tell her."

"It'll be okay." He assured.

"I believe you." She stood. "I'm off to bed. Thanks for a great night out. See you in the morning." She strode off the porch and up to her room. *Bodyguard.* That's what he thinks. Thank God she never made her feelings known. Damn Sophie anyway for making her think his feelings were more than just professional.

She closed her bedroom door.

"How stupid am I?" she said into the silence of her room. She got ready for bed turned her bedside light off and thought about what she'd say to Kelly when she called her. It would be an Oscar worthy performance, she was sure. But she wanted to do it, wanted to put an end to people thinking they could push her around. And maybe she'd be able to let go of the little dream she'd had about Danny.

chapter
twenty-one

"Here's your phone." Sophie slid it across the kitchen island to Abby.

Abby stared at it for a moment. It'd only been a few days since she surrendered it, but it already looked unfamiliar to her, like a leftover relic from another life.

Thank goodness she had Sophie. She had been answering messages and taking care of anything that couldn't wait for Abby. Sophie had also started to research new management for her. Weeding through all the companies was proving to be a harder task than she ever thought it would be. Sophie had really stepped up though, and it had Abby rethinking future plans.

"Thanks." Abby stared at it, and after a bit, she picked it up. It felt foreign in her hand. She knew she had to make the call, but knowing and doing were two separate things. She had sat down with Danny and Connor, and they explained their plan to her this morning. She wanted to trust Danny blindly, but couldn't. She'd been through too much and knew that anything could happen, even with bodyguards around.

"Abby?"

She looked up at Danny.

"You can do this, and everything will be okay."

"Yeah. You're sure this will work?"

"Nothing will happen to you."

She stared at her phone.

"Look at me." Her gaze automatically found his.

"I give you my word. *Nothing* will happen to you. Sean won't get near you."

This wasn't the first time Danny had said that, but still Sean managed to get close to her. He hurt her. A lot. Too much for her to take Danny's promise at face value. Abby knew he believed what he said, and she believed him too, but that didn't mean she wasn't scared. There were too many unknown variables, but if she didn't do this, she'd never get the control she desperately wanted in her life. She nodded and looked back at the phone, steeling herself.

"Act normal. You're checking in and wanted to let her know you're okay. You don't want to make her suspicious. Mention in passing how you're at the cabin." Sophie recapped for the millionth time.

"Yep." *I'd like to thank the Academy…* She took a deep breath and pressed Kelly's number on her speed dial. She hesitated only a second before putting the phone to her ear. The sooner she got this over with, the sooner she could maybe move on. From both Sean and Danny. Last night's words still hurt. Crushes sucked.

"Hello?" Kelly answered, sounding tentative.

"Hey," Abby said, glad she sounded normal. "What's up?"

"Abby?"

"Yeah, it's me. Sorry I haven't called you"

"That's all right. I lost you that night, and I was worried."

"I'm okay now. I was pretty messed up for awhile." *Oh, yeah. This was definitely an award-winning performance.* Sophie gave her a thumbs-up.

"Girl, do you remember what happened to you? The gossip is flying. I can't believe Sean could do that."

Abby wanted to reach through the phone and smack her. *Do you know what happened to you? Yeah, I do*, Abby thought. *You fucking set me up.*

She said, "Is the gossip really that bad? I've tried to stay away from it."

"Your face and name were plastered all over the place for awhile. It's died down some, now."

"Well, that's good. I guess. No news is good news."

"How did he get to you?"

"I don't know. I know what I've been told from John and Aaron. They were helping you. There was some guy getting rough with you or something."

"Yeah, that bastard I was dancing with got really upset I was talking to Aaron, and he came up and just punched him. Shit got out of hand after that." She sounded blasé, as if that kind of thing happened all the time and she was an innocent bystander. Abby knew better, but she sure as hell wouldn't let Kelly know that.

"Things are really blurry," Abby said. "I remember that Sean took me, but that's all. The doctor said memory loss is common with head injuries. After that, all I remember is waking up in the hospital."

"Damn, girl." She actually sounded a little contrite.

"It's been crazy. If it wasn't for Danny taking me away from it all, I think I'd have had a breakdown."

"He took you away?"

"Yeah. Up to his cabin. It's so beautiful up here. It overlooks Lake George." She looked at Danny to see he was nodding his head in approval.

"Well, that's good. You probably needed a break after that."

"For sure, but I need to get back to my life. We're planning on coming back to the city sometime next week. I'm getting antsy and want to get back to the tour."

"I'll bet. Call me when you're back in the city, and we'll hang. Raven is opening this weekend. We can totally check it out."

"Sounds good. Later." Abby hung up and set the phone on the table. "Nothing. She didn't give me any hints that she's in on this. She's just as fucking crazy as he is."

"You won't hear me defend her," Sophie said.

Abby shot her a look. "I should have listened to you."

"It's hard to believe the worst about someone." Sophie squeezed her hand.

"She acted like she was innocent. Like 'oh, sorry that

happened. Let's hang out.'" It hurt, knowing that. But Abby's growing anger helped burn it away.

"You did great," Danny said. "You sounded natural, and that was most important."

She smiled. "At least that's something. Academy Awards, here I come."

"For sure, girl," Sophie said with an answering smile. "So now what?"

"Everybody's here, and we're ready," Danny said. "Stick to the plan. Act natural, like nothing's up."

Easier said than done. Abby thought she saw that thought echoed in Danny's eyes. Or maybe she just wanted to believe that. She'd thought she'd seen other things in his eyes and been wrong before. She turned to Sophie. "I know you need to micromanage every last detail, and I love you for it, but maybe just let me know the big stuff for a while. I'm going to go upstairs, find my keyboard and maybe, for the first time in forever, get lost in what I love to do." She gave Sophie a small smile before she left the phone on the counter and headed to her room.

* * *

Danny figured they had, at minimum, six hours before Sean could be in the area and, at most, a day. His men were already close by, and King would be walking through his door within ten minutes. He wanted to sit down with both Connor and King to go over any last minute concerns.

He let himself think about Abby. Damn, she'd done a fantastic job. And he liked the fire in her he'd seen last night. Liked it a lot. Maybe too much for his own good. And after the phone call, he had a feeling that the fire in Abby was here to stay.

"Nucci?" Connor called from the porch.

"Kitchen."

Connor opened the screen door. "The King is in the building."

"Coming." Danny finished stirring the sauce and lowered the flame. Restaurant food and take out was getting old, and Danny was apparently the only one that knew how to cook.

He walked through the living room and out onto the porch. Connor and King were waiting for him near the front of the cabin.

"How was the ride?" He greeted King.

"Fucking long. Never drive six-plus hours with Ricky."

"I already know that." Danny chuckled. "He doesn't shut up. Stakeouts are always fun too."

"Thanks for the heads up," King said sarcastically.

"Anytime. What have you got for me?"

"We've been to every gas station and motel in a twenty-mile radius. If he shows, we'll know."

"Everyone's in position," Connor said. "Now we need that fucker to show his face."

"He will." Danny scanned the area.

"I've got Ricky and Freddie camped out at the interstate exits," King added.

"Good. There are a ton he could use to get here, but maybe we'll get lucky and they can follow him."

"That'd be good, but all this prep work could be useless if he looks online and uses his GPS rather than asking one of the locals," Connor pointed out.

"Well, we're prepared either way. We have a point man hidden at the beginning of the road. It's the only way to get to the cabin, so that gives us enough time to get the upper hand."

"We've got this covered, man." King mock punched Connor in the shoulder.

"Keep in touch," Danny ordered.

"Absolutely. Everyone has been equipped with radios." King moved away from the railing he was leaning on and picked up a pair of two-way digital radios from the steps.

"For you." He gave one to Danny and one to Connor.

"Frequency?"

"Eighteen."

Danny checked the radio and made sure his was working correctly.

"I'm headed out. There are men in the woods," King informed them.

Danny nodded. "Perfect. Stay safe."

"For sure."

"Stay alert," Connor reiterated what Danny had said.

"Always." King gave them both a chin lift and left.

Danny watched King head down the deck steps, get into his vehicle, and drive out to the main road before he went back inside.

* * *

"Why have you waited this long to cook me a meal?" Abby pushed her dish away and finished the last of her wine.

"I needed to withhold some of my talents."

"I don't think I can move. That was delicious."

"Thank you." Danny smiled.

"I'd offer to cook one night, but I might poison everyone," Abby said.

"Yeah, I think I might pass on that."

She laughed.

"We all might pass on that," Connor added with a wink.

"Who taught you how to cook?" Sophie asked as she took another bite of the pasta.

"My mom and grandmother."

"Well, they did a great job because this is phenomenal. I can't remember the last time I ate so much."

"Since you cooked, we'll clean." Abby stood with her plate in her hand.

"You don't have to do that," Danny said, reaching for her plate.

"Whatever, Chef Nucci. C'mon, Sophie."

"Ah, women's work." Connor snorted a laugh as Abby and Sophie gathered the plates.

"Screw you, Connor." Abby dipped her fingers in her glass and flicked some wine at him. "And you like him?" she asked Sophie.

"Oh my God, shut up." Sophie lightly slapped Abby on the arm and left for the kitchen.

"Whoops." Abby smiled and followed Sophie.

* * *

"Okay, for real. I'm freaking the fuck out," Abby said to Sophie as they cleaned up in the kitchen.

"I know. You wouldn't be normal if you weren't."

"I really want to run away."

"That's normal, too."

"But I also really want to *not* run. I don't want this asshole to govern my life." She finished wiping one of the counter tops down.

"And I'm proud of you for that. If it helps, the last I heard there was nothing new to report. No one's seen him

290

yet."

Abby stopped and stared meditatively at the floor. "He would've had to leave right after I got off the phone with Kelly to already be here."

"True. So let's finish here and find one of those eighties cult movies you love so much on Netflix and veg out."

"I could go for that."

"Good. Let's get the rest of these dishes loaded."

Abby looked around. "Danny's a great cook, but he used practically every pot and pan in this place for one meal."

"Men." Sophie shook her head. "Just be happy he can cook. Cleaning is pushing it." She grinned.

"So true."

"What are you ladies laughing at?" Connor leaned against the granite island and watched them work.

"Men." They said in unison and laughed louder.

"I'm not touching that conversation with a ten-foot pole. Although…" He straightened and stuck out his broad chest. "My pole is always at your disposal." He winked at Sophie and sauntered away.

Abby busted out laughing. "You wish," she hollered. She turned to look at Sophie. "So are you still denying there's nothing between you two?"

"Shut up and thanks for that comment before." Sophie placed the dishtowel on the hook and headed toward the living room.

"I'm so right," Abby said to herself and laughed. At least Connor had a knack for dispelling tension. She followed Sophie.

* * *

"One sec," Abby called from the bathroom. She was changing into a pair of sweat pants and a T-shirt for bed. She wasn't sure what was about to happen, so she wanted to be wearing something more than pajamas. It just made her feel safer.

"It's me," Sophie said through the door.

"Come in." Abby finished up in the bathroom and headed out to her room. "What's up?"

"Danny asked if I'd stay in here with you tonight. He wants us in the same room."

"Okay." She'd actually been thinking that she'd like Sophie with her. "Anything new?" Abby was completely on edge. Every sound she heard made her jump. Danny and Connor asked them to stay upstairs while they strategized and got ready for whatever the hell you wanted to call what was about to happen. All of this was just so crazy. Like something out of a bad movie where the hot chick runs up the stairs and gets killed within the first five minutes. She didn't want to be that hot chick.

"Not that I know of. He said he wanted us together. I thought it made sense. This way there's only one room to worry about."

"And you know how much I love being the subject of worry." Abby walked over to the window and peeked out the shade. It was dark so all she could see were the stars in the sky and the reflection of the moon off the lake in the distance. There wasn't a soul to be found, yet she knew Danny and everyone else was out there watching and waiting.

"Try to relax. We'll have a slumber party. It'll be fun."

"Easy for you to say," Abby muttered.

"Actually, it isn't easy for me to say. I'm here, too. If anything, I'm glad I have someone next to me to worry with me. Let's turn the TV on and watch something light and fun."

Abby felt bad for being so focused on herself. She didn't realize how this could be affecting Sophie.

"Oh, I think the Yankees are playing the Red Sox." Abby smiled. The Yankees were their team. There was nothing like the Yankee-Red Sox rivalry to distract her from a crazy lunatic heading straight for her safe haven.

"That's light and fun?"

"Far from that but we'll probably wind up yelling at the screen so it's sure to be fun." This was a far better distraction than a movie.

"Get the remote," Sophie ordered. "We have a game to watch and they better be winning."

"Got it." Abby turned on the television. "In all seriousness, though, I don't think I'm going to be able to sleep."

"Me, either, but at least we can keep each other from freaking out."

"Then it's you, me, the Yankees, and our frazzled nerves." Abby got settled in bed with Sophie next to her and though they did get into the game, Abby knew that Sophie was just as worried as she was.

chapter
twenty-two

Danny's team was at his cabin, and their trucks were hidden in his garage. Everyone was in place, hiding in the woods and waiting for Sean.

They got a huge break about an hour ago when a local store owner called to say Sean and Kelly had stopped to pick up a map and a couple of candy bars. He called the second they pulled out of his lot, giving Danny time to get everyone back to the cabin.

Since the call, they'd been waiting in the woods. Danny positioned himself behind a cluster of pine trees, glad for the extra cover of darkness. From here, he was able to watch both the road and Abby's room.

"I have a black unmarked van approaching," Freddie said over the radio.

Finally. "Copy. Showtime, gentlemen. Stay sharp." Danny hooked the radio on his belt and took a couple of deep breaths. He heard tires crunch on gravel and then the vehicle stopped.

Danny lifted his night-vision binoculars and watched as a man got out of the driver's seat. Danny studied the figure through the binoculars. Definitely Sean. He appeared to be alone, dressed in black from head to toe, and he held a backpack over his shoulder. No telling what was in it. He'd find out soon enough. Sean was his.

Danny kept his gaze locked on Sean through the binoculars as Sean cased the front of the cabin, searching for the best way in. Danny glanced at the van; there was no one else around it. Either Kelly wasn't with him or she was hiding in the back of the van. Danny turned his attention back to Sean as he reached behind his back and pulled something from his jeans. Danny zoomed in with his binoculars and saw the glint of a knife. *Never take a knife to a gunfight, asshole.*

Sean headed toward the side porch door, and Danny started to move, keeping quiet. He weaved through the trees and bushes placing his feet carefully to ensure that Sean didn't hear him. He was nearly to Sean when he charged. He knocked Sean into the garbage cans just as the outside lights came on as planned. They'd blocked the motion sensors to give Sean a false sense of being unseen. The knife flew out of Sean's hand as they tumbled to the ground.

"Motherfucker," Sean mumbled. He scrambled to his feet, but Danny stayed with him.

"You're not going anywhere." Danny took a couple of steps back, aware that several of his employees were standing behind him. "Stay back," he told them, his gaze never leaving Sean.

"He's all yours," Connor said.

"Fuck you." Sean glared at the assembled group. "All this for a lousy lay? Now the mother, she's another story. You should've tapped *that* when you had the chance." He lunged suddenly, and his fist caught Danny on the jaw.

Adrenaline coursed through Danny, and he didn't even feel the punch. He let him have the shot, then advanced on Sean, watching his position. Danny stutter-stepped, and his fast movement made Sean stumble. It was enough. Danny's right hook connected cleanly with Sean's jaw, and he grunted as he collapsed. Danny didn't give him any time to recover. He jumped on him and punched him in the face over and over, consumed with thoughts of Sean terrorizing Abby. He had weeks of built up frustration and anger, and now, finally, he had the source of that rage in his grasp.

"Enough, Danny," Connor said. He sounded as though he was far away, calling to Danny from the other end of a tunnel. Danny brought his fists down over and over. He thought about Vanessa, how he wasn't there to save her, and about her bloodied, broken, and lifeless body. He'd let her down, and he wasn't going to let Abby down. Not again. Sean would never hurt her again. He'd make sure of it. "Nucci. Stop. The guy's fuckin' done."

Danny drew his fist back again, but he didn't finish the blow. Sean deserved much more. But there he lay, mumbling and groaning, face smeared with blood. Danny got to his feet. "Fine. Call 911."

Sean rolled to his side. Danny put his foot on his chest and pushed him back to the ground. Danny bent down, "It's your lucky day, asshole," he whispered into Sean's ear. "You get to live a little longer."

Sean stopped trying to get up, and two of Danny's employees stood nearby in case he tried anything. Sean couldn't even catch his breath, let alone move enough to be a danger. Still, with someone like Sean, it was better to be vigilant.

Danny moved to Sean's van and opened the back doors. No Kelly. He walked over to the passenger side where he found zip ties scattered across the seat and a bag on the floor. He reached into his back pocket and pulled out a small flashlight. He used the grip of the flashlight to move around the items in the bag, making sure not to touch anything. His stomach plunged when he saw what was inside. There was rope, duct tape, a bottle of some sort of liquid, and rags that could be used for a blindfold or a gag. Danny ground his teeth together. Sean was going to use all of this on Abby. He clenched and unclenched his fists.

"Chill, man," Connor said. "He's down. No point getting arrested for murder."

"It'd be worth it in this case." Danny shined the flashlight on the seat of the truck.

"Damn," Connor said. "The guy's seriously fucked up. And now I kind of want to finish the job, too. What a sick son of a bitch. Fuck, man, how long does it take the cops to get here?"

"There are some disadvantages to living in the woods. Just make sure the asshole doesn't move." Danny walked away from the van. He needed a moment to cool off; otherwise he might do something he'd later regret.

Flashes of blue and red lights broke through the forest.

"Cops," Connor said. "And about fucking time too. I was getting worked up again." He came up behind Danny and clapped him on the shoulder.

Danny met the first patrol car and briefed them. "He's over there on the ground," he said, motioning to the prone Sean. "That's his van. All his gear is on the seat. Other than opening the door, we didn't touch it." One of the officers nodded and directed the other to assess Sean's condition. The ambulance arrived a few minutes later.

"Got a receipt for a local motel in town," one of the officers said from Sean's van.

"You'll probably find a woman named Kelly West there," Danny said.

"What's her relationship in all this?" the officer asked.

"The hell if I know. That seems to be the million-dollar question. My guess is some infatuation with either Sean or Abby. I'd like to know what you find out."

"Will do. We'll need to speak with Ms. Murphy."

"She's in the house with her assistant. I don't really want her to see him. Can we meet you down at the station?"

"I'll need to speak to her tonight."

"Absolutely. I'll get her and bring her down as soon as the ambulance clears out."

"Appreciate that."

Danny turned and started toward the house.

"Dude, you can't go in there looking like that."

Danny looked down at his chest. It was covered in dirt and splatters of Sean's blood. "Shit, I'll scare the fuck out of them. I'll get a new one first."

"Wash your face before you go in there too." He gestured at his own lip.

Danny touched his bottom lip. His fingertip came away with a streak of blood. Sean's initial punch. And now that he thought about it, his lip hurt a little. *No biggie*, he thought as he pictured Sean's crumpled form on the ground earlier. A split lip was a small price to pay for getting that freak show locked up. He took the stairs up to the second floor two at a time before stopping in his room to clean up and get a new shirt.

* * *

"Did you hear that?" Abby sat up and shook Sophie.

"What's wrong?" Sophie mumbled.

"Did you hear that?" she repeated. There had definitely been a noise and now her heart was pounding in her chest. What if something went wrong? What if Sean made it inside the house? What if he had a gun? What if Danny's hurt? Or worse?

"I was sleeping. Hear what?"

"That noise."

"What did it sound like?"

"I don't know. If I knew, I wouldn't be asking you."

"Slow down a second and take a breath. Giving me attitude at," Sophie glanced at the clock, "three in the morning is not going to solve anything."

Abby was about to respond when a loud crash from outside interrupted. Abby swung her legs to the floor.

"Where are you going?" Sophie grabbed Abby's arm.

"I need to see what that was." She tried to pull away. Danny could be hurt.

"Shit," Sophie said.

"I need to find Danny." Abby pulled away from Sophie's hold. She needed to know what was happening. Why didn't Sophie understand that?

"No, you need to get down." Sophie was out of bed now, too. "Get down," she pulled them both to the ground. "We need to get to the closet. Go."

"Don't you want to know what's happening?" Abby looked over at Sophie. She didn't even want to think of all the horrible things that could be going on down there, but her imagination wouldn't rest.

"Of course I do, but right now I want to get us somewhere safe."

Abby stopped arguing and crawled to the closet. She really wanted to know if Danny was okay, but self-preservation won out. She couldn't let Sean find her.

Sophie closed the door behind them. "We need to stay here until the guys come and get us."

"I want to find Danny. Don't you want to know where Connor is? If he's okay?" Abby fought the panic she felt rising in her chest. She just couldn't shake the feeling that something horrible was happening downstairs. She needed to know.

"Abby, you need to stop." Sophie grabbed Abby's hands. "Of course I do, but do you think us running around the house or outside is going to be helpful? Think. Take a second and think. The guys are trained in this sort of thing. We aren't. We need to stay here and keep out of the way. This is the only way we can help them." Sophie moved closer to Abby and wrapped her arms around her. "It'll be fine."

"Liar."

"Stop it. Calm down."

"I want to know what's going on."

"I know you do, and so do I, but we need to stay here. Listen…it seems to have calmed down."

They stayed huddled together for a few more minutes. It was eerily quiet, and the lack of noise was working Abby's last nerve. Her imagination was running wild. Was Sean out there? Had they found him?

"I hear something," she whispered.

"Me too. Stay quiet."

"Fuck." She moved closer to Sophie.

What sounded like footsteps thudded through the ground level and then up the stairs. Was that furniture getting moved around? Abby clutched Sophie tighter. She prayed Sean wasn't fumbling about, looking for her. Danny *had* to be fine.

The waiting was horrible. Why did she agree to call Kelly? She was happy living up here in secret. Lake George was beautiful, and there was a ton of things to do. She could've spent the summer up here in ignorant bliss.

Hysterical thoughts continued to flood Abby as she waited for something to happen or for someone to open the door.

"I can't take this anymore," Abby whispered. "I think we should at least check to see if they're in the house."

"Stay—"

The door opened, and someone flipped on the light switch. Abby squeezed her eyes closed at the sudden glare.

"Shit," Sophie said.

"It's us," Danny called out. The sound of his voice, familiar and comforting, relieved the pressure in her chest, and the tension slowly drained from her body.

Before Abby could process what was happening, Sophie let go of her and hugged Connor. Abby stared at Danny. He seemed to be in one piece, except the bloody lip and dirty jeans.

"It's over. You can get up now." Danny held out his hand to her.

Abby stared up at him. After a moment, she took his hand, and he pulled her to her feet.

"Are you all right?" She didn't let go of his hand, and they hadn't moved from the closet.

"I'm fine."

"Are you sure?" She traced her fingers along his jaw down to his lip.

"He got one punch in. He looks a lot worse. Trust me."

"He hit you?"

He nodded.

"Danny beat the crap out of him," Connor said matter-of-factly.

"You're not helping." Danny glared at him.

"You're not hurt?" Abby asked, searching his face.

"No. I'm fine, and it's over."

"We heard banging. I thought it was gun shots."

"Come sit down," Danny said, his voice gentle.

She let him guide her out of the closet, their fingers still entwined.

She sat on the edge of the bed.

"Everyone's fine," Abby repeated Danny's words, hoping that maybe if she said them aloud, they'd register in her head.

"Except Sean," Connor said.

She didn't care what happened to Sean. She looked at Danny to make sure he was telling her the truth.

"We need to go down to the police station so you can give your statement. There's nothing to worry about. You're safe."

"And you're fine?"

"I'm perfect. We need to go back outside, and you need to get dressed. Come down as soon as you can."

"'Kay."

Danny didn't move. "It really is all over. You're safe

now." Danny's fingers lightly traced Abby's cheek.

A chill ran through Abby, and she closed her eyes. When she opened them, he was gone.

* * *

Paramedics were strapping Sean onto the stretcher when Abby walked outside. Danny had told her to stay inside until everyone left, but she had to see things for herself. There were people everywhere. Some she recognized, but most she didn't. She looked around for Danny, but saw Sean first. She strode deliberately toward him.

"Abby," Danny called. She ignored him. She stood over Sean and stared at his bloodied and bruised face. She forced herself to look at him, to keep herself from running away. His eyes were swollen shut. He couldn't even see her, and he appeared to be barely conscious. She stared at him for what seemed to be a long time. This was the man who had tormented and assaulted her. This piece of battered meat.

"Ma'am?" one of the paramedics said. He looked at her, a question in his eyes.

"I'm fine." She stepped aside as he and another paramedic loaded Sean's stretcher into the ambulance and closed the door. She whispered, "I hope you rot."

"Abby?" Danny stood beside her, concern in his voice.

She exhaled as the ambulance drove away.

"It's over?" Abby said.

"It's over." He squeezed her shoulders from behind.

"Part of me doesn't want to believe it." She stared down the road, in the direction the ambulance had gone.

"Believe it. They'll soon both be behind bars."

"Both?" She turned to him.

"Kelly. I'm sure she's being arrested as we speak."

"Do we know why?"

"No, but hopefully we'll find out. I told the officers we'd meet them down at the station to give our statements. Maybe they can shed some light on things. We can leave whenever you're ready."

She managed a smile. "I'm ready."

"Let's go then."

She followed him to the garage, feeling a lot lighter than she had in weeks.

* * *

Abby walked slowly behind Danny into the police station with Connor and Sophie close behind. King and Freddie stayed outside to wait.

The officer at the front desk ushered them through the main area and into a private conference room.

"Someone will be with you in a moment." He left before Abby could thank him. Not long after he left, another man, balding and wearing wire-rim glasses, came in carrying a couple of folders. His shirt and tie looked freshly pressed. Either they didn't get too much action up here, or he had just arrived for his shift. "Ms. Murphy. Mr. Nucci," he said with a nod. "I'm Detective Mathews. I have a few questions for you."

"Sure," Abby said. Danny nodded back, and Mathews took a seat across the table from them. He set the folders on the table, and for the next hour, he listened to what the ugly saga Sean had turned her life in to.

"So Kelly West is someone you thought was a friend." Mathews looked up from his paperwork at Abby.

"Yes. But not much more than someone I would hang out with on occasion when I had time. She was not involved at all with my work."

"Hmm," Mathews said, but Abby couldn't tell if he was agreeing with her or puzzled. He looked first at Danny then back at Abby. "We have taken Kelly West into custody."

"Was she helping Sean?" Abby asked.

"Very much so."

"Why would she do that?"

"From what she told us, she's infatuated with him." He tapped his pen on the table. "She blamed you for ruining his career and claimed she and Sean had been a couple for years, and he was only with you to climb the ladder to success."

Abby sat back. "Unbelievable. The whole time we were hanging out, she was probably thinking that."

"On the plus side, they're both in custody, and between the evidence we've gathered and Ms. West's loose lips, they won't be going anywhere for quite a while."

"That's very reassuring." Abby fought back her tears. She was done crying, but shit if she wasn't relived. "Thank you for everything."

"Absolutely. If I need anything else, I'll be in touch, but for now, go home and get some rest." He slid his papers back into the folders and stood. "I'll show you out."

"Thanks." Danny stood and waited for Abby to precede him from the room behind Mathews. As they left the police station, Abby wanted to laugh, celebrate, and sleep for a week, all at the same time. Instead, she looked over at Danny. "I really want a milkshake. Chocolate."

He laughed. "Let's see if we can find a place that'll do that for you."

Abby got into the SUV. "Y'know," she said as she buckled her seatbelt, "I think I'm hungry, too. Maybe we can find a diner. I'd love some really salty fries. Oh and a bacon cheeseburger."

Connor grinned at her. "Atta girl."

"We have a new mission," Danny said to Freddie and King. "We must hunt down some food for Ms. Murphy." He drove out of the parking lot. A few minutes later, they pulled into the only twenty-four hour gas stations that had a small convenience store.

chapter
twenty-three

Abby packed the last of her things. She was almost ready to head back to the city, but she didn't want to forget anything important.

"Is this the last of it?" King asked from the doorway to her room.

"I have this bag, but I can bring it down. Thanks for the help. I'll be down in a few."

"Sounds good. I'll let the guys know."

Abby zipped up the small suitcase, gave the room one last sweep, and then headed down to the car.

"We never got to go to The House of Frankenstein." Sophie pretended to pout.

"You're joking, right?" Connor turned in his seat to look back at them.

"Not really. It looked fun."

"It's not like you can't come back up," Danny said. "Now that the summer is here, everything will be open, and you can really experience all the area has to offer."

"I might take you up on that."

Abby listened to them banter back and forth. She'd love to come back up here but didn't see that happening.

"You okay back there?" Danny asked. He was looking at her in the rearview mirror.

"I'm good. Not excited about going back to the city and facing the mess that's waiting for me."

"It'll be fine. You're a badass. And we have a ton of meetings set up. You'll have new management before you know it." Sophie smiled, encouragingly.

"I don't doubt I can find someone, but first I have to get rid of the current one. I'm not looking forward to that conversation." Not at all. On the plus side, her mother didn't have Sean to play off of anymore.

"I know you're nervous, but I also know you can do it." Sophie reached over and squeezed Abby's hand.

"I hope so." She chewed her lip and stared out the window, listening to Danny tell stories with Connor about their Army days. Just another day for them. And though she felt as if she was finally free of Sean, she was pretty sure things would get ugly with Vivien. Finally, she dozed.

* * *

"Okay, there's a lot of press and fans outside the main entrance to your building," Sophie said.

"Figures." Thank God for the underground parking. She'd be able to avoid all of that.

They took the service elevator up to her floor. Home sweet home. She looked around her apartment and didn't get that warm, fuzzy feeling she'd always experienced when entering. She already missed the cabin.

"There will be two men at your door at all times," Danny said. "Please don't leave without them."

"I'm not about to go anywhere without having someone glued to me."

"Good. And if you need some privacy or alone time or if you want to see some friends, let me know, and we'll figure something out."

"Yeah," King said as he walked into the room. "It's nuts down there."

"I miss my bubble. Reality sort of sucks." Abby moved a pillow out of the way and plopped down on the oversized chair in her living room.

"It'll die down eventually." Sophie carefully moved the curtain aside and peered out.

"Not for a while. Tomorrow a whole new layer of crazy gets added to the mix." Abby imagined the conversation with Vivien. No matter how she spun it, it went bad every time.

"It'll be fine." Sophie continued looking out the window.

"I hope so."

"Speaking of Vivien, I'll be here at ten to take you to your office," Danny said.

"You're coming too, right?" Abby looked back at Sophie.

"Duh. You'll have to chain me to a wall to stop me from being there." Sophie teased and turned away from the curtains.

"I could do that," Connor said.

"God. You two should get a room already and get it over with," Abby said.

"In his dreams." Sophie picked up her bag. "I need to go. I love you and all, but I need a break. No offense."

"None taken. I'm done with you, too." Abby blew her a kiss.

"Ten tomorrow morning," Danny said. "And don't leave this apartment on your own."

"Yes, sir." She saluted and watched as everyone left. Alone, she stared glumly around her apartment. At least she felt safer than she had in a while. She did hate not being able to go down the block for coffee and a bagel, but she understood, finally, what her life was about and that she needed to take some responsibility. This was her reality, and she had to figure out how to make it work. It occurred to her that it would probably be pretty hard to date anyone with Danny around. It would feel weird, too, like she was somehow betraying him.

Stop it, she said to herself. *He's your bodyguard. Not some ex-boyfriend.* But it was sad to think that. She got up to unpack.

* * *

"You can do this," Danny whispered in Abby's ear right before the elevator doors opened to the offices of Murphy Entertainment. She looked up at him and managed a smile.

"Yeah. I know. Doesn't make it much easier, though." She knew she was well within her rights to fire her mother. After everything that went down combined with the fact that Abby wanted a say in her career and creative control over her music, she knew there was just no other option left.

She took a deep breath, and it calmed her for a moment. She walked into the lobby with Danny and Sophie. She was glad she had their support, but this was her meeting. She was the one that needed to set things straight.

"Ms. Murphy, it's so nice to see you back. You're looking well." Dawn, her mother's choice for assistant, greeted her with a fake smile.

"Is my mother in her office?" she asked. There was no time for small talk. She wanted this over and done.

"I'll buzz her and let her know you're waiting for her."

"No need." Abby walked through the double doors of Vivien's office and marched in. Danny and Sophie followed close behind, and she knew a few other guys would wait in the front office. As she passed through the doors, a wave of calm overtook her. She was ready and didn't need them for support, but they deserved to see this too.

"How nice of you to announce your visit," Vivien said,

a hint of mockery in her voice.

Vivien was sitting on the sofa sipping coffee in her large corner office. It overlooked the city skyline.

"You can't barge into my office with your flunkies." Vivien glared at Danny and Sophie.

"From what I remember, I'm the one who pays for this office." Abby snapped back.

Vivien stood, an uncertain expression in her eyes.

Abby squared her shoulders and took a deep breath. "In light of recent events, I've decided to end my management relationship with you. I'll expect that you'll have your personal effects cleared out by the end of the day."

Vivien stared at her as if she'd been slapped. "Now wait a Goddamn minute," she started.

"No. I've thought about this long and hard, and this is what's best for me. I can't continue to let you make all the choices. I'm old enough to make my own decisions and have a career that's truly my own. The only way to do that is to cut ties."

"You can't do this without me, Abigail," Vivien pleaded.

"I can't do this with you anymore. I won't. I'd rather fail then have you running my career."

"Abigail, we can work something out. What if we let you pick a song or two on the next album? I'm sure we could figure something out." Vivien sounded flustered.

"There's nothing you can say to change my mind."

"This business will swallow you up. You have no idea what goes into running a career like yours. I've done nothing for the last sixteen years but make sure you succeeded."

"You've done nothing but take from me." Abby paused to regroup but couldn't stop her mind from thinking about how she had been a product of some trick. She could sympathize with a mother who was truthful, but to lie and cover up the true nature of her birth was something Abby had a difficult time forgiving. She didn't want this to get personal, but it was impossible to avoid. It was another reason she needed to get away from her mother. "You took away my childhood. It was always practices, performances, and auditions. Then I find out that you lied about my past and my father. You took advantage of me."

"Don't you give me that crap. You wanted your career just as much as I did."

"I was seven years old when I went on my first audition. What child at that age knows anything? I wanted to make you happy. I was too young to know what I was getting myself into. It was your job to be my mother, but you opted to be my manager. Instead of your unconditional love and support, I got your bitching and the back of your hand when I didn't get the part."

"Ungrateful—"

"Nothing I ever did was good enough for you. If I got the part, I didn't work hard enough for you. When I got my recording contract, when I went on tour, when I won awards, when a song hit number one—nothing was ever good enough. There was always more I could be doing. Accolades I should be receiving, standards I wasn't measuring up to."

"You—"

"Be quiet. Never once did you say 'good job' or tell me that you were proud of me. Never did you acknowledge anything I've achieved. Strangers," she pointed behind her at Danny and Sophie, "are more supportive and more like family to me than you ever were."

"You can't fire me. I'm your mother."

"I just did. I can't change the fact that you're my mom, but I don't have to let you control my career...my life." Abby was on a roll now and needed to get it all out if she ever wanted to move on. She was done expecting her mother to care but still, she needed this for herself. "And as if you hadn't done enough already, you slept with my boyfriend and encouraged the bastard to hurt me. He tried to rape me. How could I ever trust you after that? You didn't protect me from Sean. Mothers are supposed to protect their kids from people like that. But you...you worked with him to hurt me and fed him lies about a career you were never going to give him. Do you hate me that much that you wanted to see him destroy me? Don't you love me at all? Or has it always been about what I can give you?"

Vivien's eyes narrowed. "What you can give me? What about everything I gave you? And gave up for you?"

"Like what?"

Vivien had no response.

"We're done here. Get out."

Vivien didn't move.

"I think you were asked to leave." She heard one of the

men say from behind her.

"Without me, Abigail you have *nothing*."

She smiled and meant it. "You know what? I'm fine with nothing."

"How dare you? Don't you touch me," Vivien snapped at King as he reached for her arm to escort her out.

He pulled his hand back and motioned her to the door.

She waited as King escorted Vivien out of the office. "Sophie?"

"Yes?" Sophie's eyes were as wide as dinner plates.

"One more thing to do." Abby glanced toward the front office where Dawn was sitting.

"Right. On it." She left.

"You okay?" Danny said. He looked like he wasn't sure what to do with her.

"Actually, I'm really good. That felt…awesome. And amazing." Was this empowerment? Because damn, she wanted more.

"It was." Danny smiled at her.

"I feel like a huge weight has been lifted from me."

"You were incredible. I'm actually speechless." He sounded impressed.

"You? Who knew that could happen?" She let a breath out and collapsed onto the couch. "Once I started, I let it all go."

"She deserved every word."

"Oh, I know."

They looked toward the door when they heard the commotion in the reception area.

"Dawn was not happy with being kicked to the curb. Oh well." Sophie shrugged.

Abby grinned. "They're gone?"

"All gone. The guys are escorting them out."

"Perfect."

Sophie plopped down next to her and gave her a side-hug. "I can take it from here."

"You sure?"

"Girl, I got this shit covered. If I need you, I'll call. You need to bail before Vivien calls the press and you're stuck in this building."

"Good point." And her mother would. She was probably calling right now. Abby got up and gave Sophie another hug and quick kiss.

"Okay, the guys are waiting downstairs for us." Danny placed his phone in his pants pocket.

"Great. Let's go."

* * *

A couple of days later, Abby packed her bags again. This time, however, she was heading to her small house on Long Island Beach in New Jersey. She loved it there because it was peaceful and the locals left her alone. She had a separate guesthouse in the backyard that she had converted into a state of the art recording studio and that's where she wanted to be.

"Abby?"

She turned and looked at King.

"Ready?"

"I'm gathering a few more things. I'll be good to go in a few."

"Great." He retreated.

She threw the last of her things in her suitcase and headed out to King and Freddie. Danny wasn't going with her to New Jersey. He needed to check in with other clients. Abby was a bit disappointed but she understood. He had a successful firm that dealt with many high profile clients and he couldn't devote all his time to her. She had been lucky that he had taken the lead on her tour but all good things must come to an end. Still, it felt bittersweet.

The ride to her house took nearly three hours and when they finally arrived Abby was itching to get out of the car. She waited with Freddie as King did a walk through before she helped them bring in her luggage and groceries.

"I haven't been here in a long time," Abby said. "So, it's a bit stuffy but once I open some windows we should get a nice breeze."

As she walked through each room she pulled off the sheets that had been covering the furniture. Abby loved her house. It was one of the few places she owned that her mother had never been. There wasn't one piece of Vivien in this entire house. Abby's style was comfortable and relaxed with light wood floors and white walls. The soft white furnishings were accented with various shades of red, from light to dark, on pillows, frames and curtains.

"Hey, guys. I'll show you the best part. You'll probably want to check it out anyway." She motioned for the guys to follow her through the kitchen and out the back porch doors. "Isn't it amazing?" She headed toward the pool. "I bought this house for three reasons. The view, the pool and this." She motioned toward the independent building. "Welcome to Magnolia Studios, gentlemen." She unlocked the door and rushed inside to turn the alarm off.

The large room held two white couches, beanbag chairs, several small throw rugs in a red damask pattern. On the walls hung several guitars and shelves that stored notebooks, smaller instruments and a ton of candles. Chandeliers hung from the high ceilings and in the corner there was a black grand piano.

"This is pretty cool," Freddie said, his voice filled with appreciation.

"Isn't it? Do you play at all?" Abby noticed him staring at the guitars that hung neatly on the wall.

"I used to play guitar, but I haven't in a long time."

"Feel free to jam out whenever you want. My producer, Aisling, will be here in a few days to help me with a new project." Abby had spent a lot of money to get her, too. One of the hottest producers around didn't have free time.

"She's worked with some amazing artists. Jamming with her would be a dream come true."

"I know. I flipped out when she agreed to work with me on this album."

"Everything looks good in here."

They went back into the house and Abby started the tedious process of unpacking and settling in.

* * *

Abby didn't want to waste any time so the next day she went straight to work. She was determined to get the lyrics and music she'd written over the last few weeks recorded while the guys upgraded her security system.

While she was fiddling around on her piano, her cell phone rang.

"Hello," Abby answered.

"Hey, it's Aisling."

"Hi. What's up?" Abby greeted.

"I got here early and I'm settling into the house I'm renting," Aisling explained. "I wanted to touch base and see when you wanted me to come over."

"Whenever you want. I'm in the studio now just getting my bearings."

"Excellent. How about we meet up somewhere tonight and I'll introduce you to my team and we'll get to know each other a little better, see what kinds of vibes we can produce."

"Perfect. How about we meet at The Hardware?" Abby

suggested.

The Hardware was a local bar that Abby often frequented when she was at the shore.

"I'll see you at say eleven?" Aisling suggested.

"See you then."

Abby hung up, stared at the piano keys for a second, then whooped. Finally. She finally felt like she was moving on with her life.

chapter
twenty-four

"Hi. It is so nice to meet you," Abby said as she hugged her new producer. "I'm so excited to work with you." The bar was crowded, but Abby felt comfortable. She had begun to think she'd never feel that way again, but King had called for two more guards, and they surrounded her. There was no one getting next to her tonight.

"Same goes for me. I was thrilled when I got the call. Let's get you a drink."

Abby ordered a beer and chatted with Aisling and her crew. She had her assistant, co-producer, and engineers with her. They were all very friendly and easy to get along with.

"How long have you been working together?"

"The last three years." Aisling shouted over the music blaring from the DJ's speakers.

"What made you decide to reach out to Aisling?" Jax, Aisling's co-producer, asked.

"I love her work. And I need someone who'll push me beyond my limits."

"She'll do that." He smiled, and it lit up his gray eyes. He looked like a quintessential rocker dude, with his long, messy brown hair. Kind of sexy. "Let me get you another drink."

"I'm good, but thanks." She wasn't about to let anyone get her a drink other than her guards.

She had been worried that she'd feel uncomfortable around Aisling and her production crew, but that wasn't the case. The more they talked, the more excited Abby got about working with Aisling and her staff.

"Dance?" Jax pulled Abby off her seat and into his arms before she even had a chance to protest. He held her close as they danced next to their table. He ground his hips into hers, and she let herself enjoy the attention. His playfulness and flirting were refreshing. It was nice to go out and have fun.

"It's getting way too late. I'm not use to this rocker life," Abby winked. Abby hadn't ever followed a normal schedule; starting her night late and ending it in the wee hours of the morning was part of the norm. Especially when she was on tour. She and Aisling shared that in common.

"We start in two days. So make sure you're ready for me to kick that sweet ass of yours," Aisling teased.

By the time she left the bar, Abby was feeling quite proud of herself. She was finally on her way to controlling her own career and life.

This would be the first album that was totally hers. The first time she had complete control of her music and her life. She was about to find out what kind of woman she really was, and she couldn't be happier about the challenges ahead.

* * *

"Abigail, sweetie that song is amazing. I'm so proud of you. This is going to be the album that shows everyone what I already know." Ms. Sohm gave Abby a warm loving hug. Abby had invited her former teacher and mother figure to her house so that she could spend some quality time with her and show Ms. Sohm that she was healing.

"Thank you. I'm really excited to get started tomorrow." This project was a long time coming. Her music. Her melodies. Her lyrics.

"It's going to be amazing. I just know it." Ms. Sohm picked up her cup of tea and took a sip.

"I hope so. This is all so new, and it feels like it all fell into place too easily." Abby stood up from her piano seat and joined Ms. Sohm on the couch. She had a lot of nervous energy and found it hard to sit still lately.

"You'll be fine. Just let the music guide you. Now, enough about work, how are you?

"I'm good." Wasn't that the biggest lie ever? She was in one piece, but she was not good. She was scared and excited and freaked and a million other emotions that she couldn't admit to.

"You can't pull that 'I'm good' stuff on me, young lady. I followed what happened in the news."

She should have known better. Ms. Sohm knew her too well to let that line slide. "Well, I was freaked, of course, and I still have nightmares."

"That's understandable. What happened to you was horrific. Anyone would have nightmares."

"I talk with Sophie all the time, and Danny too, though not as much lately. They've been really helpful."

"I've noticed the news coverage has died down a bit."

"Yes. Since I came here, it's a lot better. I don't have to deal with crowds so much, and that's a good thing for now. They come with what I do, but depending where I am, my panic can get bad. I try to fight through it because I can't avoid crowds forever. For now, though, I don't go out without guards."

"Well you shouldn't go out without someone. Even before all this." Ms. Sohm scolded her.

"I never went anywhere major without someone with me, but I could walk around my neighborhood in the city and no one would even look twice. Now I can't leave the house without worrying about the reporters camped out in front of my apartment building. The only reason why they aren't a fixture on my front yard here is because I'm in a private community." And thank God for that. She needed time to feel free rather than suffocated and closed off from the world. Her house here was right on the beach. She could walk down her deck steps and put her feet in the sand and just be. She didn't need to act a certain way or worry about being photographed.

This is her life now. With all she'd been through, it was natural to feel scared, but she wasn't complaining about her fans. She was grateful for all her success, but it was nice to have a moment to just breathe.

"It'll get better. You just gotta give yourself some time. You were attacked, and that's traumatizing. Spend time with yourself these next few weeks. Decide what you want in your life," Ms. Sohm encouraged.

That was Abby's plan. Abby had always come to her for advice, and it was satisfying to hear those words from Ms. Sohm. Maybe Abby was on the right track. It felt like she was, but Abby spent a lot of time second-guessing herself. Making decisions shouldn't be so hard, but the fact was Abby hadn't ever been responsible for herself. Someone else made all the decisions, from the simple to the complex. She had been a follower. Jumping head first into the leader position was scary, and it should be okay to admit that she's terrified.

"I know but it's so hard. I've been micromanaged for so long I don't even know where to begin." She took a shuttered breath. She didn't want to cry *again*, but all of this unknown terrified her. "I feel lost, and it's so damn scary. I wanted my independence, and now I have it. And I'm clueless." Abby placed her head on Ms. Sohm's shoulder and tucked her legs under her. What was she suppose to do? Where did she even start? She didn't want to feel like she was some pathetic loser who had to have her mommy do everything for her. She knew the reputation she had in the industry. She wasn't deaf and certainly wasn't dumb. Everyone knew if someone wanted anything, then that person went to Vivien not Abby. Now she had to not only get her life in order, but she had to prove to the industry that she could be her own person.

"You're not clueless, but you're right; it is scary. But you're also not alone. Not having your mother around doesn't mean you have to do it all with no help. Don't use that as an excuse not to step out on your own. You'll make mistakes, but if you surround yourself with people you trust, then things will get easier." Ms. Sohm curled her arm around Abby.

Abby let that sink in. She fought so hard to break free; was she using her mother as a reason to give up before she even started? Ms. Sohm was right. Abby didn't have to do it on her own. Asking for help didn't have to mean a loss in control. But still it was hard. Abby had Sophie. That girl was the master of efficacy, knew everything that was going on, had a ton of contacts, and was a really good friend.

"I feel like I have a few people I can trust now. Of course there's you." She turned to look at Ms. Sohm. "And Sophie is amazing. She's had my back since the day we hired her." If only Sophie could manage her? She sat up. That was it. Why couldn't she? Abby trusted her, people knew Sophie, and there'd be no awkward transition or fear that her ideas wouldn't be heard. "I've just had a great idea!" Abby was so overjoyed that she wanted to jump up and down in her seat.

"What? I need to know what put that look on your face?"

"I'm going to ask Sophie to manage me. I've been so worried about who I'd find, if we'd get along and if they'd listen to me. This is the perfect solution, and really, she's the right fit. She knows me, the business, and we talk all the time, so she knows what I want out of my career. She'd never overstep."

"Oh, I like Sophie. That sounds like a fabulous idea. You need to ask her."

"I will. I'll call her later." Abby felt such relief. Now she just had to ask and hope Sophie wanted to take that leap.

"What's going on with you and that handsome man that brought you to my house last time?"

Abby stilled. That was out of left field. "Um, you mean Danny?"

"Danny. Yes. That was his name. He's always on TV with you."

Abby smiled. She couldn't help it. Every time she thought of Danny, she smiled or laughed or just felt like a school girl with butterflies racing around in her stomach. "Nothing's going on." Why would she think something was going on?

"That's a shame."

"Well, he's...he's..." Abby found it hard to describe how she felt about him to someone else. She was still trying to figure that out for herself. Bodyguard didn't cut it. Friend seemed somewhat off. She wouldn't be thinking of him like this if he was just a friend.

"You have feelings for him. Don't deny it. You know, you can't hide things from me. Besides you're blushing."

Abby felt her face warm. She was blushing, and now that Ms. Sohm pointed it out, she probably looked like a tomato. "I do, I guess. I just don't know how he feels about me. I thought he felt the same, but then he says things that make me second-guess. Plus, it's not the right time now. I need some space to figure myself out before I start a new relationship." He confused her so much. Was she just a client to him? It didn't feel that way. Sophie's comments kept playing in Abby's head. She'd employed a lot of bodyguards, and no one ever went out of their way for her like Danny. They did the bare minimum. Hanging out and bringing her to their house in the woods wasn't in their business contract.

"I agree; you need time but don't let too much pass by. If you like him, why not tell him? I've seen the way he looks at you."

"No way." She jolted up. What way? She had to be mistaken. The last time she saw Ms. Sohm was over four months ago. "How? When?" She wanted Ms. Sohm to spill every last detail she remembered.

"Listen to me. I may not be twenty anymore, but I know when a man cares for a woman, and that man has feelings for you. When you're ready, you need to take the chance."

Ms. Sohm thought Danny was into her. *Hmm...* Abby let those words sink in while they spent the rest of the day chatting and eventually made their way to the boardwalk for some shopping. Were Ms. Sohm and Sophie right? Did Danny have feelings for her? This was all too much for now, and instead of wracking her brain with crazy scenarios, Abby decided to just enjoy the time with the person she considered to be her true mom.

* * *

It had been nearly three weeks and Abby, Aisling and

her team had worked non-stop, day and night. The process wasn't easy, and often Abby and Aisling butted heads, but the results were amazing.

"I can't do another take." Abby grabbed her water and downed nearly half the bottle.

"You can. One more. You're almost there. Feel the music. Think about the lyrics. These are intense. Pull from those emotions. This is your story. Let your audience feel it too."

Abby knew that sharing her music and inner thoughts with someone would be scary, but with Aisling and her team, she was willing to try new things with her voice and was eager to get input and feedback on her music. Aisling pushed Abby to channel her pain, hurt, and sorrow into her songs. With every note, it seemed a little piece of her healed.

Aisling brought in some very talented musicians, and Abby really loved what they were doing. This was such a change from what she was used to in the studio. Abby either wrote, or had a hand in writing, every song. This entire album would be hers. Each word she sang was from the heart, and the emotions behind them were genuine. Often she had to stop to collect herself. This was the most personal work she had ever created, and as hard as it was, it was the most gratifying thing she'd ever done musically.

"Ready?" Aisling asked.

Abby took another sip of water and gave the signal for the music to start. She closed her eyes and tuned everyone else out. It was just her and the music. She pulled from her memories and focused on how she felt so alone and lost not that long ago. She thought back on how her mother lied and Sean hurt her, and she let it all go. This here was her therapy. She didn't need to sit on a couch and tell a stranger how she was feeling because music was her way. This was her way to tell the world how she felt and explain how she was coping. Music was the way she would show everyone that she could make it on her own. She was strong enough to make her own choices and carve her own path in life.

"That's a wrap, babe," Aisling called through the speaker in the control room.

"Yeah, I thought I nailed that one."

"Absolutely. Take a break."

Abby removed her headphones, walked out of the recording booth, and into the control room.

"I'm ready to dive into the next song," Abby said as she sat in the empty chair next to Aisling.

"I wish I could, but I made plans tonight to go check out some area clubs."

"Nice. Have fun." Abby smiled, but she was a bit disappointed. She was on a roll and wanted to keep going.

"Come with?"

"I wish I could, but the guys need some warning before I go traipsing off."

"Makes sense." Aisling didn't add anything to that. Everyone knew what had happened to her. "Tomorrow I have a meeting in the city, so I'll see you in two days. Sound good?"

"Absolutely."

"Awesome. I'll call you when I'm on my way."

"Have fun." Abby gave Aisling a quick hug.

"Thanks."

* * *

Two weeks had passed since her talk with Ms. Sohm, and she'd done nothing but think about what she said. She missed Danny and wanted to talk to him. But she hesitated to call. They'd texted a few times since she arrived in New Jersey but nothing beyond that.

Abby poured herself a cup of coffee in the kitchen. She stirred the sugar in and thought about the connection she'd felt with Danny, a bond that she had never found with anyone else.

Sophie called in often to check on Abby. Over the last week, she seemed determined to convince Abby that Danny had feelings for her.

"He keeps asking about you," Sophie repeated for what seemed like the millionth time.

"That means nothing." Abby sighed.

"God, you're so blind. Wake up girl. What's it going to take for you to believe me?" Sophie nearly yelled into the phone. Abby could hear her frustration. Maybe she should take Sophie's word.

Abby took a sip of her coffee. She knew that she had to

find the courage to take a chance.

Abby glanced down at her phone. What if Sophie was right? What if Danny was interested in her? If she didn't take a chance, she'd never know. She tried to talk herself out of it on the way up to her bedroom, but that nagging little voice—the one that sounded too much like Sophie—had her determined to find out one way or the other if Danny's feeling were more than just professional. She placed her coffee on a small, glass-topped, cream-colored, wicker side table before sitting down on the extra wide window bench.

Once settled she unlocked her phone, called up his contact info, and stared at the screen. Her finger hovered over his name. *Just do it.* She touched the call button and waited for him to pick up, nervously tapping her foot.

"Hey, you. Everything okay?" Danny greeted. His voice was warm, and he sounded happy to hear from her.

"Yeah. I'm fine. Everything's great here." And it was. She was really happy with how things were going recently.

"That's good to hear. So how've you been? Did you have a good Fourth of July?" he asked.

"Busy, and it was good. I had my producer and her crew over for a barbeque." God, she felt stupid. If he wanted to talk to her, he would've called, right? Suddenly, she needed to move. She stood and paced the short distance between her bed and the door. "I've been working on some new songs. We finalized two the other day."

"I heard. King said they're amazing." The warmth in his voice sent heat down her thighs.

"He told you about them?" She was surprised that King would share something like that. He didn't seem to notice anything about her, yet noticed everything about their surroundings. He made her feel safe without being intrusive.

"He was really impressed, and Freddie is in heaven. He said you let him jam once or twice with the musicians."

"He's quite good." She sat back down on the cushioned bench and looked out at the ocean.

"Don't tell him that. You'll give him an even bigger ego than he already has."

"Ha, I'll remember that, but I think it's too late. Jax already told him that he has some talent."

"Jax, huh?"

"Aisling's co-producer. He's quite the talent all on his own."

"I bet," he sounded annoyed. "How are the guys? They aren't crowding you?"

Abby paused at the abrupt change in subject.

"They're fine. Perfect gentlemen. It was a little strange for a bit, but they have their own rooms, and since you had them put in a security system that's better than the one the White House has, they don't really need to be shadows while we're on the property." She laughed.

"Yeah, well, I'm glad the system is working."

"It is." She leaned against the window and saw her reflection. She was smiling and blushing. "So..." She hesitated. Was she ready to take this step? Once she said what she wanted to say there would be no turning back.

"I…I…"

"What's wrong?"

"Nothing. I just…well, I wanted to know if you'd like to have dinner with me."

Silence.

Shit. This was not going well. "I thought maybe pizza and a movie. We can veg out here and catch up or whatever." She kept her tone light. "I get it if you're really busy, but I kind of miss having you around." She tried to make it sound as if she was teasing.

"Oh, really? After I was all up in your business for so long? You miss that?"

"Okay, maybe not that."

He laughed. "Yeah, yeah. Okay. When did you want me to come over?"

"I know it's short notice, but I have tonight to myself. Aisling is in the city today and part of tomorrow, so my schedule is free."

"Tonight?" He hesitated again. "Hmm…I can do that."

"Yeah?" She was surprised. The drive from the city to Abby was about three hours without traffic. Abby thought for sure he'd say he was busy, but he didn't. She couldn't stop her smile.

"Yeah."

"Great. How about six?"

"That'll work."

"Cool. I'll see you tonight." Abby pulled the phone away from her ear. "Yes," she said as she hung up and then hugged herself. He said yes. Now what was she going to wear? She ran to her closet to find the perfect outfit for tonight.

* * *

Danny thought he heard Abby say "yes" as she hung up. If he wasn't a manly Army guy, he might have done the same.

Finally. He hadn't wanted to push her with all that she'd been through, but it had been practically a month since he last saw her, and he was on the verge of breaking his own rules. Sophie had been pushing him to call her, but he wanted to give her time to get established. More than ever, she needed to know she could do things on her own. She didn't need anyone micromanaging, and he knew if he were around, she'd lean on him when it came to decisions she needed to make herself.

"Nucci?" Connor strolled in. He stopped. "Dude? What happened?"

"Abby called."

"Oh." He laughed. "You got this," he said and broke into an eighties snake dance move. Danny sat back and watched Connor pop and lock.

"You missed your calling, bro. So did you come in

here to annoy me, or did you need me for something?"

"The annoyance was a bonus. I told Paula I'd come get you. Our next meeting is waiting in the conference room."

Danny looked at his computer to check the time. It wasn't even lunch yet. "Let's get this meeting over with." He stood and followed Connor to the meeting. If he got lucky, this consultation wouldn't take too long and he could take his ass home and change before heading to Abby's place.

chapter
twenty-five

As Danny hit the Garden State Parkway, he wondered what the night would bring. His main role had always been keeping Abby safe. Yes, they were friends, but first and foremost, he was her guard and her protector. He didn't mind that job. In fact, he'd hated giving the responsibility to anyone else, but he knew it was necessary. He wanted to control everything, and he hated that about himself—especially when it came to Abby.

He still worried that she wouldn't see him any other way. Throughout the tour, he noticed a pattern; whenever Vivien let her wrath loose, Abby would lean on Sophie or him. They were familiar, and they let her blow off steam in a safe environment. Did she ask him over because she missed the people who were familiar to her?

Abby needed to rely on herself and her own judgment. She was an intelligent woman who managed to be successful despite her mother. She needed to see she was worthy of that success. Her accomplishments were all hers. He wanted her to see that she could do it all, and he realized, too, that he wasn't helping her by being a control freak. That was why he stepped away from her security detail.

He watched out the windshield. The traffic on the

Parkway was heavy but thankfully moving. The shore traffic could be killer any day of the week in the summer. The closer he got to his destination, the more nervous and unsure he felt. He didn't know how the night would go, but however it went, he'd let Abby lead the way.

* * *

Abby stared critically at herself in the mirror. This was the third outfit that she'd tried on. Everything looked as if she was trying too hard. Finally, she settled on a black lace, strapless bandeau and a sheer cream-colored flowy camisole. She put on a pair of jean shorts then searched her closet for a pair of flat strappy sandals before she headed downstairs. She checked the time on her phone and quickly did the math in her head. Danny had texted earlier to let her know he was on his way. If traffic wasn't too bad, he'd be here soon. Maybe she should order the pizza.

Abby went down the hall that connected the living room to the kitchen and knocked on the utility door. When King and Freddie rewired the house and updated the security system, they hijacked the small room off the kitchen and made a command center.

"Come in," King called.

"I was going to order pizza. Did you guys want anything different?"

"Danny gave us the night off so no need to worry about us."

That wasn't what she wanted to hear. "Really?" Abby wanted time with Danny the man, not Danny the security specialist. The last thing she wanted was him to be focused on the work of being with Abby instead of the pleasure. "Umm…if you've not made any plans yet, could you stay?"

"Stay?" King looked confused.

"I want to catch up with Danny, and if you guys are around, then he won't have to be Mr. Security Guard." She hoped King couldn't see her blush.

He didn't seem to notice, or he was just too professional to tease her about it. "Oh, yeah. Sure. We didn't have any plans. Do you have a menu? I'll take a look and give it to Freddie when he comes back down."

"Yes. Be right back." She left and closed the door behind her before she leaned against it and exhaled. She took a moment to let the excitement in her stomach settle a bit. Then she went to get the menu.

* * *

Abby stared at the door when she heard the doorbell. It felt like there were gymnasts doing flips in her stomach. She had performed for presidents and in the Super Bowl halftime show, and she couldn't remember ever feeling like this. She let out a deep breath, checked the peephole, and then opened the door for Danny.

She took in all six feet two inches of him. Had he always been this tall and broad? Geez, he looked good. *Really* good. He wore a charcoal-grey V-neck T-shirt and jeans.

"Hey," she said. She was so nervous didn't recognize her own voice.

"Hey." He grinned and stood there staring at her.

"Oh, sorry. Come in." She opened the door wider and moved aside so he could move past her.

"Thanks." He smiled as he stepped into the living room. He almost brushed against her as he passed, and Abby held her breath and focused on not reaching out and touching him. It'd been far too long since she'd felt his arms around her, and she hadn't realized how needy she was for the experience.

Chill out, she chided herself silently. "Didn't the guys give you the code to the door?"

She watched him scan the room and evaluate the space. Old habits. It made her smile. And those jeans fit him really well. And his cologne...how had she forgotten something as basic as his scent? She breathed him in and almost laughed when she realized how all over the place her thoughts were. *Focus.*

"Yeah. I thought I'd better use the doorbell. Be like other people." He gave her a lopsided grin. "Where are the guys?"

"In their new command center. I'll show you."

She was about to show him to the room when the doorbell sounded again.

Danny looked at her.

"It's the delivery guy. I'll go grab my purse."

"I've got it."

"No. I invited you."

"Please?"

"All right." She didn't want to argue about pizza, so she relented and headed into the kitchen to fetch the dishes and silverware.

"That's a lot of food for two people," Danny said, holding the three boxes of pizza.

"I asked the guys to stay."

"Oh?"

She gave him a playful little smirk. "I didn't want you *on duty*, so I asked if they'd stay." Abby hung air quotes around "on duty." She paused for a moment when she realized exactly how that sounded, but decided to forge ahead anyway. "I hope you don't mind, but I sort of wanted to hang out with Danny Nucci and not Mr. Bodyguard. That is if you can be just you for a few hours." She left that as a challenge.

He grinned. "That works. I'll bring them their food. Where are they hiding?"

"We actually passed them. The first door on your left." She pointed back to the hallway.

"I'll be right back."

"I'll be in the living room. Do you want a beer?"

"Yes, please."

Abby handed Danny the pizzas for Freddie and King,

then piled the dishes and silverware on top of the remaining pizza box. She had been so worried he'd object, but it seemed as though he was all for spending personal time with her, time when he wasn't on the clock and she wasn't just a job. Her small smile turned into a grin. Maybe this could really go somewhere.

"Let me help." Danny had snuck up on her. He grabbed the remaining pizza, the plates, and silverware.

"I'll be right behind you. I'll just get our drinks." Abby grabbed the six-pack and an open bottle of pinot grigio from the fridge and balanced the two, along with a wine glass, in her hands and followed him to the living room. She set everything on the coffee table. "Here." She handed Danny the TV remote. "Pick something to watch from Netflix."

"What are you in the mood for?"

"I don't care."

"Really?"

"Yeah, pick away." She placed two slices of pizza on a plate and put it in front of him.

"It smells delicious."

"It's one of my favorites in the area. I called them earlier because they're usually busy in the summer."

"Smart thinking. Okay, get ready to laugh."

"*The Naked Gun*?"

"Ever seen it?"

"No."

"Then I'll repeat myself. Get ready to laugh."

Abby served herself, sat back on the couch, and dug in.

* * *

The movie was funny, and Abby found herself, on more than one occasion, wiping away tears of laughter from her eyes.

"Told you," Danny said, triumphant.

"You did." She picked up her wine glass. It felt good, having him here and laughing at a goofy movie. It was almost like it was when they hung out late nights on the bus. Abby and Danny would stay up long after everyone else had gone to bed and just watch whatever they could find on the TV, or they'd pop in some movie that they'd seen a million times before.

"I'm really glad you asked me here tonight," he said.

Feeling shy, she blushed and looked down at her glass. "Same here." She met his gaze. Could she take the plunge and let him in on how she was feeling? Would he turn her down? Or was Sophie and Ms. Sohm right? Did he really have feelings for her? Now or never. "So, I've had a few incredibly exciting weeks, and I learned a lot about myself. I've never had to think for myself. I know I'm going to make mistakes, but that's okay because I can do it. And I've figured out at least one thing that I want."

"What's that?"

She swallowed, her mouth suddenly parched. This was it. Could she do it? She inched closer to him, her eyes automatically traveled to his alluring, full lips. Her breath quickened while her whole body began to tingle with desire. "You." Her voice came out breathy and needy.

In a rush of boldness she leaned over and grabbed Danny's shirt to pull him toward her. His eyes widened, but he didn't pull away. She leaned in.

The boldness she felt a second ago melted away when she thought of King and Freddie looking on. With the exception of the bathrooms and her bedroom, the entire house was wired with monitors.

"The cameras…"

He smiled. "If they want to keep their jobs, they'll have shut them off by now."

"Oh." His comment surprised and delighted her. She bit her lip to hide her smile.

Before she could say thank you, Danny pulled her toward him and covered her mouth with his. She hesitated for only a moment before allowing Danny's tongue entrance, and her body relaxed as his right hand pushed her hair away from her face. His kiss ignited a fire in her. Her hands traveled up his hard biceps, something that she had wanted to do for a long time, and eventually found their way into his hair to pull him closer. His arms tightened around her waist, and it felt so good and so right.

Why had she been so nervous?

He peppered chaste kisses down her neck until he

buried his face there and held her in a tight hug.

"I've wanted to do that for a long time," he said softly.

"Same here," she confessed.

* * *

"It's getting late," Danny murmured softly as he kissed the top of Abby's head. She was tucked tightly into his side, a spot he didn't want her to move from, but he had to leave.

"You could stay here," she said quietly, and her cheeks turned a delightful shade of pink.

Danny tightened his grip on her shoulder as he thought about the meaning behind her words and the blush creeping up her face. He was tempted. "I have an early meeting and no clothes."

She turned her face and looked up at him with the cutest pout he'd ever seen. He wanted to give in to her but knew staying wasn't a good idea. Not yet. He didn't want to rush things.

"So you think you might come back?" She sounded a little uncertain. "Tomorrow?"

"I'd like nothing more than to come back. But aren't you recording?"

"Yes, but I'd love for you to hear what we're working on. You'll get to meet Aisling, Jax, and the rest of her crew."

"I'd love that."

"It's Friday, so maybe we can go out after."

"Sure. Whatever you want. Just let me know so I can call a few more guys out here to check out the restaurant and make sure we'll be able to handle the weekend shore crowds. Depending where you want to go, it can get out of hand quickly."

Abby opened her mouth and closed it. He could tell she had something on her mind.

"What's wrong?"

"You know how I asked the guys to stay tonight so you didn't have to be Mr. Bodyguard and distracted? Can we do that tomorrow? I'd like to hang out with you, not him." She smiled.

"It's not that simple. I can't just turn off my instincts." He needed to explain why but not now. He needed a minute to think how to tell her about his past. About Vanessa. Damn. Her smile faded.

"I understand," she said, but judging from her tone, she didn't like it. "But I want to spend time with you. I don't want you to work. I don't want to be your job."

"You have a good point. I'll try." He cupped her face and lifted it so he could look into her light blue eyes. "I can't make you any promises about that, but I'll try."

"Thank you." She leaned into his hand and closed her eyes.

"I'll see you tomorrow."

She opened her eyes and no longer looked sad. They sparkled with excitement. "Yes. Come whenever you want. We'll be in the studio most of the afternoon and into the evening."

He stood and pulled her into his embrace.

"Will you call me when you get home? There are crazies on the road this time of night."

"I will." He smiled into her hair.

He took her hand and walked to the front door. "Sweet dreams, Abby." Danny bent down and placed a light kiss on her lips.

"Night."

He unlocked the door and turned. "Lock up behind me."

"Yes, sir." She winked.

He smiled and waited until the door had closed and he heard the lock engage before he returned to his car. He got inside and started the engine with a huge smile on his face.

chapter
twenty-six

Abby showered and changed into a pale-blue, tailored men's nightshirt. She opened her bedroom window for the cool night breeze. She loved sleeping with the window open because she was able to hear the waves hitting the shoreline. The smell of salt water floated into her room, and Abby shut off all the lights except for one small lamp.

She opened her bedside table drawer and grabbed her notebook. She'd stopped journaling during all the crazy Sean drama occurred. Since she arrived at the beach, she'd started to write nearly every night before bed. She used the time to work on new ideas and melodies, but tonight, she sat and stared at the blank page before her. She'd finally done it. She'd kissed him. And he'd kissed her back. She wanted more. Much more. She had no idea how long she'd been sitting there thinking about that kiss and what more would be like when her phone rang.

She checked the screen and smiled. *Danny*. "Hi," she answered. She glanced at her alarm clock; it was nearly one o'clock in the morning.

"Hey, I just got home."

"Did you hit any traffic?" Abby had worried about him

traveling back to the city at such a late hour.

"No, it was pretty clear." Danny yawned.

"Good." She was smiling so much her cheeks hurt.

"I had a great time tonight."

"Me, too." She admitted. Gah, she totally wanted to squeal like a teenage girl.

"So...I'll see you tomorrow. Well, technically tonight," he joked.

"Yes, tonight." She laughed softly into the phone.

"Okay. Um, I'm going to get some sleep. Good night."

"'Night." She hung up and set her notebook aside. Once again her thoughts drifted back to Danny. His smile, his laugh, and the way he smelled—clean with the soft, musky undertones of his cologne. And she thought about how he wrapped his arms around her as though he wanted to keep her safe and about the sharp tug of desire when he brushed his lips against hers.

Inspiration hit her, and she grabbed her notebook and started writing. The lyrics spilled out of her and onto the pages.

* * *

It was pushing three in the afternoon when Danny exited the Garden State Parkway on his way to Abby. He'd enjoyed such a great night with her, and all the doubt he'd had about Abby's feelings for him evaporated the moment his lips touched her.

Still, if he was honest with himself, he was anxious about tonight. He needed to open a door that he had shut firmly years ago. Before anything went further, he wanted to lay it all out there for Abby. She deserved to know about Vanessa. He didn't want secrets, and then maybe she'd understand why he held himself back.

"Hey, boss." Freddie was sitting outside.

"Are the rest of the guys here?"

"Just pulled in twenty minutes ago."

"Good. Where's King? He scanned the neighborhood looking for anyone or anything that seemed amiss.

"Control room."

Danny gave a quick chin lift of acknowledgement and then proceeded up the walkway. Everything looked good. He punched the code in the door, slipped inside, and headed straight to the control room.

"King, gotta minute?" He took his sunglasses off.

"Sure. How was the trip?"

"Fucking traffic was insane, as usual." Danny wasn't a fan of sitting in bumper-to-bumper traffic, but he wasn't about to say no to Abby, not when things were progressing between them.

"What's up?" King turned toward Danny.

"I want you on lead tonight."

"No problem. Aaron and John just got here. They're heading out in five to get the lay of the land for the restaurant and the bar."

"Good. Abby asked me to take a backseat for the night." He crossed his arms in front of him, feeling a bit awkward talking about this sort of stuff with King.

"Don't worry, boss. I got it covered."

"Keep me posted if I should know anything."

"Absolutely."

Danny clapped King on the back and went to the studio.

* * *

When Danny entered the studio, he heard Abby's melodic voice coming through the speakers. He was amazed at how rich and soulful she sounded. Definitely a departure from her previous work. He didn't want to interrupt, so he stayed near the door and watched Abby in her element.

Her vocals were spot on, and she was clearly enjoying herself. This was so different from the only other time he'd watched her in the studio. That time, she went in, belted out the vocals to go with the musical scores that were previously recorded, and then left. It was a very clean, brief experience that lacked emotional resonance the same as most business transactions.

Now, though, he watched as she suggested alternative

arrangements. It looked like she was really embracing her new role. She sang with her eyes closed, her hands extended, and her whole body vibrating with the power of the song. Danny was transfixed.

"That's a wrap on this one. Ten minute break?" Some guy called out.

Abby agreed, and then she removed her headphones and made her way to the door.

"Has my phone buzzed at all?" Abby asked as she walked out of the recording booth. Then she noticed Danny. "Oh, hey, you're here." Her face lit up as she walked over to him.

"Hey," he smiled and pulled her into his arms. "I missed you," he whispered in her ear.

She tightened her hold and looked up at him, "Me, too. How long have you been here?"

"Long enough to hear you. That was amazing." Danny smiled.

"I'm having so much fun." Her happiness was apparent on her face, in the curve of her mouth, the sparkle in her eyes, and the way she almost vibrated with excitement. Joy radiated from her.

"I can tell."

"Wanna meet everyone?" Abby pointed to the group in the control room.

"Absolutely."

Abby took his hand and led him into the next room. It

was spacious and packed with recording equipment, couches, and people.

"Hey, all. I just wanted to introduce you to Danny. Danny this is Aisling and Jax her co-producer and assistant. Then over here we have Misha, Tami, Anja, and Loredana. Poor Jax is the only guy on the team."

"It's not so bad, and Abby makes the experience bearable."

Abby laughed, and Jax winked. Danny stifled a growl. He did not want anyone else winking at Abby, especially not this guy. He slipped his arm around Abby's shoulders and stepped just a little closer to her.

"Nice to meet you, Danny," Aisling extended her hand. "I've heard a lot about you."

"Abby's said nothing but fantastic things about you. If the rest of what you're doing sounds like what I just heard, I'm sure you'll have no problem with getting the record company to pick it up." Danny complimented.

"We've sent a few songs their way and all's good so far." Abby smiled.

Danny squeezed her shoulder. "That's awesome."

"Right. Okay, we'll be back in ten. Um, maybe twenty minutes."

"Girl, if you want to cut the session short, no biggie. It's Friday, after all." Aisling gave her a knowing smile. Danny liked her.

"You sure?"

"Yeah, don't sweat it." Aisling waved them away.

"Okay. Then we're out," Abby said.

"Nice meeting you all." Danny waved and followed Abby out of the studio. He managed to not glare at Jax, but only because he got distracted by the sway of Abby's hips as she walked.

* * *

"Can I get you anything?" Abby poured the boiling water in a cup and dunked her teabag in it. She always drank ginseng with honey and lemon after singing; it soothed her throat.

"I'm good for now."

"Okay, but help yourself if you change your mind. You know how to navigate through a kitchen." She laughed nervously. "Better than I do, that's for sure."

"Don't worry. I'll make myself at home."

"Yes, please do." She finished making her tea and joined Danny at the table. She sat there in silence, waiting for something to pop in her head. She felt so shy around him all of a sudden.

"I can't do this," she blurted.

"Huh? Can't do what?"

"This. Small talk. I don't know. I'm really nervous. I'm sitting here trying to think of something to say and I come up blank. All I can think is how glad I am that you're here." She let out a breath and felt better having confessed her fear.

His shoulders relax. "It's okay. This is new for the both of us."

She looked into his warm, brown eyes, and still she had nothing to say. She didn't get this far only to have her nerves get the better of her did she?

"Look. Relax. It's just you and me. Abby and Danny. The same Abby and Danny who spent the last year together on a bus watching corny movies, playing board games, and eating crap diner food across the country. We never had a problem talking then."

"No, we didn't."

"In fact, we've probably spent more time together than the average couple that's been seeing each other for years."

"True." They'd spent a lot of time joking, laughing, and getting to know each other. "I feel kind of silly."

"Why?"

"Well, because we have hung out so much. Seems silly that I'm so nervous."

"It's not silly. I'm a bit nervous too. We'll figure it out."

He was feeling the same way too? That made a bit of Abby's nerves settle. It seems that they were both worried about the same things. "Okay, we have a reservation, so I'm going to head upstairs and get ready."

"Sounds good. Don't mind me. I like kitchens."

She smacked him playfully on the arm. "Back in a few." Abby left Danny waiting for her. Now, what to wear? Man, she wished Sophie were here.

Finally, Abby was dressed and ready, but Danny wasn't where she left him. She had an idea where he would be. She knocked on the door off the kitchen. Danny opened the door to the command center.

"Uh-huh. I thought only women gossiped," Abby teased, raising her eyebrows.

"Could you have given them a smaller room?" Danny pulled her against him and kissed the side of her head. "You look amazing," he whispered so low she doubted anyone else heard. Sparks raced up her back, and she thought about doing a lot of other things that didn't involve going to dinner.

She'd chosen a scoop neck navy blue maxi dress that faded in color as it reached the floor. It was fitted but not skintight. She paired it with sexy, high-heeled, nude-colored sandals with one thick strap across the toes and one around the ankle. She'd finished the look with a plain gold bracelet on her wrist.

She rolled her eyes. "I didn't pick this room. They could've had any room. I even offered to have a room built for them." She shifted in Danny's arms to look at King. "That offer still stands, too. But you'll have to talk to Sophie about it. She's the queen of resources and numbers."

"It is something to think about," Danny said. "If we do something like that, I'd like to talk to you about other security measures."

She looked up at him. "Whatever. If you want to talk

business with me, Mr. Nucci, you'll need an appointment. Tonight, you're off duty."

"Fair enough. I'll talk to Sophie."

"That's what I like to hear. Let's go." She pulled him down the hall to the front door.

* * *

Abby scanned the intimate restaurant as the waiter filled their glasses with water. The manager had seated them in a remote part of the dining room, and King and Freddie sat a few tables away. They were close enough to see, but not hear. She wondered what they thought of Danny and her together. She knew Sophie was ecstatic when she told her. She said something along the lines of "about fucking time you got your head out of your ass."

"I'll leave you to look over the menu." The waiter held out the menu for Abby to take.

"Thank you."

After a few minutes, Danny asked, "Do you know what you'd like?"

She blushed.

"Time for that later," he said with a sexy little smile.

"Oh, you mean dinner. Yes. What about you?"

"Yes." He waved the waiter over.

"Ready to order sir?"

"Yes, we are." He looked at Abby.

"I'd like the fresh mozzarella and tomato for an appetizer."

"The caprese." The waiter clarified.

"Yes. I can never say that right." She laughed. "I hate to mess it up." She heard Danny chuckle but ignored him. "For my entrée I'd like the penne alla vodka with grilled chicken, and a glass of white wine. sauvignon blanc, please."

"Excellent. And for you, sir?"

"I'll have the stuffed mushrooms for an appetizer, and for the entrée, I'll have the eggplant rollatini. Could you make the sauvignon blanc a bottle, please?"

"Absolutely."

"Thanks." He handed the menu to the waiter, who took Abby's as well before he left the table.

"Are you okay?" Abby asked. "You seemed distracted on the way over."

"Actually, I have something I wanted to share with you, and I admit I'm kind of nervous about it."

"You can tell me anything. I hope you know that."

"I do…But it's not something I share often, and it's definitely not a time in my life I like to relive."

The waiter arrived with their wine. Abby waited while he poured a sample into Danny's glass and waited for his approval. Danny nodded, and the waiter filled both of their glasses with her favorite wine. The show was all a bit too much for Abby. Right now all she wanted was to know what was making Danny nervous. Maybe he was having second thoughts?

When the waiter left, Danny took a swallow of wine, as if preparing himself. "Okay, you know Connor and I are Army buddies."

She hesitated a moment but then nodded, wondering what he was going to tell her. Abby hadn't expected him to talk about Connor or the Army. She took a drink from her own glass and tried to get a handle on her rising level of anxiety.

"What you don't know is it wasn't just Connor and I that stuck together from basic training. There was a third person in our group."

"A third person?" He hadn't talked about the Army much when they were touring, but since Connor arrived, he'd shared a few stories. Neither of them had mentioned anyone else. It was always just fun little stories about Danny and Connor. Why was this the first time hearing about a third person? Where did he go? Oh no, maybe he was killed? It was war after all. God, how awful. "Oh. I'm sorry. Did you lose somebody in combat?"

"No, not in combat. Her name was Vanessa." He paused and took a deep breath. "She and I were together…for a long time."

"Together?" Abby rolled that around in her mind. "As in, seeing each other?"

"Yeah."

"I thought that wasn't allowed in the military." She didn't know that, actually, but she had to say something, and that was the only thing that made it past the sudden, unexpected wave of jealousy. She sat a little straighter in her chair; she wasn't proud of her desire to fight off this previously unknown threat to her new and still vulnerable relationship with Danny. Sure, she'd been involved with Sean for the past couple years, but that wasn't the same. She tried to smile at Danny, to encourage him to continue, but she wasn't looking forward to *this* conversation.

"We were the same rank, so it was okay."

"Oh." She didn't really know what to say and was a little confused about why he was telling her this. But if it was important to him, she'd do her best to listen. She paused before asking, "What happened to her?"

"She had a stalker."

"Oh, God." And it was as if a light bulb turned on for Abby. That was why he was so intense about Sean. Had to be. He had been through this before. Where was Vanessa now? Was she okay?

"He was someone she worked with often," Danny said quietly. He stared at her, his gaze vulnerable and darkly intense.

Abby sucked in a shocked breath. "How? Why?" And of course the waiter picked that moment to bring them their appetizers. Danny thanked him, and Abby took a moment to collect herself. This new information explained a lot about Danny, but that didn't mean she was prepared to hear more about it.

"He was a Private, and they worked closely together. Apparently he thought their working relationship was

362

something more."

"She didn't tell you?"

"No."

She heard the pain behind his words.

"Vanessa kept it all from me, and by the time I realized, it was too late. Looking back, there were signs, but I was so focused on our mission, I didn't see them. She thought she could do it all, and that she could handle anything that came her way."

"Too late?"

"He killed her." He said through clenched teeth and averted his gaze. His eyes were shiny with unshed tears.

"I'm so sorry." God, that sounded so wrong, but she didn't know what else to say. This all seemed too familiar for her. She could have been Vanessa. She almost was. If it hadn't been for a little luck, Abby wouldn't be here now. She knew she'd been fortunate, but in that moment, she realized just *how* fortunate. At the time, she'd understood enough to be afraid, but it was a generalized, muted fear that came from realizing she was vulnerable. She'd never actually thought she could die. And she'd had no idea how much it had affected Danny. Fuck, she'd been so clueless.

"Can you understand now why I asked you to be honest with me and not keep me in the dark? I can't lose you like I lost her. She thought she could handle him, or maybe she thought he'd get the hint and back off. I'm not sure. What I do know is *if* I had known, she'd still be here. I could have protected her."

Everything made sense, now. The way he reacted and how he tried to deal with her. She stared at him. "I'm sorry," she said again.

"You didn't know, and I'm not big on sharing it." Danny shrugged. "But I thought that you deserved to know."

"I really screwed up." She fought back her emotions. How could she have been so blind?

"How did you screw up?"

"I should've told you what Sean was doing as soon as I started getting those calls and messages. Maybe if I did—"

"Hey. It's done." He reached over and took her hand in his. "But now you know why I am the way I am. I'd lose my mind if something happened to you."

"Well, I learned my lesson." Maybe Sean would've been arrested much sooner if she'd told Danny what was happening.

"Stop it," Danny said.

"What?"

"Guilt-tripping yourself. Everything worked out, and it's okay, now. I didn't tell you this to upset you. I just wanted you to know and to maybe understand me a bit better."

She nodded in agreement. There wasn't really anything she could say to that.

"Now eat. Before our main course comes. Don't let this great food go to waste."

She took a deep breath and let it all go, before she picked up her fork, cut into the mozzarella and tomato, and took a bite. "Mmm, this balsamic glaze is delicious. Want to try some?"

"You'd share that?"

"Only if you give me a mushroom."

"I see how you are." He laughed and speared a mushroom and handed her his fork. Abby took it and thought that right then, she didn't want to be anywhere else.

chapter
twenty-seven

Freddie stopped in front of the bar where they were meeting Aisling. She had texted earlier and invited Abby and Danny to join her at Sand and Salt, a small, but busy little bar located on the beach. King exited the car, but Abby and Danny waited for the all clear. There was a light mist of rain so there weren't too many people loitering outside, but once they saw Abby that could change.

"Let's do this," Abby heard King instruct the guys before he opened the car door. Danny slid out first, and she followed. She'd hoped he'd act like a guy on a date rather than her bodyguard, but instead of grabbing her hand or placing his arm over her shoulder, he joined the men in protecting her. No matter which way she looked there was a body blocking anyone else from getting close.

They entered as a group, and her detail led her up a narrow staircase to the second floor. They continued through a small crowd to a roped-off area that seemed to be a makeshift VIP lounge with a few bouncers dedicated to crowd control. Danny grabbed her hand, and she was finally able to take in her surroundings.

The room's light blue walls, nautical pictures, and accessories made it feel like a ship, especially with the dim lighting. The bar was outside the roped off area. Ordering drinks would be inconvenient, but not really her concern. The back wall was entirely made up of floor to ceiling windows, with a wooden deck on the other side. No one was outside due to the weather, but the view was spectacular.

She searched for the restroom sign and found it was tucked away toward the back of the bar. Luckily, not down a secluded hallway. She didn't know if she'd ever get over that fear, but she felt safe with Danny here. He would protect her and knowing that filled her with a warm sense of security.

Aisling and her gang were already partying, and from the number of empty bottles on the table, Abby doubted they'd have a recording session tomorrow.

Danny pulled her against his side, "I'm gonna grab a beer. Do you want anything?" He murmured in her ear. His breath tickled her neck.

"A Malibu Bay Breeze, please." She looked up and tilted her head so that she could give him a chaste kiss, but Danny had other ideas. He slipped his tongue inside her mouth and caressed hers. She tangled her fingers in his hair, pulled him closer, and let out a soft moan as arousal surged through her.

Danny quickly broke the kiss. "I'll be right back," he said with a knowing smile.

Bastard. He knew what he'd done to her. She watched his ass until she couldn't see him anymore.

"Holy fuck, girl I need a fan, and I think you need a room." Aisling smirked at her. Abby fought a blush and tried to shrug nonchalantly. Aisling gave her a knowing look and laughed. "I take it things are going good."

Abby smiled. "You could say that."

"Uh-huh. I don't have to. That smile says it all."

"Do you think we can cancel this weekend's sessions? I want to rest my voice."

Aisling laughed. "Oh, right. Rest your voice. Mmm hmm."

Abby's face flushed with heat. So much for not blushing. But when it came down to it, she didn't care who knew how she wanted to spend the weekend. None of that mattered compared to the thought of Danny doing…stuff.

"We'll start up again on Monday. But right now we need to party. Come on." She grabbed Abby's hand and brought her onto the dance floor.

After a few songs Abby looked around for Danny. He was tucked in a corner booth. "I'll be back," she shouted over the music. She left the floor and made a beeline toward him.

"Scoot over." She nudged him. He adjusted, and she slid into the seat next to him and put her head on his shoulder. Danny pulled her closer.

"Why are you over here?" she asked.

"I don't dance."

She laughed. "I bet I can make you."

"That's one bet I'll take."

"What do I get if I win?" She batted her eyes innocently at him.

"What would you like?"

"I'm sure I can think of something." She sipped on the fruity beverage.

"I can, too." He looked at her, his eyes dark and intense.

She played with the straw in her drink. It took all the will power she had not to jump him right then and there. She heard a familiar voice and looked up to see Aisling standing in front of her.

"I'm stealing your girl." Aisling hooked her hand around Abby's wrist and pulled her to her feet.

Abby bent down, gave Danny a quick peck on the cheek, and then let Aisling drag her away. They danced and laughed for quite a long time. She enjoyed letting go without worrying about how she should act or if her mother would bitch at her the next day. It was liberating, and she wanted more of it.

Jax joined their little group and was his goofy self. They danced and laughed like they had done before. He innocently flirted with her. Jax was a player, but it was fun to just let go. Besides, she didn't expect anything to come of his flirting since he didn't really mean it and she didn't really want it.

She laughed and twirled around and bumped into a wall that hadn't been there before. Except it wasn't a wall. It was Danny.

"Hey," she smiled up at him.

He pulled her closer to him.

"You changed your mind?"

He didn't look very happy to be standing there. In fact, he wasn't even looking at her. He was staring at Jax. *Shit.* Abby suddenly felt guilty for dancing with Jax. She hadn't thought about it at all. She was just having fun.

"Come on, dance with me. Please?" she begged.

"I don't dance."

She wasn't going to take no for an answer. She called on her inner sexy goddess and tugged on his hand to stop him from sitting down. With her other hand she pulled on his belt to bring him closer to her and pressed her body tight against his. He gathered her in his arms, and she turned in his embrace so she could slide her ass up and down his growing erection.

Abby twirled back around until they were face to face and was struck by his intense expression. He tightened his grip on her waist, and her breasts pressed against his chest. She stared into his smoldering brown eyes and licked her lips. God, she wanted him.

"Baby, don't start something we can't explore," he said, voice husky, before he leaned down and covered his mouth with hers. This kiss wasn't like any of the ones they'd shared before. It was intense, and she could taste his need mixed with hers.

When he finally broke their connection, Abby couldn't catch her breath. She rested her head on his chest as she inhaled deeply and tried to pull herself together.

"Damn. I'm going to go freshen up." She looked up into his heated eyes. "And maybe splash some cold water on my face."

"I'll be right here waiting."

Abby turned to leave. King stood nearby, ready to escort her. She looked back at Danny, and he was smiling. He was still being Mr. Bodyguard, but a damn cute one.

"Ladies room, please."

She followed King out of the roped area before the other men joined them. They checked the bathroom before giving her the all-clear and waited outside while she took care of business.

When she stepped out of the bathroom, she signaled to King that she wanted to stop at the bar. He and the others accompanied her.

"Can I get an ice water, please?" she asked the handsome bartender.

"Just a moment." He took care of another order before getting her water.

"Thanks." She took the water and made her way back to Danny. A drunk guy stopped them along the way. He tried to reach her but only succeeded at knocking her glass of water from her hands. The glass shattered when it hit the floor, and water splashed in a wide arc, soaking her ankles.

After that, everything happened in a blur. King moved toward the guy, but Danny appeared out of nowhere and pulled him from the area before King could reach him. The entire incident lasted no more than thirty seconds. She didn't understand how Danny could have made it to them that fast, especially since there had been a pretty decent sized crowd between them.

"This way." King's voice interrupted her confusion.

She nodded and followed him back to the VIP area. Patiently, she waited for Danny to return while Freddie hovered at their table. She kept her eyes on the staircase and noticed him right away when he hit the second level. He didn't come directly to her, instead went to King. Judging by his gestures and the hard expression on his face, Danny was not a happy man. Why? The guy hadn't even touched her. He touched her glass; that was it.

She never felt as is she was in danger. They had the situation under control and Danny was overreacting. When he broke away and started toward her, she turned away.

"I got this." She heard Danny's cool voice dismiss Freddie. "Are you okay?" he asked her.

"No."

"No? Are you hurt?" He sat down beside her and reached for her hand. She pulled it away.

"I'm not hurt. I'm mad."

"Mad?"

"Yes."

"I know that guy was out of line, Abby. I got to him as quick as I could."

Was he really that clueless? "I agree; he was out of line. But I'm not upset about that."

"What, then? Because from what I see I had every right to step in."

"Oh, then you're my bodyguard tonight?"

"Abby, I can't just shut this off. I explained this tonight. Keeping you safe isn't just a job to me."

She sighed, frustrated that she wasn't getting through, and he didn't seem to be open to hearing anything that meant he might be wrong.

"I understand we will have a bit of a learning curve with," she motioned back and forth with her hand, "whatever *this* is, but you have to at least try not to step in every time. You need to decide. Are you my employee or are you my date? Because at the end of the day, I'm not taking my employee to bed. Now you have to decide what you want."

He deflated a bit. "I'm trying."

"Try a little harder. Please." She paused. "I know we need to figure this out. I don't expect our transition from business to personal to be without some bumps. I'm not sure how you feel, and maybe it's too soon for me to lay it all out there, but finding this," she rested her hand on his chest, "*finding us* has been the most amazing thing for me. I finally feel like I'm where I'm supposed to be."

She waited for him to say something, but he didn't so she continued.

"You get all of this crazy I live in, and you accept it. You allow me to be me. You *encourage* me to be me. I couldn't have dreamt of a better man to be with. After we talked tonight, I understand you more and can appreciate how difficult it is to let someone else be in charge, but if you really want this to work, then you need to figure out how to do that. I know there will be times when you'll have to take the lead, but tonight is *not* one of them."

He remained silent.

She let out a frustrated breath. "I need air. Let me out." She waited for him to move. "Please."

He got up, and she scooted over on the seat.

"King?" she called.

He was next to her in an instant. She figured after he got his ass chewed out, she'd have to deal with him hovering, too. "Yes?"

"I need air."

"You got it."

King walked Abby out onto the deck, and she waited while he took a look around.

"All clear."

"Thanks. Do you mind if I have a minute to myself?"

He blanched. "I don't know. With what just happened."

"Just a little bit."

He relented. "I'll have Freddie man the other entrance, and I'll take this one."

"Thanks."

She headed to the end of the deck and let the misty sea air wash away her tension. Staring out into the dark night and hearing the waves break, she thought about what had happened. Did she miss something that only Danny saw? She had a limited view, but she didn't really have any contact with the man. She couldn't even remember what he looked like.

She heard the door close behind her and knew Danny was outside because no one else would be allowed onto the balcony with her. But she didn't turn around.

He came up behind her and slid his arms around her waist. She tried to hold on to her anger for just a little longer, but couldn't. Finally she leaned back and rested her head against his chest. She closed her eyes. She didn't want to argue with him, but this had to be addressed now before they'd be able to move on. They needed to understand each other and establish some ground rules.

"I'm sorry," he whispered and kissed the side of her head.

"Me, too." She turned to face him and wrapped her arms around his waist. "I think we still need to talk about this. I know taking a step back is hard, but I don't want another keeper. I've had too many years of that."

"I'm not your keeper, Abby. I just need you to be safe."

"You're going to have to do a better job of not acting that way. I'll work on figuring it out, too. Maybe you, me, Sophie, and King could sit down and talk it out. I don't know. I'm so terrified of falling back into bad habits."

"That won't happen, but I agree a sit-down is needed. This is new for me, and I need to make sure everyone on my team is all on the same page."

Abby tightened her hold around his waist and closed her eyes. It was a new situation for both of them, and she needed to show a little patience and understanding, and she was willing to do that. As long as Danny knew how she felt and was mindful of it, she was fine with whatever adjustments and meetings that had to take place to get them to a point where this wasn't an issue.

"Do you want to go back inside or are you ready to go?" Danny's voice broke her reverie.

"I'd like to stay for a little while longer."

"Okay, let's go dance." Danny sounded resigned.

"Ha! If only." Abby laughed at his tone.

"Well, I might try some new things now and again."

"Oh, really?" She looked up at him and smiled.

"Really." He held out his hand. She took it and let him lead her inside.

chapter
twenty-eight

"Hey sleepyhead, we're here." Danny murmured in Abby's ear.

"Hmm?"

"You're home."

"Oh." She opened her eyes and realized they were in her driveway. "I guess I fell asleep." She turned to face Danny.

"Let's get you inside." Danny helped Abby out of the car, took her hand, and she followed him to the door.

"I had a great time tonight."

"Me, too." After the "water incident," the rest of the night had been a lot of fun. They danced, laughed, and even found a moment to just talk about things. It was a start. A very good one. And she felt like they could really make a go of this. She leaned into his hand as he tucked her hair behind her ear.

"Good night, Abby." Danny's hand trailed down her neck.

"Don't go." She didn't want him to leave.

"It's late. I have a long drive home."

"Stay." She tugged on his shirt to convince him to follow her inside.

"You've had a few drinks tonight. I think I should—"

"I'm not drunk. I know what I want."

"What do you want?" he asked.

"You." She held her breath waiting for a response. Her nerves were getting the best of her.

She felt his feather light touch on her jaw, and her gaze immediately found his. His fingers continued their journey to her chin, and she instinctively stepped closer. His free hand wrapped around her waist and pulled her toward him until there was no space between them.

"You're sure?"

Tingles traveled up her spine with his intense stare.

"Yes," she rasped; her voice was thick with need.

"Come on." He tugged on her hand, and she followed him inside, across the living room, and up the stairs. Once at the top of the landing, Abby directed him to her bedroom. Danny pulled her into his arms as soon as they crossed the threshold. His light touch on her overheated skin drove her crazy. She wanted him, and he hadn't even kissed her yet.

She relaxed into his body and let her hands make the long slow trip up his sculpted arms. She pulled him down into a kiss, and he growled when her teeth grazed his bottom lip. He slowly guided them toward her bed until her legs hit the mattress. He lifted her up, and she wrapped her legs around his waist as he placed her gently on the bed. This was really happening.

"Lift your arms up," he whispered in her ear.

She obliged. Slowly his hands traveled up her thighs, hips, sides, and breasts as he pulled her dress up and over her head. The thin fabric of her bra was the only barrier between his hands and her flesh, and soon that was gone, too.

Her skin felt as if it were on fire. She was so turned on by his touch. Any lingering questions about if this was right vanished, and Abby surrendered.

He kissed, sucked, and nipped his way down her body. Taking his time. He didn't seem to be in any rush, but Abby was. She needed him...now.

Abby reached for him. He was still dressed, and she needed to fix that. She pulled at his T-shirt and freed it from his pants, but that was as far as she got. Danny gave her a wicked smiled as he pulled his shirt over his head and then continued to torture her with his hot, patient descent down her body. She lifted up onto her elbows and watched as he slowly devoted himself to learning every inch of her over-heated skin. When he got to the apex of her thighs, he hooked his fingers around the thin string of her thong and pulled them down her legs.

He stood at the foot of the bed, and her gaze raked his body as he took a condom from his pocket then removed his pants and boxers. A shiver of pleasure raced through her at the thought of what was to come. Abby licked her lips at the sight of his cock.

Abby opened her legs for Danny, and he covered her body with his. She loved the feel of his weight on hers. She felt safe and adored.

"Oh, God," she said with a moan as his mouth covered her taut nipple. She pushed closer to him. She wanted—no, needed—more contact with him. He stopped and stared at her with hooded eyes. Tentatively she placed her fingertips on his face and traced the line of his jaw. She delighted in the texture of his skin beneath her touch. He let her explore, eyes closed, mouth partially opened. She leaned closer and captured his mouth with hers. It didn't take long to get lost in him.

"Please," she begged.

"All in due time." His voice only added to Abby's want. He was driving her crazy. She wanted this. She wanted him.

She'd waited a long time, and she was ready. He lifted her pussy toward his mouth. His tongue skimmed over her clit, and she gasped. She arched into his touch, begging for more. He continued to lick and suck, and her arousal soared. He feasted on her pussy.

"Oh God, Danny, more."

His tongue continued its maddening rhythm as his fingers glided through her wetness.

"You're so wet," he said. "I love it."

"More."

She felt one, then two fingers slide inside, and her walls clamped down on them. His fingers glided in and out, stretching her, filling her. Her legs tightened around him as he continued to pump his fingers in and out. She was so close.

"Danny." She grabbed a fist full of his hair, and he stopped to look up at her. "Please don't stop."

He dipped his head to blow lightly over her clit and send wonderful shivers through her body. All she needed was the slightest touch from his mouth and she'd come. He didn't make her wait long until once again he was ravishing her, and she lost control completely. Her hips bucked, her legs stiffened, and the most wonderful wave of pleasure took over her body.

"Danny…Oh God…"

"Baby." He waited a bit and then moved up to kiss her. She rested beneath him, gathering herself. She wanted more. Much more.

"You okay?" he asked after a while.

"So good." She nuzzled his neck and felt another stirring deep inside. "I'm not done yet," she said.

"I'm not, either." He sat up and tore open the condom wrapper with his teeth. She watched as he positioned it over the tip of himself and rolled it down. When he was done, he leaned down, and as he kissed her, another wave of passion engulfed her. He dominated her mouth, and she moved so that he could position himself before he drove into her pussy.

Danny filled her, and a moan escaped her lips. It emerged from somewhere deep inside her to trip out her mouth without permission. He felt so good; pleasure coursed through her veins.

"Oh, fuck." He groaned against her neck as he rocked his hips. Her skin tingled as he plunged into her. She clutched his shoulders and met him thrust for thrust, digging her heels into the bed and panting.

"You feel so fucking good, baby," he said between gasps.

"Harder."

He pounded into her, and she swore he was swelling inside her, and she clamped down on him as another orgasm tore through her. He groaned his own pleasure moments later and collapsed on top of her. She wrapped her limbs around him and held on tight, enjoying the feel of him.

Danny rolled them over so Abby was on top. She nuzzled into his neck and kissed him right below his jaw. His grip around her waist tightened.

"That was amazing." Danny kissed her hair.

"Mmm hmm." *Amazing didn't even cover it,* she thought, but she was too exhausted to clarify. Abby had spent many nights dreaming of this moment, and it was so much better than she'd imagined. Danny was so attentive and giving.

He grinned, and the glint in his eyes told her he was quite pleased with himself. She wanted to roll her eyes at his smug look, but instead she snuggled closer. "I'll be right back," he whispered and then kissed her temple before moving her off him. Slowly she opened her eyes and admired his fine ass as he walked into the bathroom. A few minutes later he returned. He covered both of them and then wrapped his arms around her. She turned into him and tangled her legs with his and closed her eyes. Within a few minutes, she was sleeping securely in the arms of the man she was definitely, without a doubt, in love with.

* * *

"Hey," Danny said, his gruff voice near her ear.

"Mmm."

"Baby. Phone call."

Ugh. She took her phone from his hand. Danny's stubble tickled her neck as he kissed her. "Hello?"

"Girl, please tell me there's a really good reason for Danny to be answering your phone at this hour," Sophie asked.

"Um. A very good one." She held the phone away from her ear as Sophie whooped.

"Shit, you're going to blow out my eardrums."

"Oh my God, tell me I'm not imagining this. That I'm not still asleep and dreaming about my BFF and the man she's been secretly swooning over for nearly a year. Please God tell me this is reality."

"Swooning?"

Danny laughed and then coughed to cover it up. She poked him in the gut.

"Whatever. So this is for real?"

"As real as it gets." Abby was prepared this time for Sophie to start cheering again. She narrowed her eyes at Danny when he started to laugh again. "All right, the laughing at Abby's expense is done. Why the hell are you calling me at," she took the phone from her ear to check the time, "seven-thirty in the morning on a Saturday? Do you really have nothing else to do?"

"I was excited and wanted to call."

"Excited?" She sat up. She heard Danny's light chuckle but chose to ignore him. "About what?"

"Your offer."

Abby had been waiting on Sophie's answer, and it looked as if she was finally going to get it. "So you thought about it? You want to be my manager?"

"I did. I'm totally on board."

"Yes! This is going to be so amazing. I know it. You need to come here so we can celebrate. I have the entire day off."

"You *sure* you want company?" Sophie snorted into the phone with laughter.

"Shut up." And then Abby heard someone talking in the background. Someone who sounded a lot like Connor. "Mmm hmm. Kettle, I'd like my pot back please."

"I have no idea what you're talking about."

"Tell Connor I said hi and get your annoying ass over here. We'll have a barbeque and hang by the pool."

"I'm in, but I'll have to call Connor because he's not here."

"He totally is, so stop denying it."

"Whatever, see ya later." She hung up before Abby could continue teasing her.

Abby placed her phone on her bedside table and snuggled back below the covers with Danny.

"Hey." He tucked her hair behind her ear.

"Hey." She smiled.

"So, barbeque with O'Brian and Sophie," he said.

"Mmm, seems so. We need to go shopping."

"Yeah?"

"Yes."

"Too bad. I had other plans for us this morning," he said, trying to sound sad.

"Really? What?"

"Let me show you."

He rolled on top of her, and Abby let him show her exactly what plans he had in mind.

chapter
twenty-nine

The steaks were on the grill, Danny had a beer in his hand, and Abby was relaxing on a lounge chair by the pool. Life was pretty good. He closed the top of the grill and took a long swallow from his beer.

"How are those steaks coming along?" Connor patted him on the back.

"Another few minutes."

"Excellent. I think it's time for a swim." He discarded his shirt and cannonballed into the pool. He soaked both Abby and Sophie in the process.

Danny laughed as both women yelled at Connor for the unexpected shower.

"I saw you laugh, Nucci." Abby said as she came over and planted a kiss on his cheek. "I'm watching you."

Danny admired the view as she sashayed through the screen door and into the kitchen. Abby was wearing a pretty green halter-top bikini that accentuated all the positives. Danny particularly loved the bows that kept everything in its place.

Connor splashed again, and Danny jumped out of the

way. Connor nearly soaked Danny and the barbeque. "Connor, you done?"

"I am now."

"Watch the steaks. I'm going to help Abby bring the rest of the food out."

"Yeah, sure you are." Connor gave him a knowing smile.

Danny looked back at Connor and narrowed his eyes at him.

"Abby?" He called as he walked into the kitchen.

"In here," she called.

Danny went into the living room where Abby was pulling on a beige cover up that was lined with silver beads and hugged her curves. He took a moment to admire her.

"I can feel you ogling over there."

"I no longer have to hide my ogling anymore. I can ogle out in the open." He chuckled.

"Well then, ogle all you want." She laughed and freed her hair from underneath the cover up.

"Oh, I will," he promised. He took Abby by the waist and pulled her down with him onto the couch.

He turned them so that Abby's back was against the pillows before he captured her mouth with his and got lost in her sweetness.

"Ahem, am I interrupting anything here?" Connor asked.

Abby froze in Danny's arms.

"No, not at all." Danny added extra sarcasm.

"Well, when you have a spare minute, dinner's ready. Or I could get some popcorn and watch."

"Yeah, that's not going to happen." Danny got up and pulled Abby with him.

"Can't blame a man for trying," Connor said as he left. "Stop necking like teenagers and come out and eat."

"Whose idea was it to invite him here?" Abby asked as she followed Danny out of the room.

"Don't make me come back in there and separate you two." Connor poked his head out from the hallway.

Danny scowled at his friend. Unaffected by Danny's nasty look Connor laughed. At that Danny took off after him, and Abby decided she might have fallen for a teenager.

* * *

The rest of the day was filled with more childish antics that had Abby bent over in stitches from laughing so hard. She really enjoyed having Sophie and Connor over, and she was so excited for Sophie. Not only was her best friend about to start up her own management company, but she seemed happy with Connor.

They had a few minutes alone while they put away all the leftover food from the barbeque.

"Today was so much fun." Abby hugged Sophie.

"It was. We need to do this more often. It's nice to relax."

"Relax? You, Miss Workaholic are talking about relaxing. Are you feeling okay? I think all that sun got to you today."

"Hey, even I need a day once in a while to chill out."

"You do, and we should do this again. Maybe next weekend?"

"Sounds good. You know I love the beach." She looked past Abby at Danny. "Good night, Danny."

"Night. Safe trip home." Danny gave her a quick hug before she followed Connor to the car.

"Alone at last."

"Mm hm." Abby wrapped her arms around Danny and leaned her head on his chest. "Where are the guys? I don't think I saw them all day."

"Their job is to be ghosts until it's their job to *not* be one."

"I felt bad that I didn't offer them anything to eat."

"They ate. Don't worry."

"Okay." She hugged him tighter.

"It's time for bed."

"You think?"

"Oh, I know." Danny lifted her over his shoulder and headed straight to her bedroom.

* * *

Monday morning came way too soon, and Danny had to leave for the city. Abby dove back into her work, and before she knew it, Wednesday was upon her and she was missing Danny something awful. They talked a lot and texted often, but it wasn't the same. That night she went to sleep with her phone tucked close beside her because she hadn't heard from him since he said he had had an emergency he needed to attend to. She reached over and turned off her bedside lamp and did her best to find sleep.

She woke up, startled. "What—"

"Hi," Danny said in the dark. "Sorry. Go back to sleep."

She felt the bed dip, and then Danny's arms were around her as he spooned her.

"I missed you," she mumbled before she fell asleep again.

The next morning her bed was empty, and she thought she had dreamed Danny waking her up late last night, but when she turned over to his side of the bed, she found a note on his pillow.

Baby,

Sorry I woke you up last night. Text me when you're awake. Missing you.

Danny

She clutched the small piece of paper close to her heart. She sat up and reached for her phone. She opened up the text app.

Abby—*Morning.*

She brought her knees up to her chest and sat there waiting to see if he'd respond right away. *God, I'm acting like a schoolgirl.* The thought made her smile so hard her face hurt.

Danny—*Hey baby. Did you have a good night's sleep?*

Abby—*I did once I got over getting the shit scared out of me.*

She laughed because she totally didn't mind getting scared if the reward was Danny's arms around her.

Danny—*Sorry about that but I sure did enjoy the feel of you around me.*

Abby—*Oh, I'm not complaining. ;)*

Danny—*What are your plans today?*

Abby—*Recording. I think we're nearly done. You?*

Danny—*I got shit brewing here with a client. If I can get it resolved I'll be there tonight. If not, I'll see you tomorrow night.*

Abby—*KK*

Danny—*I'll try to call you later. Have fun today.*

Abby—*I'll miss ya.*

Danny—*Same here. Keep your phone close.*

She jumped out of bed, feeling like she was ready to conquer the world.

* * *

"Girl, you're on fire today." Aisling's voice echoed in Abby's headphones.

"Thanks. I feel like I'm in a zone." Abby said into the microphone.

"Well if this keeps up, I think we can call this baby a wrap tonight."

"Really?" Abby was in shock. They were really done? All these years she had dreamt of recording an album that was completely hers, and now she'd finished it.

"Fuck, yeah." Aisling sounded almost as excited as Abby felt.

"Awesome. Let's get to it." The end was in sight, and she wanted to get it completed.

It seemed like everyone was on fire today. They were flying through the songs, and Abby focused on the end game.

When Aisling and her crew left, Abby heated up some food and spent the evening relaxing on her deck. She looked out at the ocean and missed Danny. He hadn't called all day and only sent a brief text or two. The breeze off the water made it feel more like fall than summer, but with September around the corner, that was expected. Abby picked up her mug. It was filled with her favorite blend of tea.

She felt a bit lonely without Danny; after all, she didn't really see him last night. It was nearly eleven, and she had to face the possibility that he wasn't going to show tonight. She settled into the lounge chair and pulled her sweater tighter. A few minutes later, the back porch doors opened.

"Hey," Danny said.

She placed the mug on the small glass side table and dashed toward him. She jumped into his arms and held on tight as he swung her around the porch before setting her down and taking her hand.

"I thought I wouldn't see you tonight."

"King let me know you wanted to head back to New York, so I made sure I was here."

"Oh." She was surprised King had told Danny. "He stole my news."

"What news?"

"I'm done! Well, mostly. Now the mixing and post-production stuff needs to get done, but Aisling and I agreed we can do that in New York."

"Excellent. He didn't tell me any of that." Danny sat down in the chair Abby had vacated and took her with him.

"Good. Because I wanted to tell you." She relaxed into his lap and admired the peaceful ocean.

"You must be excited."

"I've been on a high all day. I can't believe that it's done *and* that it's a record full of songs that I created. I can't wait until it's released to the world."

"I'm so happy for you," he murmured into her ear and gave her a light kiss on the side of her head.

They were silent for a few minutes, and she looked out at the spectacular sky and reflected on how far she'd come in such a short time. She was happy that her relationship with Danny had come together naturally.

"What are you thinking about?" She whispered into his ear and snuggled closer.

"Us."

"What about us?"

"I'm so happy that we're together, and after everything you've been through, you still trusted me enough to take a chance."

"Of course I trust you. You and Sophie were the only people in my life that always have my back." She hesitated. She wanted to tell him how she really felt about him, but what if he wasn't ready yet?

"What's wrong?" He placed a finger under her chin and guided her gaze back to his.

"Nothing. It's just…" She took a deep breath and let her confession roll off her tongue. "I love you." She watched his face transform into a dazzling smile, and it gave her the courage to go on. "And finding us through all the chaos and crazy that my life has been has made all that other stuff worth it. I'm happier than I've ever been, and that's because of you. I…" She turned in his lap to straddle his legs. "I never thought I'd find someone like you. No one's ever cared about me for me. It's always about my fame and what they can get from me or gain from being around me. With you I know it's only about us, and that's worth more to me then fame or any amount of money."

"I love you too, baby," He whispered before capturing her mouth with his. She melted into him. He tightened his hold, and before she could protest, Danny was on his feet and walking them back into the house.

"I don't think your neighbors would appreciate the PDA."

She laughed as he closed the door and headed toward the stairs.

chapter thirty

By noon the next day, Abby was in Danny's car heading back to New York. King and his team acted as escorts in vehicles ahead of and behind them.

Abby phoned Sophie after receiving a text message from her a few minutes ago. "Hey, we're headed back now. What's up?"

"An executive at MTV called, and somehow they heard that you were recording new music. I explained how it was totally different than your current stuff. The whole 'new sound, new management, new you' kinda deal. They want you to open up the awards this year. I know we canceled everything after your attack, but I think it's a good idea. Plus you're up for a couple of awards."

They wanted her to be the opening act? *Awesome!*

"I like the idea but what do you think, Miss Manager?"

"I think it's the perfect platform for you to kick-off promotion. I have your photo shoot scheduled for Monday. We can conference call with Emma about maybe coming up with a new look to go with the 'new sound, new you' campaign we have going on." Sophie was in her element now.

"I agree, and I love the idea of the new look. Set up the call and add it to my calendar, please." Abby was nearly bouncing with excitement in her seat. She was going to perform her new music on the MTV awards. The idea of updating her look just sort of made sense too. And besides, Emma was a kick-ass stylist. Abby knew anything she'd come up with would totally rock.

"Of course. When will you be back in New York?"

"A few of hours if the traffic stays light. We're heading in the opposite direction of traffic so we might get lucky."

"Safe travels and let me know when you're back."

"You got it."

Abby placed her phone in the middle console between her and Danny.

"New look?"

She glanced at him. He was smiling at her while waiting for the traffic light to change.

"Maybe. Would you mind?"

"You could wear a sack, and I'd think you were the most beautiful woman I've ever laid eyes on."

"Flattery? Mr. Nucci, that might get you places." She unhooked her seatbelt and leaned over to kiss his cheek.

"Put your seatbelt back on, baby. The light just changed."

Abby did and relaxed into her seat while Danny drove them back into Manhattan.

* * *

When Monday rolled around, Abby left with King to meet Sophie, her stylist Emma, and her hair and make-up crew at Emma's office. Emma had styled Abby for the last two years. She was excited to see their ideas in person. They didn't have much time to pull a complete presentation together, but she had full confidence in them.

"I got you a tea, no milk." Emma handed Abby the steaming cup of coffee.

"Thanks." Abby sat down at the round conference table in Emma's office.

"Okay, here are some ideas on dresses for the event." Emma opened up her portfolio and dove into dozens of designs. They didn't come up for air until Abby selected a very sexy, floor length, black dress with a deep V-neck in the front and two thin straps that crisscrossed the back.

"Very cutting edge," Emma said. "I like it. I'll contact the designer and give them your measurements. Also, Amy's waiting in the studio to do your hair. Time for your transformation." Emma sat down at her desk and picked up the phone.

"Off to become a brunette or red head or who knows. Oh, what about silver. That seems to be all the rage." Abby laughed.

"Um. No." Emma and Sophie both looked at each other before answering in unison.

Abby laughed and left Emma's office. She turned right and moved down the long, narrow hallway until she reached the studio. It was a large room with several stations filled to the max with everything a hairdresser could ever dream about.

"I have a vision," Amy announced when Abby sat in the chair.

"I hope the vision is of me with fabulous hair," Abby teased.

"Ha! You'll soon find out."

"Do your worst, girl."

"You got it." Amy winked, and Abby closed her eyes, waiting to see what the stylist would come up with.

* * *

"Baby, where are you?" Danny called from the living room.

"In my room." She was searching for a light sweater to put on.

"How'd you make out today?"

"You tell me." She shook her hair out.

"Wow. I like. A lot." He took her in his arms. "I'm not sure what color it is, but it makes your eyes stand out." He bent down and claimed her mouth, and she willingly opened her lips to allow his tongue access.

"It's called black cherry." She explained breathlessly

without pulling out of the kiss. She loved the feel of his mouth against hers and didn't want to surrender the contact for even a moment.

"You look hot." He released her. "We need to go, otherwise I don't think we'll make it to dinner. Ready?"

"Yes."

They left through the garage exit. Per Emma's instruction, Abby was trying to avoid the press so that her new look wouldn't be unveiled until she hit the red carpet in a few days.

"What did you ladies decide on for dinner?"

"Sophie's cooking," Abby said with a straight face, but Danny's horrified expression made her laugh so hard she couldn't breathe.

"That's not funny. That's terrifying."

"Truth. But don't tell Sophie I said that." She hopped in the car and waited for Danny to get in before she continued. "I think she ordered an assortment of food from the local deli. Their food is really good."

"Thank God. I didn't feel like spending the night getting my stomach pumped."

"Ha, sad but true. How was your day?"

She listened while Danny chatted away about some new clients and how he finally resolved the issue that had kept him so busy over the last week or so. She loved to listen to him talk about work, but she loved the way he seemed to have adjusted to having King in charge of her security detail even more.

"No King tonight?"

"No. They all have the night off. It's just me protecting you. Hope I live up to your standards."

"My standards are quite high, Mr. Nucci."

"I'd expect nothing less." They were stopped at a traffic light, and she glanced his way. His gaze was heated and full of promise.

"Anyway…I do like King. He's on top of his shit, and I feel safe with him."

"He's very good. It's why I allowed him to take the lead. Connor is the only other person I'd trust with you. I want to talk to you about something before we get to Sophie's. This way we talk about it and then you let it go and have fun with your girl."

"Okay." Abby didn't like Danny's demeanor. Something was definitely up.

"I have an update on Sean and Kelly. They are both pleading not guilty. So unfortunately you might have to testify if it makes it to trial."

She groaned. "Great."

"Hopefully, the DA can get their lawyers to talk some sense into the two of them."

"I sincerely doubt that."

"We can keep our fingers crossed. I wanted to make sure you heard this from me."

"If I do have to testify, you'll be there, right?"

"Of course. I wouldn't let you go through that alone."

She relaxed a little. "I'll try to stay positive. I'm not thrilled to have to see either of them again, but I can do it if necessary."

"You don't have to do it today, so relax."

They walked into Sophie's Manhattan apartment, and Abby smelled something good heating in the oven.

"What's that I smell?"

Sophie emerged from the kitchen. "I'm heating up some appetizers. Mini quiches, pizza roll ups, and mini chicken parm balls."

"Chicken parm balls?" *Yes!* Chicken parmesan was one of Abby's favorites.

"Yeah I ordered them for you. There's a whole smorgasbord of food in the kitchen. Help yourselves. Hi, Danny."

Abby moved into the kitchen and filled a plate with a variety of foods, especially the chicken parm balls.

"Holy shit, look at your hair." Connor said as he entered the room, then he made a weird choking, coughing sound as he stifled a laugh.

Abby glared at him.

"It's purple," he teased.

"It is not. Are you color blind? Or do you need glasses, old man? It's called black cherry." Abby gave it to him right back. She was used to his teasing sense of humor by now.

"And I love it," Sophie said. "So leave my friend alone."

"Looks purple to me." Connor shrugged and piled food on his plate.

Danny playfully slapped Connor on the side of his head, and Abby laughed.

"It's a wonder you're still not single." Abby shook her head at him in mock annoyance and left for the living room.

"He might be after tonight," Sophie added with a little laugh as she followed Abby.

"Pfft, you'd be crazy to leave all this." He motioned to himself.

"Don't be so sure." Sophie smiled.

"Come on, the game's on." Connor settled onto the couch.

Five minutes later, Abby was yelling at the screen. "Come on! Did you see that? He was clearly safe. That ump needs to fuckin' pay attention."

"You're adorable when you watch baseball," Danny said. "And that filthy mouth of yours is especially tempting," he added in a whisper.

Connor started to say something, but Abby interrupted him. "Don't talk bad about my Yankees," she playfully threatened.

"They suck this year." Connor said, bravely.

"They what?" Abby moved out of Danny's arms.

"You heard me."

"You don't like breathing, O'Brian?" she threatened, teasingly.

"I'm breathing fine." He took in a big pull of air and smiled at her.

She narrowed her eyes and pointed at him. "Keep it up and you won't."

Danny must've had his fill of her antics because he laughed, a real belly shaking laugh, and when she turned to look at him, he was wiping away tears in his eyes.

"What's so funny, Nucci? Because I know you ain't laughin' at me. Or my Yankees."

"You know you're not a member of the team, right? They aren't *really* yours."

"Unbelievable. Have I entered another dimension?"

"I'm an Angels fan." Connor's smile grew even broader.

"Gah, why are you even here?"

"I'm dating your best friend."

"I so don't like him anymore," Abby said to Sophie.

At that comment everyone laughed, including Abby. Danny pulled her back to his side and kissed the top of her head.

"You all suck," Abby added.

"Love you, too." Connor threw a potato chip at her.

But she wouldn't have it any other way. She threw the

chip back at him and, lucky for him, the Yankees won.

chapter
thirty-one

"You're done," Emma said as she stepped away from Abby.

"And with ten minutes to spare." Sophie smiled at her friend. "Take a peek. You look absolutely stunning."

Abby smoothed her hands over the dress and went over to the full-length.

"I love this dress, and my hair looks amazing. Thanks so much, Amy." She turned to check out the back, which really was nothing but two very thin straps. She turned away from the mirror. "Okay, are these babies going to stay in place?" She glanced down at her chest.

"You're glued and taped. There will be no 'wardrobe malfunctions' tonight. Not on my watch." Emma gave an emphatic nod.

"Excellent. Let's get this show on the road."

Sophie handed her a small gold clutch that paired nicely with the very thin necklace she was wearing. She opened her bedroom door and walked down the hallway into the living room where Danny was waiting for her.

"I'm ready," she called, as she entered the room.

"Oh, my God." Danny said, his voice raspy and needy.

"What?" She looked down at her chest to make sure everything was in place.

"You look…words fail me. Beautiful doesn't cover it." His tongue darted out between his teeth, and he slowly licked his bottom lip.

"You think?" Abby smiled and walked toward him.

"I don't think. I know. Exquisite might come close." He moved closer to her.

"As much as I'd like to stand here and watch you both eye fuck each other, it is time to roll," Connor said with a laugh. "Plus, I don't have any popcorn."

"I guess that's our friendly reminder that we are about to be late." Abby kissed Danny and let him guide her to the car.

* * *

"Five minute warning," King called from the front seat of the limo. They needed to rush through the red carpet because Abby was opening the show. Sophie had prepped everyone earlier that day, but King still took a moment to review his instructions "Remember that we have to wait until the team gets to the car before I'll let you out. Once you're out, I know you need to stop for pictures and press, but I'd like to keep things brief. Any questions?"

"Got it," Abby said. "And Sophie will shut the press

down if they try to keep me."

"I know she will, but I wanted to make sure you were good."

"I'm good. Thanks, King."

"Showtime," King announced and opened his door.

Abby was getting nervous. Not about the performance, but about walking the red carpet with Danny. Once they stepped out of the car together, the entire world would know that they were a couple. It was a lot of pressure. She knew how it felt to be under constant scrutiny, but it would be new to Danny. She waited for King to close the car door before turning to Danny, "Are you ready for this?" She tried to get her voice to sound light but it betrayed her; she was worried.

"Ready for what?" Danny looked confused by the question.

"Going out there. Staying with me." She shrugged, trying for indifference but not succeeding.

"You ask now?" Danny chuckled. "Of course I'm fine with it. We're together. Why should we hide it? Right?"

"Yes." Abby smiled.

"I'd kiss you, but I think Sophie would kill me if I mess up your make-up."

"She probably would."

"Nervous?" Danny asked.

"Not anymore. Just excited to see how everyone reacts to the song. I don't even care if I win anything," she admitted.

"I think tonight is more about the performance, don't you? I know I can't wait to hear it."

"I agree, and I'm *really* curious to hear if you like it." Abby gave him a look.

"What does that mean?"

King opened the door. "Time to move."

"Saved by King," she teased and blew Danny a kiss as she stepped out of the car.

Abby and Danny were bombarded with reporters yelling their names and asking them prying questions about their relationship. Camera flashes went off in her face, blinding Abby for a brief moment. Abby loved the red carpet, but between the reporters and fans, it was overwhelming. Everyone was calling her name and begging her to stop. She followed Sophie's lead with interviews and also paused for photos and signed a few autographs before being ushered inside. Everything after that was a blur. Danny kissed her cheek and left for his seat, and then she was whisked away to prep for her performance.

"Here is your mike pack, Ms. Murphy."

"Thank you." She tucked it into the pre-made holder that was sewn into her dress. Sophie helped her set the wires in place and within minutes she was ready for her performance. A producer knocked on her dressing room.

"Ms. Murphy, five minute warning."

"Thanks."

"Showtime," her drummer said, and she followed the band to the stage.

The house lights dimmed. The audience started to scream and chant. They didn't know who was scheduled to open the show, but the blog-o-sphere was littered with rumors that Abby would be performing tonight. Officially, she was only marked as a guest.

Those butterflies she loved were dancing in her stomach. This was the part she enjoyed the most. Right before the lights went on. It was always rush, rush, rush to get to the stage, but once she was on her marker, the chaos around her simply fell away, leaving her a few precious seconds to take it all in. This was her life. And tonight she would be performing her music and her words. She couldn't wait for Danny to hear it. She'd let him listen to a few songs from the album but held this one back. The intro to the song started. It was finally time.

* * *

Danny sat alone with several empty seats around him for Abby and her entourage. Letting someone else take the lead when it came to Abby was still strange, but he was trying and thought he had adjusted quite nicely. At least Abby seemed to feel better about it. Tonight he really wanted to sit back, enjoy her performance, and celebrate with her. He had no doubt she'd nail it.

The room went completely dark, and the announcer's voice boomed through the speakers. Once Abby was introduced, the place erupted in cheers even louder than before.

When the curtain lifted, he was mesmerized by her

beauty and her voice. She was an amazing talent who had been held back by a jealous mother for years. Now she was shining, and he couldn't have been prouder.

He watched in awe as she sang from her heart. She was hitting every note, and had the crowd cheering and swaying along to the music. He hadn't heard the song before, but Abby had hinted that the words were significant, so he tried to pay attention to what she was singing and not get swept away by her beauty. He closed his eyes for a moment and let her voice move through him.

He opened his eyes in time to see Abby look over toward their seats. Her happiness was unmistakable. It radiated off her and made it hard to fight the lump in his throat. All around him, the crowd was screaming for more. They were all on their feet, but all he could see was her.

* * *

"Holy shit, that was amazing!" Sophie pulled Abby into a tight hug. Abby's body was charged with adrenaline, and she needed to move. She managed to extricate herself.

"Ohimgod, did you see them? They gave you a standing ovation." Sophie cheered.

"Yes." Abby yelled over the noise and chaos of the people around them backstage. She was overcome with so many emotions. "Sophie, I need to get back to my seat. I want to see Danny."

"Let me see if we can go now while they are on

commercial break."

Sophie disappeared, and Abby took a few pictures with backstage hands while King stayed close.

"Okay, we got the all clear if we go right now." Sophie explained.

"Let's go." She needed to see Danny.

He was waiting for her with open arms. She ran to him, and he lifted her off the floor and held her tightly.

"That was fucking amazing." Danny whispered in her ear and gave her a kiss right below it.

They sat down in their seats and finally she had a moment to just breathe and take in what just happened. "What did you think?" she asked Danny.

"Abby, I was blown away. And just so you know I love you too," he winked.

Abby beamed. The song was about them and their journey. She had been scared to share it, but the look on Danny's face said it all.

She moved closer to him and whispered, "I can't wait to get home."

The night was filled with crazy acts and drunken musicians, but Abby didn't care. It was all par for the course when you were in the music biz. She was up for a few awards, but those things weren't something she ever really strived to get. Those were things her mother wanted.

"The next award is for video of the year." Abby looked toward the stage when she heard a familiar voice boom through the speakers.

Aisling.

"The nominees are…" Aisling turned to watch the videos displayed on the stage screens. Abby looked over at Danny and felt overwhelmed with the depth of her feelings for him.

"And the winner is…" Aisling struggled to open the envelope. "Abby Murphy!"

She heard her name, but it sounded like Aisling was in a tunnel. If it wasn't for Danny's strong arms helping her from her seat, she would've believed she was dreaming. She felt like her feet weren't even on the floor.

"You won!" he shouted. "Go up there." He let go of her hand.

"No." She pulled him along with her. "Come with me."

"This is your moment. Own it."

"No. Danny, without you none of this comes true for me." She pulled him up on the stage with her where she took the award from Aisling and gave her a fierce hug.

"Thank you so much," she said into the microphone. "I know time is running out so I'll keep this short. Without the man standing beside me, none of this would be possible. Danny, you taught me to believe in myself again. You gave me the courage to take a chance. You made me feel special and you cared when very few really did. You encouraged me, loved me, inspired me, and I thank God every day that we found each other, because without you, there is no me. Thank you."

THE END

Debra Presley

Coming Soon
Coming Soon

Saving Us
Sophie and Connor's story

acknowledgements
acknowledgements

I started writing *Finding Us* nearly two years ago. Writing a book was always this dream in the back of my mind yet never talked about. I started a few times, and I stopped soon after. I felt so lost and had no clue what I was doing.

When I started blogging, I discovered the indie book world, and my little dream resurfaced. I still didn't have a clue, but the more I blogged and read indie authors, the more I thought about trying again. I mentioned it to an author friend one day, and instead of laughing, she encouraged me and helped me. Before I knew it, I was writing the story of Abby and Danny.

Since then, I've had the help and support of many people, and I'd like them all to know just how thankful I am to have them in my life. Most of them I've never met, but we've become such great friends I don't know what I'd do without them in my life.

Mom—You've always encouraged me to follow my dreams and supported me in all my crazy ideas. I could never express to you how much that means. I love you so very much.

Dad—I wish you were here to see this, but I know you

are up in heaven watching. Thank you for always supporting me in my dreams. You spent countless hours driving me back and forth to voice and piano lessons, rehearsals, auditions, and concerts, and you never complained. I miss you every day.

Vinny and Joanne—Thank you for your encouragement and understanding when I would visit only to disappear for hours to write. Vinny, you're the best brother a girl could ask for. Thank you for answering my EMT questions and for risking your life daily to save others. I like to tease you a lot, but that really is an amazing job, and you're awesome at it.

Genna, Vincent, and Vanessa—I love you three more than my own life. I'm so lucky to have you as my nieces and nephew. I love watching you grow and mature into such wonderful people. You make me the proudest aunt in the world.

Sheri—Thank you doesn't seem to cover it. You encouraged me to try and write. You said you just sit down and do it. You shared your knowledge and never got annoyed with my million and one questions. Your generosity is like none I've known before. Without your help and support I wouldn't have a book or a business. Thank you for all you do. I appreciate you more than I could ever say in a few sentences.

Andi—Thank you for sharing your time and knowledge with me. You answered all my questions, let me work through ideas, and guided me in the right direction when I went totally off track. You didn't make me feel like I was some newbie that knew nothing. Instead you encouraged me and made me feel like mistakes were okay and rewriting was fun. Thank you for making my first experience with an editor a positive one.

Scriptease Editing—I spent countless hours trying to find a copy and line editor. Every website I looked at made me wonder about why they were editors. You're answered all my questions and when I reached out to you I was immediately comfortable. I loved how not only edited by book but you shared useful pieces of knowledge with me that I'll always keep. Thank you for an amazing experience. I can't wait to work on my next project with you!

Lannah—Thank you so much for the wonderful job you did proofreading *Finding Us*. I really appreciate everything you did.

Cover Me, Darling—Thank you for the kick ass cover. I love it so much! Also, thank you for being so professional and patient with me. Working with you was effortless.

Brenda Wright – Formatting Done Wright—Thank you for being great and doing a fabulous job. Also, for walking a newbie like me through the process.

To my Street Team—Thank you for all your support. You rock!

Stephanie (of Stephanie's Book Reports)—Thank you for all your support. I loved your Beta Ghost program and took so much of the feedback I got from that group. Your friendship means so much to me.

Tonya—Thank you for being such a great friend. You started following my blog when it was brand new and somehow we developed a friendship that I truly cherish. Your constant encouragement and enthusiasm has meant so much to me.

All of my co-bloggers on <u>The Book Enthusiast</u> (TBE)—Paula, Kelly, Cindy, Erin, Tami, Cyndi, Anja, Loredana, Nikki, Misha, Dawnmarie and Nicola. Without the help from you all I'd never have been able to keep TBE active while working on promotions and writing. I really appreciate and love you all.

Emma—Thank you so much for all you do. You work tirelessly behind the scenes at <u>Book Enthusiast Promotions</u> and your support and friendship means so much to me.

To my nurses, Beth and Nikki—Thank you for chatting with me and answering my endless questions. Nikki you were also my go to girl for all things Army. Thanks so much to both of you.

Finally, I'd like to thank you for taking the time to read *Finding Us*. I truly appreciate you taking a chance on a new author like myself.

Made in the USA
Middletown, DE
14 August 2015